THE SHOCK OF NIGHT

Books by Patrick W. Carr

The Staff and the Sword

A Cast of Stones

The Hero's Lot

A Draw of Kings

The Darkwater Saga

By Divine Right (e-novella only)

The Shock of Night

THE SHOCK OF NIGHT

PATRICK W. CARR

BETHANYHOUSE
a division of Baker Publishing Group
Minneapolis, Minnesota

Published by Bethany House Publishers
11400 Hampshire Avenue South
Bloomington, Minnesota 55438
www.bethanyhouse.com

Bethany House Publishers is a division of
Baker Publishing Group, Grand Rapids, Michigan

Printed in the United States of America

Library of Congress Control Number: 2015015397

This is a work of fiction. Names, characters, incidents, and dialogues are products of the author's imagination and are not to be construed as real. Any resemblance to actual events or persons, living or dead, is entirely coincidental.

Cover design by LOOK Design Studio

Author represented by The Steve Laube Agency

15 16 17 18 19 20 21 7 6 5 4 3 2 1

To my father, Major Joe William Carr, USAF,
and to all the other men and women who
carry the wounds of war on their body and in their spirit.

Thank you

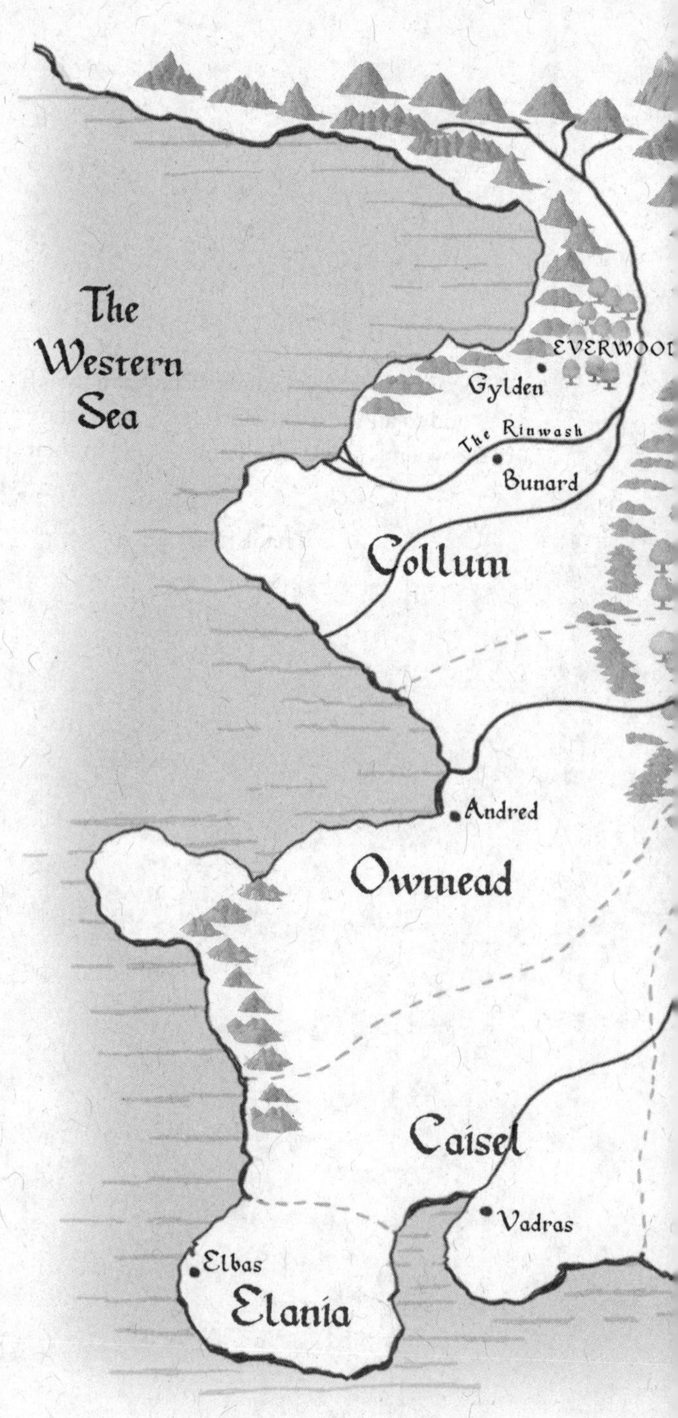
The Western Sea
EVERWOO
Gylden
The Rinwash
Bunard
Collum
Andred
Owmead
Caisel
Vadras
Elbas
Elania

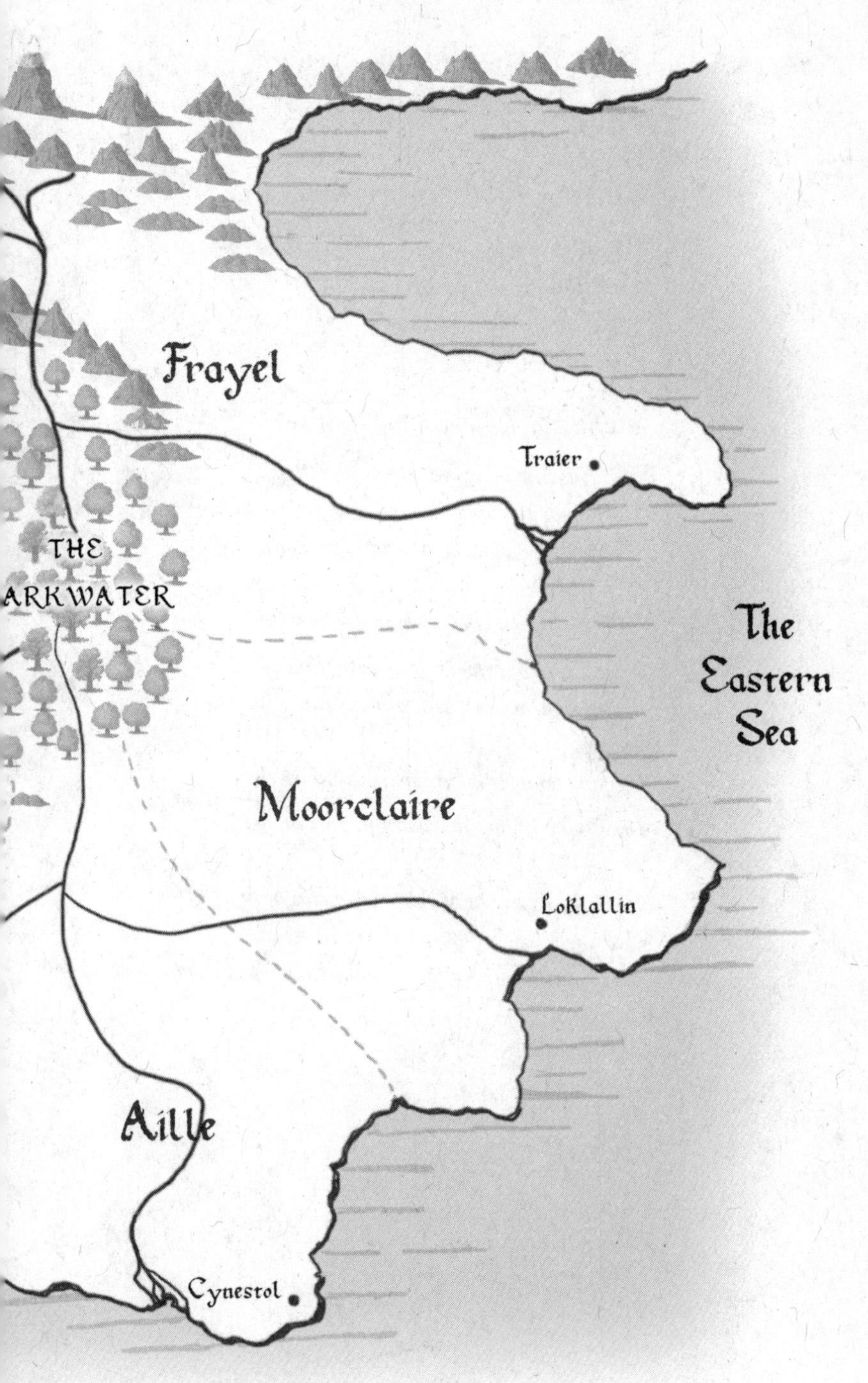

Frayel
Traier
THE
ARKWATER
The
Eastern
Sea
Moorclaire
Loklallin
Aille
Cynestol

The Exordium of the Liturgy—

The six charisms of Aer are these:

For the body, beauty and craft
For the soul, sum and parts
For the spirit, helps and devotion

The nine talents of man are these:

Language, logic, space, rhythm,
motion, nature, self, others, and all

The four temperaments of creation are these:

Impulse, passion, observation, and thought

Within the charisms of Aer, the talents of man,
and the temperaments imbued in creation
are found understanding and wisdom. Know and learn.

PROLOGUE

Elwin stopped at the edge of the forest, his eyes scanning the trees for any movement that might presage an attack, though the man at his right, Robin, would surely be doing the same and better than he. Still, no one living stood in a better position to appreciate their danger. Within the shadowed canopy of twisted black-leaved trees nothing stirred. No bird called its summer cry, no squirrel foraged the floor, no fox hunted.

Elwin almost touched the sliver of metal tucked away in his cloak, stopping just short of brushing the shiny yellow fragment of aurium, afraid to confirm its impossible existence.

"A blacksmith," he muttered.

Robin turned from his inspection of the cursed forest to give him a questioning look. "Eldest?"

For a moment he considered brushing aside the invitation to explain, but Robin's insight had proven valuable before, despite his youth. "The dead man back there was a blacksmith. Soot marked the scars of old burns on his hands, and his clothes still held the smell of fire and quenching oil." Elwin tapped his cloak pocket where the shard of metal rested, the man's death sentence had he not already been dead. "That still doesn't explain how he managed to survive as long as he did."

Robin nodded. "How does a blacksmith come to be in possession of aurium?"

Elwin nodded and then shook his head. "How does anyone come to possess the forbidden metal?"

They continued riding north, their horses ascending out of the fertile valley stretching east and west that marked the border between Owmead and the northernmost kingdom on the continent, Collum. The question lay between them, unanswered, like the death of a patriarch no one dared mention, but they'd left the torn and mauled body of the blacksmith behind as a warning, according to the law of the kingdoms that bordered the Darkwater Forest.

They kept to the edge of the forest as the landscape grew rockier, defying the efforts of those who farmed it. After another mile, Robin pointed. "There. Another one," he said in a tone of voice like the crushing of rock.

The mound of torn and matted fur, buzzing with flies in the sun, brought a surge of bile to Elwin's throat, and he looked away to bring his stomach under control. "Check it," he ordered in a voice that sounded hollow and strangely far away.

Tying a strip of cloth across his mouth and nose, Robin dismounted. The flies shifted at his approach—and for a moment Elwin's guard wore a dark halo—but no other carrion eaters defiled the carcass. The body of the sentinel, larger than a wolf by half and more heavily muscled as well, had been left untouched this close to the forest. The sentinels sparked fear even in death.

Elwin nodded to himself—animals were wise in such things. He saw Robin's chest rise and fall in a sigh even before he turned from the body.

"Like the others," Robin said. "It bled to death. There are cuts all over it." He stooped to pull the lips back from the muzzle, its triangular shape a testimony to the power in the jaws. "Clean. Whoever killed it managed to do so without taking any injuries."

"Any sign of the pup?" Elwin asked.

Robin surveyed the landscape for a moment, then pointed to a smaller mound some twenty paces away. "There."

With a mental wrench that rose almost to the level of physical pain,

Elwin abandoned another hope. Fantasies and delusions would no longer help them. "Could you do such a thing, Robin?"

To anyone else the question might have been an accusation. That Robin had never left his side since becoming his protector cast the query in a different light. His guard cocked his head, his eyes growing distant, and Elwin knew he fought the beast at his feet within his mind, playing stroke and parry before answering. "Yes," he said finally. "But not alone."

"Are you saying there is someone out there better than you?" Elwin asked.

Thankfully, his guard shook his head, leaving him one of his few remaining hopes. "No. Some of the wounds on the sentinel are on the back flanks and legs. I would think three or four men attacked it. I do not think any one of them to be my equal."

He caught the slight emphasis on *think* and tried to keep the surprise from his face, but Robin had only paused.

"I wouldn't want to come up against these men without my brothers to help. They're certainly gifted."

Elwin growled a curse that had nothing to do with his time in the priesthood of the Merum order. "Or something like it. That's a half dozen sentinel deaths in the past year. We don't have the replacements." He tapped the sliver of aurium in his pocket and looked at the forest as if the trees might uproot themselves and attack there in the noonday sun. "Faran can't keep up. It takes years to breed and train a sentinel." Despair clogged Elwin's throat, and for a moment it broke free of his ability to contain it. "I wish Cesla were here."

Robin turned away at the mention of Elwin's brother, unwilling, perhaps, to intrude upon the grief that still seemed so recent. "What of his gift?" he asked softly.

Elwin nodded in approval. His guard possessed a talent for knowing others in addition to his more obvious physical ones. Descending into that familiar grief wouldn't serve them. "We follow the trail as best we can," he said with a sigh. "Sometimes I think we did our job too well. We've hidden ourselves so completely that the gift becomes difficult to find if it goes free." He patted a pocket. "But there's a rumor from the village of Cryos."

"Convenient," Robin said without explaining.

Elwin nodded. "Yes, we can visit Faran and see if there is any way he can replenish the sentinels more quickly." The thought of the journey north wearied him. He carried too many memories, and his mind bowed beneath their weight, like a wagon axle trying to support too many bags of grain.

Elwin held out his hands to survey them in the muted sunlight that filtered through the cloud cover. The prominent veins and the skin, as thin as the papery outer layer of an onion, still surprised him. "I'm almost ready to move on, Robin. I've used the gift too often, and now it's used me up."

The sentinel lying dead at their feet brought a surge of anger, and he straightened in his saddle. "But before I go, I need to bring justice to the men who did this."

He twitched the reins, and they rode northwest, following a trail only he could sense, deeper into the kingdom of Collum.

CHAPTER 1

The Twentieth Year of King Laidir's Reign

The pounding on my door pulled me from slumber, and I drifted toward waking, my mind a piece of sodden wood floating toward the surface of a lake. I had one hand on the door latch and the other clutching a dagger behind my back before I managed to get both eyes open. Through the peephole I saw a guard—one of the king's by his dress—standing next to Gareth, a night constable. I snuck a glance out the window of the apartment the king provided me as a lord of his employ. The glass wasn't of sufficient quality to offer me anything more than an impression of what lay beyond, but I could tell the sun wasn't up yet.

The remnants of some dream I didn't want to remember cracked my voice as I opened the door. "What?"

The guard gave me an almost imperceptible bob of his head. My title was the least in Laidir's court. "You're needed, Lord Dura."

I tried to keep my temper in check. My unique position in service to the king seemed to require the same hours as a midwife's. "What about Jeb?" I asked, mentioning the chief reeve, the one who should have been awakened instead of me.

Gareth shook his head. "We thought we should wake you first. There's been a killing in the lower merchants' quarter."

A thread of panic shot through my chest, filling my heart with ice, but I kept my gaze on Gareth with an effort. What had I dreamed? I kept my voice steady and played the part of the interrupted sleeper as best I could. "So? What's so dire about some fool shopkeeper who can't keep his money safeguarded?"

Gareth's plain soldier's face lost what little expression it held. "It's a churchman."

I stifled my next comment and turned back into the apartment to get dressed. It took me a moment to realize I already was. Only my cloak and boots were missing. Another surge of panic brought me to full wakefulness, and I moved quickly to prevent the guards from entering at my delay. I lit a candle and spotted my cloak lying across a chair on the far side of the room. I crossed over and lifted it.

An oath crossed my lips before I could prevent it at seeing spots of blood on the hem. I rolled it into a bundle and shoved it beneath the armoire before retrieving another and picking up my weapon. All of the city's reeves wore a sword, but most of them didn't expect trouble. Except me. I attracted it the way a lodestone drew iron. I moved to a small stand and tucked a pair of daggers into leather pouches stitched into the back of my belt and slid another into the inside of my right boot. Then I tried to reconcile myself to being awake before dawn.

Jeb ran the city watch and did it well. If it came to brawling or persuading some poor unfortunate to confess, Jeb's methods yielded results. His fists served as a fair approximation of iron, and he enjoyed using them to convince people to mend the error of their ways. It was amazing how the sound of his knuckles popping loosened a man's tongue.

But murder presented a different challenge, particularly one without witnesses or one involving people of importance. Jeb's persuasion couldn't quicken the tongues of the dead, which explained Gareth's presence at my door. And I had proven my worth to the king. A year prior, I'd had the mixed fortune of solving a crime that earned me his favor. Over the objections of the rest of the nobility, the king raised me to lordship, though without lands or gift. I became the least in his service. My current duties were the price I paid for my nobility and another reward he'd given me that I esteemed more highly.

We exited the halls of King Laidir's stronghold and came out onto one of the blocky staircases that led downward, descending the massive tor on which it had been built, carved from gut rock. Enormous granite stones merged with the mountain that defined the ponderous edifice of Laidir's seat. The vertical walls were high enough to be impervious to ladders, and the surrounding landscape made it difficult to bring siege engines close enough to do any real damage.

The massive city of Bunard, King Laidir's seat of power, spread beneath us. The Rinwash River curved around the stronghold to the north and west, but the river had been diverted into channels to supply water to each quarter of the city. If the sun had been up I could have seen the bridges connecting each section of the city, but in the darkness only the ends were visible, illuminated by the watch fires at each bank.

I followed Gareth downward until we arrived at the king's stables, the smell of horse strong in the still air of the morning. Mounting quickly, we set out for the lower merchants' quarter as the sky showed hints of slate in the east, riding southwest, passing by the four massive cathedrals of the divisions of the church, each with their criers' stand out front—thankfully empty. I appreciated the silence. By the time I returned, the day's chosen lector would be out front, declaring each division's interpretation of the Word for the unbelieving.

After crossing the first bridge, we rode through the opulence of those living nearest His Majesty, structures just short of castles, with broad sweeping arches and stained-glass ballrooms. The scarcity of land precluded the types of formal grounds many of them maintained in their holdings, but their meticulously groomed gardens exuded wealth and order just the same.

They were as welcoming as iron.

We crossed the next bridge over the Rinwash, heading into the upper merchants' quarter, and turned south, passing homes nearly the equal of the nobility, though they lacked the space for private gardens and they held about themselves the concentrated energy of those focused on profit.

When we passed over the next bridge, the buildings changed from heavy-cut granite to wood, first with several stories, then with just two or one, their plain windows already glowing as those within began preparations for their day in the marketplace or at their craft. The ring of a hammer started somewhere off to my right, and the smell of bread drifted to me, reminding me I'd yet to eat.

Gareth took the opportunity our travel afforded to provide what little information he had around mouthfuls of dark bread. "We found two men, one dead from blood loss, the other nearly so." His mouth pulled to one side beneath a nose that had been broken so many times that it changed directions often. "A seamstress heard the clash of steel and started screaming, but by the time the night watch arrived, the attackers had fled."

I logged Gareth's pithy summary away. My heart beat faster with each step closer, and the abstraction I felt in the presence of the dead commanded my attention. I concentrated long enough to ask a proper question. "Do you have any names?"

He nodded. "The watchman recognized them. The dead man is Robin. He's the menial of Elwin, the man who got hit on the head. They're Servants."

I pulled the mist of predawn into my lungs and squinted through the darkness. Some might resent the studied aloofness of a Merum priest or the zeal of the Vanguard, and others might even take exception to the aggressive mercy practiced by the Absold. But no one in their right mind begrudged a Servant. They seldom preached—the only exception being their crier—wouldn't fight or try to change anyone. They served others. But for some reason, two men of the most humble of the four orders on the continent had been attacked. My heart quickened again.

We rounded a corner and came to the edge of a small grassy area bordering a clump of plain wooden buildings that huddled against the dark. A stone wall about eight feet high separated the area from the bank of one of the man-made branches of the Rinwash River.

Gareth pointed to a pile of limbs and cloth sprawled against the base of the wall. Here and there pale white skin showed against stone or fabric. Dark wet blotches covered the tunic. Gaping wounds assaulted my vision as the smell of blood hit my nose, and I fought to keep the remnants of my last meal in place. Gareth said something that almost penetrated the spell cast by the dead man, but none of the words registered as important.

I ignored him. Distraction was the enemy. Death begets death, and my job was to bring the killers to the gallows. I knew one thing immediately—Robin had been taken down by at least two men, maybe more. Deep slashes on his legs that matched those on his torso testified to as much. A single fighter would never risk a low-line attack that way. I pulled a breath heavy with mist off the river into my lungs as I counted the wounds. "They didn't just kill him—they cut him to pieces." Even his face. "How did anyone recognize him?"

Gareth shrugged. "I asked Ahden that same question. He recognized Robin's clothes and the chip in his front tooth—and knows of his service to Elwin."

I bent and shifted the hair to see his eye. I signaled Gareth closer with his torch. The details of death and the shadowed surroundings faded as I gave myself to Robin's stare. Identical to the others I had seen at the end, regardless of the why or how of their passing. His eyes—a startling blue, like a potter's glaze—focused on something so impossibly far away in death that he appeared to see through me, the city, and the kingdom. Even the stars were too close to capture his attention. A familiar longing awoke in me at the sight of it, and I desired nothing more in that moment than to somehow pull his attention from eternity so that he might answer my question. "Tell me, Robin, what do you see?"

Robin didn't answer, of course. I was too late, as I always was.

"Milord?"

Gareth's voice pulled me from myself. He stood with the torch, shifting his weight from foot to foot, discomfited. No wisdom had been forthcoming from Robin, just as none had come to me from my family, Duke Orlan's brother, or countless others. "Scan the area, Gareth. Tell me what you find."

He wandered from spot to spot on the grounds, careful to avoid touching the body or disturbing the scuff marks in the turf where the earth bore witness. I turned from the pull of Robin's gaze with an effort and climbed the steps to the top of the wall, my mind split between trying to understand what lay before me and worry. There'd been blood on my cloak.

From my elevated vantage point, the extremity of Robin's defense became clear. The grass, trampled by the attack, flowed back and forth like the strokes of a painter. My experience in battle didn't rival Gareth's, but even I could see Robin had fought bravely and well, very well. That last fact struck me, and I stopped to consider its implications. Too well for a Servant.

I descended the heavy granite steps, my breath misting the air before me. Gareth stepped to my side. The presence of Robin's corpse didn't prevent him from munching on his bread, his face impassive. "Reminds me of the last border war. Even after the bodies had been hauled off and burned, you could tell where the worst of the fighting was by looking at the grass. Rough business. Robin didn't go down without a fight. He gave as good as he got, or nearly so."

I nodded to acknowledge Gareth's confirmation and reminded myself I only had three more months of duty as a reeve of the city watch. After my marriage to Gael, I would be more elevated among the nobility that despised me. I blew air through my hands trying to warm them. "What do you see?"

He smiled at the chance to display his veteran's knowledge once more. "Come. I'll show you." He led me toward a patch of earth. "Trace the scuff marks." He bent. "See how the grass is bent and torn, pointing toward the river? Robin and Elwin were backing away with a pair of men following. There's a bit of blood here. Robin's, I think, because just after you can see the scuffs turn a bit. I think Robin was trying to protect his wounded side. And then we come to this." Gareth pointed to a pair of bloody splotches on the ground. "See the space between there and here? Both Robin and his assailants found their mark." My lieutenant knelt and touched the grass. "They all struck hard."

Two puddles of deep vermillion, almost black in the predawn, each almost a foot in diameter, discolored the earth, perhaps a cupful, maybe two. "It doesn't look like so much."

Gareth shook his head. "When a man's bleeding through his clothes and moving, Lord Dura, this is enough to kill."

I nodded, convinced. He pointed at another spot between us and the body a few feet away. "Robin got marked again."

We traced and read the desperation of Robin's defeat written in splashes of blood on the ground until we stood over him once more. A few feet away to Robin's left the grass had been flattened and a sluggish pool of blood marked one end of the spot. I knelt, searching the ground under the yellow light of Gareth's torch. Droplets of blood littered the grass, smudges really.

"This is where they found Elwin?"

Gareth nodded, but something seemed wrong. Elwin should have been behind Robin, but from the scuffs in the grass and the blood spatters, it appeared he'd been out to one side or possibly in front when his enemies took him. "Why would he be here?" I muttered, not meaning for my voice to carry, but Gareth heard me anyway.

"Men do strange things in the rush of battle, my lord."

My misgiving remained despite my silence. "Is there anything else?"

Gareth led me to a spot several paces away, pointing to a pair of shallow grooves on the ground running parallel to each other. "Someone was dragged away."

This was why I needed Gareth. Whatever he lacked in insight or intuition, he made up for in observation. With ten years more experience in the king's service, he'd seen enough dying to make him an expert, but the stares of the dead held no interest for him.

I retraced the track of Robin's struggle over to his body, where I rolled him over and searched his clothes. A heavy jingle drew my attention, and I cut his purse free and dumped the contents. My pulse quickened once more as a glint of yellow, so rare as to be almost illegal, tumbled into my hand.

I almost stood then, but something about the rents in Robin's clothing stopped me. I'd been in the last border war and had seen plenty of dead and injured, but the holes in in his tunic and breeches were unique in their similarity. I examined a pair of wounds on his right thigh before unfastening the buttons of his coat and lifting his shirt to inspect the damage on his stomach and chest.

I shifted the body to get a better look. Whoever had cut him up had tried to kill him quickly and obviously failed. I probed one of the wounds on his chest. A slash, not a thrust, about a hand wide ran horizontally, or nearly so, across Robin's right side, the wound much deeper in the center than either side. Curious, I checked a couple more, then compared them to the wounds on his thighs. Every wound appeared the same, a clean cut nearly a hand wide and almost as deep, like sword or dagger slashes, but something about the depth bothered me—like a face that should have been familiar but wasn't—and I stared, trying to place it.

Robin's fist still clenched a sword, and there was blood on the blade. By the light of Gareth's torch, I inspected the nicks on the edges. No, not nicks, something else. Nicks from sword parries left small triangular notches in the edge of a blade. Instead, Robin's blade had small arc-shaped dents, as if he'd tried to hack through the bars of a prison. I pried the sword from his grasp and tucked it into my belt, behind my own.

"Interesting."

Gareth looked at me in surprise. "Lord Dura?"

I replaced Robin's tunic, my movements as respectful as I could make them. This was why I was here. Despite Gareth's experience, he lacked the ability to extrapolate his observations. "You say Robin marked a man badly enough to kill. Yet there's no one else here. And his purse was full, very full."

I shook the purse and noted the clear ring of silver along with a richer sound I'd rarely heard. "So that leaves us with a set of attackers who have no interest in money and whose identities are so important they're willing to spend the time and effort necessary to drag away their dead comrade."

I pointed a finger at Robin, trying to accuse him of something that would matter. "He was a Servant of all things. They don't fight. They don't strike back when struck. But he fought." At this point Robin's death didn't bother me nearly as much as his occupation.

"People kill for all sorts of reasons," Gareth said. "Not all of them make sense."

The education I received before becoming a reeve gave me a perspective on history. In the life of the church, I knew just how short a few hundred years could be. The Order Wars represented a long and lurid part of history on the northern continent. No sane man would ever wish their return, but the Servants had refused to fight, even then. I sighed. "Does the king know about this?"

Gareth nodded his head. "If he doesn't, he soon will. The castellan was writing his report when I came to get you."

Tension crept its way up the back of my neck, and I kept myself from using Gareth's soldierly vocabulary, barely. The best I could say about the new castellan was that he didn't come from the Orlan family. Being gifted, he'd never gone to war and didn't have the experience to understand the kind of violence Robin's death represented. I'd served in the last fight with Owmead almost a decade ago. A stab of pain shot through my head at the memory.

I focused on the scene before me. Blood soaked the earth and stones like spilled communal wine. What I saw made me wince, but it wasn't the violence or the blood. "Where's the other man—Elwin?"

Gareth made a vague gesture with his hand toward the southwest. "They took him to the House of Passing."

I chewed my lip. Elwin had been wounded in the attack and survived it, at least temporarily. But instead of taking him to the succor of his order, the city watch had taken him out to the House of Passing. "He's a churchman. Why didn't they take him to a healer? For that matter, why didn't they take him to the Servants' cathedral? They're the best healers in Bunard."

I led Gareth back to where I'd tied up my mount, my pace urgent. I needed to see Elwin's body, and if the slim chance remained that he still lived, I wanted to take advantage of the opportunity to question him or observe his passing. "Has anyone else come forward as a witness?"

Gareth snorted. "In this part of the city? No sir. These aren't the type of people that take an interest in another's business."

His reply failed to discourage me. There were more witnesses—they would just be harder to get to. Nothing happened in the city of Bunard without someone seeing. The observers might not be the type the king's magistrates would hearken to, but they were there. Whether they were beggars, pickpockets, thieves, or prostitutes, someone had seen the attack.

"I'll be married in three months, Gareth, my year of betrothal completed, the husband of a lady and a man with responsibilities within the nobility." I spoke to my fear. "I'll learn the work of a respectable lord."

Gareth blew air through his lips. “Why would the king allow that? There’s no one else that has your talent for seeing the way of things.”

I shook my head. There was no use in putting it off. Gareth might not be able to see the problem, but the king would, and I’d learned firsthand the difficulty of shading the truth with him in any way. Gareth would have to make report for me. “How long has Robin been in the city, Gareth?”

He shrugged and took another bite of bread. Dark crumbs littered his pale beard. “About five years.”

“What were a church functionary and his helper doing out at night? How does a menial Servant come by the skill to fight more than one opponent and kill one of them? Did you see his wounds?” I tried not to leer at the memory of his stare. “He bled to death. Against two or more swords, intent on killing him, he bled to death, meaning they weren’t good enough to land a killing stroke against a *Servant*.”

I turned a slow circle, searching out the closest buildings. This section of town was home to many of the shopkeepers, those less-prosperous merchants who worked without ceasing but managed to maintain their status. Most of the buildings close by housed the proprietor’s business in the front and their living space in the back. Some few possessed a second story. I pointed them out. “Start with those. A few of them would have a view of the fight. We need information.” I didn’t bother sending Gareth after those who filled the shadows of the city at night. They’d never speak with him. Skittish, sometimes they wouldn’t even talk to me. I nodded toward the dead man. “And have someone take care of Robin.”

Chapter 2

I pushed Dest to a gallop in the hope of reaching Elwin before he died. I knew the place and the path well enough to make the trip in the dark. The House of Passing sat in its crevice between the hills, a gateway to eternity against the banks of the Ende River. The rocky path to it was lined with flowers, even in the winter, flaunting their colors—blue, yellow, or pink, but never red. The preceptors of the dead never allowed the color of blood.

Those who were gifted didn't always use it for a profit. Some, out of conscience or guilt, used their gift in the service of the church, mostly those with the gift of helps. I couldn't imagine the effort it took to grow flowers in the winter, no matter how talented they might be with nature, but I was grateful for it just the same. The trip to the House of Passing was often the most beautiful the dying ever took.

Laidir funded the house out of taxes levied on the four orders to provide death with dignity, even for the least of his subjects. The religious orders resented the tax, enough so that some had attempted to refuse payment, but the Vanguard had been forcibly disbanded and expelled for a year when they'd tried. The loss in revenue, and souls, of course, became unacceptable. Everyone paid promptly from then on.

No one order ran the house. It seemed death was one of the few things the four could agree on. The expanded structure had grown along with the city until it boasted two levels and four wings. Rich green grass surrounded the stone edifice, and more flowers created a carpet of brilliant blue and yellow against the solid backdrop of masonry.

As I approached, light fog rolled in from the river behind the house, shrouding the landscape in tendrils of mist that brushed the stone pier with ghostly caresses. In the gray of predawn I could see half a dozen flat-bottomed coracles, each a little wider than I was tall, stacked beneath a simple shed. After someone passed, the brothers or sisters would say the antidon in the tradition of their order. Usually the dead were buried or burned, according to the tradition, but every now and then the old beliefs sprang forth and the dying requested the journey west in their attempt to join the mythical Fayit, the eldritch beings who'd supposedly walked the earth before Aer created man.

The brothers and sisters in the House would load the body into the coracle and send it down the Ende, which meandered through the lowlands to the west, without falls or rapids, until it emptied into the Western Sea. From there the current caught it and carried it toward the setting sun and into the unknown.

I pulled my attention back to the house. The brothers and sisters who worked there volunteered in turns from the segments of the church that resided within our kingdom. They all had cause to know me. A candle shone in the window to the left and a shadow moved within. Care for the dying didn't follow a merchant's schedule. I checked the moon. It wouldn't be full for another seven days.

I dismounted and stopped, my ears straining. An echo of sound, the distant crunch of gravel beneath a hoof, came to me, but dawn still lay some minutes away, and I could make nothing out except the dim outlines of the trees lining the path. My heart worked against my ribs, and I pulled my sword and backed my way into the torchlight of the stone entryway.

Geoffrey, wearing the white armbands of the Vanguard and carrying the smell of death on his clothes, greeted me just inside the door. He gave me a polite nod and a heavy-lidded blink that always took a split second longer than it should have.

"Lord Dura. I wondered when you would return to us." The subtle note of disapproval in his voice drifted to my ears as if he had to bribe the air to carry it to me. "Jocelyn has been asking after you. None of the other visitors will read the tales to her, it seems." He paused to check the moon. "She's trying to make it to the next festival of Bas-solas. She's close, but I'm not sure she'll make it. You'll wish to escort her, I assume?"

My head had nodded assent before I remembered why I had come. I'd escorted a dozen or more of the residents of the House to the threshold of eternity, reading them their favorite story or holding their hand, each time waiting to catch some hint of what they saw as they stepped through the door to forever. So far their blank stares defied me, refusing to surrender the knowledge. I hoped someday one of those passing to the other side would return long enough to give me some hint. I'd heard of it happening in tales and rumors until I thirsted for it with the desperation of a man in the desert. Geoffrey's disapproval failed to shame me—my need was too great.

"I can't read to her," I said. "At least not now. I'm here on the king's business. A man was brought to you a couple of hours ago. He's probably passed, but I'll need to see the body."

Geoffrey's eyes almost sharpened into interest, and he turned, crisp, like a soldier toward the east wing. "I'll take you to him. He's still alive, though we are at a loss to understand it. Sister Iselle believes he may pull through despite his grievous injury." He sighed, a whisper of sound that carried mourning in it, though I knew from experience it wouldn't be for the dying. "Her duties here weigh heavily upon her. She hopes and prays for each resident's recovery." His shoulders shifted beneath his cassock. "Servants often have difficulty with death. The Vanguard know better."

I followed him into a long ward with a row of plain elevated beds on each side of a wide aisle running the length of the room. Cries filled the air, and I stutter-stepped at the unfamiliar sound. People didn't suffer pain in the House—the brothers and sisters were skilled at easing it. We passed by a number of men whose injuries had fouled past the healer's art, and the smell of infection hung heavy in the air despite the vinegar used to mask it. Then we came to the source of the cries.

Elwin, his head swathed in several feet of blood-soaked bandages, tossed on his bed, his back reflexing in arced tension, caught in his dreams, his head shaking from side to side. Sister Iselle stood over him with her weight forward, calling encouragements, trying to calm him, but each time she reached out to him, he flinched, recoiling from the prospect of her touch.

Disappointment settled onto my shoulders like a cloak. The blow to his head hadn't killed him yet, but there would be no information coming from Elwin. "How long has he been like this?"

Geoffrey shrugged. "It can't have been long. He was unconscious just a few moments ago."

Elwin's eyes opened, but his gaze passed through his surroundings with the stare of the unseeing. Then his arm reached toward me.

Iselle followed the gesture, her blue eyes shining in a heart-shaped face that would make most men jealous of the church she served and resentful of the vows of celibacy her order required. She straightened to face me, her expression welcoming but tinged with sorrow as always. "Willet, it is good to see you again." She glanced at Elwin. "You've always done so well with the passing. Do you think you can calm him? If we could get him to rest, he might recover. I'm hopeful—"

"Sister Iselle, you know that—"

"We do not know the future, Brother Geoffrey." She thrust her chin in defiance toward Geoffrey and his condescension. "No one dies until they have breathed their last." She faced me, her arm beckoning.

I stepped toward the bed. As much as I disliked Geoffrey, I couldn't help but agree with him. Elwin's soaked bandages stated plainly he would die from blood loss even if the blow didn't kill him. I saw now why the watch, peopled with veterans from the last war, hadn't bothered the healers. They'd recognized the certainty of Elwin's death.

He stilled as I approached, the arch in his back easing and his arms coming to rest on the blankets. I couldn't help but sigh at his passing. For a moment I had dared to hope I might be able to question him.

I turned back to Geoffrey and Iselle. "I'm sorry. I'll need to search him." I shook my head. "And I'll have to look at the wound as well." Geoffrey gave me another of his slow blinks and a nod I would have expected from any of the Vanguard, but Iselle turned from me, scattering tears.

Starting at Elwin's feet, I worked my way up, feeling along his legs for anything he might have tried to keep hidden. Nothing beyond the bony ranginess of an old man came to me, until I came to his cloak. A lump made of tight layers of cloth lay within a small pocket stitched to the inside. I took it and tucked it into my belt, waiting for a more opportune and private time to see what I had.

When I looked up, Elwin's dead stare caught me, and I placed my mouth close to the bandages covering one ear. "Elwin, can you tell me what you see?"

He didn't answer, of course, and silence settled over the room once more. I shifted my feet in preparation to unwrap the bandages on his head.

Elwin's body convulsed, lurching forward, and he grasped my head, the nails digging into my flesh. "Domere!"

The room tilted and went black.

Chapter 3

Screams brought me to consciousness. I scrambled to rise from the floor and draw my sword at the same time. Knots throbbed on my head, and I squinted, struggling to bring the room into focus.

Geoffrey and Iselle stared at me while I tried to steady myself against Elwin's bed. I brushed one of his arms, still warm with a mockery of life. His eyes called to me a second time, but a scream of fury from the house's entrance pulled me away.

Steps echoed and reechoed through the building as Geoffrey and Iselle ran with me toward the sound. I could hear pounding now, a deep boom coming from the entrance. I turned the corner to see a man I did not recognize struggling to hold the door closed. His feet skidded back against the stone a few inches as something hit the door.

He spared enough time to face me. "Drop the sword, man, and help me hold them out!"

Tortured growls and curses came from the far side of the door, and I knew that to surrender the door was to die. I ignored the stranger's order as it slipped open another inch and threw myself at the heavy planks. It closed enough to touch the frame, and I jammed my sword under the bottom, wedging the blade between the wood and stone.

The man nodded in approval and put his feet on the hilt. "Clever."

Howls of pain from the far side of the door pulled the air from my lungs, and I heard a snap and the ringing of metal as the blade broke. The stranger looked at me, ready to call instructions, but the sharp retort of wood cut off whatever he might have said next, and an arc of steel appeared through the thick boards near the man's head. Deep growls of rage on the other side of the door raised the hair on my arms.

Weight hit from the far side, and the door shifted, the hilt of the broken sword sliding toward my feet. I turned to find Geoffrey and Iselle, but Geoffrey was gone—hiding, no doubt. My opinion of the Vanguard, the fighting order, slipped somewhere beneath the soles of my boots. "Sister, we need weapons."

Another blow shook the door, and the stranger cursed. "They're going after the hinges." He paused to turn his dark eyes to me. "Weapons won't help us. We have to hold the door."

The next blow fell against the wood like a death knell. With a few more strikes they'd be in our midst and at our throats.

Geoffrey came at a run, his robes flying behind him, a large wooden mallet in one hand and thick wedges gripped in the other. He didn't stop until he crashed into the door, his teeth clenched in savagery. The impact reset the door in its frame, and he bent, pounding a pair of wedges beneath it with quick, vicious strokes. Then he did the same to the top.

My estimation of his division changed in that moment, and a flash of shame forced the next words from me. "Ably done, brother."

He nodded, giving me an almost-smile. "By Aer in heaven, I've missed fighting." He pointed to the wedges. "They won't keep them out forever."

A cock crowed, and frantic screams came from behind the door as a flurry of blows hit the wood on the hinge side. A crack appeared and a portion of a man's hand, the skin pale as a maggot, became visible on the other side.

A touch on my arm pulled my gaze to Iselle. She stood, slight and frail, no more than half my weight, but her eyes blazed as if the attack had refined and distilled the courage she used to face death day after day.

Another blow from the axe fell, and two planks across the top hinge gave way, the door slanting in with the weight of the men beyond it. The stranger, Geoffrey, and I threw our mass against it, but this time the door refused to close. Sister Iselle thrust her hand into the pouch at her waist and darted forward to toss a handful of yellow powder through the opening.

Coughs and curses in a strange tongue came from the far side, and another blow from the axe hit the wood, but without strength.

I sought Iselle's gaze. "What was that?"

Her smile turned triumphant. "Somnal powder. We give it to the patients for pain. It acts very fast."

My expression mirrored hers. "Throw some more."

She shook her head. "That's all I have."

I looked to Geoffrey, but he shook his head. "I have none. Sister Iselle is more skilled with the powder than I."

The brother's frank admission raised my estimation of him even as hope flared to ashes and died in my chest. The cock out back crowed again, and I wondered absurdly if the men on the other side of the door would kill it as well.

The pounding stopped.

The three of us kept our shoulders to the door, waiting, but no more blows or axe strokes landed. A hint of orange sunlight showed, lining the door in radiance. Outside, the air stilled and quieted, as though the attack had never been. I waved a hand for silence and listened, but not even the sound of breathing could be heard.

"A ruse?" I asked the stranger.

In the depths of those eyes I saw doubt, but behind it there lurked a deeper knowledge. "I don't think so."

The thought of opening that door to whatever lay beyond hollowed out my stomach. I had no intention of moving until I was sure the threat had passed. "I don't fancy falling for a child's trick."

"Wait," Iselle said as she darted away. I heard her footsteps ascending the stairs and then descending again after a pause. "They're gone."

"Hiding?" I asked.

The stranger shook his head. "No." He straightened and stepped away from the door—leaving Geoffrey and me to brace it alone—and addressed Iselle. "Where is Elwin?"

The sister's eyes clouded. "In the west wing. I'm sorry, sir, he's just passed."

For nearly a year, I'd been the king's reeve, assigned to seek out the truths within the city of Bunard that might endanger Laidir's rule. For eight years prior I'd worked the poor quarter, learning to read what passed in the stranger's eyes in that moment. I stepped away from the door, and Geoffrey did as well. It rocked from top to bottom on its one good hinge, fragile and useless, but there was nothing beyond the battered wood except the breaking daylight. I bent to retrieve my shattered sword blade and made to follow the stranger out of the House of Passing.

I put my hand on his shoulder. "Maybe you'd like to tell me who you are and how you know the dead man's name."

I saw him work to put a smile on his face, but the loss in his eyes, the look of a man whose last hope had died, drowned his countenance in sorrow. His gaze drifted across the badge on my cloak, and he gave a small nod. "Peret Volsk." He stuck out his hand. "Well met, reeve."

I took his hand in mine and the room spun. By the time my eyes stopped turning circles in their sockets, hoofbeats were thundering away from me.

"Are you hurt, Lord Dura?"

One of Iselle's hands came forward to brush another swelling on my forehead, the touch cool and gentle. Light flared in my vision and I winced, closing my eyes to ward away the glare. For an instant I had the sensation of falling through her gaze before vertigo darkened my senses.

A moment later my sight returned to normal and I found myself on the floor, a couple of feet farther away from the door, with Iselle still looking at me. I gasped for air.

Geoffrey came forward to offer me a hand up. "Lord Dura, are you well?"

I ignored his hand for the moment and shook my head, trying to clear the pain and glare from behind my eyes as I probed the knots forming on my head. The room's spin slowed and stopped at last and I plotted how I might find Peret Volsk and question him properly. He represented my best clue to finding Elwin's killer. He'd known his name and where he'd been taken. "I need to see Elwin."

The world held a strange cant to it, as if someone had shifted it off its axis. I rolled to my feet. My knees trembled, and more than anything I wanted to leave, to be free from the House of Passing, but Elwin's body might provide some clue or evidence that his voice had not. His last desperate call still echoed in my hearing.

"What did he say, there at the end?" I asked.

Geoffrey shook his head, but Iselle bit the corner of her lower lip in thought. "I wasn't always a sister of the Servants," she said. A tinge of rose colored her cheeks at the admission. "My family placed me with the Merum when I was just a girl. I had to learn the liturgy in the original tongue." She shrugged. "Domere—it's from the rite of absolution, but the meaning of the word changes depending on the context. It might mean *bestowed* or *granted*, or even *forgiven*."

I grunted. Iselle's family must have been quite wealthy. Only a few schools taught the dead language, certainly none of the ones available to lower merchants. Even so, her interpretation didn't make sense. It didn't sound quite right, but with my head pounding I couldn't argue.

Someone had caved Elwin's head in with a sword. In his last moments, almost any thought or impulse might have come from his wounded mind. I took a deep breath and locked my knees to keep my trembling legs from dumping me back on the floor and strode back into the house to Elwin's deathbed to unwrap the bandages that covered his wound.

"Context?" I said. "What does it mean when a dying man has your head clenched in a death grip?" I didn't expect a reply, but I needed something to distract me from the task at hand.

Geoffrey didn't answer, but whether in ignorance or disapproval, I couldn't tell. Iselle just watched me, looking uncomfortable.

Then I saw Elwin's eyes. When had the stares of the dead become so important? I thought back, but I couldn't place the moment. Priest or prostitute, noble or commoner, man or woman, aged or young, they all held a vision of something I could almost understand were it not so impossibly far away. Elwin's eyes nested in a batch of wrinkles, and age spots covered his face like random spatters of ink. Why would someone fight so hard to kill a man who would have died in a couple of years anyway? His eyes, blue and remarkably clear for someone his age, provided no clue. "What's out there, old man?"

Then, because Iselle and Geoffrey stood watching me, I removed the last of the blood-soaked cloths covering Elwin's head and looked upon his wound.

One thing became apparent immediately, though it might not be of much use. Robin had gone down before Elwin. The gouge across the old man's head looked as deep as a furrow from a freshly sharpened plow, and bits of crushed bone in the wound testified to the strength behind the blow. Robin had taken his wounds to keep the attackers from his master. When he'd gone down, they'd made short work of the defenseless old cleric.

"I'm sorry, sister," I said to Iselle. "There's no way he could have survived this." I nodded my acknowledgment of Elwin's feat and patted him on one gnarled hand, the flesh already cool to the touch. "He must have been as tough as boot leather. I don't know how he lived long enough to make it to the house."

Dest broke into a trot as soon as I had him turned north toward the city, away from the house, eager to leave the smell of death and dying. The cool air served to shake some of the cobwebs I'd gotten by way of hitting my head. Anger cleared the rest. Fury at the attack, the indignity done to Robin, and the thought that people existed who were willing to take the lives of defenseless old men burned in my gut. I savored the feeling, reveling in the thought of unleashing a portion of my anger on the men who'd brought death into my city.

But I needed answers. Our city wasn't as big as those of the kingdoms to the south, but Bunard boasted over a hundred thousand souls, and finding the stranger would prove difficult if he didn't want to be found. Once I found him, I'd have to find some way of squeezing information out of him.

The house didn't get many visitors. The brothers and sisters there admitted as much. And though some of them looked askance at my interest, they welcomed my assistance. The stranger hadn't looked like the type to visit the sick. His dark hair showed the cut typical of nobles. His clothes had been well cut but without ornamentation. The gifted didn't use the charity of the king's hospice. He had money—but without a merchant's desire to market himself and lacking a noble's proclamation of ancestry.

That left the church. But which order? He wore no sign or sigil that would offer a clue. His clothes were too fine for him to be of the Servants, but he could belong to any of the other three.

As I considered him, I realized it was his face that I remembered best—the expression at learning of Elwin's death had held rage and desperation and loss.

I leaned forward to give Dest a pat on his forequarters. "What do you make of our stranger?"

He never answered my questions, but I was used to his silence and made a habit of offering his speculations for him. "Perhaps he's a preceptor of one of the churches?" I shook my head. "No, he's of an age with me, perhaps no more than thirty."

No echoes came to me of other horses, but I looked ahead and over each shoulder anyway as I pulled the tight bundle of cloth I'd found on Elwin out into the morning light. Unwinding each layer as carefully as if the fabric held jewels, I held my breath to see what a dying man might consider precious.

A shard of metal with a faint yellow cast more subtle than gold lay in my palm. I pushed against it with one thumbnail, but it refused to yield. Then I tried my dagger and got the same result. Not gold then, or silver, or even an alloy of the two. A fear and reverence shrouded me as I tried to argue with my suspicion. *Aurium*? That in itself might explain much about Elwin's death. Had the stranger at the House of Passing known of it?

The temptation to marshal the watch and roust him out of whatever hole he might be hiding in tugged at me, but I had to report to the king. Since the deaths that resulted in my elevation, any murder in the city got his personal attention, but the death of a pair of clerics carried threats and reminders of the unknown, and Laidir had reason to distrust ignorance. Had either of the men owned a gift?

"Not again," I breathed.

Dest flicked an ear back at me but didn't bother to answer.

Chapter 4

I passed through the gates on the southern side of the city. I acknowledged the guard's recognition with a nod that sent my head reeling and began the ascent up the streets of Bunard to the king's fortress, where it squatted atop the mammoth tor. The people filling the markets and alleys—hurrying or sauntering as their temperament and schedule dictated—the buildings and even the sky overhead all held a strange tilt to them.

"Ho, Willet," a voice cried out. "Good morrow. Figs today?"

I reined in Dest, turning to see the face of a man I'd known for years, his bulbous nose and too-large ears suddenly unfamiliar. I smiled and shook my head as I struggled to recall his name. The faces of the hawkers with their wares and the city guards on watch struck me as wrong, as if the thousands of images that made up their memory were locked away.

I spurred Dest forward, crossing the successive bridges over the Rinwash until I came in sight of the cathedrals and heard the yelling. The noise of the criers grew, accompanied now by the sound of a muttering crowd, and I considered going another way. With a sigh, I continued on despite the weariness that dropped on my shoulders like a bag of grain. I needed to get to the king, and a detour would waste time.

I turned a corner in the road and hit the edge of the crowd. The Servants' crier was on my left, the Vanguard's on my right. The edict of tolerance had forbidden fighting amongst the orders, but that didn't keep their adherents from going at it by proxy.

"The purpose of man is to serve others, placing them above himself," the Servants' crier proclaimed, his brown robe ruffling in the breeze. "If every man looks to use his gift in his own interest, we will descend into selfish barbarity." His clear tenor carried above the crowd. Many in the loose assembly that filled the large square framed by the cathedrals nodded their heads in agreement.

"I must take issue with my brother," a brazen-throated woman in white declaimed. "While service is a noble goal, there will always be evil in this world. Unless we are bold in confronting the enemy's malice, servanthood will only provide fuel for its excesses." Tall, her auburn hair floated in the breeze, wreathing her head in a flaming halo atop her spotless white robe. "The gifts of Aer are given so that we might eradicate evil from the world."

I dismounted and led Dest through the crowd on foot, grinding my teeth at the delay. Yet it would be quicker than having to apologize to some merchant if my horse stepped on his toes. The criers for the Absold and the Merum loomed ahead. I looked around at the throng. I'd been through Criers' Square any number of times. Most of the faces never changed, but even in their newfound strangeness, I noted the presence of new adherents.

The Absold's crier—they were almost always attractive blue-clad women—had the largest portion of the crowd. Many of the men gazed at her with something other than religious fervor. I moved to my left to get by.

"While I can sympathize with the desire to serve and to fight evil, as my brother and sister so eloquently express, I must disagree. Our principle purpose here is not dependent on what we do, but on what we are. We are all fallen. Only by extending forgiveness freely to each other, in imitation of Aer's forgiveness for us, can we free ourselves from those internal chains that make us less than we are. Then you will see your gift shine forth."

The Merum priest, dressed in red, waited for her to finish. The crowd in front of his stand, a simple stack of granite slabs at odds with the massive cathedral behind it, was smaller than the other three, and most of them waited passively, their faces neither pained nor expectant. "The strictures are these," the priest intoned, reciting the daily office. "You must not delve the deep places of the earth, you

must not covet another's gift, and above all you must honor Aer, Iosa, and Gaoithe in all." He stopped. The Merum never debated. They quoted the office in pieces between the proclamations of the other three. Most people, even those who didn't adhere to their division, had heard it so many times, they could recite it themselves.

Before the Servant could speak again, a rough voice hurled itself at the crowd from just ahead of me.

"Look at you!" A red-faced man standing atop a collection of crates just beyond the criers' area stood, his finger pointing at the crowd. "How many of you actually have a gift?" He pointed at a man, bearded, broad and heavy across the shoulders. "You! Do you have a gift?" When the man shook his head, the speaker laughed. "And how many of you have waited on your knees with your prayers turning to ashes in your mouth, hoping that somehow your talent and work might be enough?" His derisive laughter could have tanned a hide. "Or that you might become one of the gifted?"

"What of it?" the bearded man asked. "Sometimes gifts come to those who wait."

The man on the crates shook with dismissive glee, his thick dark hair waving with the motion. "Sometimes?" He stabbed his finger in the air, picking out people in the crowd. "Is that what you're hoping for? That someone will die unexpectedly or without an heir and somehow a gift will come to you?"

He pointed down from his crates at the bearded man. "I speak for the Clast, and I'm here to ask you this: What right does some rich man's family have to hoard their gifts from generation to generation and keep you poor?"

A few of the people in the crowd nodded their heads, and a few more shifted to move closer. Some of the faces in the crowd turned ugly. I knew that emotion. I'd owned it often enough myself, but I didn't trust where it would lead. I led Dest around to one side until I stood next to the speaker's makeshift platform.

"Excuse me, friend," I said as I tapped his leg. "You might want to ease up on the rhetoric."

He looked at me as if I'd given him a gift. "Is this not Criers' Square?" He pitched his voice to reach the next kingdom, and I winced.

"Aye," I said.

"Then what is your problem with me?"

I looked at the people around the speaker. A couple of the men, including the bearded fellow, had edged closer to me, their hands not quite in view. Hoping for subtlety, I moved to put my horse between them and me. I'd seen plants before—people who appeared to be just random parts of the crowd but weren't.

I held up my reeve's badge. Anyone from the city of Bunard or anywhere else in the kingdom of Collum would know what it was. The bearded fellow stopped edging toward me, and I allowed myself to relax. The badge didn't always work.

"I've got no problem with you, neighbor," I said. "Unless you mean to do something more than just air your views peaceably."

The speaker laughed, sweeping his eyes over the crowd. "How like the gifted, to desire peace right up until war breaks out." He stabbed a finger at me. "Then it's the ungifted who fight, dying for the kings of Collum, Owmead, Caisel, and Moorclair while you stay behind with your gift."

This brought an angry mutter from the crowd. The man's words were true, and everyone in the square knew it. No one with a verified gift went to war anymore. Too many times the gift had passed to the enemy, diluting a kingdom's resources once the war ended.

I couldn't refute him on his main point, but he'd made a mistake. I mounted Dest so the people in the crowd could see me better. "I am Willet Dura. You know me, and you know that I fought in the war. It's true the gifted stay behind. They stay because the kingdom—"

"You heard him!" The speaker raised his arms. "If you are ungifted, Dura, you belong with us. I speak for the Icon, leader of the Clast. There is a place for the ungifted within our order, a place where you will be the equal of any other man or woman."

He turned away from me and leveled a finger at the crowd. "And for those of you within reach of my voice who are gifted, I say this: Come join us. Renounce the gift that sets you unfairly higher than your fellow man and become one of the Clast. Rely on the talent and temperament that is given to any man."

The criers for the four looked on in horror. I pitied them. Trained and instructed to give the daily homily in cooperation with each other, they froze beneath the verbal onslaught the man brought upon them—puppies facing a wolf. I spurred Dest away from the square and flagged down the first man of the city watch I saw, a young long-limbed fellow named Ahden. Why did I remember him being taller?

"Lord Dura?"

I pointed behind me. "Keep an eye on Criers' Square this morning. There's a new guy there."

He sighted along my arm, squinting for an instant, and nodded. "You mean that fellow from the Clast?"

"He's been there before?"

Ahden spat in disgust. "Every morning for the last two weeks. Always railing about how the gifted are keeping the rest of us beneath their heel." His eyes narrowed. "He doesn't come right out and say it, but he's hinted at forcing those with gifts to let them go free or split them among the entire city."

I hadn't heard of any disturbances, but the uneasy feeling in my gut didn't go away. "Any trouble?"

Ahden shook his head. "No. So far he's been pretty careful to limit himself to words, but every day a few more follow him from the square with the look of men and women who have a score to settle."

I nodded. "Ahden, I'm changing your assignment. From this point on I want you in the square." At his look of protest, I raised a hand. "I'll clear it with Jeb, but I want you posted with the criers each morning. Don't do anything, but keep your badge out and make sure this fellow with the Clast can see you."

He bowed from the neck in confirmation of the order, and I turned Dest toward the base of the tor and Laidir's keep.

Chapter 5

I turned right and traced my way along the circular wall of dark granite that formed the outer defense of Bunard's stronghold. Twenty paces high and six wide at the top, in the entire history of the continent the wall had never been breached. Guards patrolled the height with the relaxed, loose-limbed strides of soldiers during peacetime.

The entrance to the guardhouse and the prison cells beneath the tor loomed on my left, and I passed into darkness beneath archer slits in the heavy rock above. Torches licked the darkness with yellow-tongued fire that cast dancing shadows around me.

Sevin manned the open archway that framed the entrance. I liked him. He didn't bother to show any deference to my title, small as it was, but he didn't respect anyone else's either. "Is Gareth within?"

Sevin nodded, his mouth pulling to one side to speak around the scar that puckered the length of his left jawline. "Aye, he's with a merchant." He paused to spit his opinion across the floor. "The goat's get says one of his servants is a thief." Sevin's scorn pulled his damaged face into a leer. He barked a laugh as he let his eyes roam the bruises on my face and the knots on my head. "The next time you go brawling, take me with you. I'm getting out of practice."

As I moved past him, I sighed with relief. One of the other reeves could handle the merchant, maybe even Jeb, if the man refused to be put off.

I passed into the sprawling guardroom, the light from a dozen lamps lost in the height of the dome overhead. I dismounted and gave the reins of my horse to a stableboy, and Dest shook his head, looking relieved to be free of my weight for a while.

Weary, I put out my bare hand against the rough granite walls. Desperation and gloom leeched into me, as if the collected misery of accused and accuser had etched itself into the stones. I swallowed bile and tottered to the nearest table, where a guardsman scratched pen against parchment, and reached out to steady myself.

"Lord Dura?"

The voice sounded distant, and I squinted to bring the room back into focus. Gareth beckoned from the far end, flanked by a raven-haired young woman hardly more than a girl and a man dressed in gaudy reds and yellows of merchant's dress.

I gave my head a shake and focused on the steps I needed to take to reach him. The room refused to still, but I reached the table set aside for Gareth's use and managed not to spill his inkpot when I grabbed the smooth wood to keep myself from reeling.

Gareth stood and inclined his head toward the merchant, a paunchy, sweating man who looked as though he cherished every insult ever laid to him. "Lord Dura, this is Master Merchant Andler." He sighed and gestured toward the comely young woman with delicate features and a thick wealth of dark hair. "And this is Branna, one of his servants. Master Andler insists that she has thieved against his interests." Even Gareth's raspy voice couldn't make the charge sound less ridiculous. He gave Andler a stony-faced look that did nothing to hide his contempt. "Naturally, Branna denies the charge."

I retreated a step to distance myself from their dispute. Even with my tilted vision I could guess the real source of their conflict. "Let Jeb handle it. I have to report to the king."

Andler's chins wobbled with his indignation. "I will not be put off. I demand this woman be released into my custody to return my property, or else I shall petition the king directly."

I did my best to ignore him and his complaint. "Gareth, were there any other witnesses this morning?"

He looked at me for a moment before his vision cleared in comprehension. "No, Lord Dura, just the seamstress. And her story keeps growing."

The merchant's words finally penetrated the fog in my brain, and I shook my head. "Why is Master Andler asking for her release? Didn't he bring her in?"

Gareth shook his head. "No. The girl came here asking for protection."

I shook my head. "Protection from what?"

My lieutenant's beefy hand indicated the merchant. "Him, Lord Dura."

Andler, his face florid, reached for me, grabbing my arm below the elbow. "I care nothing for your trumped-up title! I want that thieving girl released into my custody so that I can reclaim my property. You will listen to—"

I grabbed his hand, twisting it at the wrist so that he buckled. I'd never cared for people touching me without permission. His face floated in front of me, twisted with malice, like the heads of fiends carved into the towers of the old churches to keep evil spirits at bay. Obsidian clouds in my head roiled with the desire to see Branna dead. The muscles in my legs turned to water, and I staggered away, my vision spinning. Gareth, his face wavering and shifting as if seen through the heat of an oven, pulled, grabbed me, and threw an arm around my shoulders.

"Willet, what's wrong?"

I swallowed bile and panic in equal measures, staring at Andler's bare hands. The clouds in my mind receded and my vision crept into focus, bringing a semblance of balance back with it. "I'm all right," I said to Gareth and stepped away from him to prove it. My guts churned. If I released Branna to the merchant, she wouldn't survive the day, but I needed a reason to keep her.

That's when I noticed Branna's clothes, not quite those of a noble, but too fine for a servant. The dress clung to her, and the bodice hinted at too much to be considered proper. Her boots were fashioned of soft leather and were turned down to allow more than a hint of her calves to show. The scent of orange and rose petals, expensive and uncommon perfume, wafted from her skin. She had her chin set the way people do when they've made up their mind not to cry. A tremor in it showed she might lose the battle.

I pointed at her and tried to force my voice steady. "What's her defense?"

Gareth's head shifted back and forth. "She's offered none except to say she hasn't stolen anything."

I moved away from the table and beckoned to the girl. The question I had to pose would be shameful to her or any woman. It would be better to keep others from hearing it. She followed me, her eyes fastened to the floor. Tremors worked their way up and down her arms, matching the ones in my legs. I pitched my voice so it would reach her ears alone. "How many times has the merchant offered you to others?"

The dam of her resolution broke, and she clutched at me, shaking her head and scattering tears across the stones of the floor. Somewhere deep in my chest, rage, hot like a blacksmith's furnace, began to build. My imagination conjured images of her family held in debt to the merchant and Branna's body taken and bartered as recompense.

Perhaps this time she'd refused. But I had no proof, and the king would flay me himself if I brought charges or violence against the merchant without it. I didn't have time to sort the truth, and I no longer wanted to leave this to Jeb.

"Trust me," I whispered to the girl.

Turning to Gareth, I did the only thing I could. "Branna has offered no defense. Have her imprisoned until I can verify the truth of the merchant's charge." I tried to ignore the startled weeping behind me.

"My lord?" Gareth's voice held more than questioning.

I turned from his disbelief. "Does this satisfy you, Master Andler?"

From the look on his face, I could see it did not, and that was enough to salve my conscience at having the girl thrown into prison. With a stiff nod and as much dignity as his soft posture could conjure, Andler departed. I pulled Gareth out of their hearing. "See to it that she is kept alone with whatever she requires." Gareth's confusion knotted his gruff soldier's face, so I continued. "The merchant means to kill her. To release her before we can prove he's bartering her means her death."

Gareth gave me a slow, dubious nod. "I can see it might be possible, but how do you know?"

I fought a sudden discomfort. Away from the merchant and the girl, the room had resumed its accustomed solidity, but I didn't want to give credence to the intuition that had driven me. "The dress and the boots. Branna could never afford that kind of finery on a servant girl's wages. And every time I looked at her calves she squirmed, trying to hide the skin that someone else had obviously wanted her to show."

I took Gareth's nod as agreement and left. The king would expect me to report, and Gael would be waiting for me at court. Branna's predicament should prove easy enough to unravel. It could wait while I tackled the far more difficult problem of Elwin and Robin's murders.

Chapter 6

I exited the guardroom on the north side, came out onto the broad arced plaza that circled the base of the tor, and set my feet on the wide street that spiraled upward toward the stronghold. Offices and living quarters passed by me as I ascended, each a bit larger than the last. Wary of a fear I couldn't name, I kept my bare hands in the folds of my cloak.

The sun, weak behind a tenacious fog, indicated noon, and a small knot of worry blossomed in my stomach. King Laidir was a fair man but tended toward bursts of impatience, and nothing shortened his temper more than murder in his domain. I had no illusions about my position or the influence that my title carried. I was the least of the king's nobility, a lord without land, hardly more than a servant, and while the means of my elevation had earned the gratitude of the king, it had also garnered me the enmity of the other nobles.

I entered the shadow of the stronghold as I came around to the north side of the tor. Even this close to noon the shadow stretched away from the monolithic blocks of charcoal granite with omens of judgment. As I passed through the large stone arch, I stopped to speak with the men and women on guard duty.

I nodded to a pale-haired man with oversized hands. "Greetings, Linan."

He took enough time to glance over my shoulder, but the foot traffic remained light. "Lord Dura."

He didn't drink, a fact that made him difficult to bribe. I liked him anyway. "Is the king holding court?"

Light gray eyes flicked over to me and held mine for an instant. "No. He's in his private audience chamber."

I breathed a sigh, relieved at being spared the public spectacle of presenting myself before a full court. Not so bad as nighttime, when the nobles gathered to feast and dance, the throne room still presented danger. My first impression months earlier had been a riot of color and sound, a feast for the head as well as the stomach. It had taken two days for the reality to assert itself. Court was actually more like the surface of a beautiful lake with eels swimming just beneath. Only Gael's presence and the king's command, in that order, compelled me to attendance whenever my duties as reeve did not interfere.

"You are ordered to see him the instant you arrive," Linan added.

Invisible hands reached inside my gut and started kneading my stomach like dough. "How long has he been waiting?"

He gave a slight shake of his head, and the hands folded my insides again. "Too long."

Regardless of who manned the entrance, whether I found them to be amiable or contentious, I made it a habit to buy them drinks, along with the other servants of the stronghold. Nobles seldom took notice of servants, but those who manned the entrance, tended the chambers, or performed any of the other thousand small tasks of the city noticed everything. I flipped the guard a silver half crown. If he didn't want to spend it on drink, so be it.

I passed through an oversized arch and into a thousand years of history at a jog. The stronghold occupied the summit of the highest hill in the region, a flat-topped peak that necessitated a myriad of stairs, keeping the less-determined supplicants away. But the same design that frustrated opposing armies now conspired to delay me. The lords of the land were supposed to show more dignity than to run through the hallways.

The main passage, one level below the king's audience hall and private offices, was lined with weapons from a thousand years of intermittent fighting. I ran past a sweeping chronicle of the blacksmith's art, noting the change in weaponry. Huge two-handed broadswords that could chop through armor gave way to smaller swords and wicked-looking crossbows. Light mail changed to plate, and pikes changed to halberds. Black flecks of blood-rust remained on most of the weapons.

Upon my ascension to the nobility, the king's chamberlain had spared enough time for my education to keep me from embarrassing myself in front of the other nobles. His instruction had included a lesson in the history of the kingdom of Collum. The weapons displayed in the hall hadn't been donated—they'd been scavenged. With the blood still on them, they were placed here beneath the king's seat of power to honor the dead. I tried to ignore the images the spots and streaks of rust conjured from my own wartime experience.

The main stairway at the middle of the Hall of Remembrance ascended into luxury, the floors lined with polished stone and the walls adorned with tapestries, many embellishing the kingdom's long bloody history. This is what most of the gifted nobles saw—glorious scenes of battle without the grisly reality of the hall beneath. The view from the field had been altogether different.

I skipped the main entrance to court—a tide of noise and light and the smell of food washing over me—and came panting to a stop before a wide pair of double doors, the kind people opened together when someone important made an entrance. More than anything I wanted to slip inside with as little disturbance as possible.

Four guards stood watch, a pair on each side of the doors. Only two should have been there—the rest belonged inside with the king. I spoke to one of the guards on the left. "Shouldn't you be with His Majesty?"

He nodded but didn't speak. His face had taken on the stillness men wear when they've no choice but to swallow their anger.

"What's his mood?"

His expression shifted for a moment. "Strange."

I slipped through the door into the king's private chambers. At the far end three large arched windows with clear panes of leaded glass faced west, overlooking the main flow of the Rinwash as it meandered toward the sea. Shelves, black with aged lacquer, lined the other three walls, their contents a semi-ordered mix of books, parchments, and oddments—baubles and devices that never failed to catch my eye.

A low dais less than a foot high ran beneath the windows, and a well-padded chair occupied the center for those occasions when Laidir wanted or needed to remind those in his presence of his position.

The entire room stood at odds with the kingdom's perception of Laidir as a military man, but I knew this place defined him more accurately. Most of the real work Laidir accomplished happened here, not in the audience chamber. The gift of kings, a compilation of the gifts the orders called the six charisms, allowed Laidir to run a kingdom with hundreds of thousands as easily as a proprietor ran a business.

Two steps into the room I faltered. The guards outside the door weren't the only people sent from Laidir's presence—the king's personal attendant, the chamberlain, was nowhere to be seen, and his castellan, too, was noticeably absent. Instead, a brown-garbed Servant with more years than most people would get stood on his left, wearing a closed expression and the sigil of her order—a foot resting on a hand, a symbolic washing that emphasized their interpretation of Scripture and the church's mission. The yellow pendant hanging from her neck brought me up short—not just any Servant, then, but *the* Servant. I tried not to gape, but the proscription against delving made gold as rare as a lightless day.

But that wasn't what set me on edge. Overtopping the church woman by three hands stood a man dressed all in black—the same man who'd fought beside me in the House of Passing.

I fingered the knots on my head as I went forward, stopped five paces short of the king, and touched one knee to the floor. "Your men told me you wished to see me, Your Majesty."

Instead of replying, Laidir looked to his left, seeking permission from the Chief of Servants to speak in his own chambers. The woman made a vague gesture. Briefly, she cut her eyes to the man in black. "I pray you, Lord Dura, continue." Her voice mirrored her features—dry and shriveled, as if the weight of her years had leeched the moisture from her throat.

With an effort, and out of pique, I kept my gaze on the king. I was offended on his behalf. Until he decided to tell me why he'd emptied his chamber of his most trusted aides and replaced them with strangers, I'd pretend everything was normal. "Two men were killed in the lower merchants' quarter last night. A man named Robin and the man he served, Elwin. We think they were attacked by at least two men, possibly more. Robin died there, Elwin later at the House of Passing."

I pursed my lips, unsure of how much to say before continuing. I didn't know these people, and I'd learned to regret misplaced trust. "There's something strange at work here, Your Majesty. From what we could tell, Robin appears to have killed at least one of the attackers, but no other bodies were found. They hauled the body away and left Robin his purse, a purse holding more coin than a menial of the church should have. Some of it was gold."

I watched the Chief of Servants and the black-garbed man out of the corner of my eyes as I spoke. I didn't mention Robin's skill with the sword or Elwin's strange behavior on his deathbed, and I mentally clamped my mouth shut against speaking of the sliver of metal I'd found on Elwin, metal I suspected to be aurium. I hoped mentioning gold would put Laidir's visitors on the defensive, and I had no intention of revealing my deeper suspicions.

The man in black whispered something to the Chief of Servants, who in turn leaned in to mutter something to the king. The hackles on the back of my neck urged me to leave.

Laidir's mouth compressed, and I saw his eyes flash at the indignity of being reduced to speaking for others. "What of Elwin?"

The Servant and the man looked at me with bright, intense eyes, and I concentrated on keeping my arms and feet still, as though nothing untoward had occurred or ever would. Then I shrugged, pretending the question was unimportant. "He died at the house, Your Majesty. I examined the body to see if his wounds could tell me anything." I shook my head, trying very hard to appear to be nothing more than a frustrated reeve. "I don't know how he ever made it there. He took a sword stroke to the head that opened his skull."

The man in black leaned over to whisper to the Chief of Servants again, his eyes glittering with impatience. Once more, the Servant bent to pass her order through the king.

"I'm right here in front of you." I straightened, stiffening my spine against the rebuke that was coming. I wasn't disappointed.

The Servant's mouth compressed, lines of displeasure radiating outward from it until it resembled the center of a web. "I am used to being treated with respect, Lord Dura."

I laughed. "If you know enough of me to use my title, then you know I'm not overly impressed by them." I allowed a hint of a smile to touch my face. If Laidir couldn't or wouldn't defend his position, perhaps I could make his visitors a little less sure of themselves. "Or you might not have heard people refer to me as the king's dog, Laidir's assassin, or any of a dozen other ridiculous titles." I let my expression go blank, a look I gave people to let them know I considered them nothing more than an object, a thing that I found unworthy of emotion or feeling.

The Chief of Servants pointed at me, her mouth tight and her arm trembling. "You will recount your visit to the House of Passing in minutest detail, Lord Dura. I speak for the church."

I turned from her as if her presence was already forgotten. "Your Majesty, do you desire to hear the account of my visit to the House of Passing?"

He nodded at me, his expression almost neutral, but I could see his pride and joy for what I had done gleaming in his eyes. "By all means, Lord Dura."

I described what had happened, changing the order of events so that it seemed as though I'd inspected Elwin's wound before the stranger's arrival and the subsequent attack on the House. With a nod toward the Servant, I described Elwin's wound in painstaking detail until I saw her pale. I finished by relating how the stranger had helped defend the house against attack, but had left before I could question him. The man in black gave me a nod of acknowledgment but didn't reply.

The Chief of Servants sighed, and the tension flowed from her until she no longer resembled a spider hovering over its capture. She looked to the man, waiting for him to speak. If he went back to check my story, Geoffrey and Iselle would tell him what occurred. They served the dying, not me or Laidir, and had no reason to keep information from anyone. The need for silence or adjusting the facts would never occur to them.

But the man in black didn't speak. He paused instead to gaze at me, his manner friendly. I felt myself sifted and weighed down to the last dram.

The king nodded, but I saw his jaws clench. "Very well. Your service in this matter is concluded, Lord Dura. The Chief of Servants and her assistant will be handling the matter of Elwin's death from this point."

I tried to make sense of what I'd just heard and failed. A flash of anger heated my voice. "Your Majesty? I'm not sure what you've been told, but that man knows something about Elwin's death." I thrust a finger at the stranger in accusation. "He arrived at the House of Passing just after I did. By what authority does he refuse the king's reeve?"

The man in black commended me with another of those looks that held camaraderie, but he turned from my anger to nudge the old woman once more.

"By the authority of the church." The Chief of Servants turned to the king and gave a slight bow, acknowledgment given to an inferior. "Your lord's concerns do not involve the church, Your Majesty. We'll take our leave now."

The door closed behind them, echoing in the emptiness of the king's chamber.

Chapter 7

King Laidir rose from his chair and descended toward me. I had not been dismissed from his presence, and he made no move to send me away—regardless of the fact that hundreds of people awaited him in his court.

Despite his fifty years, his chest was still as broad as a stump, and the sword at his side owned little in common with the ornamental affairs worn by the kings to the south.

He put a thick hand on my shoulder. "Lord Dura, your service to me is without question. I owe you my life and my crown. I have a request to make of you—a request, mind you, not an order."

I knew that this was part of his gifting—this ability to give and receive loyalty—but I would have walked through fire for the look he gave me then. Any of his men would have. It was part of who he was.

"I am always at your service, Your Majesty," I said with a bow.

He shook his head. "No. I will not accept your service until you understand what is being asked of you." Letting go of my shoulder, he paced away from me and then returned, his eyes on the floor, his brows furrowed. His heavy hands, more a blacksmith's than a king's, flexed as if he wished to draw steel, and shoulders as thick as hams testified to the years he'd labored with the weapon, but his frustration was deprived of adversaries.

"That church woman," he said, his voice at odds with his posture, "was from the order of the Pueri—a Servant."

I nodded. Anyone would have known as much upon seeing her clothing and emblem. The Servants traditionally wore brown.

The king chewed the inside of his cheek, not gently, and his eyes, a color somewhere between green and brown, searched for answers. He worked the muscles of his jaw with one hand, pulling the tension from them. "She had letters from the other three orders. They all said the same thing." He raised his head to look at me, his gaze intense, fired with the towering curiosity we shared. "Have you ever heard of all four orders agreeing on anything, Lord Dura?"

I shook my head. Outside of providing priests for the House of Passing, I hadn't. The king held me by my curiosity now. His entire stable of horses couldn't have dragged me from the room. "No, Your Majesty, not unless it comes to fighting, with words or otherwise."

"They all requested—ha, *ordered* is more like it—that the investigation of Elwin's murder be turned over to them, completely over to them." He pulled a sheaf of parchment loose from his belt and waved it at me with a nauseated expression. Glimpses of the four sigils of the divisions passed in front of me. I didn't doubt Laidir, but my curiosity burned with the desire to read the orders for myself.

I blinked. "The orders don't have reeves in their service, Your Majesty. How do they expect to investigate Elwin's death?" Something occurred to me. "Is that exactly what they said, Your Majesty?"

He cocked his head at me. "Yes."

"It's strange that they would make no mention of Robin," I said. "What makes Elwin so important that Robin has become an afterthought before his corpse is cold?" Robin's purse, the one with real gold in it, jangled as I hefted it. "And they never asked for his purse. Why not?"

The king looked at me, his eyes burning. "That's what I want you to discover. I don't like things going on in my kingdom without my knowledge. There's a tale here that needs to be told."

I nodded, eager at the opportunity to discover the man in black's role in this story. "Gladly, sir."

The king sobered. "If they catch you, I'll have to make an example of you, Willet. The four orders together wield enough power to topple me if they wish."

I shook my head. "But you hold the gift of kings. The right to rule is yours."

Laidir's smile held a hint of indulgence. "All the gifts in the world can't stop a war, Willet. Far from it. Many times the covetousness they engender can cause it. Nearly every soul on the northern continent worships in one of the four orders. If the heads of each order will it, they can foment war or rebellion and force me from rule."

His assessment shocked me—both for its stark outcome and for the casual way he described it. "They would do such a thing?"

He shrugged. "It depends on how important the outcome is to them. I don't think this situation merits the desperation of such a response, but the threat remains. Therefore, I need you to be circumspect in your duties. Do you understand?" When I nodded, he stuck out his bare arm.

I gripped his forearm, humbled at the gesture that acknowledged me as a friend.

The room pitched in my mind, and I locked my knees against the sensation of falling. Behind the warmth of the king's hazel eyes, I saw a resolution as hard and unyielding as iron. For years I'd heard the people of the kingdom attribute the king's success to his divine right. Through the touch of his handshake, I could sense the enormity of the gift he'd been given, but with it I sensed a towering resolve, a perseverance, that made the stones of the keep seem weak. In the exordium of the liturgy there existed no explanation, no talent or temperament to explain Laidir's strength of will.

He released my hand and I blinked, trying to right myself and smile.

The king preceded me to the door, peering over one shoulder to look at me on the way. "What will you do first?"

The room still flowed like water in my vision and I pulled a deep breath, stammering my answer in time to the frightened pounding of my heart. "Even if the orders hadn't intervened, solving Elwin's death would prove difficult. Before, I would have scoured the city, trying to find a witness. There must have been at least four men involved, three with swords, maybe more. That kind of noise doesn't go unnoticed."

King Laidir grimaced. "You won't be able to make those kinds of inquiries now. What will you do instead?"

The king was correct, insofar as he knew, but the people I sought didn't usually attract the church's attention. The witnesses I spoke of required my discretion. Any unwarranted attention from the city watch or the king's other reeves and they would never talk to me again. "The orders' interest is a clue in itself. The head of the Servants petitions you and asks you not to investigate the murder of one of her clerics?"

Laidir grunted and gave me half a smile. "You don't need to dance around the truth, Lord Dura. They didn't *ask*."

Anger on his behalf coursed through my chest. King Laidir was the best man I'd ever met. "The point, Your Majesty, is their behavior tells us Elwin was much more than a simple church functionary. If I can discover what made him so important, we'll know why someone wanted to kill him."

"And you think to make those types of inquiries without arousing the suspicion of the church?"

I nodded with more confidence than I felt. "I was almost a priest." The familiar ache of what I'd lost in the last war pulled at my insides like scar tissue covering a wound in my soul, but I shrugged it away. "I still have some friends in the order." I didn't mention my desperate need to see one in particular. Ealdor.

The king nodded with understanding. "Ahh." He squeezed my shoulder. "Fortune, Willet, and make haste." He sighed. "The court will wonder at my absence. I'll leave orders with the guard to have you brought to me here if you discover anything."

I drew a breath at the note of dismissal, and the king's smile returned. "Pardon my oversight, Willet. Accompany me to court. I'm sure the kingdom's need allows you a few moments with Lady Gael before you begin your work."

I nodded my thanks and we entered the passage. The king's guards, all four of them, fell in with us as we walked, two in front and two behind. They were good men, but we didn't speak on the way.

When we arrived at the court's side entrance, I stepped aside to allow the king and his guards to enter. I circled around to use the main entrance, resigned to running the gauntlet of minor and not-so-minor nobles, each of whom held more wealth and prestige than I.

I stepped through the oversized doors to bright candlelight combined with lilting strains of music and the scents of perfume and food to overwhelm the senses, but the candelabras and stained-glass windows held no attraction for me. I sought something more luminous.

Gael would be close to the center of court. According to the chamberlain, there was no set protocol governing the arrangements of nobles at leisure, yet by instinct or unspoken agreement they ordered themselves in close approximation of their estates in the city—those with the most power were closest to the king.

I passed a man whose fingers flowed over the strings of his mandolin, notes cascading in perfect harmony to fill the space around him. And to one side a singer, her voice flawlessly tuned to his instrument, sang a song of unrequited love that could have reduced the sternest cynic to tears.

But the nobles in their vicinity carried on their conversations as if unaware of the gift and talent and work that had been provided for their pleasure. The music washed over them without effect. I had no time or energy to spare for their practiced indifference. A few paces farther on I passed a juggler who balanced himself on a large wooden ball while keeping seven daggers aloft in a weave, the blades flashing in the reflected light. I'd seen better once, but he would never return. A girl, no more than a dozen years old, was his only audience. She clapped her hands with each new trick, and her startled jumps at his feigned mishaps made her thick brown curls bounce in sympathy.

The gifted filled the alcoves between the hall's giant buttresses, each as startling in their skill as the one before. They offered their acts to nobles largely unaware of their presence. Blue bloods and courtesans alike, selectively blind and deaf, reserved their attention for their private conversations.

I kept to the edges of the grand hall, my motions discreet. I had brought death here, and the dead man's allies sought recompense.

"Ah, the king's jackal graces us with his presence once more."

I winced at the sound. The voice belonged to Lord Baine, a cousin to the man I'd killed. Baine owed his fealty to the Orlan family, but by the complicated rules that governed Laidir's court, he was forbidden to challenge me. I had, after all, proved the duke's brother guilty, albeit by less than straightforward means.

Although court protocol kept Baine from challenging me on the matter, it didn't keep me from challenging him. Each time I appeared at court he made it his mission to provoke me to that end. As challenged, he would be allowed to choose weapons, and Baine was deadly enough with a sword to be almost gifted.

I had my suspicions on that account, but proof was another matter. I tried to ignore him.

"Come, Lord Dura, grace us with your presence."

My wince deepened. Second only to the king in power, when Duke Orlan spoke, etiquette demanded I respond. I sighed and changed course to join the broad circle of nobles clustered around Orlan and Baine, his hired killer.

Caution stopped me a few paces short and I bowed. "Your Grace."

Duke Orlan had been bestowed with the type of visage sculptors sought for the face of their conquering hero, but those works done in white marble only accentuated the darkness of his heart. "Tell me, Sir Jackal," Orlan purred, "how do the kingdom's pickpockets and prostitutes fare?"

I could have ignored the address—protocol only required I answer to my given title—but silence would only prolong the conversation. Instead I made a point of letting my gaze linger on the handful of courtesans within the duke's circle. All of them stood in contrast to the duke—young against middle-aged, smooth-skinned versus weathered, soft versus hardened. That he kept known courtesans so close while his wife hung on one arm testified to his arrogance. Even so, his brother, subtle and deadly, had almost exceeded him. "I'm sure Your Grace knows as much of the kingdom's affairs as I."

The women looked at me with naked hatred, but it took a moment for the duke's eyes to widen. He would not challenge me. "You dare to insult your betters?"

"Have I?" I asked. Again, my response took a moment to register, and the duke's face progressed through different shades of rage.

"You forget your place, jackal," Lord Baine hissed.

I nodded my agreement. "Yes, I usually do, my lord." I turned back to Orlan and smiled. "I crave your pardon, Your Grace. Please, allow me to fetch you a drink."

I watched his eyes widen in shock and left while he spluttered. I slipped through the crowd and back to the edge of the hall, ducking behind one of the mammoth columns that supported the lofty ceiling overhead.

There was no doubt my insolence would cost me, I just didn't know how much. I pushed the duke and his hired sword from my mind and resumed my search. When I found her, my body reacted in contradictions, as always. The hole in my chest, the emptiness at her absence, filled while my heart struggled to find its rhythm. I drank in the sight of her.

Gael Alainn and her sister, Kera, gathered admiration and jealousy in equal parts. Both of them had been raised in their father's ventures as buyers and sellers of fine cloth, and their gift of craft created a business built on the creation of clothes and dyes whose depth of color far surpassed others. They imbued silk and satin with colors that seemed lit from within. Today, Gael wore a royal blue dress that accentuated the taper of her waist before flaring to shimmering folds of rippling color that did not reflect the light so much as it gathered and focused it. Kera wore matching green. The rest of the ladies at court tried to ignore them, but they inevitably made their way to the sisters, drawn like vagabonds to a campfire, and the house of Alainn was enriched.

Unlike the ladies of court, I cared little for Gael's dress, choosing instead to focus my attention on the woman. Her face didn't inspire awe as so many beauties at court, but rather inspection. Every time I gazed upon her I discovered some new grace to the strength of her features—the arch of her brows, the sweep of her jawline, the fullness of her lips. It was a face I could love and look at forever, and I intended to do so with whatever fraction of eternity Aer granted me.

Her nose might have been considered too aggressive by the standards of court, but the wealth of dark hair that accented her perfect skin brought harmony to her features. If other men at court lacked the vision to appreciate her beauty, so much the better. My gaze slid from her face, and I nodded a greeting to her sister.

I bowed and kept my gaze proper, just. Her uncle, guardian over both her and her sister, stood to one side. "Count Alainn. Ladies Kera, Gael. It is good to see you, as always."

The count gave me a cool nod, his gaze checking over my shoulder, looking to one side, but never quite meeting mine. I took no offense. The count, like every other noble present, outranked me, and he desired nothing more in that moment than to attach himself to someone of higher rank so that he might reflect a greater light.

Fortunately for me, he succeeded and moved off to accost them, leaving me in the presence of his nieces. I sighed and made a conscious effort to let my shoulders settle back into place.

Kera gave me a teasing smile, her pale cheeks dimpling. "If you expect to move among the nobility, Lord Dura, you'll need to learn to relax." Her face, wan in the light, held the gentle mocking I'd come to appreciate in her and her sister.

I cast a look around me. "I am among the lowest-ranking nobles here, Lady Kera. The others have no wish to have me move among them. There is no gain or profit to be made by associating with me. And there are other reasons as well."

"Nonsense," Gael said, laying a hand on my arm, her touch warm through my sleeve. "At the least some of them should seek your good grace for the day you end up arresting them."

Our laughter, sudden and loud, drew stares until a fit of coughing interrupted Kera's. A sensation of pain bolted across my mind, a knot of black that ate at me when Kera gripped the bare skin on my arm and I clasped her hand. Gael's brows furrowed and she held her sister until the spasm passed. "Still, sister?"

Kera fluttered a hand, dismissing it. "Just until the weather warms." She pulled her shoulders back and brought forth a lady's kerchief to dab the corners of her mouth, and her smile returned. "I simply refuse to be ill just now. My wedding precedes yours by a month."

Gael's hair floated, catching the light, as she gave her head a small shake. "Uncle and his ambition."

"Now, Gael," Kera said, "we can't all marry for love." She grinned. "Not that I won't love spending a bit of my betrothed's money. Besides, Rupert will need me to manage his southern interests. Between his access to the courts of the south and our craft, our family fortunes will be assured for generations." She sniffed. "I'm more than happy with uncle's match if it will get me out of Collum and this drafty old keep."

I nodded and tried not to let my shock or embarrassment show. The touch of Kera's skin had staggered me to the point that I didn't trust my knees to keep me upright. I focused on the conversation with an effort. Count Alainn had managed to arrange an advantageous marriage for Kera to a noble with a growing cloth trade from the southern kingdoms and access to the silk markets. Only the intervention of King Laidir had secured Gael's hand for me. I suspected a rather large sum of money had changed hands between them, but I had no desire to shame Gael or myself by asking.

Kera winked at me and drifted far enough away to maintain the fiction of watching over us without being able to overhear.

"And are you happy with your match, Lady Gael?" I asked.

She sniffed and gazed over the rim of her wine toward the king's dais. "I never expected love within marriage." The glass tilted, and she took a lingering sip. "Mostly, I hoped not to be too bored." The look she turned on me could have lit tinder. "You will try not to be boring, won't you, Lord Dura?"

I kept myself from laughing, just. My engagement to Gael had been granted just after I'd killed Duke Orlan's brother, the marquis. Very few people knew or suspected that the woman in front of me had assisted that endeavor. I stepped closer than was proper for court or public, my lips almost brushing hers. "That's hardly a promise that needs to be made. I think surviving until our wedding will prove to be more difficult." I gave Gael a dose of her own medicine and let my gaze and voice dip. "Three months seems a very long time," I said.

A blush crept into her cheeks, turning her face from luminous to radiant, and I longed for nothing more in that moment than to throw protocol to the wind and feel my lips against hers.

She lifted her chin, her deep blue eyes burning, and gave me a smile that held a fiery challenge. "Then I will have to ensure I am worth the wait." And before I could respond, she curtsied, looking up at me.

I floundered, cudgeling my brain for some rejoinder that would extend our customary duel of words, but it was hard to be clever when breathing was so difficult. Then I caught sight of the king behind her, on the dais across the room, and the moment melted away as if someone had dumped snow down my back.

"Lady Gael." I bowed. "I regret I must take my leave. There is a matter I must take care of for the king." The nobles who stood close to us gasped, and I bit my tongue at my choice of words, but to her credit, Gael didn't flinch or turn angry as so many others in the room might have.

She bowed from the neck, granting me leave to go. "Until later," she murmured.

I stepped close so that no one would see the wrapped cloth I held. "Get this to Myle," I said, pressing the tight bundle I'd taken from Elwin into her hands. "I need to know if this is what I think."

I kept my hands in my cloak, avoiding the incidental touch of others as I sauntered from court, but inside I struggled to breathe. Nobles and courtesans alike held a tilt to them, and I struggled to put one foot ahead of the other. By the time I reached the door, sweat plastered my shirt to my back. I had to find Ealdor.

Chapter 8

Bunard was the center of the kingdom of Collum. The king's keep, and my quarters as his personal reeve, sat on a vast bluff overlooking the Rinwash River. The road from the castle spiraled down the sides of the overlook, the slope crafted so that horses and carts could bring goods and food to the top. Steep alleys and granite steps cut across the road throughout the tor, allowing our fair denizens to shortcut their way to the base of the hill where the majority of the king's subjects lived.

As I walked, my view alternated between the river to the west, where barges drifted south, and the Cibus Plain to the southeast, where we grew our food. Here and there in the distance, villages dotted the hills whose ripples flattened little by little until they disappeared entirely. Beyond sight at the far end of the plain, the Darkwater Forest stretched away to the east and south without light or village to interrupt it. I suppressed a shiver and focused on my destination.

The chief offices of each order were dispersed in a broad square below the keep, clustered just outside the main wall as if watchful of each other. They all kept parishes in each part of the city, sometimes right next door to an order of different interpretation. Perhaps in their choice of location they longed for the reunification the Merum order spoke of.

After catching a glimpse of snow-capped peaks in the distance to the north, I turned south and trekked along a winding cobblestone road that took me past my favorite inn, Braben's, and through a marketplace. My stomach growled, but my need for Ealdor's counsel surpassed my hunger at the moment and I entered the small run-down church belonging to the Merum at the edge of the lower merchants' section, just north of the branch of the Rinwash separating it from the poor quarter.

I didn't see Ealdor at first, and I took a moment to search the inside of the church, moving toward the altar and the prayer rail, brushing my fingers in reverence over the weathered wood and grieving the profession that had been denied to me. I saw him then, emerging from the gloom into the beams of sunlight that came through the patchwork roof. He gave me a smile tinged with sadness and moved to the double-sided rail. I came forward to join him.

"It's been a while," he said without accusation. He stuck his hand out to shake mine, but I avoided his touch, hoping the friendly tug I gave his cassock seemed natural.

I twitched my shoulders. "I've been busy."

"I understand you're spending a lot of time at the House of Passing."

I nodded. "Sister Iselle says it comforts those crossing to have me read out loud or just sit with them."

His eyes, a gray so light they were almost silver, locked on mine. "And is that why you go there so often?"

I laughed, trying to ignore the familiar question. "We've talked about this before. If what I do is the right thing, do I have to do it for the right reason?"

He tilted his head to one side in that way I knew meant he wasn't conceding the point but didn't think it worth arguing about. "And have any of the dying returned to tell you what they see on the other side of eternity?"

I curled my shoulders in an attempt to deflect the question. "Not yet, but I've heard tales of those who've come back."

"And you believe them?"

I shook my head. "No, but I don't disbelieve them either."

We knelt in silence for a moment, just the two of us in the empty space of the church, before Ealdor spoke again. "Do their deaths still bother you?"

Most of their names I'd never known, and nearly ten years of living had erased the few I had. Guilt cut across me, and I engaged in the only penance I could practice—I called up the faces of the mercenaries I'd tried to save in the last war, focusing on the way they looked, young and trusting or old and cynical, just before the column of Owmead soldiers caught us close to sunset and drove us down the slopes and into the Darkwater Forest.

Their caustic laughter rang in my ears, and I winced, rocking back and forth, the memories running forward of their own volition, sweeping me along despite my resistance. We clustered together with our shields raised as bow fire pushed us ever lower until it was either enter the Darkwater or die. We scrambled between the giant boles that marked the border between light and malevolence.

I blinked and saw Ealdor looking at me as the memories wound down and stopped like a child's toy.

"How did they die, Willet?"

His probing frustrated me. "How does anyone die? Something happens and they stop breathing." Curse him, I tried to recall their passing, but I couldn't. The memories refused to come. "I can't remember their deaths. The day was spent. Every time we tried to exit the forest, the archers were there to force us back in, until the light died completely. Blurs of darkness took them one by one after the sun set, but I remember the screams."

The familiar knot of grief lodged in my chest, and my voice grew thick as I tried to speak past it. "I tried to lead them out, but things dropped out of the trees behind us and we were down to nine before we knew what was happening." I shook off the memories like a servant shaking out a blanket. "I'm not here to talk about deaths we've hashed over before."

He nodded in that noncommittal way that either comforted me or irritated me, depending on my mood. He reached out a hand, but I folded my arms across my chest. "Then why are you here, Willet?"

My mouth went dry, and I found myself thinking I'd rather talk about the squad I'd lost, but I didn't have time to indulge my fear. "I need information about the church."

"You don't need the binding of the confessional for that, Willet.

We could have had a nice cup of tea in my chambers. The chairs there are more comfortable too."

He stopped when he saw the look in my eyes, then levered himself up with a sigh. "I see. Wait here while I seal the church."

He closed and barred the front doors and did the same with the side entrance near the altar. Without the light from the open entryway, the church darkened into gloom. Only the holes in the roof permitted shafts of wan gray illumination into the sanctuary. When he knelt across from me again, I decided to ignore my fear for a moment longer. "What do you know of a cleric named Elwin?"

Ealdor smiled. "I've run into him a few times. He's an interesting character. He argues theology with the skill of the best-trained seminarians."

I nodded. "Not anymore. He's dead. Do you know who might want to kill him?"

Ealdor's face blanched, and I waited while he bowed and recited the antidon.

Now that I had broached the topic, I gave myself over to my experience as reeve. I watched and catalogued every reaction on Ealdor's face, hating myself as I did, but I'd learned even people I trusted held secrets. "Someone bashed his head in with a sword. He was old, Ealdor, really old. I can't imagine he had that many years left. His servant Robin was killed with him."

Ealdor nodded. "Not surprising. I never saw one without the other."

I leaned forward though no one could hear us. "This might surprise you. From what we can tell, Robin was a pretty fair swordsman." I scrutinized Ealdor's face. "Actually, he was probably better than pretty fair. I wouldn't have wanted to go up against him."

Ealdor's brows knit, but the revelation seemed to have less impact on him than it did me. "I'm not sure why he would need a swordsman," Ealdor said. "I'm sorry I don't have more to offer. The Servants and the Merum are on cordial terms, but we seldom seek each other's company."

I pushed harder. "But that's not the strangest thing about their deaths. Elwin took a sword blow that caved in his skull, but he lived long enough for the night watch to take him to the House of Passing. He was still alive when I got there."

"Did he say anything?"

I exhaled my disappointment. "He passed without regaining consciousness, but when I returned to the keep, the Chief of Servants directed the king to keep me from investigating Elwin's death. She ordered the king as if he were some menial who threatened to displease her."

His eyes widened—it seemed I'd found the means to surprise him at last. When he spoke, he pitched his voice as if to keep the empty benches from overhearing. "Then the most prudent thing to do would be to let the church handle it." He forced a smile that wilted at the corners of his mouth. "And don't you have more important matters to consider? How is Gael?"

Ealdor had helped me in the past, and not just with my work as reeve. When I'd returned from the war with the guilt of eleven deaths and the accusation of their families on my conscience, Ealdor had come to my aid and defense. I owed him too much to let his dismissal make me angry, but I required information. I was too scared to admit I needed help. "How does gifting work?"

He blinked a couple of times. "The gift is passed from one individual to the next, usually from parent to child. Sometimes the parent chooses to split the gift, but it weakens." Ealdor frowned at me. "The intersection of Aer's gift, the charism, with a person's talent and their temperament determines their ability. A gift of beauty with a talent for visualization gives us a sculptor. A gift of craft with that same talent gives us the premier builders on the continent." He shrugged. "You know how gifting works as well as any, Willet. Why are you asking?"

I licked my lips. "Because I think Elwin was gifted and he was hanging on until he could pass it to someone."

He nodded. "Those who carry a gift often fight to keep death at bay until they can surrender it, but that doesn't make sense." He shook his head. "Very few people in the church are gifted. Even the ones with the charism of helps usually end up as healers."

That drew me up short. "Why is that?"

"Because of how most people come to us. Those with a gift are intended to carry on the family business. Even the minstrels are careful not to split their gift. It usually goes to the eldest." Ealdor gave a soft laugh. "Finding a gifted firstborn son or daughter who happens to be a cleric wouldn't be impossible, but it would certainly take you a while."

The stab of jealousy every ungifted man or woman felt hit me again. "Sometimes I think the Clast makes sense. Why should some other man come into a gift and set himself over me?"

My priest and confessor shrugged again. "Aer places the free gifts where he sees fit, but you've done all right for yourself. You've won the king's favor. You would have been wealthier as a silversmith, but you wouldn't have been a noble."

I couldn't keep the derision from my voice. "It's a mixed blessing. Most of the other nobles would like to kill me. A few have tried already. It's probably just a matter of time before some hired footpad gets lucky and puts a knife through my ribs."

I thought about the screaming man in the square and the people he drew to him. How would it be to live in a world without gifts, where every man rose or fell on his own merit? "How come some families don't have a gift?"

Ealdor shrugged. "That's a short question with a long answer. Libraries are filled with the conjectures. Most writers agree that the gifting is limited. It doesn't seem to grow with the population. As the number of people has grown, so has the number of families without a gift."

I licked my lips. "Are there any gifts we don't know about?"

Ealdor laughed, but not in derision. "Gifts interact with their owner to create something unique. Why are you asking, Willet? Any child over the age of twelve could tell you this."

"I want to make sure I haven't missed anything." I looked at the arched windows with their simple stained-glass patterns, not the intricate pictures and scenes of the cathedrals.

"Very well," Ealdor said. "The gifts are split into three groups based on the body, the mind, and the spirit: beauty and craft, entirety and minutiae—also known as sum and parts—helps and devotion. Each of those creates a specific ability based upon the intersection between the gift and a person's talent. And the ability is shaped by their temperament. For example the gifts of the body—"

"What about the gifts of the spirit?" I interrupted.

Frustration showed in the clench of his jaws. "Most of those gifts center around helps, leading people to become healers or administrators. Some few receive the gift of devotion, but that one is harder to predict and even harder to test." He shook his head. "Of all the gifts, it is the one most easily turned from its intended path."

I nodded, trying to feign casual interest, but my heart hammered against my ribs. Ealdor's description didn't come close to describing what had been happening to me. His hands were still resting on top of the bench. I reached out and took one of them, the gesture nothing more than a prelude to parting, and braced myself.

Chapter 9

The interior of the church faded from my vision as awareness fled and I drifted through Ealdor's gaze. I couldn't describe what I perceived, unable to name it as mind or personality or spirit. Instead of the thoughts and impressions I'd felt with others, I saw an image of myself—as if my perception existed outside the confines of my body.

I moved to release Ealdor's hand, but he broke contact before I could complete the motion.

His voice came to me. "Willet, are you all right?"

I struggled to make sense of what had just happened in light of my impressions in the House of Passing, the jail, and the king's tor, but the puzzle pieces refused to fit.

I blinked and found Ealdor looking at me, his expression wondering. What I was about to do frightened me. Every human touch since the House of Passing had sent me reeling, leaving me vulnerable but showing me the essence of the one touched. I could continue to pretend it was the aftereffects of Iselle's drug if I said nothing, but if I spoke and Ealdor confirmed my suspicion, I would have a problem on my hands that dwarfed finding Elwin's killer.

I'd always been smart, but not too many people accused me of being wise. "Elwin touched me, Ealdor. Men attacked the House of Passing, trying to break down the door to attack a man who was already dying." I gripped a fistful of his cassock and pulled him forward, turning my fear into anger. "I can't so much as brush against someone without seeing into them," I growled. "Who was Elwin?"

Ealdor didn't bother to echo my anger. "Do you think the bishops share their counsel with simple priests?" He glanced up toward one of the holes in the roof that let in both light and rain. "You're asking me to trade in tales and gossip, speculations."

I ignored his subtle accusation. "If it's just speculation, it can't do any harm for you to share it with me."

He pulled his cassock gently out of my fist, his face sad. "This is what comes with your preoccupation, Willet."

I ignored the deeper imports of his sympathy. "I'm the king's reeve. I went to question a dying man who grabbed my head and screamed at me, and now I can see into people."

I watched him consider me before he spoke. "There is a gift mentioned in the church history. But it's supposed to be lost." He gave a small shake of his head. "Some gifts are more dangerous than others."

The air of the little church began to grow stale. I pulled a pair of breaths before I pressed him again. "Dangerous for whom?"

Ealdor pushed against the bench, rising to his feet. "Pull your sword." When I did, he pointed at the burnished steel. "How many edges does it have?"

I grimaced at him. "I've heard the adage, Ealdor, and yes, I've cut myself a few times sharpening it. I don't need proverbs."

"How do you think they become proverbs? This gift you have is dangerous to you, Willet, because it's dangerous to our enemies. Do you need me to remind you that when people feel threatened, they seek to eliminate the threat?"

I lived that reminder every day I went to court and many days I didn't. "No, I don't, but this gift is dangerous to *your* enemies. It doesn't have anything to do with me. I'm no priest, remember?"

His eyes flashed at me. "Do you think the people trying to kill you will make that distinction? If you can see into the heart of any man or woman simply by touching them, how long will it be before those who harbor evil decide to protect their intentions?"

I tried not to believe him, but the cave that bloomed in my gut, where I kept my intuition, confirmed everything he'd said. As crazy as he sounded, the incident at the House of Passing and the Chief of Servant's involvement made sense. "Does this gift have a name?"

"Domere."

Was that what Elwin had screamed at me? Ealdor wouldn't lie. I knew that, but that didn't make him right either. I needed confirmation. For all I knew Iselle's drug had skewed my perceptions. Even now, I might be imagining the whole conversation or dreaming. I set aside the possibility for the moment. The king had given me a job to do, and the implications of owning a gift that would preclude me from human touch scared me more than a little. "Who was Elwin?"

He looked at me and gave his head a little shake. "If what you're telling me is true, he was your predecessor, the man who held the gift before you. By the right of succession, it's come to you."

"By the right of succession?" I almost laughed. "He grabbed the closest head!" But even as I said it, I knew this wasn't true. Iselle had tried to approach Elwin several times before and after I arrived. A thousand times a thousand questions fought for attention in my head, but Ealdor turned his back on me to open the doors and let the light back into his little domain.

As I walked toward the side entrance, I realized I had a weapon in my possession, a way to find Elwin's killer. Even more, I had a way to ferret out every enemy the king had. I stroked the dagger at my belt. With a single touch, I could determine the innocence or guilt of every soul in prison. My head swam with the possibilities. I would fall on the criminals of Collum like an avalanche. I need only convince the king of my ability and I would roar through Laidir's court like a gale. Plotters like the Orlan family would live the rest of their lives in fear and regret.

Ealdor's voice stopped me as I entered into the light. "Willet, be careful."

I turned, not bothering to hide the wolfish smile that showed my teeth. "I'm not the one who needs to be careful now, Ealdor. Not me. Not ever again."

In the dimness of the interior he might have shaken his head. "Don't forget your sword, Willet. Every gift carries two edges. Every gift has a price."

Before I turned on my heel and walked away, I made an answer with what I held in my heart. "Then I will make sure someone else pays it."

Pellin sat close to the fire in the common room of the Solstice, fingering his ale and staring at the worn parchment. The words were as familiar to him now as his name, but no amount of scrutiny could unlock his dead brother's intent. Deep in his middle, locked away until the day he made time for it, sat a knot of grief so black and intense it threatened to block his gift.

He pulled his eyes from Elwin's last words to consider his surroundings. The tavern floor had been swept clean and wide windows let in the early spring sunshine, but the air this far north still carried a tinge of cold and necessitated the fire that crackled and popped. The smell of burning oak and walnut drifted to him.

Yet the tavern lacked something. The owner's ale was smooth and the food tasty enough, but instead of feeling at home or as a welcomed guest at a friend's house, he felt as if he were just another customer. The owner's gifting, if he had any, didn't seem to include helps, and his talent appeared to run toward something besides others. He took a pull from the metal flagon and watched the door.

The man on his right ran his eyes casually over their surroundings, noting the men at the long bar and a young couple giggling with the flush of infatuation, before settling on the door once more. "He's late."

Pellin took a deep breath, fighting the temptation to agree or complain. "There's no timetable, Allta. Better that the information is sure than to rush." His guard didn't fidget, their training precluded allowing nerves to influence their single-minded focus, but the tension Allta held within heightened until it was almost palpable. A hand taller than most men, he carried more bulk as well, but in compact form, a design that spoke of speed and force rather than brute strength. As pure a gift of beauty as possible coupled with considerable physical and spatial talents and temperaments of impulse and thought made the man at Pellin's right one of the most dangerous in the world. Yet his better, Robin, lay dead from a score of wounds, strokes that never should have landed.

"Yes, Eldest," Allta said, resuming his scan once more. Beneath the table he fingered a dagger. "How could they have killed Robin?"

The question hardly reached Pellin's hearing. How indeed?

The door of the tavern opened, and a draft of air swirled through the opening to accompany a man dressed in black. He closed the door and stood in the reduced light of the tavern, waiting for his eyes to adjust before making his way to the corner where Pellin sat.

Without waiting for an invitation, he pulled up a chair. To any who didn't know him, the stiff lines of his face would have been characterized as impassive, perhaps even stoic. Pellin knew better. Peret Volsk had trained for over two decades as an apprentice to the Vigil, with all the sacrifice required against the day when one of them must surrender their gift and depart.

Volsk's stiff countenance contained a grief and disappointment so large it might have matched Pellin's. Pellin had lost a brother, but Peret Volsk had lost a father figure and mentor.

"What of the men who attacked the House of Passing?" Pellin asked, choosing the easier question.

The Vigil's apprentice shook his head. "They melted away just before first light. I've been unable to find any trace of them."

Inside, Pellin stifled the worst of his fears. "Perhaps Bronwyn can help track them down." He swallowed, forcing himself to the real reason Volsk was there. "Free or rogue?" he asked.

Volsk's face, dark with several days of beard, twisted. "Rogue. Both of the clerics at the House of Passing confirmed it. I spoke with them separately to make sure."

Pellin released a sigh of relief. "Praise Aer," he breathed.

"For what?" Volsk asked.

Allta's voice rumbled across the table, the thunder of an approaching storm. "He is Eldest now."

Volsk shot Pellin's guard a look but nodded a moment later. "Your pardon, Eldest, but either outcome seems a disaster."

Pellin nodded. In truth they were arguing over the extent of the catastrophe, not whether their present circumstances qualified as one. "Consider what would have transpired if the gift had become free."

Volsk gave one savage nod of his head. "Yes, it would have come to me."

"No. It *might* have gone to you, but in the end it is the same with all gifts. Aer will give it to whomever he sees fit. Then we would have to wait for word to come to us." He shrugged and nodded to a man across the room, his head lolling from too much drink. "Perhaps it would have landed close to us, but more likely it would take months for its nature to manifest."

He sighed. Long ago, before Volsk had been chosen, one of their number had died, by falling from his horse of all things. The gift had gone free and it had taken over a decade to find and vast resources to quell the rumors it had started. Of course, no one had suspected its recipient to be from the only kingdom on the continent that *didn't* border the Darkwater.

Volsk leaned forward. "What am I to do if the gift does not come to me?" Threads of desperation wove their way into the tenor of his question.

Pellin kept his face neutral to avoid giving hope or disappointment. "You know our history, Peret. Rogue gifts have a tendency to turn on their owner."

His dark eyes widened at the matter-of-fact tone. "But not always. You mean to leave him to the gift?"

Pellin shook his head. "No, of course not. We will bring him in. Most of the Vigil is in the city or on their way."

"For my ascension." Loss threaded its way through his voice.

"Yes." Pellin nodded. "But it's a long road that turns only once, as they say."

Chapter 10

My euphoria faded on the trek from Ealdor's church to the poor quarter. Whatever gift I might or might not have, I needed information about Elwin's death. Even if Aer or fate had seen fit to allow me to see into the hearts and minds of others, I didn't have time to solve Elwin's death by touching every soul in Bunard.

The buildings grew decrepit as I looped around to the south of the city, the owners unable or unwilling to part with enough coin to repair them. Walls leaned against each other for support, and stairs tilted to one side, forced to follow the slanted floors to which they were attached. Warped wood predominated, but the calls of the people who lived or worked there rang with the simple truth of those who had no need for pretense.

I turned left toward an alley whose precarious balconies blocked the sun, casting the infrequent cobblestones into perpetual gloom, and drew my sword as I entered the shadows. The watch tried to weed out most of the cutpurses, but the unsuspecting could still wind up face-down in the muck with a knot behind one ear and their purse missing.

A form bathed in sunlight broke away from the edge of the ramshackle inn on my left and approached, her steps spilling down the porch to the sound of strident voices inside. "Hello, Willet."

Constance—she didn't have a last name anymore—greeted me the way she greeted every man, with an unspoken offer in her smile and a voice clothed in velvet. A desire to touch her, to see if Ealdor's judgment proved correct, stole over me, but I folded my hands in my cloak, pretending to fight off the chill of dusk. I already knew Constance's story, and I was unwilling to intrude on her private grief.

Not many of her customers bothered to discover she cared for two children at home because her husband, Rolfe, had been conscripted after the last war and killed in a border skirmish. Her story echoed dozens of times in the poor quarter. Friends for Constance were few. Most men looked at her as a thing to be taken, but in my ignorance I'd once assumed that the other women of the poor quarter might help her. Her predicament must have cut too close to the bone. The married women in the poor quarter, unskilled and untutored, were one accident or skirmish from joining Constance in her profession.

I flipped a silver half crown toward her and shook my head at the offer implicit in the saucy lift of her brows. I nodded to the spot where she'd been standing, visible from the street where the watch and lower-class merchants conducted their trade. "That's not where you usually stand, Constance." I snuck a glance down the alley. "I'm looking for Rory."

The sauce and smile melted off her face, and I saw a tremble begin in her hand before she clenched her fist, stifling it. "He's not down there, hasn't been all day," she said in a normal soprano. "I saw him next to Grim's this morning."

I gave Constance a polite nod of thanks and turned right, but inside my instinct screamed something was wrong in the poor quarter. Prostitutes didn't barter themselves on the main street, and pickpockets didn't practice their trade near Grim's. The moneylender took pains to discourage the urchins from robbing his customers. His knuckles probably weren't as hard as Jeb's, but no one wanted to put the theory to the test.

I passed through a narrow alley that smelled of human waste on my way to Grim's place on the next street. Bodies blocked the far end, facing away from me. I put my hands on my weapons. Street fights were common in the poor section, but I could tell this was something else. Spectators to fights were rowdy, but the men and women blocking my view stood entombed in silence.

I forced my way through and found myself looking down at an

urchin, not Rory, face down, but judging by the size, the boy or girl couldn't have been older than ten. A tough-looking woman of the city watch held a cudgel in her hand, enforcing a circle of space around the body as Jeb stalked the onlookers, his lean face thunderous and hands clenched.

I stepped around the child and the large pool of blood and tapped Jeb on the shoulder. He scowled down at me, his brows meeting over his hooked nose. "Did the king send you to relieve me?"

I held up my hands. From the side, Jeb's face resembled the edge of a hatchet. It didn't look much friendlier from the front. "No, I'm looking for information on the Servant's death." I didn't bother to explain. As head of the reeves, Jeb knew about every death in the city almost as soon as it happened.

His laugh sounded like the bark of an angry dog. "In the poor quarter? Since when do Servants consort with prostitutes and cutpurses?" His arms hung loose at his side, but he clenched his hands over and again, his knuckles cracking.

I ignored the invitation of Jeb's question and pointed to the child. The blood on the stones looked fresh. "How long ago did this happen?"

"Not long, right about sunset." Something dreadful appeared in Jeb's face and I offered a quick prayer for the success of his investigation.

"You got here awfully quick."

He spat and growled a curse that could have stripped paint from wood. "I was already here." He nodded his head toward the ramshackle front of Grim's across the street. "I don't know why the king wastes our time trying to police theft in the poor quarter."

My gut instinct started yelling at me again, but since I wasn't there to take Jeb's job from him, he was more forthcoming than usual. "The boy was taken down with a single cut to the throat, nearly took his head off." He glared at the crowd. "Not a scratch anywhere else on the body—and not one of these lousy *kreppa* saw a thing."

Despite his size, a couple of men in the crowd looked angry enough at the insult to take a run at him, but the woman slapped her palm with the cudgel and they backed off.

"That's strange," I said.

"Are you daft?" Jeb hurled his derision at me. "How often do we get a good witness in the poor quarter?"

I shook my head. "That's not what I mean. A single cut to the throat?"

Jeb nodded, the glare easing a bit from his eyes.

I gnawed on the inside of my cheek. "How many men do you know who can sneak up on one of the urchins?"

He stared at me for a moment, and I could almost hear the wheels turning as he struggled to reconcile opposing facts. It looked painful. "Pah! Everyone gets careless sooner or later."

I moved over to look at the body, trying to ignore the blood beneath my boots and hoping to be wrong. I knelt and, as respectfully as I could, I shifted the still form until I could see the wound that had taken the boy's life.

I swore under my breath. Jeb's description of the wound had been spot on. It exactly mimicked the wounds I'd seen on Robin, a smooth gash a hand across and almost as deep.

I nodded and stepped away. Torches, more than usual, appeared on the street as night deepened. By the flickering light I scanned faces for Rory but couldn't find him. I'd have to come back the next day.

The urchins, a loose collection of thieves and pickpockets under the age of fifteen, lived on the street, orphans unable to find a home, the detritus of violence or disease. Now one of them was dead, killed in quiet, the night after Elwin and Robin had been murdered. I couldn't see a connection yet, but the similarity of the wounds screamed for my attention. The king's city of Bunard might go a month between murders and now we'd had three in the space of a day with what appeared to be the same weapon for two of them.

Deep in my chest, embers burned. Everything had begun with Elwin's and Robin's deaths, and the leaders of the four divisions of the church knew it. Worse, they not only refused to share what they knew, but they'd ordered the king—ordered him!—not to investigate. If some old man had done something to displease the other orders, that was his business, but now someone was killing street children.

My hands hurt, and I concentrated on opening the fists I'd made.

I hoped for a chance to use them, but right now I'd run out of time. Looking for the urchins at night was a good way to acquire a permanent disability. I turned north and began the long trek to the nobles' quarter.

Count Alainn, Gael's uncle, kept his business and his estate in close proximity halfway to the tor in the nobles' quarter. Like many of the second tier of the nobility, Alainn derived most of his income from his business rather than his lands. The death of his elder brother had given him control of the family's fortune and gift, split at death, weakened by a dual blessing.

Of course, that gift was now shared between Gael and Kera. Alainn, with all the warmth of a fish, had evaluated the situation and decided that the most expedient route to even greater wealth would be to align his nieces in marriage, beginning with Kera.

His plans to profit from Gael's marriage as well had been scuttled by a series of improbable events that had left him grinding his teeth. My boon from the king, Gael's hand in marriage, had come with an unexpected elevation to the nobility. After a private audience, I'd hit my knees in front of the entire court like the most desperate supplicant and begged for the younger sister to be my wife. Only Kera's lucrative betrothal, already secured, had made it possible, but I'd earned the count's undying enmity ever since.

I approached the estate to the sounds of stonemasons and carpenters putting away their tools by torchlight. Alainn intended to show the city of Bunard and all of Collum just how wealthy he would become. The guards at the gate and at the door, virtual copies of each other in stiff blue livery, nodded me through.

The count's hall reflected his ambition. Tapestries from the kingdom of Aille and artwork from the southern continent, stark figures in impossible landscapes, filled the walls. A pair of gilded chairs offered beauty but no comfort for those who were forced to wait. I glanced up. Perhaps visitors amused themselves by playing with the echoes in the cavernous chamber.

I knew where Gael and her sister would be at this hour, but custom and the count's orders kept me in the hall until one of the trusted servants could escort me. Once again, I resolved to ignore the slight and the implication that I couldn't be trusted.

"Good evening to you, Lord Dura."

I turned from a feigned contemplation of a painting I would never understand at the chipper greeting. Marya stood before me, and I sighed in relief. Better her than Padraig.

"Good evening," I said. "Would you be so kind as to escort me to Lady Gael? I believe she wanted to discuss our wedding."

Marya winked as she turned. "I'm sure. If you'll follow me."

She guided me through opulence until we came to the shop at the back of the count's estate. We passed through a vast hall filled with innumerable bolts of cloth and spools of thread categorized by type and color. A long row of silks shimmered in the light, and I put out a hand to feel their caress as we passed.

Marya escorted me into Gael's presence, pausing long enough to ensure Kera would serve as our escort before leaving. Gael came to me, and I felt again that twinge of surprise at finding she nearly matched my height. Her memory always receded in absence, becoming more fragile and precious. I reached out to let my fingers brush a cheek that made the silks feel coarse by comparison and stopped just short, halted by a stab of fear at what I might see.

"Enough," Kera said. "The two of you can give each other your calf-eyed looks in a moment."

I turned, a smile spreading across my face . . . and then had to work to keep it plastered there. Even in the yellow warmth of candlelight, Kera looked spectral. Smudges of fatigue lined her eyes like portents, and lips that had held a blush of youth a few weeks ago were bloodless around her smile. I darted a look to Gael. Her eyes showed signs of weariness as well, and I thought for a moment—hoped—it might be nothing more than the aftereffects of a restless night, but behind the weariness lay desperation on behalf of her sister that bordered on frantic.

She pulled me into a fierce embrace, her arms gripping me in the extremity of her fear. "Say nothing," she whispered.

We parted as a wracking cough doubled Kera over and Gael darted from me to help. When Kera straightened she wobbled, nearly falling until Gael took her weight. Kera turned her head to face me, struggling to muster a saucy smile. "I think I should rest. Take me to the anteroom, sister. That will allow me to be close enough to claim I've chaperoned you and your handsome visitor without impeding your conversation."

Gael walked Kera from the room, her steps short and abrupt from bearing her sister's weight. When she returned, tears tracked down her cheeks, but I resisted the urge to brush them away.

"Is it always this bad?" I asked. Gael knew the context of my question. Kera struggled every year with the cold and damp of winter.

Gael shook her head, scattering tears to spot the floor. "The healers don't know what to do. Her lungs won't clear, even with the warmer weather coming. Sometimes I think the only thing keeping her going is her upcoming wedding." She turned to pace away from me. "She's not getting better." I had to strain to hear her. "I walked in on her one morning before she got dressed. She was wearing nothing but her shift and she rushed to cover herself, but not before I saw her." Gael turned toward me as her face crumpled like parchment in a fist. "She's lost so much weight."

She held out her arms.

Haltingly, I came forward, but my heart quailed within me and I berated myself for my cowardice. The touch of Andler, the merchant within the prison, had nearly overwhelmed me. Yet it failed to frighten me half so much as Gael's need for solace, a request I couldn't bring myself to deny.

What so many had desired over the centuries, to know their lover's thoughts completely, scared me so absolutely that my hands shook as I raised them to cup her face, as I leaned forward to kiss her tears from her lips.

Gael's sob faded, cut off as I fell through the startling blue of her eyes as through a tunnel. I would have shuttered my mind to keep myself from knowing her, but I didn't know how. Her thoughts and emotions pierced me, sharper than a surgeon's needle, before they merged with my own and I recoiled from discovering what I didn't want to know.

Unfamiliar memories swept my sense of self away until Willet Dura became the merest phantom. My arms and legs held the coltish awkwardness that I hoped would someday settle into some semblance of elegance. I reached up to touch the nose I'd inherited from my father, remembering his admonition. *"Never trust someone with a small nose. They have no sense of direction."* I played with other children, watching as they visited their petty cruelties upon each other. I stood there, impelled by guilt and remorse, defending and comforting a waif-like boy with dark hair. Memory shifted and I stood aloof from the rest of the daughters of nobility, refusing to engage in the tests of wit and will that determined their pecking order.

It went on until the image of a dying man formed within my mind. *Father.* I stood at his bedside, pleading with him to split the gift he intended for me alone. I heard his voice, the reedy whisper of a man about to die, desiring to provide for me, his second born. Kera, as eldest, would carry the obligations and wealth of the family. I would have the gift. Somehow, I prevailed. The scene shifted and I saw father's hands on both of us, pronouncing the ancient rite of blessing.

The memories flowed past me like paints running in the rain until I saw a reeve in Laidir's throne room, his accusation against the duke's brother proven, shock still written on the marquis's face at his unwilling confession. I watched as Dura stepped forward with the knife I'd given him and, with a single thrust through the heart, took the gift thief's life. Heat flashed across my mind, fierce and exultant, rejoicing at the justice of his death.

Other images flashed past as I, Willet Dura, rose above the flood of memories that served to make up her life, but since that day in the throne room, the images Gael held of me were coupled with as much warmth and intensity as her sister's.

My fingertips lingered for a split second before they fell from her face.

I came out of the bond, her lips still against mine, and pulled a deep breath in relief. Gael's wealth of dark hair covered our faces—hers wreathed in grief and mine in relief. Her memories still washed through me, but unlike the others, I welcomed them and placed them at the forefront of my mind.

"I shouldn't have come," I said at last. "But I needed to know what

Myle said about the package I gave you." A twinge of guilt at asking the question in the midst of Gael's distress tightened my throat. Bless her, she didn't accuse me of anything.

She shook her head. "He's still checking it. It's small so he has to exercise care not to destroy it by his alchemy."

I nodded. There hadn't been much to the sliver, but if anyone could pull information from that minuscule amount, Myle could. Giving Gael a quick embrace, I stepped toward the door. "It's getting late, and you should see Kera to bed. She needs to rest."

Gael pulled an intake of breath. "She needs . . ." She stopped, then nodded a moment later. "Yes. She needs rest."

I passed from the halls of Count Alainn's estate and ascended toward the keep. The circumstances of our betrothal had left a kernel of doubt in my mind, a doubt that a single touch had managed to dispel. Whatever else happened, I now possessed something precious. I skipped the hall where the nobles would doubtless be assembled, drinking and shaping their plots, and sought my bed.

They came for me in the hours before dawn, taking me while I slept. I woke to the sound of a key turning in my door and the glare of torchlight as men rushed me and placed a hood over my head, heavy with a scent I recognized from the House of Passing. Perhaps a dozen heartbeats passed while I thrashed in their grip before losing consciousness.

I came to with the effort of pulling air into my lungs through the hood. A rough wooden chair supported me, but ropes bound my ankles to the legs, and my hands were tied behind me. Whatever drug they'd used had faded enough to regain awareness, but dizziness lingered and I lolled in my bonds. Somewhere in the back of my mind I tried to make peace with my regrets. People who took me in secret surely wanted me dead. I tried to concentrate on what I would find on the other side of death instead of how long they would take to kill me. The chair and the bindings were a bad sign. Quick deaths didn't require them.

I waited, but no blows or voices relieved the silence. A trickle of water sounded off to my left, and a draft of cold lifted a few of the hairs on my arm. "Greetings," I called. My voice faded, echoing within vast space around me. I listened and thought I caught the intake of breath, but the hood skewed my senses. The ropes around my wrists and ankles refused to yield. If I was alone I might be able to rock the chair enough to tip it over and break it. I threw my weight forward and the rear legs left the floor until hands grabbed me from behind and pushed me back down.

"We wouldn't have gone to the trouble of bringing you here if we meant for you to leave without hearing us." Hands rolled the hood up over my head to uncover my mouth and nose, and the musty smell of old water and earth drifted to me. I was somewhere in the caves beneath the city.

I digested that, and somewhere in the panic I was trying to keep in check, it registered that I might get out of this alive. "Then talk."

A woman to my left, her voice precise with the clipped accent of one of the southern kingdoms, spoke. "With your permission?"

"By all means," a man directly in front of me said.

"Willet Dura, least of King Laidir's court and chief reeve of his kingdom, and some say, a murderer," she said with the precise cadence of someone reading from parchment, "you've made some very powerful enemies."

I didn't care for the accusation in her voice, and I didn't see the need to defend myself. "You seem to know who I am, but a five-minute conversation with any of the king's guards or nobles could have gotten you that much and more. I hope you're not waiting for me to be impressed."

Soft laughter came from my right, and I stilled, waiting for the familiar voice to continue. It didn't, so I replayed the comment and the conversation with the man in black back at the House of Passing.

"Silence," the woman to my left ordered.

My mind raced. If they'd meant to kill me immediately, they would have done it by now. That meant they wanted something, but I had no idea what it might be, and giving it to them might end my usefulness, and my life. I sat in ignorance, but in the past I'd noted people often revealed information when they were angry. Of course, sometimes they just expressed their irritation with a dagger and walked away.

"No, Lord Dura," the woman continued. "Whether you're impressed is not our concern. What you do from this point on, however, is."

I heard a rustle of movement that came from all around me and tried to guess the number of people in the room. Five? Ten? Twenty?

I tried to face the speaker. "I'm the king's reeve, and what I do is up to him." I ran my tongue over my front teeth and spat on the floor. "Your potion tastes like manure." Two people on my left made sounds of distaste at my coarseness, and I made a note. At least some of those who held me were highborn.

"Someone is killing children in the poor quarter." I tried to give the appearance of seeing through the hood and traced an arc, looking left to right. I forced disdain into my voice, past the fear that made my mouth dry. "Unless you've got information that will help me . . ."

I stopped and took a breath as I shook my head. I was about to get really insulting. "No. I don't suppose the deaths of pickpockets and whores or children matter much to the four orders. Funny. When the Chief of Servants was talking at me, not once did she show concern for Robin's death, only Elwin's. I don't think I care much for you people. So get to the point and let me get back to my work."

Silence. I'd hoped for yelling and screaming to verify my thrust in the dark, but I heard nothing. Then I heard a sharp intake of breath.

"You dare to accuse us?" a woman's voice said, different from the one before. But above her protest I heard the man behind me snicker.

"You may call me Bronwyn," the first woman said. There was a hint of a smile in her voice, but whether it was intended for me or for the other woman, I couldn't tell.

I snorted. "And you can call me Arin, last emperor of Caerwin." The man behind me chortled again.

"I can see how your impertinence would amuse the nobles at court," she said. "Now, are you prepared to listen, or do you have additional insults for us?"

Chapter 11

I'd run out of ways to put my judges off balance, and I'd already picked up something I might be able to use later—the man in black clothes from the House of Passing might be involved. If I could find him, I might let Jeb have an extended conversation with him.

"All right, Bronwyn," I said. "I'm listening."

"You went to the House of Passing to investigate the deaths of Robin and Elwin. While you were there, the house was attacked." She paused. "You and another man managed to hold them off until sunrise."

I looked to my right, pretending to make eye contact with the man who'd laughed first. "I know that. I was there."

"Yes, and you were touched by Elwin."

"Because he could not touch anyone else!" the second woman put in.

I tried to feign indifference. "He was dying and in pain. People pass over in all sorts of ways. Sometimes they have something that needs to be said or long for one last touch. Talk to Iselle or Geoffrey if you're not familiar with death."

Bronwyn laughed at me, but it didn't hold humor, only mockery. "You would be surprised to know how familiar with death we are, Lord Dura. But you are correct—Elwin needed to touch someone and say something with a desperation you cannot begin to fathom." She sighed, her breath hissing between her teeth. "Elwin chose you."

"And ever since, you have seen into the people you touched," the man in front of me added.

I closed my eyes and concentrated on listening as closely as I could. I bowed my head, making a show of humble acknowledgment. "Yes. Does this gift have a name?"

The man in front of me answered. "A few actually. Originally it was called domere. Those of us who hold it call it dema."

My lessons as an acolyte in the Merum order came back to me by reflex. "Truth," I said.

"Or judge," the man in front of me amended.

I'd been prepared for anger but not the sob of wrenching loss that came from the woman on my right. The man in the center pulled my attention back to him. "The gift comes with risks, Lord Dura. We are the Vigil, those who remain in the kingdoms who possess it. As you might guess, your presence in our number is unexpected. Until we are sure of you, you will not be permitted to see us. I am Pellin. Would you like a drink?"

I shook my head. "What I'd like, Pellin, is my freedom so I can do my job."

He grunted assent. "Here our purposes align. What you wish is also what we desire, Lord Dura—to find Elwin's killer."

"Enough, Pellin," the woman on my left said. "This dissembling is a waste of time. Let us put him to the touch and be about our business."

I stiffened, and a hand made of fear and anger reached into my chest to take hold of my heart and squeeze it. "No."

"It has been decided," Pellin said. "Each of us has endured the touch of the others upon joining the Vigil. You will do the same."

"Were you hooded and tied to a chair when it happened?"

"No," Pellin said, his voice unconcerned. "But it is not unheard of. The circumstances of your selection are somewhat unusual. We will not risk ourselves with you, Lord Dura."

I heard the scrape of chairs moving across the rough floor, and people gathered round me. I flinched, drawing my shoulders up to my ears, trying to prevent their touch in spite of my bonds.

"It's been too recent for me," Bronwyn said. "I will rely on your impressions."

They took turns, each touch briefer than expected, their hands cool or warm against the back of my neck. One hand jerked in surprise, but the owner made no comment. I had expected to be able to see into them as they were surely seeing into me, but my mind remained blank.

The swish of cloth moving against cloth sounded as the members of the Vigil resumed their seats.

"We will return you to your quarters, Lord Dura. Though you are not one of our number, you are entitled to a guard. Bolt will be with you and will answer such questions as he is permitted."

I was still angry with their touch, though I had no idea what they'd seen. "Yes, thank you," I said, sarcasm lacing my voice. "That certainly helped Elwin."

Pellin's voice tightened as he spoke. "Take him back."

The hood descended over my nose and mouth, and the sticky sweet scent I'd smelled before brought a growing darkness in my mind until awareness faded.

Pellin leaned back in his chair and pulled a hand over his face. The nest of wrinkles that shifted under his touch shouldn't have surprised him. When had he gotten old? The look of shock on the faces of Bronwyn and Toria Deel echoed on his own. First things first. He signaled Peret Volsk, hovering near Toria Deel, and pointed after Dura. "Peret, follow them. Stay close, but unseen. You are to be our eyes and ears."

"How can this be?" Bronwyn asked after Volsk left the room.

"It's a mistake," Toria Deel said.

Pellin sighed. Young, as the Vigil counted age, Toria Deel still held about her the intractable certitude of youth. "The liturgy of the Word tells us that Aer does not make mistakes."

Toria Deel's dark eyes flashed above her delicate nose. "Then it is a temporary gift, like Danel's at the end of the empire, or Ranwyn's before then."

"That is not for us to decide," Bronwyn said. She shivered. "Did you really see it?"

Pellin shook his head. "How could I not? There is a black scroll in his mind, locked and stronger than any I have felt since I came to the Vigil." He stopped, unwilling to voice the connection they all knew existed.

Toria Deel, her eyes flashing, stabbed a finger at him. "If you will not say it, I will. Willet Dura is insane."

Pellin chopped the air with one hand. "No! There is a vault within his mind. Even he is unaware of the events he's locked away." He sighed, suddenly lacking the energy to maintain the battle of wills with her. The effort it took to keep from crushing her hopes tired him. "We all own circumstances in our past we would rather forget."

Bronwyn shook her head, adding her denial to Toria Deel's. "You know that is not the case, Pellin. Willet Dura's mind has been broken. Whatever's behind the door drives him, though he is unaware of it. We've all seen such before in those we've hunted, those who preyed on others. How many like Dura have you had to kill, Eldest?" Bronwyn asked.

Pellin closed his eyes against grief and pain at the unaccustomed title. "I never wished to be Eldest."

"You knew this day was coming." Toria Deel said. She paused to open her hands, stretching fists unwilling to relax. "Elwin used himself mercilessly for the last ten years, and with his death you are the most senior of us. Who will lead us if you do not?"

The mention of the rest of their number, including those too distant or too committed to make the journey for Volsk's ascension, brought him up short. A chair to the right of Bronwyn, still cold, shot a thread of foreboding through him. He shivered. The last ten years had taught him to be afraid. "Where is Laewan?"

Bronwyn and Toria Deel shook their heads. Their ignorance placed another burden upon him that couldn't be denied. Laewan, stationed for the last ten years in Owmead, had worn his gift even less than Toria Deel. Brilliant but brash, he often loosed his arrows before testing the wind.

Pellin looked back across his life with a jaundiced eye, watching memories of himself dispensing Aer's justice in lurid detail. Iosa have mercy, weariness ate at his bones like a disease. "I do not desire the position of Eldest." He almost whispered.

Bronwyn's voice, when it came, reminded him of her presence and of the rest in the ancient cavern. "No one with a shard's worth of sense does. But we must act. There are rumors running through the kingdoms to the south of gold in the forest, and more of the sentinels on the border of the Darkwater with Collum have died."

Toria Deel picked up Bronwyn's protest without pause. "The Clast convert more and more to their liturgy of the ungifted every day, while the four orders are unable to convince the populace of the truth." She spat. "The Clast! I did not think to see the day when men would lap up lies like cats in front of a bowl of cream, forsaking their gifts. How much craft and learning has been lost already? We have yet to touch their leader. Who knows what kind of heresy lurks in that man's mind?"

Pellin tried to make a gesture that would be interpreted as calming, but his hand jerked at the end of his wrist, as if he were warding curses. The fire in Toria Deel's eyes told him she'd found it dismissive. Ah, well, perhaps she saw more clearly than he.

Bronwyn, ever the peacemaker, interjected, "The Icon and his sheep can wait. It is the death of the sentinels that is the most troubling news of all. How will we be able to protect the forest?" She stopped to pull a shuddering breath. "Cesla ten years ago, and now Elwin." Her gaze sought his but slipped away after an instant. "I'm sorry, Pellin."

Everyone struggled with their memories. He leaned back, ignoring the momentary discomfort of the rude chair. "Elwin never came to terms with Cesla's passing." He shook his head with a bitter chuckle. "It's strange. After all this time we were still the same three brothers who grew up together, Cesla impossibly good at everything, and Elwin always there at his right hand." Pellin paused to meet Bronwyn's gaze. Unshed tears hung in her eyes. "They were a bit older than I, as things are usually counted. Even after the gifts came to us there was a bond between Cesla and Elwin that defied definition. They were more than brothers."

Toria Deel stirred on his left. Perhaps his pain struck too close to her own. "Elwin was the most experienced of us. If he can be found, then none of us are safe." She spoke in the reverential tones people reserved for funerals.

Pellin tried to appropriate the peace of Aer he knew he should feel, and failed. The most permanent fixtures of his life had been taken from him in the last decade, thrusting him into leadership he never wanted. "The most immediate threat is from Elwin's killer. Lord Dura will serve us well."

Bronwyn snorted. "His blundering leaves a trail any idiot could follow. I've never seen a touch so clumsy."

Pellin shrugged. "How could he be anything but? When was the last time the gift went free? Peret spent the last two decades preparing to receive it." He faced Toria Deel squarely. "You were counseled on the risks of falling in love with him. It is not unheard of for the gift to pass to someone else."

Her eyes blazed at the rebuke. "And how many hundreds of years ago did that last happen?"

"What are we to do with Dura?" Bronwyn interrupted. "His ham-fisted use of the gift threatens to expose us all. The Vigil spent centuries hiding, letting people believe the gift had died out, then spent centuries more letting even the rumors of it fade from memory."

Pellin nodded. "Yes, but that may be turned to our service. Elwin's killer cannot fail to note the passage of the gift to Willet Dura. When he thinks to strike, we will be there."

"And if we are too slow?" Bronwyn asked.

Pellin shrugged, not willing to voice the relief he felt when he pondered the possibility of Dura's demise. He turned, catching Toria Deel's gaze in his own. "If we stay close, it may be that Dura's gift will not go free. The gift to judge carries its own strange compulsion. It wants to be passed on." He turned to speak to his guard, a man who radiated physical power despite the peaceful expression he wore. "I will leave it to you to communicate with Bolt. He must not reveal our deeper purposes to Dura unless he survives."

"Bronwyn, I want you to find Laewan. He should have been here for Peret Volsk's ascension. Perhaps he was detained. If you find him on the road, advise him of our counsel and have him return to Owmead. I want him to find someone from the last war who saw Dura and his men enter the Darkwater. There is nothing he can do for us here, but bring his journals. I want to know why Willet Dura has been walking the streets of Bunard."

"You don't trust Laewan," Bronwyn accused.

"Not true." Pellin shook his head. "I don't trust his youth. At the very least, Dura is a night-walker. Laewan should have delved him long ago."

Bronwyn pursed her lips as though she meant to argue the point but conceded with a nod a moment later.

Pellin caught Toria Deel's attention. If he was to be Eldest, then he needed to salve her feelings, but he could not trust her here in Collum, so close to Dura. "Take your guard and ride to the forest. Appropriate some men from the Vanguard. I want to know how many sentinels remain here in Collum. Discover who's killing them and how. I will send messages to Faran. We will need more. We will watch Dura and keep Peret close to him. Perhaps his elevation and your wedding have only been delayed."

"You're staying here in the city, Pellin?" Bronwyn asked.

He nodded, feeling every one of his years. "Peret will be busy, and as you say, the vault within Dura's mind presents a problem. I'll be at the Eclipse Inn. It's removed enough from my old stomping grounds to keep me from being recognized. You and Toria Deel can find me there."

His sigh seemed louder than he intended. "Just who is Willet Dura?"

The blurred light of the sun through my window roused me, and I stirred, shaking my head to scatter the fog that enveloped it. Other than myself, my quarters were empty. For a brief moment I wondered if I'd dreamt the whole episode, but bands of scraped flesh around my wrists told me I hadn't.

Still fully dressed, I stumbled to the hallway intent on the kitchens. Complications were cropping up faster than I could take care of them, but my growling stomach made a mockery of other priorities. A shadow detached from the wall as I left my quarters and fell in beside me.

My hand jerked toward the dagger I kept at my side but stopped halfway there. He made no threatening move, just walked by my side as if he'd always been there and always would be. A little over medium height, he carried a taut strength his clothes couldn't disguise.

Sprinkles of gray salted his hair, but his face had that ageless quality that could have put him anywhere between thirty and sixty.

"Name?" I asked.

A grin snuck up the sides of his face, and a network of lines bunched around his eyes. I adjusted my thinking. Whoever he was, his prime lay well in his past.

"They told you last night. I'm your guard, Bolt." Lean and spare and deadly, the single name fit him well enough.

Our gazes met. The fine white line of a scar tracked its way next to his hairline over light blue eyes. "You must have really annoyed somebody. What pasture did they call you out of for this duty?"

His grin deepened. "Arinwold."

The village lay forty leagues to the south, near the western edge of the valley between Collum and Owmead. It was literally a pasture. That explained how he'd gotten to the city so quickly after Elwin's death.

"And how am I supposed to explain your presence to the king?"

He grinned, showing teeth. "You won't have to. I've been hired by the city watch. They thought it would be a good idea to have me accompany you. For some reason, there are a lot of people who think you need protecting but not a lot of volunteers for the duty."

I shrugged. "I killed a man who needed it. He happened to be a marquis and he didn't have the opportunity of escaping justice by buying his way out of it. For some reason I can't discern, being a commoner who cut down a duke's brother in the king's throne room has made me unpopular with the other nobles."

His eyes twinkled. "That's a mystery, true enough."

We made our way to the kitchens, avoiding the large hall, opting instead to take our meal near one of the innumerable arched fireplaces where hordes of cooks worked to keep the king's household fed. I sat across from Bolt at a small wooden table tucked into the shadows of a corner near the vegetable bins and worked my way through a wedge of cheese and a bowl of thick porridge. I liked it here. No matter how damp or cold the weather, the kitchens radiated warmth and light.

In my head I ticked off the problems vying for my attention. First, there was the matter of Elwin's and Robin's murders, but that task also included the gift that had landed me in trouble with the Vigil and made me an enemy of some or all of its members. Then there was the attack on the House of Passing. What made a dying man so important his killers would return to hasten his death?

If that weren't enough, someone had killed one of the urchins. My head started to hurt. I had the feeling I was sitting in front of a conjurer who showed me a tenth of what was really happening, and I didn't have the slightest idea how to comprehend the rest. Where could I begin?

Bolt sat across from me, eating spare amounts. His eyes nestled beneath his age-furrowed brow like a pair of robin's eggs.

"What can you tell me?" I asked.

He cocked his head to one side without changing expression. "You're in trouble."

I let my eyes grow wide with feigned surprise. "Really? I had no idea, because I almost always start my day by being kidnapped and interrogated by zealots."

A smirk grew on his face, but his eyes stilled until they might have been carved from agate. "Hold on to that spit, son. You're going to need it." I saw him scan the kitchen, exercising mild curiosity, but he waited until a nearby cook moved off until he spoke again. "They killed Robin."

Impatience got the better of me. "I know that," I snapped.

"Yes, but you didn't know Robin. Elwin was eldest of the Vigil. That meant he was accorded the best guard."

I shrugged. "He was attacked by at least two men, possibly three. That's usually a good way to come down with a fatal case of dead."

Bolt's sneer mocked me as I took a bite of cheese. "Son, Robin was the best we had. His gift had probably never been split, and he had all the talents and temperaments swordsmen crave and more. He would have gone through half a dozen of Laidir's best men like a blade through water."

"So what are you saying?"

"Someone knew how to make Robin vulnerable." He leaned back. "They concentrated their assault on Elwin, forcing Robin to defend him even if it meant exposing himself to attack, and those attackers must have been gifted. That means they knew who Elwin was."

I paused to finish my porridge and to think through what Bolt had said. It all sounded dire, but he hadn't told me anything I didn't already know—except that Robin was more skilled than I'd suspected. All of Bolt's words could have been designed to keep the conversation away from the Vigil, which meant I could no more trust Bolt than any of those who'd hidden their identities. Bolt spoke of Robin, but said little of Elwin.

"What does the Vigil want from me?"

His smile held all the warmth of a Collum winter. "The same thing you want—to find Elwin's killer."

My shoulders itched with the feeling that someone behind me held a weapon, but no one in the kitchens wanted me dead, at least as far as I knew. I wouldn't be getting anything useful from my guard. That left me right where I would have been if last night's incident hadn't happened.

I stood and breathed the warm air of the kitchen fires deep into my lungs as I settled my cloak onto my shoulders. "Come on."

Bolt stood, leaving the food on his plate behind like a man who'd never been hungry. "Where are we going?"

I debated keeping him in the dark but didn't see any point to it. He'd know soon enough, and this way he'd be ready in case his skills were needed. "To find the urchins."

Chapter 12

We stopped by the guardroom along the way. With the inadvertent help of the Vigil, I had a better understanding of what I'd seen when I'd touched Andler. He wouldn't hesitate to buy his way into the prison. I couldn't prevent it without raising more suspicion than I already owned due to my night walks, but I could rob him of his target. We descended through each level of the keep, the sensation of weight overhead growing until my shoulders tightened with it. The granite blocks grew larger the lower we went until the stones were as long on a side as two men were tall.

We passed by Sevin at the entrance, and I saw his gaze run a slow sweep of Bolt from head to toe and back again before straightening as if he'd been caught slouching on parade. I stepped into the flickering torchlight of the prison and noted Jeb. He spared a glance for Bolt that held recognition before turning away. When I saw Gareth, I pulled him aside. "Do we still have Andler's girl in prison?"

Gareth nodded, but uncertainty clouded his gaze. "Aye, she keeps to the far edge of her cell when any of the guards come near. That soft merchant has her so scared she's frantic. Should I cut her loose?"

For a moment I was tempted to say yes and let her run, but I hadn't even started my investigation into Andler's affairs. She wouldn't be safe, but it wasn't practical to keep her in prison either. "No, after I talk to her, take her to the chamberlain. Tell him I want her placed with the servants at the top of the tor and have her watched." I thought for a moment. "And have her use a different name."

At the north end of the rock dome that formed the guardroom, a rectangular cut in the wall opened onto a long corridor filled with the cells where we kept the king's prisoners. Two guards at the door kept any from entering save those who were to be released or interred there . . . and me, of course. As the king's reeve I held the authority to bind or loose prisoners based on my investigations, bypassing the magistrates.

Though our prisons might have been smaller than others, some of those within had been kept behind the cold iron of its bars for months while we searched for the truth. Staring down the uninterrupted length of misery, I stood amazed at the stupidity of the idea taking form in my mind. *Foolish,* my better sense chided. If there existed a better way to draw attention to myself and Elwin's gift, I didn't know what it was.

The first few steps into the cells brought me in sight of a young man, his skin sallow from lack of sunlight, his eyes as dull as those of a broken-down horse being led to slaughter. For a moment the old hunger stirred, but whoever he was, he still lived. There would be no answers about eternity from him—at least not yet. He could do nothing for me in that regard.

But perhaps there was something I could do for him and the rest of the prisoners. I retraced my steps to the entrance and summoned one of the guards. Maybe I could minimize my exposure. "Bring Gareth to me. Have him bring the list and a quill."

When Gareth arrived a moment later, I had the guard lock the door behind us so that only I, Bolt, and Gareth would witness whatever followed.

Bolt grew still as the door clanged behind us and a hint of displaced rust mingled with the stench of unwashed bodies. "What do you mean to do?" He paused when Gareth turned toward him and the tone of interrogation in his voice. Bolt ducked his head with all the grace and compliance of steel. "Lord Dura."

I stored his reaction away with all the other things I needed to handle later and turned to face my subordinate. Bolt's refusal to answer questions required nothing of me in return.

"Lieutenant Gareth," I said. "Please attend and place a mark next to each name you give me."

Bolt's hand clamped on my arm, and my surroundings blurred as he spun me around to face him, his face stiff with anger. "You fool! Are you trying to get yourself killed?"

I tried to jerk my arm away. I'm not small, and no one who fought for Collum would ever be considered weak, not after drilling for months on end with the sword, the bow, and the pike, but my arm might as well have been encased in stone for all the effect I had.

I jerked again, turning toward Gareth, who stared at the pair of us open-mouthed. "Gareth," I ordered, "if this guardsman does not immediately release me, you will summon as many of the watch as it takes to intern him here." I locked gazes with Bolt. "Indefinitely."

He sneered at Gareth and threw my arm contemptuously away.

I knew the implications of what I meant to do. Those prisoners who were released would talk. Few of them would be believed if I could help it, but some would be, and there would be no way to stop the rumors that the judges' gift might yet live. "I know they're scared and value their secrecy, but I can't let innocent men and women suffer if I can do anything about it." I shook my head. "I can't."

Bolt pinched the bridge of his nose. "You think I'm scared? Son, I gave up being scared on my own behalf long ago. What you intend to do is dangerous for you. Not me—you."

He had my attention. "Explain."

His gaze took in the prisoners and Gareth, who stood waiting with the list and a quill clutched in his hand as though he might have to use it as a weapon. "You don't have the experience to understand."

I snorted at his slippery answer. "Perhaps I will surprise you."

"Oh, you've already been a surprise, Lord Dura," Bolt said. It wasn't a compliment.

I stepped to the bars—black iron as thick as my wrist spaced a hand's width apart ran the length of the hall. Anchored into the stones of the floor and the ceiling, they had proved equal to the ravages of time and every attempt at escape. Doors constructed from those same bars every four paces marked the entrance to each cell. Only the locks offered the prisoners any hope of escape, but should one prove successful at picking it, the locked door and the guards at the entrance refuted all hope.

"Name and charge?" I asked Gareth.

"Oberd Hanson. He killed one of the healers' guild."

I nodded. Behind the bars, Oberd stared at us, his eyes slowly coming to life, flickering back and forth between us, interest showing at the break in the routine. "Come here, Oberd."

He stepped to the bars, his eyes darting, trying to see everywhere at once.

I tried to look officious in spite of the trickle of sweat that inched its way down my back, chilling me as it went. "Empty the contents of your purse into your hands, Oberd."

His face clouded with confusion, but he reached through the slit in his cloak and pulled out a small cloth bag. I watched him empty what remained of his life into his hand. Prisoners surrendered any coin to the crown when they were interned, but they were allowed to keep whatever keepsakes they possessed so long as they couldn't be used to escape.

Trinkets of memories and a former life ended up in his sweaty palms. A pair of tarnished medallions showed that Oberd might have worshipped in the Merum order once. A good-luck charm, a seven-pointed star, testified to his more ecumenical beliefs in the Fayit. The old superstitions died hard.

I took a deep breath and reached out to grasp his hand, the picture of a man who wanted nothing more than to inspect his meager belongings more closely.

The torchlight narrowed, blocking my vision of Bolt, Gareth, and the rest of the prison until only the image of Oberd remained. I put my free hand out to steady myself against the bars as the light dimmed further, leaving me with nothing to see but his eyes. The sensation of falling strengthened, and I fought to retain the feel of cold iron in my hand, but it faded as I plunged into the haunted visions of Oberd's life.

Images and scenes played before me as I walked his past: I was a child of two or three, holding the frayed and dirty tail of an apron, toddling after a plain woman with kind eyes. Then the woman, older and thinner, surrendering silver coins to the hand of a tall man with a healer's sigil on his clothes in exchange for a small blue bottle. An older boy, I wept by a simple pine casket with the body of an emaciated woman inside. A man with grief-etched lines in his face lashing out with his fists at me, over and over and over. The man, withered as a stalk, lying very still next to another blue bottle. Running the streets as one of the urchins.

The scenes flowed past, coming too quickly to pull meaning until one last vision—entering a healer's shop by the light of a crescent moon to find a tall man mixing poison with honey into a small blue bottle. Fury filled me.

I came to myself, one hand still holding his and the other on the cold truth of iron, knowing what the boy Oberd had not, could not, have known. Blue was the healer's color for vaperin sap. Every adult knew it was poison, given to help those with the wasting disease or some other hopeless cause function until the death took them.

I stepped back. Bolt eyed me as if he might have to kill me any second, but Gareth only waited. What had seemed like hours to me must have taken no more than a moment. The pain of Oberd's loss closed my chest, and I struggled to breathe. Worse, I could do nothing for him. Oberd was guilty, but I would not testify against him. His guilt, wrapped around the innocence of his pain, required death, but I had no desire to be the means of its delivery.

I moved to the next cell, but when I motioned Gareth forward with the list, Bolt put his hand on my shoulder, tense but not threatening.

"This is unwise, Lord Dura."

I heard the hitch in his voice, knowing he would not speak in plain terms before Gareth, counting on it. "I am merely checking the contents of each purse to ensure they have no means to escape."

Bolt snorted his disgust, and I ignored the questioning look from Gareth to point between the bars at a heavyset man with the scars and ears of a brawler. "Name and charge?"

"Erich." Gareth shook his head. "No last name that we know of or that he'll admit to. He's accused of beating a man to death, supposedly for cheating at dice." Gareth shot a look through the bars as the prisoner rose from his pallet, rising as he stood until he overtopped us both by a head. "Be careful of this one, my lord."

I nodded, making sure none of the menace I felt coming from the boulder of a man before me reached my face. "Empty your purse into your hand and extend one, and only one, through the bars."

Coarse laughter scraped its way free of his throat. "You can trust ol' Erich, my lord. 'E wouldn't 'urt a flea." His hands groped through his pocket slits and he leered at us. Undoing the drawstrings, he emptied what remained of his possessions into one hand. Grime covered most of it as though even his belongings carried the taint that stained his soul. I stepped forward, bracing myself against the tunnel and flood of visions I expected at his touch.

As my hand neared his, Erich dropped his belongings and lunged, moving faster than anyone with that bulk should. He threw himself backward, and I raised my free arm against the impact as the bars raced toward me.

The pain shooting toward my shoulder did nothing to stop the prison from blackening down to the pinpoint of Erich's eyes. I passed into a series of images and scenes from child to boy to man. They never varied, never wavered. Somehow I became aware of gorge rising in my throat. I vomited, and light returned to my vision.

When I straightened, I saw Bolt standing at the bars, his sword against Erich's throat, the giant trying in vain to see the edge of the blade against his skin. Gareth stared, not at me, but at Bolt, his mouth agape. "I never saw him move."

The time spent delving Erich's memories could have been measured in less than a handful of heartbeats or less, but the filth of his deeds coated my mind like hot tar. Erich measured his pleasure by the amount of pain and power he could exercise over others.

I took a step back from the bars, and Bolt moved to join me, removing his blade from Erich's neck when distance forced him.

"What's his situation?" I asked.

Gareth shook his head. "We're still gathering evidence. Nobody wants to testify."

Erich leered at me with his broken teeth. "Pardon my trip, milord. Ol' Erich is a bit clumsy at times."

I made a show of looking at his hands. "Clumsier than you know." I turned to Gareth. "He has a lot of dirt crammed under his nails."

I pulled one memory loose from the fetid swamp that constituted Erich's life. "Have the watch pull the stones of his hearth and check the dirt beneath them."

Erich's eyes widened as his twisted smile slid from his face.

I tried to ignore the grim satisfaction that bloomed in my chest.

"Let's move on," I said.

Bolt stepped in close on my right. "Don't you think this has been tried before?" he murmured. "How many times can you swim through the ache and loss of another mind without rest?"

Somewhere deep in my chest a mulish refusal to surrender to Bolt, to the Vigil, took hold. "As many as I have to. Your precious council may not care for such as these, but I know at least one innocent is imprisoned here, and there may be others."

I forced my trembling legs into motion and met Gareth at the next cell, though my mind screamed at the prospect of another touch. A spinster, wrinkled and withered, pushed her arm toward me, her milky-blind eyes squinting in the dim light.

On and on it went, until Branna came into sight. I never made it. Three cells away, the room darkened and refused to lighten again.

Chapter 13

Pellin waited until three hours after dawn to move from his secluded room at the Eclipse and weave his way through the press of people crowding the market. The sounds of goats and chickens mixed with the cries of hawkers selling fruits and vegetables already in season in the southern kingdoms with winter crops still being harvested in Collum interspersed between. Merchants jostled with customers, making it difficult to move in the crowd.

Which was exactly the way Pellin wanted it. His guard drifted behind him, agile in the press despite his size but frowning just the same.

"Tell me again, why did we choose to move through the city at this hour?" He pivoted to squeeze through two clusters of customers in front of a stand bearing figs and dates. "We can hardly move."

Pellin smiled at Allta's discomfort. The crowd would make it all but impossible for him to draw steel without injuring innocents.

"Too little time has passed since I lived in Collum, and the city of Bunard in particular. I have no wish to be recognized."

Allta nodded, but his frown remained until they cleared the crowd and were able to move more freely. Pellin kept his head down and concentrated on guiding himself and his guard to a small Merum church on the edge of the lower merchants' quarter. His route was simple—use deserted streets or packed ones. At this hour, that meant packed.

They turned a corner and left the crowd behind, venturing onto a side street. At its end, no more than a hundred or so paces from the bridge leading into the poor quarter, they came to a run-down parish. Pellin stopped outside the door, noting the splitting wood and the holes in the slate roof above. No smoke came from the rectory's chimney. No candles illuminated the windows. The entire block surrounding the church remained abandoned, testimony to the fact that Bunard's population had yet to recover from the last war.

He paused. Nothing in the air or feel of the building hinted at occupation, but somber familiarity nagged at him as if he'd come upon a friend grown unexpectedly old.

"Are you sure we're in the right place?" Allta asked.

Pellin nodded. "Apprentice Volsk was very specific in his directions." He gestured toward the run-down church. "According to the guards at the tor, Willet Dura makes it a habit to come here every few days for confessional. Perhaps his priest is something of a hermit," he added, but inside he didn't believe a word of it. "Let us see what sort of man holds Dura's confidences."

Allta stepped in front of him and pushed the door to the small church open with his left arm, his right holding his sword at ready. The creak filled the air, and a crow fled at the sound, its indignant squawks piercing. They stepped into gloom relieved only by diffused lighting allowed by the windows and the holes in the roof. Still, it was plain by the thick dust on the floor that haeling hadn't been held in the church for some time.

"Here," Allta said, pointing to a single set of tracks that led to the front of the sanctuary. Pellin and Allta followed them like dogs on a scent to where they ascended the customary three steps to the altar, circling it. Then the tracks moved to the left, toward the confession rail, the veneer splitting from the wood, marked and worn by thousands upon thousands of penitent confessions. Pellin traced it with one gloved hand, careful not to touch it with his bare skin.

The tracks—Dura's, he assumed—stopped at the rail, the dust scuffed on the kneeler where his knees had hit it, before they exited the building through the side door.

"Should I search the rest of the church, Eldest?"

Pellin pursed his lips in thought and nodded. "As you wish, but I don't think you'll find anything."

Allta dipped his head. "We should be sure."

"Oh yes," Pellin said. "Make it as sure as you can."

Pellin stood in the aisle, considering the identical tracks leading to the rail and away from it, mulling over what it meant. He didn't have long to wait. The church wasn't big, nor were the grounds. Allta returned before three minutes had passed.

"There's no one else here," his guard said, shaking his head. "I don't understand."

Pellin pulled a lungful of musty air and sighed. "Unfortunately, I do. There is no priest, no confessor, that Dura comes to."

"Why would the guards lie to us, Eldest?"

He shook his head. If only it could be so simple. "They didn't. They reported exactly what Willet Dura told them—there is a parish on the edge of the poor quarter where he comes to celebrate haeling and offer his confession."

Allta's face closed in frustration. "But that means Dura is lying to the guards, but to what purpose? There's nothing and no one here."

Pellin shook his head. "Look at the tracks in the dust, Allta. Dura came here a day ago, and he officiated over haeling before offering his confession at the rail." He swallowed against the emptiness that had bloomed in his chest. How could things get worse?

Allta shook his head. "But there are no implements, and there's only one set of tracks in the dust."

Pellin nodded. "You're quite right, of course, but Dura's not lying. When I delved him, I lived his memories of this place." He peered into the gloom. "It looked a bit better." Pellin turned to face his guard. "And I saw his last visit here, the celebration of haeling, the confession. And Ealdor, a narrow-faced man with eyes the color of palest sky." He sighed. "The newest member of the Vigil is quite insane."

Allta drew a slow measured breath. "But he has the gift."

"Yes," Pellin sighed again. "And there's a vault in his mind that hides something, something horrifying. Willet Dura is two people—we must guard ourselves."

Allta loosened his sword in the scabbard. "If you order it, I will kill him. Better the gift should be freed than we hug a viper to our chest."

Pellin hung his head. The guards of the Vigil dedicated themselves to developing their natural physical ability with the sword to something almost beyond human, but their mission tended to blind them to the nuances of humanity. They saw the world in two categories, threats and non-threats, and threats needed to be dispatched.

"No," he said at last. "The water grows murkier. We will have to wait for it to clear before we know what must be done."

I drifted in and out of consciousness, aware in the faintest of ways of blankets around me. Light dimmed and brightened without reason, and the passage of time progressed in disordered pieces like shards of glass strewn across the rocks. Memories of the prisoners in the cells far below mingled with my own, and I fought to separate myself from those different personalities, each with innumerable moments of kindness or cruelty attached. My shoulder ached.

Voices called out to me, unrecognized, adding to the mental weights that held me captive. Who was I? Erich?

I recoiled at the thought, but his memories chased me through the corridors of my mind, latching on to me, calling to me with their joyful cruelties and the pleasure that comes with power, whispering in my ear, "This is who you are."

"No!"

Thrusting the recollections away, I sought peace. I opened a door along the corridor of my mind and stepped through to light and warmth. A chair waited by a fire, and I sat, alone. No. Not alone. A woman sat across from me, her face familiar, reminding me of one I'd seen in the cells.

But this woman lacked the gray hair and wrinkles of the other. She rose from her chair, lithe and sinuous, and came to me. "It's done. Now we can be together." I saw the empty cup in her hand, knowing the poison it had held. I lifted my hand in warding, but the color and veins on the back of it were strange, unfamiliar.

I fled back along the corridor, my arms held protectively in front of my face as phantoms appeared, clutching, whispering their seduction as they sought to merge with me.

Light, real light, stabbed my eyes, and I tried to block it with one hand only to find my arms bound. There were no blankets. Instead, I sat upon the chair in my quarters facing the window and the blurry dawn that shone through it. My hands were tied.

A voice spoke behind me. "He's coming around."

"Aye," Bolt said.

"How many did you say he touched?"

"At least a dozen."

"Interesting," the voice spoke again. "Few on the council would have lasted so long, even with our experience. It would seem he's possessed of talent and temperament as well."

"That surprises you?" Bolt said. "Aren't you the ones who say Aer chooses his servants?"

A soft grunt came in reply. "Well spoken. I have to admit we've said it so often that we no longer consider its implications. Still, his recklessness in the dungeon will be some time in paying."

I believed him. My head felt too small for the crowd of memories that fought for attention within it. The horrors I'd seen didn't surprise me, at least not much, but I'd been unprepared for the intimacy those experiences inflicted upon me. So much hate and loss and despair had soaked into me that I wondered if I could ever be clean again.

"I don't think Lieutenant Gareth or any of the prisoners realized what was happening," Bolt said. "And none of them were innocent. There won't be any opportunity for them to speak of their suspicions, if they even have any."

"For which I'm thankful, but the danger I'm speaking of lies within Lord Dura."

A suspicion grew in my mind. The tones of the voice were strange, deeper and raspy, as though the speaker were taking pains to avoid recognition. Yet the cadence of his words, the oddly formal lilt to his speech, and the rhythm of his thoughts sounded familiar to me.

I turned my head, not enough to see him, but enough to let him know whom I addressed. "Are we ever going to have a conversation where I'm not tied up? Speak plainly, Pellin."

I felt rather than saw him jerk, and a sigh of displaced air rose and died before he came around my left and into view. "Perhaps it's time for forthright discourse, at that."

A man of slightly more than middling years stood within the wan yellow light. Thinning white hair still showing hints of the jet color it must have been in his youth showed over light blue eyes. His nose was strong but slightly bulbous at the end, giving him a look of mirth rather than strength, and that impression was reinforced by a slightly upturned mouth that seemed on the verge of smiling. His gaze looked old beyond its years.

I'd seen that look before on the faces of men who'd endured the horrors of war and spent their time trying to blink away the images they carried with them. Yet one look at Pellin's hands told me he'd never been a soldier. The calluses a man at arms would have kept at the base of each finger were noticeably absent. His hands were more suited to the lute or the mandolin.

When I met his eyes again, he smiled as if amused by my inspection. "We've never had a reeve join our ranks before." He paced back and forth between me and the window, sunning himself first on the port side, then on the starboard. One hand traced a negligent wave as he spoke. "Oh, we've had soldiers—and a few nobles have come into the gift, mostly those too far down the line of succession to have any hope of inheriting. And those of the priesthood, of course," he sighed. "I was one such."

"Which order?"

He looked at me a moment before he answered. "Merum. The first and oldest. What about you, Lord Dura? What division do you claim as your own?"

I shrugged, but inside I resolved to keep a part of myself private. "Does it make a difference? There are some things I admire and dislike in each."

"And what of the Clast? What do you think of them?" The casual gestures he used to accompany this last question failed to convince me. His hand carried tension, and he jerked his wrist. Something about the Clast concerned Pellin.

I debated my answer, to see if I could frustrate him into revealing something I could use, but he'd already committed to the discussion. I only hoped my opinion wouldn't change that. Besides, with a single touch he could determine how I felt, no matter what I said. "I don't care for them."

Pellin's eyebrows rose in curiosity. "And why is that?"

I cocked my head. "Have you ever been to Braben's Inn, Pellin?" When he shook his head, I went on. "It's not much of a place for nobles. It's too low down in the city. But when you walk into his tavern on a night when the wind is slicing its way down the northern cut, you step into light and warmth, and Braben is there with a smile and a tankard of ale or hot mulled cider almost before you've asked for it. And almost without knowing it, you've found your way to your favorite bench and there's a meal at your elbow."

Pellin smiled. "It sounds wonderful, but I don't understand . . ."

"Braben has a gift, a partial one, of helps, actually, and any of his customers would tell you the same." I shook my head. "I can't countenance some fool trying to tell people that there's no such thing or that we're not supposed to use them."

Nothing in Pellin's expression changed, but a subtle shift in the set of his shoulders, a slight easing of tension, told me he approved of my answer. "It may be that you will become a valuable member of the Vigil someday."

My response left my mouth before I had time to stop it. "I don't care to be part of your group, Pellin."

The tone of my voice alone should have roused some ire in him, but he chuckled as if I'd assayed some mild jest. "I think I remember feeling the same way, once. Your gift may make you a part of us whether you will or not. How long you share our company is up to you, of course. If you wish to be rid of us in short order, I must say you've gone about it the right way. At this rate you'll be dead in a matter of weeks."

I'd been threatened several times over the course of the months since I'd been raised to the nobility, and a few times those doing the threatening had tried to back it up either in person or by proxy. None had carried the casual certitude of Pellin's statement.

I tried to moisten my lips. "I'm listening."

He nodded once, short and sharp. "It's about time. Lord Dura, you have a gift, a gift everyone in the Vigil shares, to see into the minds and hearts of any you touch. You're not the first to attempt to bring justice to the world overnight. We've had others." His eyebrows lifted to accent the roll of his shoulders. "Your gift carries a price. Each time you touch an individual, you partake in their strongest memories and thoughts. You walk through their mind. You know them as truly as it is possible to know. Domere."

He smiled. "Do you think it's a coincidence that the word we translate as *judge* is also the root for *dominate*? But it is *we* who are dominated by the gift."

I tried to swallow. The effort resulted in a cough as I recalled some of the memories I'd waded through. My stomach twisted. Gorge rose, and the room danced in my vision like tongues of fire. I bent against the ropes and vomited, bile burning my throat. I turned my head, wiped my mouth across my sleeve, and blinked away the tears that filmed my vision.

"You see," Elwin said, "even the recollection is more than you can stand at this point. The gift must be used with care. Our group carries a long history—though with fewer members than you would think." He paused as if considering what to say next, then gave his head a small shake, leaving me to wonder what he'd omitted.

"What happened to them?" My words rasped over my strained vocal cords. "The ones who tried to save the world?"

He looked at me with those old, old eyes and pursed his lips. "Every man and woman eventually went insane, Lord Dura, driven mad by memories that weren't theirs, their minds broken because they couldn't hold on to themselves. Each one was killed by their guard, struck down by their friends to release them from their raving.

"Every member is trained and cautioned, but we've had a few—those such as you who came into a free gift—who refused to believe the danger such a course presents."

I tested the ropes and succeeded in making them tighten around my wrists. "I'm not a danger. I have no intention of attacking you or anyone else. You can cut me loose."

At Pellin's nod, Bolt drew his dagger and sliced through my bonds with an almost thoughtless overhand sweep that deposited pieces of rope on the floor. I checked my suddenly naked wrists for blood.

"We were never in any danger from you, Lord Dura," Pellin said.

I didn't care for the note of dismissal in his voice. I wasn't accustomed to being taken lightly. "Other men have made the mistake of thinking that." I stood, trying to work the circulation into my numbed backside, and noticed I still had my sword. I stepped over to join Pellin by the window. Bolt still stood behind the chair, some four paces away. "If I wanted to draw on you now, Pellin, I could cut your throat before he could save you."

I heard Bolt chuckle, but the sound shifted, changing pitch just before I felt a sensation of cold against my throat and looked over to see him a pace away with his sword in hand.

Very slowly, I lifted my hands away from the weapons at my belt and Bolt sheathed his blade. I smiled as if I'd just won a large wager. "You wonder why I don't trust you, Pellin? You've set a man as my guard who's faster than anyone I've seen, and his loyalties are elsewhere."

Pellin's eyes narrowed at me with the realization he and Bolt had been tricked, but Bolt laughed and retreated a step.

"I think I like this one," Bolt said.

Pellin smirked, but there was a sour cast to it. "Yes, I can see why you would. You always said those in the Vigil hold too high an opinion of themselves."

A bark of laughter greeted this. "You've dressed it up. I said you were all insufferable and that you needed to be humbled."

The smile slid from Pellin's face, and a muscle jumped in his left cheek. "It seems you've gotten your wish." He turned to face me. "And this would appear to be the means of your answer."

Bolt's voice was placid. "If you're going to war, you look for weapons. After you've won, you can worry about whether or not you were justified in using them."

"You know, I listened to you spout soldier proverbs at me for decades. I never liked it," Pellin said.

"That was one of the reasons why I did it."

I waited for their conversation to run its course. It held a familiar sound to it, a verbal dance the men had been through many times before.

With a shrug that almost appeared to be a surrender of sorts, Pellin turned to me. "With Elwin's passing, I am Eldest of the Vigil. The responsibility for the success or failure of your actions belongs to me."

I nodded to show I understood. Those who employed military men used a military chain of command. "If there is something you want from me, you need to tell me what I need to know." I thought for a moment. "And if you want anything from me in terms of loyalty, you better tell me what I *want* to know as well. Right now, I'm the king's reeve, nothing else."

"Very well," he said, "though much of it you already suspect. Bolt's loyalty is to the Vigil, not to you. What you did in the prison was noble"—he nodded—"and incredibly stupid. Listen to Bolt. He's there to keep you alive if he can."

I laughed, but I wasn't amused. "But he's here to kill me if I put my foot wrong."

Pellin nodded. "If by that you mean endanger yourself or the rest of us, then, yes."

I felt a trickle of sweat begin to trace an icy path down my spine. I was decent with a sword and creatively ruthless in a fight, but if Bolt drew on me, I would die without my so much as marking him. I'd seen what a pure physical gift could do. No amount of talent or training could hope to defeat it. Even so, Pellin's agreement meant he was willing to give me the truth—a part of it anyway.

He sat, dropping into the chair as if the burden of his knowledge or the conversation had become too heavy to bear. "For the past decade, the Vigil has been working to uncover the reason behind the growth of the Darkwater Forest."

I interrupted him before I could stop myself. "It's not growing. The six kings check the boundary stones every year just before the planting. The forest is no bigger now than it has been for the last century."

Pellin stood and paced the floor, staring at the threadbare carpet covering the stones in my room, his gaze on the pattern worn into it by countless footsteps. "A belief we encourage, but the truth is the six kingdoms bordering the curse are measuring the wrong thing. The actual Darkwater is only a part of the larger forest, but it's been growing. We keep our own boundary markers hidden within it. Each year it encroaches upon the rest of the woodlands, adding to its blighted domain. With every passing season more and more of the territory that borders it falls to its evil, and it's accelerating."

Chapter 14

Bolt's face confirmed Pellin's assertion. I still had reason to mistrust the eldest of the Vigil, but I'd taken the measure of Bolt. He wouldn't bother to lie. "Why?"

"We don't know," Pellin said. "But we believe Elwin was close to finding out."

"And was killed for it," I said. I thought of the shard of aurium I'd taken from his body and then thrust the memory away. I wouldn't trust Pellin. Not yet. My training and experience as reeve took over, and in my mind I stepped back, seeing the players in the scene, even myself, as pawns on a ficheall board to be moved. I checked that. I might be a pawn, but Pellin and the rest of the Vigil carried a much higher rank. Even so, he appeared to be a man who'd just had his strongest piece swept from play—and he looked at me in expectation.

"Who would profit from such a thing?" I asked, but a moment later I began answering my own question. "The southern kingdoms might possibly have some motivation." I stopped, shaking my head. It didn't make sense. "No. Political alliances change far too often. A kingdom that is today's rival could be tomorrow's ally. Besides, the four divisions have sealed a truce on the continent. Even the boundary skirmishes are fading, at least until the droughts return."

Pellin nodded. "Our thoughts ran in the same direction." He held out a hand, beckoning. "Continue, Lord Dura. Perhaps your perspective will see something that ours could not."

I let my frustration show. "There's no point. If it's not a kingdom, then you're saying there's an individual to blame, but if a single man could unleash the Darkwater Forest, surely it would have been done long ago. We've never suffered a shortage of insanity."

I stopped myself. I'd gone too fast. We'd likely ruled out the kingdoms, but that didn't necessarily mean we were left only with individuals. My stomach, still queasy, started tumbling in my gut, like an acrobat but not nearly as graceful.

"What about the guilds?" I asked.

Pellin, for once, looked genuinely surprised. His brows rose. Even the lines that littered Bolt's forehead crinkled in curiosity. "Explain."

"'Money buys everything,'" I quoted. "If the Darkwater Forest starts to cut into the crops in the valley between the four northern kingdoms, I can think of several possibilities for profit. The price of food would skyrocket off the panic buying alone. Then there'd be an exodus toward the southern kingdoms." I laughed, but I couldn't bring myself to feel amused. "You've heard the merchants. 'Desperate men make great customers.'"

It sounded good, but I was missing something, some angle or perspective that I hadn't considered. I could dress the motives up in pretty words, but the Darkwater Forest wasn't just a dangerous piece of ground, it was insanity incarnate. Mothers didn't use tales of it to frighten their children, and toughs didn't try to prove their courage by venturing into it. It was too deadly for such games.

A decade ago I'd been forced beneath its branches by poor tactics and worse timing. Cut off from our forces, a full squadron of Owmead troops penned my men up against the forest. Our choices had been death at their hands or retreat into the Darkwater far enough that the enemy wouldn't follow. A few of the men had voted for a last stand, but my voice prevailed.

At first, I'd believed the tactic had worked. We circled into the forest and back toward our line, skirting the shadows that ate the light.

Pellin and the room wavered in my vision as the memory took over. In the light of dawn I alone came out from beneath the black oaks to the safety of the meadow. Just me.

I shook myself out of the past to meet Pellin's gaze. "It sounds good, but no sane man would try to use the Darkwater for any purpose."

His blue eyes became calculating. "We are in agreement—no sane man would."

I caught the stress he'd placed on the word *sane*. "You want me to find a madman."

He cocked his head to one side as he shrugged. "Perhaps, but to find anyone, you'll have to survive your own recklessness. Bolt can protect you from most attacks, but short of throwing you in prison, he can't keep you from using your gift."

He didn't bother to wait for my reply. Bolt moved to block the door after Pellin slipped around him, standing there for several minutes before granting me permission to leave. There would be no following the Eldest. He had said a lot without answering my deeper questions, but I did my best not to react to being held prisoner in my own quarters. I needed space away from my guard to delve deeper into the truth behind the Vigil.

I hadn't been allowed to touch any of them, and I knew from bitter experience that any man, king or reeve, could be deceived.

Bolt's steady, emotionless gaze seemed to indicate that he neither knew my thoughts nor cared what they might be. "What now?" I appreciated the fact that he didn't bother to use my title. It would have made me suspicious.

I nodded toward the window. "What's the hour?"

"Almost noon."

We had enough time if we hurried. "We have to go down into the city. I need to know what happened the night Elwin and Robin died, and I think there's someone who can point me in the right direction." I didn't bother to add that if everything went according to plan I would be free from Bolt's presence, at least for a while.

We made our way to the lowest levels of the tor, descending long flights of dark granite stairs that served to keep those with minor complaints from the king's presence. When we emerged into the greasy half light permitted by the cloud cover, I looked back at the keep. King Laidir's seat thrust its defiance like a fist against the broad bowl of gray sky. "It's never been taken."

Bolt's lift of his shoulders accented his rebuttal. "There's a first time for everything."

I tried to ignore the chill.

This time I found Rory without any trouble, and for once luck seemed to be with me. He and his group of urchins were at the end of the Potter's Way. Olwen, a skinny—all the urchins were thin—boy of ten with hunger-sharpened features led me along the alley. The squish of muck beneath our boots intensified the smell of sewage.

"Charming," Bolt commented. "The poor footing and worse lighting will make it hard to defend you if it comes to fighting."

"You'll have no need for your sword, master," Olwen said. His fingers brushed almost negligently across Bolt's cloak, and I clamped my hand around the sleeve on his arm before he could stop me.

Olwen's eyes lost their good-natured gleam, and for a split second, something hungry and feral looked back at me. "He's faster with the sword than you can imagine, Olwen." I dug a silver penny from the purse I'd tucked well inside my cloak and gave it to him. "Besides, I'm willing to pay a little extra this time."

Our eyes hadn't adjusted to the gloom, so Bolt couldn't see what I knew to be there—half a dozen urchins hidden in the shadows with daggers, knives balanced for throwing with disconcerting accuracy—but this time I was wrong. As we moved I noticed at least a full dozen places where the shadows didn't quite match the object casting them.

I didn't bother to say anything to Bolt. I couldn't afford to have my guard precipitate a fight over a misunderstanding. He shrugged as if he'd met Olwen's kind before. We came to a seeming dead end, blocked by a wall of stone with discarded bits of rotting wood leaning against it at random angles.

Olwen ducked and circled around behind the collection of timber and disappeared. I'd been here before, and by now Rory would be expecting me, but even so I suppressed the urge to draw my blade. Olwen glided through the break in the masonry wall with the slippery grace of an otter sliding down a snowbank, but Bolt and I had to hunch over and duck walk through the narrow opening.

We came into a broad cellar lit by a pair of candles that guttered in the draft, not so many to spoil the night vision of any living there. Rory greeted me, leering at me through one good eye and one swollen almost shut by a lurid bruise. As always, I looked at his hands, struck again by the slender strength obvious in the tapered fingers. He should have been a musician instead of a pickpocket. With those hands and a physical gift of beauty, he could have made stones weep.

He smiled and dismissed Olwen back to the alley before assessing me with a pair of brown eyes filled with more calculation and cunning than any lad his age should possess. And something more this time. Fear.

"I need information, Rory."

His gaze passed over me and settled on Bolt. "Yah. Who's this?" His voice dipped in the singsong of the southern kingdom.

"My new guard."

Rory's face closed. "You know the rules, yah? We don't allow the growlers in here."

I shook my head. "He's not with the watch. He's *my* guard."

Coal-black eyebrows lifted a fraction, and his swollen eyelids parted for an instant. "You're in danger again, Willet, yah?"

I couldn't deny it, and Rory would have sniffed it out if I tried. "Yah." I lifted my left hand palm up, a gesture that would have been insignificant to anyone else, but Rory caught it.

He eyed my guard with suspicion. "We don't talk in front of people we don't know, Willet."

I turned to Bolt. "Wait outside. This will only take a minute."

His eyes narrowed, but I couldn't tell if it was from being ordered out or being forced to leave me unguarded that put his back up, but after looking the rest of the cellar over and tapping his sword so Rory would notice, he left.

"Things must be really bad for you, Willet," Rory said, all trace of his accent gone.

I chuckled, faking more humor than I felt. "You have no idea. I need two things, Rory."

He smiled. "I know one of them is to ditch Stoneface out there. What's the other?"

"Witnesses to a murder."

He tried to keep his face neutral, but a tic in his left eye gave him away. Rory was scared.

"Is the watch interested enough in the poor quarter to have you investigate?" he asked. Anger made his voice warble between a boy's range and a man's. "Jeb's threatened to put his knuckles on every urchin in the district and more than a few of the ladies."

I didn't doubt it. Jeb didn't handle frustration well. "He's angry, Rory. He doesn't like to see children killed. He probably thinks the street people are hiding information so you can go after the killer yourself." My hands twitched at my sides. I didn't know how to placate either of them. "I'll see what I can do." I pulled a pair of silver half crowns from my purse and offered them in an open palm. It might have been okay to toss money to Olwen, but Rory ran the urchins, and I wasn't about to treat him like a servant.

"Which murder, Willet? Your merchant or Nick?"

He must have seen the look of surprise on my face.

"That's right, Willet. The murderer you're looking for managed to kill the best thief we had. Nobody should have been able to sneak up on him."

Now I understood the fear I'd seen lurking behind Rory's eyes. Nick wasn't just a name—it was a title the urchins gave to their best. The Nick carried the responsibility of high-gain theft. To earn the title, one had to be light and nimble enough to work across the rooftops and skilled enough to get through locked windows and casements.

Rory wouldn't let the Nick work so often or steal anything valuable enough to attract unwanted attention to the urchins, but something had gone wrong.

It didn't require much wit to puzzle out what had happened.

I paced the cluttered cellar. "Nick witnessed something he wasn't supposed to see, Rory. I think he saw a murder, and the killers saw him."

Rory shook his head. "He would have told me, Willet. That kind of information is valuable."

I stopped pacing long enough to face Rory again. "Unless something he saw kept him quiet. He was in the lower merchants' quarter three nights ago, wasn't he?"

He gave me a slow nod.

"Two men were attacked there that night."

Rory didn't bother to answer. He fixed me with a stare that belonged on the face of someone a lot older and waited for me to explain why his best thief was dead.

"One of the men killed was gifted, Rory." I paused, trying to gauge how much to tell him to enlist his help without putting him and the rest of the urchins at risk. "Pure, and I'm told he had the talent to go with it. They didn't just kill him, they cut him to pieces. I need to talk to any of the urchins or ladies who worked the area."

Rory pocketed the money, but his expression darkened. "I'll see what I can do, Willet. Nick's death isn't going down easy. What you've told me isn't going to help your case any. The rest of the urchins are already scared, and the ladies have their own guild. They don't answer to me. Did you see Constance on the way in?"

When I shook my head, he went on. "It's hard to get people to talk when they're afraid of dying for it. I won't do it." Rory turned away from me, and I reached out to grab his bare arm before I could stop myself.

The room narrowed as I realized my mistake, and my awareness fell headlong through his eyes into the mind beyond, trying to let go but unable. Images raced past me—of a woman dressed in provocative clothing tucking me in for the night; a parade of men, some highborn, most common, visiting our cramped apartment; later, enough shame to start a bonfire; the woman's body, dead from fever in the House of Passing.

Interspersed through it all, a man's face showed over and again, first young, then older, narrow to the point of being severe but owning hands that flowed and blurred across the strings of a harp. Then I saw the man dying, his hand on my head, his whispers low and unintelligible.

One final image seared itself in my mind—combing the city, collecting ragtag boys and girls, many of them begging for crusts in the street, abandoned, orphaned by circumstance or design, then bringing them in, saving them.

Chapter 15

I stumbled backward, letting go of Rory's arm. His eyes narrowed and his fingers slid to the knife tucked at his belt. This adolescent thief with harpist's hands was my only means to finding Elwin's killer. I wondered if he'd puzzled out the gift he held.

His gaze went flat, and he stared through me. "Are you trying to help us, Willet? Or are you just looking for information?"

I knew the smart thing to say, but I'd just seen more nobility of character in the dingy rat-infested cellar than I was likely to see in the entire court aside from Laidir. I couldn't bring myself to lie. "Both." I dug into my purse and pulled out my last two silver crowns and held them out.

Rory looked at me as if I'd slapped him.

"I've already paid for the information, Rory. This is for you, to help take care of the boys and girls you've taken off the streets."

His eyes widened, and for a moment, an all-too-brief moment, he looked his age. I got a sense of the burden he'd taken unto himself, a responsibility that had forced him to be a man and surrogate father. The moment passed and he tucked the crowns out of sight in such a way that I never heard them clink against each other.

He licked his lips. "I was the Nick once, when Ilroy first headed the urchins. We train our replacements, Willet. It's not so different from being one of king's guards. After three months I couldn't sneak up on him anymore." Candlelight reflected the anger shining in the depths of his eyes. “His murder is trouble, Willet. There’s something out there that can see better in the dark than we can.”

“But that’s . . .” I stopped myself at the look on his face. Rory didn’t have any education, but he was smart in a way most men would never be. Even so, growing up in the street wouldn’t have given him any means to know about the things in the Darkwater. I tried to keep myself in the present, but memories overwhelmed me.

The scent of decay filled my nose, and I peered so hard into the darkness my eyes hurt. Twisted oaks blocked the setting sun, reducing the forest to a sickly purple twilight. I led my men into the Darkwater, away from the column of Owmead soldiers and their crossbows. The twelve of us walked in two groups of six, one man to check each direction, one to check the canopy overhead, and one to watch the floor. I put myself in the van, drifting north and west toward Collum’s lines, thinking to protect my men or warn them if something came at us. Foolish. The six men in the group trailing us a few yards back disappeared without a sound, as if they’d never been.

“Willet.”

I felt a tug on my arm, blinking to bring Rory’s face into focus.

His narrow face became pinched, wary. “You don’t look so good. You’re not ill, are you?”

I didn’t bother to answer. I didn’t *know* the answer. “I need to get out of here, Rory. Keep all the urchins and the ladies off the streets at night until you hear from me—you understand? Get to someplace that has light, lots of light, and you stay there each night.” I put my face close to his. “Keep everyone out of the dark. If I don’t make it to Braben’s tomorrow, check for me there each day at noon.”

Rory nodded, his eyes wide. Something I’d said managed to frighten him. He had a lot to choose from.

I fought to ignore the twisting in my gut that said events were spiraling out of my control. “Keep everyone out of the dark, Rory.”

He bit his lower lip. “They won’t like it, Willet. We can’t beg enough during the day to keep fed.” He pointed to the back of the room, hidden in shadow. “There are stairs back there.”

I slipped around a stone column in the center of the cellar, just managed to make out a narrow flight of granite steps leading to a concealed door. I paused to give Rory one last admonishment. "They'll like it a lot better than being dead." Then I slipped away.

I came out into afternoon sunshine, but the wan light through the clouds failed to illuminate my dilemma. So far I'd done pretty well as the king's reeve. Attention to detail and a bit of luck here and there along with some decent contacts had helped keep me alive and put a few criminals before the magistrates, but I was out of my element. Up until now I'd only hunted ordinary men, however gifted they might be. Not something that could see in the dark.

As soon as the thought entered my mind, I felt a hollow spot blossom in my middle. Not necessarily someone. Old superstitions had a way of taking root, even after hundreds of years of liturgy and daily offices. I shook off the recollections of tales of eldritch beings and witch light in the dark places of the earth and focused on the more tangible present.

The worst part of my current situation was the Vigil. I didn't have anything to go on except Ealdor's sketchy information on the gift and what the members of the Vigil and their leader, Pellin, had told me about themselves.

Maybe they were all being perfectly up-front and honest about themselves.

Assuredly.

Just like everyone else I'd ever talked to in my whole life.

I made my way out of the poor quarter, walking quickly and cutting back and forth down the safer alleys and streets north toward the edge of the more prosperous part of the city, where the four divisions of the church maintained their headquarters. Flanking the square, the newer buildings of the Absold and the Vanguard had been built to impress, and even the Servants' edifice held about itself an almost luxurious solidity to accompany its soaring tower. Yet I passed by each of them to make my way toward the second-oldest building in the city, after the king's citadel itself.

The Merum cathedral. For a thousand years before the church split into the four orders, the enormous blocks of cut stone had housed all of the worshippers of the northernmost province of the empire in the vaulted basilica. On the eastern side of the nave, massive offices housed the local bishop along with his administrators and servants.

The structure remained, and supplicants still flocked to it each seventh-day, though not nearly so many as before. Yet the cathedral maintained something from its storied past that I'd found useful on more than one occasion—the library, or more accurately, its keeper. I detoured from my mission long enough to stop by the closest market and then approached my destination.

A broad rise led to the grounds of the massive church that had been erected by thousands of the faithful countless years before. The steps were broad and shallow enough to make ascending them appear elegant, but I felt the need for haste and took them two at a time.

Custos, the dry wrinkled man who documented the exhaustive records of the Merum and the entire kingdom thereby, had seemed old when I was an acolyte, but the eyes of my youth had deceived me. He possessed perhaps no more than fifty years, though he displayed the meticulous care in motion of a man much older.

As if the evil of the Darkwater prowled behind me, impatient, I sprinted up toward the massive building that housed thousands upon thousands of scrolls, books, and parchments. A pale-skinned acolyte opened the door and confirmed the keeper worked within, and I breathed a sigh of relief. He escorted me through the narrow aisles of shelves lined with ancient writings, some of them so yellowed with age they might have been dyed. I grabbed a book at random.

"Is there something specific I can help you with?"

I shook my head and smiled. "No. Specificity is exactly what I'm trying to avoid." I couldn't help but enjoy his look of confusion. He appeared new to the library and its keeper and unacquainted with our game.

We turned a corner and came in sight of a stooped figure in a faded red cleric's robe, thumbing through a small leather-bound book. Custos. In his own way, the withered little man was invaluable to the kingdom, though none could have guessed his worth by looking at him. A fringe of iron-gray hair clung precariously to the sides of his head all around, leaving his age-spotted dome bare. His nose, always bulbous, had drooped, unable to defy the forces of age and gravity that pulled it downward. But his mind and his eyes remained as sharp as ever. I'd had need of Custos before, and he smiled at me in welcome.

"Willet, my lad, welcome." His voice drifted to me in time to his breaths, a perpetual whisper that proved his reverence for his surroundings.

I pulled him close and kissed him loudly on the top of his bald crown. "I have need of that mind of yours, Custos."

He waved me away, his hands fluttering. "Have you no respect for a servant of the church?"

I returned his smile. "No, but I have plenty of respect for you."

He flapped his lips. "Your blasphemies will be your undoing, boy." His eyes grew sharp. "And you know the price for my assistance."

I mocked his seriousness. "I do indeed, you old bandit, but let us test to see if you are still worthy of the ransom you demand."

"Ha. You doubt?" He pointed to the book in my hand. "Read the description. Hurry, it's been too long since your last visit, and my avarice grows apace."

I opened the text and picked a spot about halfway down the page. "'The three brothers of iniquity are bound in the deep places of the earth, exiled from the presence of light until . . .'" I stopped reading, smiling at Custos despite the subject matter. It was just a random scroll, and the early church fathers often engaged in dire portents.

Custos blinked several times in quick succession before speaking. "'. . . the end. Therefore do not delve the deep places of the earth lest iniquity consume all,'" he recited.

His words matched exactly what was hidden from him halfway down the page. I would have said the dry little man in front of me was *gifted* but I'd never heard of such, and his ability defied my attempts to comprehend it according to the strictures of the exordium.

"It was hardly much of a test," I said. "Every church father I've ever read blathers on about not delving the earth."

Custos harrumphed at me. "That was what made it so difficult. They all sound so similar that reciting the exact verbiage is quite challenging." He leered at me, searching for the bribe beneath my cloak. "Now, my price."

He rubbed his dry hands together as I reached into its folds, his eyes gleaming with undisguised greed. I placed a leaf-wrapped packet of sweetened figs rolled in crushed almonds in his hands. "There's something I need to know, Custos."

He gave me an impatient wave as he took two of the figs and popped them into his mouth, setting one in each cheek and chewing slowly as his eyes fluttered in ecstasy. I gave up and settled myself to wait. I knew better than to try to get anything useful from him while he indulged his vice.

"All those sweets can't be good for you," I said after a moment. He ate with the deliberate motions of a man engaged in a sacrament.

He swallowed with an effort, ignorant or uncaring of the juice that dribbled down his chin. "At my age, Willet, it hardly matters. Come. Concern is scrawled all over your face, like a novice's clumsy pen strokes. Tell me what troubles you."

I cut my eyes to his acolyte, who still stood, waiting for orders.

"Ah," Custos said. "Yes. Passen, go to the north wing and shelve any of the scrolls the brothers have left lying about." Custos shot a look at me before continuing. "And then check to make sure none of them have inadvertently placed a work in the wrong location."

Passen padded off, a puppy happy to do its master's bidding, and Custos faced me once more. "Whenever you ask for secrecy, I worry. It usually means someone's trying to kill you." His voice was serious, but I could see his eyes dancing, afire with curiosity, and he kneaded his hands in anticipation. This was his real price.

"I don't know if you can help me this time, Custos," I said. I knew his pride would never admit to something he didn't know, and in truth I was certain he knew something of the Vigil, but I had no desire to put him in danger. To most of the people in Collum, he was just the records keeper, one of the innumerable parts of the Merum order in a menial job that required nothing more of him than to organize the writings of others.

But they didn't know what I knew. Custos had read every scroll in the entire building, no matter how trivial or mundane. A centuries-old census or an obscure treatise on the reasons behind the split of the church were both devoured by his incredible mind with equal relish. And he remembered it all.

"Nonsense, Willet." He drew himself up in mock offense, straightening the stoop of his back a fraction. "If the information you seek has been recorded, then the information is here." He tapped his head. "Everything you see in the library I've duplicated in my mind—sheaf, book, and scroll."

Not for the first time, I was amazed that the local bishop of the Merum had never made use of Custos's unique gift. "Why do they leave someone with your mind to gather dust here in the library, brother?"

He laughed at me and popped another fig in his mouth. "Because I don't dare tell them how much I know." His brows climbed his head as if shocked at his own confession. "They might take me away from the books and scrolls and make me work with people. I don't like people."

"You work with me," I protested.

He nodded, the gesture filled with the exaggeration of the aged. "Men and women are stories. The tale of their lives contain triumph and tragedy, but far too many of their stories end long before their hearts have counted their allotted number." He smiled. "But you're interesting, a story that changes each time it's read. Now, stop trying to use your wiles on an old man who knows better and tell me what you need."

I tried not to hope too much. "Have you ever heard of a group called the Vigil?"

He stared at me, blinking as he perused books and scrolls in his mind's eye. A frown grew on his countenance, deepening until his grizzled brows all but obscured his eyes. "Curses, lad. Not in any way that might help." He stroked the dome of his head with one hand, coaxing his thoughts. "I mean, there have been groups who have called themselves by that name, but none of them carried any import that history took more than passing note of them. They are given casual mention but just as soon forgotten. Do you have anything else?"

I didn't want to speak of the gift I'd been given. Other people's memories still swirled around my head, and I could almost feel my mind trying to erect walls to separate them from the core of who I was. But I didn't have any choice. "How much do you know about the gifts?"

He laughed and gestured to the countless shelves and books surrounding us. "Possibly more than anyone living—including what is true, what is false, and what is conjectured."

"What do you know of the gift called domere?" I took a deep breath and held it.

Chapter 16

If the question startled Custos, he gave no sign of it. He'd heard any number of strange questions from me in the course of my investigations. This one appeared to be no stranger than the rest.

"There's a name I haven't read in quite some time, hardly more than the phantom of a rumor, supposedly given to man at the beginning of creation," he said, "but lost in the millennia since." He sighed. "There's a lot of very dry theology on the shelves debating whether it ever actually existed. Most point to the absence of its evidence to prove it is nothing more than fancy."

"If it *did* exist," I asked, "why would it disappear?"

He laughed and pointed to a distant corner of the library. "Most of the books over there deal with the questions of how a gift might be destroyed." He shuddered. "Dry reading, it is, like eating dust." He gave me a coy smile. "Sometimes when I'm bored, I cross-reference the lists of the gifted with each census, but the oldest records are too incomplete to draw any conclusions one way or another. There are sporadic mentions of the gift of domere in the oldest texts, but then nothing." He lifted a hand that dangled at his wrist and rubbed his head. "That would seem to be proof enough that it never really existed. Everything in the library says that if a gift isn't passed on for any reason, it becomes free, coming to any by the will of Aer." He sighed. "But not that one. It just disappeared sometime in the third century of the church, just before the north-south split."

Something in what he said tugged at me, but I couldn't afford the time it would take to place it. Bolt would track me down sooner or later, and I didn't want him or anyone else within the Vigil to learn of my connection with Custos or his abilities. "What about the gift itself? What does it do?"

He nodded and his eyes grew sharp. "Ah, there we have a bit more to go on." He turned. "Come. I'll take you to the sanctum."

We passed through motes of dust that danced in beams of sunlight, ignoring shelves whose lacquered wood had aged almost to black, and came to an iron-bound wooden door set in stone. Custos dug in the folds of his cassock and pulled out a heavy brass key. The mechanism voiced a token complaint, and we passed into a round room, its walls lined with more shelves and a trestle table in the center.

There were no books. Instead, sheets of flattened parchment were tucked into square slots that filled the shelves. I gazed in astonishment. There must have been hundreds of them in that room, each with their own shelf. Notations had been written beneath each one in a neat hand. Even those gave the appearance of great age.

"The scrolls in here are centuries old," Custos said, "some over a thousand, and a few more than that. They're too fragile to be handled. Only I am allowed to touch them." He walked over to the table and donned a pair of clean linen gloves. "I think you'll find this interesting."

I followed him with my hands clasped behind my back. His reverential attitude forbade foolishness or jesting. We stood in the presence of history, and I didn't want to damage any of the ancient texts, not even by accident.

Custos moved without hesitation to the northern end of the room. "We keep the oldest parchments here, where they'll get the least amount of light." He raised his gloved hands, pulled a sheet from its nook, and moved to lay it gently on the table. "Read this."

I tried to read the first paragraph three times before I gave up. "It's gibberish. I can't make sense of anything except a word here or there that's so badly misspelled it could be almost anything." I scanned another two-thirds of the way down the page before I stopped. "I surrender."

He stepped in beside me and placed a finger under a passage about the middle of the page, reading aloud.

"'Se aegift ouf domere gerad ael ist wodan.'"

He pointed to each word as he translated. "'If you push the gift too far, you'll go insane.'" He raised his head to look at me, the light in his eyes brighter than any gift of sweets could account for. "Be careful with it, Willet."

"Me? What makes you think I have the gift?"

Custos put the last fig into his mouth and chewed as he eyed me. "For one thing, the fact that you didn't bother to deny it just now. For another, I never believed the gift had died out. Too many times I've read texts chronicling the history of medicine in our world that spoke of those who went mad with some sudden malady, screaming names they never knew, calling out to family members they didn't have. The physicians universally described it as insanity or possession, depending on their theology, but I've always wondered at the resemblance to the warning on this parchment."

I stood there with Custos looking through me as if he possessed the gift himself, but I was unwilling to surrender yet. "That's pretty rough information to go on, my friend. There are a lot of things I don't bother to deny about myself. If you doubt, go up to the tor and listen to what the nobles have to say about me." I snorted my contempt. "They can't even agree with each other." I waved my arm at the multitude of parchment around us. "Your scrolls say the gift is dead. Why would you doubt them?"

Custos smiled at me. "Tell me, Willet, how do you search for clues to solve a crime?"

I took a deep breath, thinking back to the scene of Robin's body. I ignored the temptation to lose myself in the memory of his distant gaze. "I look for something out of place, something that shouldn't be there, a splatter of blood in the wrong spot, perhaps a scrap of cloth in a dead man's grip."

Custos's head waved on his neck like a blossom on a weak stalk. "Exactly. Which is why I believe the gift of domere is still with us."

"I don't understand."

He clapped me on the shoulder. "I've spent my life in this library, Willet. Copies of writings from all over the northern continent make their way here—and even a few from the southern continent. There's a pattern to the writings of the church fathers and theologians, a rhythm to the written record that we've collected over the long centuries. The writings on each and every gift follow that pattern, except for one. Yours."

I knew he had me, but I no longer cared. "Go on."

He smiled, enjoying my curiosity. "A search through the library will reveal any number of writings explaining why a gift might die, or referencing the fact that it has died."

"And?" I prompted him.

"That's all. With any other gift, real or rumored, you could find hundreds of scrolls explaining how it works, its theological significance, and its intended value to mankind." He tapped my chest with a thick knuckle. "You seek what's there and shouldn't be, but I had to do the opposite. I had to see what should have been there but wasn't."

I gaped at him, stunned in the realization that only Custos had the skill and the means to come to such a conclusion. Only his mind owned the capacity. I bowed, bending at the waist until my chest was parallel to the floor. "If you ever petition the king to become his personal reeve, I'll be out of a job."

He laughed, but I didn't join in. A thought came to me as my training asserted itself. "But if the scrolls describing the gift are gone, someone must have removed them."

Custos nodded.

I went further. "And they must have worked at it for centuries, at least at first. People would have written their own memories of it in the beginning, but then others would have referenced their accounts."

He smacked his lips as if he'd just sampled another treat. "The Vigil, you say? It would seem they've worked very hard over the centuries to keep themselves a secret."

I pointed to the flaking piece of parchment on the table beside us. "But they missed at least one."

Custos grinned. "I found this when I first came to the library, misplaced between the pages of a book on ancient farming practices."

I had no choice but to trust him. He knew already, the old bandit. "I need you to keep this secret, Custos. There are people hunting me, and they won't hesitate to kill you."

His eyes sparkled. "What's it like, Willet? How does it feel to see inside someone?"

The memories of a dozen people swirled around my head like a murder of crows in flight. "You drop into a cave and become someone else. It isn't as if you read their life's record, it's more as though you become them for a while. When I come out of it, it's difficult to remember who I am."

I nodded to the parchment. "Is there anything in there that can help me?"

His grin dropped away. "I've told you most of it already. It's in our tongue, but language is a fluid thing, and this scroll predates the church—so old its meanings are obscure, though your description of the gift and the parchment's version are close. You describe it as going into a cave, while the language in the treatise describes it more that the person is tunneling."

I sighed. "That doesn't help much."

I could see my disappointment pained him, and I regretted showing so much of it. He pushed the sleeve of his robe up and put his arm out. "Knowledge is power, Willet. I can't give you information I don't have, but I can give you everything else."

The sight of his bare skin, held as an offering, started a tremble in my knees. Custos's gesture scared me. I didn't know if I could sort his memories and keep myself intact. And he might be a benign servant of the church now, but what might lie in his past?

I wanted to deny him, but could I afford to? Information was critical to my success, and Custos was offering more of it in a moment than I would be able to amass in the rest of my life, a dozen lives.

He patted me on the sleeve. "I don't think any of my memories will trouble you, Willet. Except for the occasional stolen kiss when I was a lad, I've lived my entire life in the company of books." He glanced around the library. "This is the only real love I've ever had or wanted."

His encouragement only daunted me. The contents of an entire library and more were contained in his memories. When I was a boy I saw a man hook a bladder to the spigot of a huge water barrel. When he turned it on, the bladder filled and continued to stretch, thinning until I could see the outlines of the barrel through it. Then it exploded, spewing its contents.

I suppressed a shudder. My experience in the jail had taught me to be afraid. "I don't have your ability, Custos. How am I supposed to hold everything you know without bursting?"

He pursed his lips, considering. "I think I can limit the information you get. I'll just put the other shelves away, locked within rooms I'll create in my mind." He smiled at me. "Just don't go busting down any doors."

I nodded, still feeling less than confident.

I peeled the glove off my right hand and placed it on his age-spotted arm. His watery brown eyes appeared to leap toward me, and I understood what he meant about tunneling. I had the sensation of burrowing through the layers of his mind until I came into his thoughts.

Only this time, instead of chaotic images of the past or visions of wounding that rewrote any definitions of self, I stepped into a replica of the library, secure in my knowledge of its contents. But no books, scrolls, or even shelves marred the pristine emptiness of the vaulted spaces where myriad volumes should have been. A stab of fear lanced through me. What had happened to the Merum library, the jewel of the north?

I slowed, my steps reflecting my disbelief until I noted the closed doors of the library's innermost sanctuary in the distance. Hurrying now with the careful steps of a crone, I made my way to the locked doors that held the very history of the world within its confines. My hands fumbled for the key as whimpers of panic clogged my throat.

When at last I managed to open the doors, emptiness within hit me with the finality of a headman's stroke, and I sobbed for the lost knowledge. Then I noticed a single case to the side, a solitary set of shelves with a few score volumes, all of them with the yellowed fragility that proclaimed their antiquity. Even in the midst of my relief, I wondered why these should be spared.

As I reached out to take one from its place, curious as to why it and its brothers should be spared, my mind exploded in light. The texts and scrolls flew from the shelf to disappear at my touch, imprinting themselves on my memory, each one leading to the next in a chain. Comprehension formed within my mind at each touch, like a sun dawning, the gray of predawn giving way first to the subdued crimson and then complete illumination. I understood.

The stream of parchment ceased, and I blinked, finding myself standing among the dry, dusty shelves with their contents and an image of myself looking at me. No. Custos looked at me—Willet Dura. *Who?*

Memories roiled and seethed in my mind, but they refused to commingle into identity, boiling together, oil and water that refused to mix. Why was I looking at myself?

I reached out, expecting my hand to hit the mirrored glass of my reflection, but instead finding the flesh of my visage on another. And the hand at the end of my wrist had never belonged to me. "What sorcery is this?" I panted. "Who are you?"

Panic wreathed the features that should have belonged to me, and my stomach heaved as I strove to reclaim myself. I turned from the table and sprawled across the unforgiving stone of the library's sanctuary, my hands scrabbling across the gritty surface, impotent.

Weight held my arms pinned to the floor, and hands cupped my head. "Close your eyes."

I squeezed them shut, and the turbulence within my mind receded. But two sets of memories still strove for dominance, and I lay helpless with their uncompromising refusal to mix. "Oil and water," I moaned aloud.

"I understand," my own voice came to me. "Librarian, which are you?"

Falling into the flood that circled my mind like a maelstrom, a memory washed over me, mine as a librarian, yet unfamiliar. "Oil," I sobbed. Water hit me, and the image of a woman, tall with hair the color of midnight, stole my breath.

"Librarian, make a shelf in your mind." In the eye of the whirlpool, I heard, envisioning one of the countless black-lacquered shelves in the library. "Place all the memories of yourself as Custos upon it."

I placed my hand into the swirling torrent of memories and pulled a memory, the smallest that I could see, but slick as oil, from the flood, freeing it from the mix. Forcing it onto the shelf, it became parchment, a single sheet with ancient writing on one side. Pulling another and repeating the process, the maelstrom shrank by almost imperceptible degrees, and as it diminished, identity began to coalesce within my mind.

In the end there was only one, a book large enough to require both hands in order to place it next to its brothers. I gazed at the shelf in my mind, knowing myself as Willet Dura, trembling with fear lest I touch it, even by accident. When I opened my eyes, Custos, the real one, was looking down at me, his face bare inches from mine.

"Your breath smells like figs."

He smiled. "I wonder why."

When I moved to sit up, the room spun, my eyes fighting to reconcile two sets of perceptions of the Merum sanctuary. I pulled myself up to a standing position and placed a hand on the trestle table to steady myself. I looked down at the feel of the shallow ridges of wood grain beneath my fingertips. My gaze alighted on the ancient parchment, written in a language I couldn't understand.

Or hadn't been able to.

I read through the strange characters and words twice, even though the memory of the text lurked somewhere in the vaults of my mind. The tangible reality of the script comforted me, or would have if that piece of parchment hadn't spelled out the dangers accompanying the use of my gift.

A passage caught my attention. "I can speak into the mind I'm viewing?"

Custos smiled at me as if I were a dense schoolboy. "Possibly. But wouldn't you have done it just now if you could? The text says you must grant the person foreknowledge of your intent, and they must grant you permission. You had both of those things."

A paragraph toward the end of the page stood out, and I went over it twice before I spoke. "Am I reading this right?" I asked him. "Can I train my gift to absorb the knowledge of memories without the emotions?"

He nodded. "If the text is correct. But be careful, Willet—just because something is very old doesn't mean it's infallible." He pointed to the parchment. "There's no record of Tiochus having any gift at all, much less *domere*."

I thought back to my interrogation with the Vigil. "One of them didn't want to touch me. She said it had been too recent." I looked at the yellowed sheepskin in front of me with disappointment. "It seems that there's more to learn than what's contained within the writing here."

I tried to take a step away from the table and lurched back toward it for support. My head pounded with the effort of keeping all the memories I'd absorbed sorted. My mind felt as if my skull had suddenly become too small. The beat of my heart sent black waves of pain across my vision.

"Willet?"

I sank to my knees. "I can't keep them all back."

Custos knelt beside me. "Make a room of your mind."

His voice sounded thin, far away, but I latched on to his instruction, feeling I had no other recourse. "What room?"

"Any room," he said.

Looking around his sanctuary made me dizzy enough to put me on the floor, but I copied the domed cavern into my mind. The memories of everyone I'd touched pushed against the walls, working to crack the stone and be free. "Hurry," I said, not sure I'd spoken aloud.

"Make doors in the walls," Custos said. "One for each set of memories you've taken. Put the bookcases behind the doors and lock them."

One by one I pushed the memories of others out of my mind's copy of Custos's sanctuary, the pain and dizziness receding with each effort until only one set of memories remained, my own.

I sat up and reeled with the effort, but only one perspective remained. "Where did you ever learn to do that?"

He smiled at me with his owlish brown eyes. "My youth was—" he paused, searching—"different." Then he shrugged. "It doesn't really fit into a tale. When you're ready, I'll let you into those memories if you wish."

We exchanged farewells, and I left the library by the northern exit, the one facing the long climb up to the keep. A sliver of crimson sun still shone above the horizon, and I could see purple-gray shadows lengthening as I mounted a flight of granite steps. I needed to return to court. It had been too long since my last appearance, and I needed to tell King Laidir what had transpired since.

I wrestled with myself every step of the way over how much to reveal. Distracted as I was, I didn't notice the empty alley or the men coming for me until it was too late to run.

Chapter 17

A shadow detached from the walls, a stain that blocked the fading sunlight at the end of the alley. Out of reflex I drew my sword. The shadow parted, resolved into two figures who crouched to put the fading sun into my eyes, each armed with an anlace, the long dagger preferred by the cutthroats who fought in close quarters.

Not soldiers, then. I might be able to take them both, but some of the thugs were decent with a blade, and I didn't see the need to take the chance. If either was gifted, they would have me down before I knew it.

I was already two steps into a run for the other end of the alley when another pair of figures with daggers stepped in. I didn't hesitate. Pulling a deep breath into my lungs, I continued racing for the second pair of men, screaming the entire way. "Guards! Guards of the watch!" I threw empty crates and anything else I could put my hands on behind me as I ran, trying not to think about the pair running me down from behind.

I kept screaming right up until the sound of steel rang in the alley. I hoped my charge might convince the footpads in front of me that I meant business and wasn't worth the risk, but I underestimated them. They set themselves, spreading as far apart as the alley would allow. I stopped ten paces short, pulling the dagger from my boot and throwing it at one of the men behind me. I missed his vitals, but the blade buried itself in the shoulder of his sword arm.

I darted to the side of the alley and wedged myself into a shallow corner where two buildings met. The footpads closed in, spreading to come at me from all sides. I pulled my last dagger and gripped it in my left hand. It wasn't long enough to stop anybody for long, but I might get a couple of parries out of it before they cut it out of my hand.

I gulped air. "Guards!" I had to play for time. My sword had more reach than their daggers, and I wove an endless series of figure eights to keep them at bay. They stayed just out of reach. I growled curses under my breath at my helplessness. A lunge could dispatch any one of them, but then the rest would have me.

The man on my far right, the dim light showing one eye gone white, darted in for a stroke at my legs. I let the tip of my sword fall enough to slice through the soft tissue of his neck without breaking my defense. He fell with a gurgling sound to the stones, his feet drumming as he bled out.

"That's one," I said to the other three. "You should leave before this gets any more expensive."

None of the footpads bothered to answer, but the one next to the man I'd dropped moved to pick up the extra dagger. He had sandy hair and a boyish face. My figure eights slowed, and sweat gathered on my brow. If I didn't get help soon, they'd have me.

Without warning, the sandy-haired man cocked his arm and threw the extra dagger at me. I managed to put my sword on it, but the point caught my shoulder. The other two men darted in and screamed with the effort to close my defense. They took a step back, their faces a mix of disappointment and grim determination.

But blood ran down my sleeve and my sword arm dipped as my breath came in ragged heaves. I couldn't last. I had to create an opening and get out of the alley. Hoping for surprise, I threw the dagger in my left hand, but the blade went wide.

I moved my sword from my right hand to my left, making frantic cuts to keep them at bay. In seconds I would die.

Spots danced in my vision, and my breath whistled in and out of my lungs. The man on my left, dark-haired with broken teeth, came in for the kill.

A dagger blossomed in his neck, and he toppled.

I stared. The last two attackers pounded away from me, and I fell to my knees next to the dying man. Booted feet ran toward me, but I ignored them. My attacker's breath came in gasps, his life pulsing out around the dagger buried in his neck. I could see his eyes start to empty.

His focus shifted from me as I reached out to touch his face. "What do you see?"

"Fool." A heavy foot kicked my arm away, and hands like clamps pulled me to my feet to face my rescuer.

"Bolt."

"Aye." He cut a strip of cloth from the dead man's cloak and bound my shoulder. "Can you walk?"

I nodded. I hadn't lost that much blood. One of the city watch pounded up at that moment, grim and out of breath. "Lord Dura, what happened?"

I looked at the two dead men, not bothering to keep the growl of pain out of my voice. "You're late."

Bolt pointed to the west end of the alley. "The other two went that way."

I stopped him before he could move. "No. You'll never catch them now. It's getting dark. They'd cut your throat before you knew they were on you." I pointed at the dead men. "Get these two out of here and see if you can find out who they are." A wave of nausea, leftovers from the rush of battle, made the alley spin. "I think I'd like to get to the healer now."

We left the alley and commandeered the first horse we found, a bony nag that might have been a year from the tanner's. I set the mount at a walk with Bolt keeping pace on foot beside me. A thin rivulet of blood worked its way loose of my sleeve and ran down my fingers, the color stark against my skin.

Bolt insisted on chattering at me the whole way.

"For somebody who's supposed to be the king's smartest reeve, you're awfully stupid. It makes me wonder about the rest of the people in Bunard."

My shoulder hurt too much for me to be polite, and I wasn't interested in deceiving anybody at the moment. "There are things I needed to know, and I don't trust you or the people you work for to keep my friends safe."

He barked a laugh to show what he thought of my opinion. "I'm not talking about you leaving me behind." He looked up at me, his eyes gleaming beneath the craggy lines that creased his forehead. "What do you think would have happened if you'd touched that man as he died?"

The lonely clop of the horse's hooves against the stones marked the time as the question sunk in. "Has it ever been done?"

Bolt nodded. "Only twice that I've heard tell of."

Would I have seen eternity? Longing awoke in me at the thought. "What happened?"

"Their minds were burned out." He said this with all the emotion a man might use in remarking that the sky was blue. "They didn't die." He shrugged. "At least not in the ways most men think about death, but there wasn't anything left of them. They didn't even have enough sense to keep themselves fed without help. People who worked for the Vigil took care of them, putting food in their mouth and changing their clothes when they soiled them. They even tried using their gift on them."

"What did they see?" Fascination gripped me.

Bolt looked at me without blinking, but behind his stony countenance I sensed him weighing alternatives. "Nothing. Their minds were completely empty. Not one memory remained."

I suppressed a shudder. My time with Custos put color and depth to the sparse brushwork of Bolt's warning. "You could have let me touch him," I said. "Then the Vigil wouldn't have to worry about whether I could be trusted."

He shook his head, but it might not have been me he argued against. "That's not my decision. My orders are to protect you."

I believed him, but there was more. There had to be. I reined the horse to a stop. "That's it?"

His eyes narrowed slightly. "Do I need to save you again?"

Sometimes people pretended to be offended when they wanted to hide something. "Do you think I don't know how gifting works? For all I know the Vigil is setting me up to die so their precious gift will go to someone of their choosing."

Bolt didn't move, but he blinked. "That would be out of character for Pellin or any of the others."

Which wasn't quite the same thing as saying I was wrong.

I nudged the horse's flanks with my boots and started the climb to the citadel again. "And how long has Pellin been Eldest of the Vigil?"

My bodyguard didn't bother to meet my gaze. "I'm told there are quite a few people who want to see you dead."

I couldn't help but agree. "Probably more than you know, but I'm not a big believer in coincidence, and we know these weren't the same men who killed Robin and Elwin."

"How do we know that?"

I laughed. "Would I still be alive?"

"That doesn't mean it was anyone in the Vigil," Bolt said. "I know those people. I spent decades guarding them." He gave his head a little shake, as if he were arguing with himself as well as with me. "They're all proud. Some are arrogant, and others have lived for so long with their ability that they don't really understand normal people anymore, but they're good, Willet. Deep down, they're the best people I know. They have to be."

I reached down and grabbed his shoulder with my good arm. "Why? Why do they have to be? What makes them so much better than the musician or alchemist or tavern owner?"

He looked at my hand as if he couldn't decide whether to break it or not. "Because only someone exceptional can absorb as many tortured memories as they have and stay sane."

I didn't have an answer that I was willing to share, but I probed the wall in my mind that kept those other personalities at bay and wondered how many someone could take in without breaking. What was the limit of the mind? We rode up to the keep through the increasing prosperity of the city. My shoulder throbbed in time with my heartbeat, but the bleeding had slowed.

I dismounted at the south end of the keep and sent the horse back to its owner with one of the guardsmen. The royal healer kept his apartments one level below the king's. He might not have been nobility, but he lived like it, and I couldn't help but admire the small egg-shaped man's quarters.

He took me into a small room where he kept the implements of his craft. Shelves lined the wall reminding me of the library, but instead of books, they held earthenware jars filled with pungent herbs and liquid concoctions. A long table held a broad assortment of knives and needles. Off to one side lay a wicked-looking saw, its teeth hungry and gleaming in the light. I'd seen such instruments far too often in the last war, to cut off the limbs of men whose wounds surpassed their healer's talent.

Galen pulled out a stool from beneath the table. "Have a seat, Lord Dura." His voice warmed the room, and I wondered if that was part of his gifting.

I reached up to untie my cloak.

He put just enough pressure on my arms to stop me. "You'd better let me do that. Let's not make the bleeding any worse."

His hands floated over my clothes as he undressed me, and before I realized it, I was bare from the waist up. Softly, he probed the wound, searching. "How'd you collect this?"

"A couple of footpads tried to cut me into chunks." I shot a look at Bolt. "I'm still not sure why."

"Hmm," Galen said in a distracted voice. "Probably because you insulted someone. Again."

Bolt laughed his agreement.

I shot Galen a sour look that he found amusing, and he smiled. "I speak with the servants whenever one of the nobles gets overzealous with their displeasure. They relish your visits to court, you know. Evidently, there's an organized wager on your death."

He paused to spread the cut with his fingers, and I gasped. "It looks clean, but I think I should wash it with spirits before I stitch you up to be sure." He pulled a clear bottle from the shelf and uncorked it. The smell of strong drink filled the room. "This will sting a bit."

An idea occurred to me. "Wait." I craned my neck to the side to look at the cut running down my shoulder. The center of the cut was deeper than the beginning and the end but not by much. "How many wounds like this have you treated?"

He pursed his lips. "Hundreds, maybe thousands. Not so many in the last few years, but the last war with Owmead was bad, and the one before that was worse. There were days at a time when all I did was practice embroidery on the king's men, using boiled cloak thread for stitches."

I reached across the table with my good arm to grab a piece of parchment and a writing stick. "Have you ever seen a cut like this?" I drew a half moon shape. "The center of the cut is very deep, while each end is as shallow as this." I tapped my wound.

Bolt stood at my shoulder, quiet but looking at my sketch.

Galen frowned at me. "It would have to be a dagger wound, not a thrust but a swipe."

I shook my head. "I thought so as well at first." I drew my one remaining dagger and flexed my wrist to move my hand in an arc. "See? Even if the swipe was no bigger than this, the wound would still be longer and shallower. That or the dagger's blade would be no more than a hand's breadth in length, and nobody would carry that."

He nodded without looking convinced. "I've seen a lot of strange wounds when men are fighting, Lord Dura."

Clear liquid burned through my shoulder, and I hissed and saw stars for a moment. When I could speak again, I pushed through his objection. "Yes, but *all* of the wounds were like this. I found them on his legs, his arm, and his torso. He died from blood loss." I still faced Galen, pretending to watch him tie the knots in the thread as he stitched up my wound, but out of the corner of my eye I saw Bolt go still.

Galen lifted one soft hand in a gesture of surrender. "I can't speak to what you've seen, Lord Dura, not without inspecting the body myself. It may be as you say. What do you think caused the man's wounds?"

A sigh whispered across my lips. Robin's injuries sparked something familiar in my mind, but every time I reached for the memory, my thoughts stopped, hitting a wall. "I don't know, but I saw the same wound on a young pickpocket soon after, a boy scarcely more than ten."

CHAPTER 18

We left Galen's chambers a few moments later with my shoulder stiff beneath the bandages and swelling, but I could pull a sword if needed. When we turned into a long deserted corridor, I waited until we were halfway down it before I stopped. "I need to know what you know," I said. "There are people dying in my city, and I can't help them if you and the rest of the Vigil keep me in the dark."

He shook his head. "My orders are to make sure you don't come to harm. That's all."

I tapped my shoulder. "That didn't work out so well in the alley."

Bolt hissed his disgust. "That wouldn't have happened if you hadn't ditched me."

"Fair enough," I said, "but you've already admitted that the people who killed Elwin and Robin would be more than a match for you, so your offer of protection rings a little hollow." I leaned in, trying to use my words to cudgel some admission from my guard. "You don't have to tell me everything, but Elwin's killers are going after children. Children."

He gave me a tight smile that didn't show any teeth. "You seem to do all right at finding the truth even without the gift." The smile faded, and he sighed. "The weapon is called a crest. I'm sure you can see why. It's not used much in the northern continent, but the hill people in the far south are quite skilled with it." He spoke in the clipped tones of a man who'd decided exactly how much to say. Bolt gave me what he intended and not a single word more.

An image sharper than imagination could create burst into my mind. My head erupted in pain, and flares of light stabbed my eyes. I squinted and forced myself to speak past them. "What does it look like?"

He held out his arm. "It's a tube that fits over the forearm with a bar for grasping on the inside. At the end of the tube is a round bar of metal that flares out into a half-moon blade. It's quite sharp, and even small blows take their toll."

I nodded past the agony in my head that blotted the last of Bolt's sentence. Now Robin's wounds and the dents in his sword made sense. "Let me guess—men are trained to block and thrust with it."

He nodded, studying me. I dared to hope that I might be able to extract something more from him. "But how would a crest end up here in the far north? Most of the people of Collum are barely aware the southern continent exists."

Bolt's mouth tightened as if he had to struggle to keep himself from speaking.

I pulled my thoughts from the crest, and the agony in my head receded to a dull throb. I tried to use the awkward silence to pry the words from my guard, but he remained silent. Pain and frustration made my voice sharper than I intended. "For all your protests, the Vigil reminds me of the worst nobles I've seen here in Bunard. You're supposed to protect me, but they ordered you to kill me if I lost myself in other people's memories. *Kreppa.*" I turned my back on his mute protest and outrage to head for the stairs to the upper level of the tor and the king's throne room. "Come with me if you want to do your job."

He stepped in beside me, staring straight ahead. "Where are you going that you need protection?"

"Court," I said. "Most of the people there would love to put a knife in my ribs."

Bolt drawled his response. "I wonder why. You're so good with people."

The massive doors of the main entrance at court, iron-bound oak timbers three times my height fitted to match the arched frame, yawned open at our arrival in greeting or hunger. Guards at either side dressed in Laidir's spotless red livery and holding halberds nodded us through, and Bolt and I stepped into a riot of sight and sound. The lights and music of court dazzled as always. The most gifted musicians, acrobats, and singers in the north filled the massive hall, taking turns trying to impress the bored-looking nobility in attendance with unique combinations of gift and skill.

On my left, in the nearest alcove, a thin intense-looking musician played an endless cascade of notes on a mandolin, his fingers moving so quickly across the strings they almost disappeared. Bolt and I watched in rapt attention, but as far as I could tell, none of the nobles standing near him appeared to be aware of the musician or his gift.

Bolt shook his head slowly back and forth in wonder. "I might have seen his equal down in Aille, but that was years ago." He looked around at the nobles in their brightly colored finery, intent on their semiprivate conversations. "Don't these people know what's in front of them?"

I nodded. "They do—a man whose gift can be bought and sold so that he can provide background music they can listen to whenever *they* want."

Bolt's mouth tightened into a thin line of disapproval. "What a waste."

He had my agreement and my sympathy, but his lack of understanding told me Bolt had spent little time in the courts of the kingdoms he'd traveled. I swept my arm in an arc that encompassed the room and its occupants. "There's a spiritual lassitude that comes with wealth. When you can have anything you want, anytime you want it, very little is precious to you."

We passed by a group of nobles, men and women who dressed in gaudy attempts to measure their wealth. Most of the men this close to the entrance were minor nobles, not much higher than me, but they had lands and income.

One of them, Lord Fellin, met my gaze. "Ah, the king's hound comes to court."

Fellin's girth testified to one of his appetites. The courtesan who lounged on his arm testified to another. Her thick auburn hair caught the light, but rouge couldn't disguise the fact that her most profitable years lay in her past. Tightness at the edges of her brown eyes showed a hint of panic. I pitied the future that awaited her when the blush of her youth faded once and for all.

Fellin shifted his bulk to stage whisper to the whippet-thin man on his right. "Perhaps *hound* is too generous. I have dogs, and I'm quite fond of them."

Bolt growled at my side. "Are you going to let that pass?"

I shrugged. Fellin outranked me, a lord without land or servants. I raised my voice so that it wouldn't be missed by Fellin's group or anyone else within five paces. "Laidir made me the least of his lords for good reason. A lesser noble is forbidden to challenge one of higher rank."

Fellin smirked at me, the fat in his cheeks bunching until piglike little eyes glittered. "I think you've skillfully mastered the lesser part, jackal."

His entourage erupted in fresh laughter.

Bolt's gaze went flat. "Are you going to let that pass as well?"

Now it was my turn to laugh. I pointed to the other end of the throne room, over fifty paces distant. "Do you have any idea how many times we're likely to hear this same conversation before we get to the other end?"

Bolt's eyes widened until his customary squint almost vanished. "Don't you have any friends?"

"Ooh," Fellin said. "This is touching. The jackal's guard pities his master's solitude." He pulled a scented handkerchief and dabbed his eyes with a flourish.

I put a hand on Bolt's elbow and guided him farther into the hall, dropping my voice to a whisper. "The first time I came into court after my elevation, I expected to be greeted as one of the nobility. That was foolish and naïve in the extreme. I killed a man to get here, the brother of the most powerful duke in Collum." I paused and then amended that. "I killed a man *in* here, a man who held the allegiance of Fellin and his kind."

I shrugged. "The first time one of them ridiculed me, I thought to challenge them, but Laidir prevented me. The proscription against challenging a higher noble is there with good reason. A lord who's decent with a sword could manufacture a few grievances and destroy one of the houses in a fortnight. Court politics are deadly enough as they are."

Bolt gaped at me. "You mean you've just taken all these insults?"

I exhaled in frustration. "Not at first. I couldn't challenge, but I managed to get my point across just the same."

"Good," Bolt said. "You should do that to Lord Pig over there."

"Do you know what I did?" I asked, but I didn't wait for an answer. Without calling attention to myself, I moved closer to Bolt until my nose almost touched his. I saw him tense. "Exactly. I did this. Then I delivered an insult so vile, no man would let it pass." I rubbed a spot on my coat, scratching an old scar beneath.

"But I underestimated these nobles." I growled the last word like a curse. "He didn't bother to challenge me. The next day a pair of toughs caught me in an alley. They made it plain that they weren't impressed with my recent elevation." I rolled my shoulders, shedding Fellin's insults. What I didn't say was that I was terrified of touching some of the men and women in this room.

Understanding dawned in his eyes, and he surveyed Laidir's throne room like a cat that had just fallen into a pack of dogs. "No one here is your friend?"

I shook my head. "Actually, quite a few of the higher nobles here are, but they don't know me."

"What?"

My boots made comforting sounds as I moved toward the king once more. "I have a simple definition of *friend*. It's anybody who doesn't want me dead or isn't actively trying to kill me." I sighed. "You'd think with such simple requirements I would have more than I do."

Bolt walked beside me, but I hardly noticed. I'd hoped to find Gael in attendance, but I couldn't see her. I spotted her uncle off to my right and veered toward him. Judging by the way his mouth constricted, he'd spotted me as well.

"Count Alainn," I greeted and bowed. "Is Lady Gael here at court?"

His scowl might have been carved from stone, it looked that permanent. "She attends her sister, Kera."

A stab of fear and recollection knifed through me. "Is Kera well?"

The count sniffed as if the matter were of no consequence or I had no business asking—perhaps both. "She struggles to recover from the winter, but she is none of your concern, Lord Dura."

He pronounced my title with a cough of disapproval.

I nodded and withdrew. It would be a bright day in the Darkwater before I found his favor, but I wasn't about to jeopardize my betrothal for the sake of repaying his manner.

Bolt and I wove a path through the knots of chatting courtiers and stands of burning candles toward the front of the hall, where rows of tables stretched toward the dais of Laidir's throne. A multitude of servants swarmed over the trestles, moving in and out of the doors on the left that led to the kitchens, preparing for the afternoon meal. I circled around until I stood with the knot of people who waited to petition the king. I recognized the ambassador from Owmead.

I caught the king's eye, and he nodded. A few minutes later he rose and the hall quieted.

"Friends." His bass voice filled the hall without effort. "Let us repair to supper." He waved at the tables. "The affairs of court will resume after the meal."

He rose, surrounded by his escort of four guards, and left.

I tapped Bolt on the shoulder. "Come. He will be waiting for us."

We left the way we came and circled around to the king's private audience chamber. Two of his guards, Adair and Carrick, stood outside as usual. I nodded a greeting to them as Bolt and I approached. Their flinty stares put me on edge. Neither of the guards were jovial men—their duties precluded a sense of humor—but they knew me, knew I was the king's man through and through. They'd been privy to most of the conversations I'd had with Laidir. While the puffed-up nobles in the king's hall might suspect everything I'd done, the guards knew.

And they respected me for it. Almost, they considered me one of them, but as Bolt and I stepped forward, they drew swords, edges toward us. Adair, flame-haired and bearded, loomed over us. "By order of the king, you are not allowed to come into his presence armed. You must surrender your weapons. All of your weapons." His green-eyed gaze flicked over the two of us.

Chapter 19

We left our swords and daggers with the guards outside and came into Laidir's presence. Adair and Carrick remained without, but the other two guards, Niall and Ronit, posted up in front of the richly appointed chair where Laidir sat, were scowling. They had their swords out, and they held their weight on the balls of their feet.

The king beckoned us forward, and out of the corner of my eye I saw Bolt coiling as he walked, gathering tension in preparation. His hands were loose at his sides, but by the time we stopped he looked like a wound spring. We bowed, but Laidir waved our obeisance away, his eyes stabbing at me.

"I am displeased with you, Lord Dura."

I bowed again, but lower this time, searching my mind for what I might have done. "In what way, Your Majesty?"

"In some fashion you have managed to secure the permission of the four orders for your investigation of Elwin's death." His voice rose in volume. "Yet for three days you did not see fit to inform me of this?"

I stammered as I tried to put the hints and pieces of the king's speech together. Bolt stepped around in front of me and the eyes of the king's guards went flat.

"Your Majesty." Bolt bent from the waist. "I may be of some service. Lord Dura has been ill and was unable to communicate the change in circumstances to you."

I saw Laidir take Bolt's measure, his eyes drifting down to my guard's feet and back up again. "I don't know you, but you will be silent in my presence until you are commanded to speak. Lord Dura, who is this?" Laidir's gaze sharpened. "I saw a man move that way before, once. Can you vouch for him?"

I paused, stammering for an answer to a question that had caught me by surprise. That was a mistake. The gift of kings gave Laidir insight that no reeve could match.

"Remove him," Laidir ordered.

Perhaps Niall misunderstood the order, but I saw his sword arm flex and heard the whistle of his blade as he moved to bring his weapon in line. If Bolt had been beside me instead of in front, perhaps he would have simply backed away out of reach. Instead he lunged, catching Niall's wrist in his right hand and twisting. His left swept in a blow I almost missed, catching Niall beneath his chin. By the time Ronit managed to bring his sword in line, Niall was on the floor and Bolt had Niall's weapon out in front—trained on the king's guard.

He bounded back, pushing me off to one side of the room between two of the king's writing tables and away from the door.

"I'm not here to kill anyone," Bolt said. "But if you call for the guards outside the door, people will die, Your Majesty. I'm sworn to protect him."

To his credit, Laidir didn't stir. "If that's true, then you're not one of mine, despite the watchman's badge you wear. My guards vow to protect me and no one else. Niall and Ronit are the best in my command. Their gifts haven't been divided for the past three hundred years. I saw another with the same intersection of talent and purity of gift you possess, once when I was young. He held out his hands and boasted no man could touch him. Five of the best swords in the kingdom tried. None of them succeeded."

Niall came to his feet, moving his jaw, testing it. Ronit positioned himself in front of the king with the look of a man prepared to die.

Something inside me broke at the look Laidir gave me just before he said, "Your loyalty has been a blessing to the crown, Lord Dura, but it appears that is at an end. Whom do you serve now?"

I reached around Bolt and placed my hand on top of his sword arm. At first he refused to surrender the weapon. "Kings hold the power of life and death, Willet."

I nodded with my hand still on top of his wrist. "I know, but this one holds it best."

With a shake of his head, he relented, and I slid Niall's sword across the floor to him. I shouldered Bolt aside and knelt before Laidir in the center of the room. "I have never desired to serve any but you, Your Majesty."

"Ah," Laidir sighed. "I believe you, Willet, but we don't always get to choose." He reached into his coat and withdrew a piece of parchment. "I have a letter from the Chief of Servants. She delivered it personally two days ago. That shriveled little woman ascended the entire height of the keep to summon me to my own audience room when she could have simply summoned me to her cathedral. Servants have a strange notion of humility. This is twice she's brought me to heel. I'm beginning to develop a dislike for her."

I kept my head down, my eyes burning. I'd never sought to be Lord Dura. Serving King Laidir had been my only aim, and its fulfillment had brought me something I'd thought unattainable—the hand of Lady Gael. Inside I raged as if I'd been nothing more than a boy required to watch his father's humiliation. In that moment I hated the church with everything I had within me.

"What does it say, Your Majesty?" If Laidir heard the crack in my words, he gave no sign.

His voice, deep and resonant enough to be felt as well as heard, fell on my ears like an axe. "It requests that you be assigned to the church in order that Elwin's killer might be brought to justice."

"Requests?" I hoped that he might refuse.

Laidir laughed, short and without the gales of humor genuine mirth carried. "They always *request*, Willet." He sighed. "But the truth is, their request presents an opportunity. Sometime soon—perhaps two years, possibly five—our summers will be too harsh to grow all the food we need, unless we can find a way to cooperate with Owmead. This may provide me the leverage I need to forge peace."

I nodded without looking up. The transfer of my allegiance would be a small price to pay, and he was right to pay it. Still, I felt like a piece of garbage being kicked into the gutter.

Tears gathered in my eyes, but I fought them back for the sake of my king. Laidir was the closest thing I had to a father. My own had died twenty years prior in a border war with Owmead in a fight over food.

I knew this. I knew that Laidir was trying to prevent the very thing that had taken my father from me when I was ten. If he succeeded, any number of boys would be saved from that fate, any number of women from Constance's. They would have a chance to grow up with their fathers and become the men they chose to be instead of the men they were forced to be.

"This doesn't change anything between us, Willet," Laidir said.

I nodded with my gaze on the carpet, accepting his lie and wishing to heaven it was actually true. "I will always be your man, Majesty."

My king left his chair to grip my shoulders and urge me to a standing position. I gasped as his fingers found my wound and took an involuntary step back. Laidir seemed older than last I'd seen him, his hair mostly gray, though streaks of dark brown still fought against the tide of time. Lines creased his forehead, but the hazel eyes beneath were still clear.

"No man can divide his allegiance, Willet. I can see the church has need of you, though I may not know the exact form that need may take. Serve her with the fervor and zeal you have given me, and she will have no cause for censure," Laidir said. "When your time with them is done, come back. I have too few friends among the nobles."

For a moment he looked past me to Bolt, considering. "Have a care. Secrets are dangerous, and the men and women you work for have more than their share."

My own secret burned in my chest. At the moment Aer had seen fit to give me a gift—me, one of the ungifted—I'd been removed from Laidir's service, a man who would know best how to use it. With the power of domere I could have kept him safe. But even this was secondary to my greatest dread. I hesitated to speak of it. At heart I harbored the superstition that speaking my fear would conjure it into being. Yet I was too afraid not to speak. "Will I still be permitted to marry Gael, Your Majesty?"

Laidir's laugh cut the flesh from my bones before I realized it held no malice within it. "Lord Dura, I do not raise men to the nobility on a temporary basis. That title and the hand of Lady Gael are yours."

A shuddering sigh of relief escaped my lips. "Thank you, Majesty." I took a moment until my breathing settled. "Have I your permission to withdraw?"

Laidir smiled at me, and I watched as he worked to show nothing in that gesture except his best wishes. At his nod, I led Bolt out of his presence. Outside his chambers, we retrieved our weapons. My eyes burned with the need for sleep, and I retired to my quarters. Bolt folded himself into one of the small couches near the fireplace. I prayed nothing I would do that night would wake him.

Sensations of struggle invaded my dreams, dim impressions of conflict with an enemy I couldn't see, only felt. The first conscious thought that penetrated the shroud of darkness in my mind was the awareness of sunlight peeking through the glass of my bedroom window.

After that, fatigue so deep it came from my bones dropped me to the floor. My tunic clung to my skin, and I blinked away sweat that rolled down my forehead and into my eyes. Bolt took a step back, breathing hard.

"Welcome back, Dura," he said.

Inside I groaned at the circumstances and timing of my latest night walk, but I kept my face smooth as I answered Bolt's unspoken accusation. "I didn't even know what a night-walker was until I came back from the war," I said, rolling my shoulders.

His unblinking gaze went through me as if I were made of glass. "How big a fool do you think I am?" He lifted one hand to point at the skin around his eyes. "Do you think I lived long enough to collect these wrinkles without learning *anything*? I've got at least three decades on you. I've seen night-walkers before—that's not what's happening to you."

I rose to my feet over the protest of my legs. Being that far below Bolt's head while he questioned me set me at a disadvantage. "How do you know?"

The way his face twisted told me he didn't care for the challenge in my question or tone.

"Because, *Lord Dura*, people who night-walk can be wakened." He stepped closer until his nose almost touched mine. "And night-walkers," he whispered, "don't fight in their sleep."

I blinked. Evidently, he didn't need any more in the way of encouragement to go on.

"That's right, Dura. We're covered in sweat because I had to wrestle you for the last two hours. You woke at the first light of dawn."

I shrugged with a diffidence I didn't feel. "A coincidence, nothing more."

He sneered at my protest. "Not likely. I'm your guard, but my loyalty is to the Vigil. It's been my job to take the measure of you since the first. Something in your mind doesn't care for sunlight. Where have you seen that before?" He stopped, drawing breath, leaning forward as if he had more to say.

"And . . . ?" I challenged. "Finish it, *guard*. You don't have the face for wordplay."

He nodded. "And sometime today, I'll meet with Peret Volsk. He'll report to the Vigil so that they can figure out what to do with you."

My mouth went dry. Pellin and the rest of his company didn't seem overly burdened with a sense of grace on my behalf. What would they do? I needed an ally within the Vigil, but the only candidate stood in my apartment, prepared to testify against me.

"Have you ever had something bad happen to you that turned out to carry a blessing with it?" I asked.

His eyes narrowed. "More times than I can count, Dura."

I nodded. "I started night-walking right after the war. It took me a few years to piece together why."

Bolt folded his arms across his chest. "It's not any night-walking that I've ever seen or even heard of."

I lifted a hand palm up. "It doesn't matter what it's called, only when it happens." Now I had his attention. "I only walk when someone's been murdered." I swallowed, not bothering to share my deeper fears.

He shook his head at me. "You're a fool for telling me that, Dura.

You—" A knock at the door cut off whatever he'd been about to add. I followed him to the antechamber, where he opened the door to admit Peret Volsk, the man I'd seen at the House of Passing and then later in Laidir's audience chamber.

He smiled as if I were a friend he hadn't seen in weeks. "Well met, comrade," he said to me. "And under more favorable circumstances than at first. No attackers this time."

I smiled my agreement, but questions came first. They always did. "Who are you?"

He looked to Bolt. "You haven't told him?"

Bolt shrugged. "There hasn't really been time."

"I understand," Volsk said, turning back to me. "I'm the apprentice to the Vigil. To safeguard the gift, there is always an apprentice who stands ready to receive it against unexpected necessity." He shrugged. "What it really means is I run a lot of errands."

I tried not to stare. The man in front of me had ordered the Chief of Servants and my king as if they'd been menials, and that was his idea of running an errand. "Shutting me out of investigating Elwin's death was an errand?"

He blinked. "I see your point, but yes. Of course I spoke with the authority of the Vigil then. I'm just Peret Volsk, but the Vigil . . . Well, it's hard to describe how much power they can wield when they need to." He turned to Bolt. "I need your report for Pellin."

There was no deciphering the look Bolt gave me, and I didn't want to be present when he decided to tell Volsk just how broken he thought my mind was. Apprentice or not, I didn't doubt Volsk could have me imprisoned on the Vigil's behalf if he wished.

"I'm going to change," I said and left the antechamber for the bedroom, shutting the door behind me.

Chapter 20

I waited in the bedroom until Bolt knocked and opened the door. I had Robin's sword belted to my waist and daggers hidden in my boot and belt, resolved to stay free as long as I could.

"Where to now?" Bolt asked.

"What did you tell him?" I kept my hands in plain sight.

His gaze went flat. "That you night-walk." When I exhaled a sigh, he went on. "That's enough for now. Even that much, Dura, might land you in a cell." He sighed. "But for now you're still free. After Volsk reports to Pellin, it may be another matter."

I took a deep breath. "I want to drop by the guardroom to see if they know of last night's murder."

"You're that sure?" Bolt asked.

I found something to do so that I didn't have to meet his gaze. "It's never been wrong. After that we need to go back into the city. We have to find Rory. We need a witness, and he's our best chance of finding one." I turned toward the nearest staircase to begin the descent. "The only problem is that he may put a higher price on the information than I can pay. My wages as the least of the king's lords are fairly meager." I'd used the silver within Robin's purse. All that remained within it was gold, and I had no desire to put my life or the lives of the urchins in danger by giving them a metal so rare it was practically forbidden. I shot Bolt a questioning look. "What are they as a member of the Vigil?"

Bolt tossed me his purse. Inside was as much silver as I would receive from the king in two months. He coughed. "You're not a member of the Vigil yet."

I hefted the purse. The contents would buy me all the information I needed from the urchins and then some. "I'll try to bear up somehow."

We stopped by the guardroom, but the calm measured paces of the guards and lack of commotion around Jeb's office told me there'd been no report of a murder. I had no answer to the doubtful looks Bolt cast my way, so I didn't bother to attempt one. If no one had turned up dead, it simply meant the body hadn't been found yet. I'd long ago given up the hope that I would be proven wrong.

"Lord Dura," a voice called.

I turned to see Gareth flagging me down.

He came close enough so that his voice wouldn't carry past the three of us. "You have to do something about Branna."

I shook my head. "Not at the moment, I don't. She's safe where she is, and I don't have time to go after Andler just yet."

"That's just it, Willet," Gareth said, dropping his voice into a whisper. "She's not safe. I caught a couple of men inquiring after her." His mouth tightened into a rictus of disapproval. "I don't think they got any information, but they managed to talk themselves pretty close to the cells."

Every organization had people who could be bought. The reeves and guards were no exception. I'd left Branna's name on the list of those interred in the cells as a decoy, but if anyone got inside, they'd know she'd been moved.

I trusted Gareth, but past him and Jeb, I couldn't vouch in absolute terms for anyone else. Moving to a table, I grabbed pen and parchment and scribbled a note to Gael. After I folded it in half, I handed it to my lieutenant. "Get this to Lady Gael as quickly as you can. We're going to put Branna beyond Andler's reach once and for all. But leave her name on the rolls of the imprisoned. Let's see who else shows up." An idea occurred to me. "Have one of the guards follow them at a distance."

Gareth smiled, a gesture of pride. "I did."

Bolt's fidgeting reminded me of an appointment I hoped to keep, but I took a moment to nod my approval at Gareth's unexpected foresight. "Perfect. Let me know what he finds."

Braben's Inn sat on the border between the upper and lower merchants' sections, overlooking a bend in one of the branches of the Rinwash. The location and Braben's gift of helps, which made regular visitors and complete strangers alike feel at home, meant the place held at least a few patrons at all times. Braben himself, a large bluff man with a florid complexion under thinning blond hair, possessed a hearty laugh and a capacity for quelling arguments just by placing his thick arms around the participants. He'd put them on me a few times when some of the nobles at court sent their hirelings to goad me into a street fight. I could testify that peace flowed through those hands.

We stepped through the wide door into warmth and light and the smell of nut-brown ale that always carried a hint of almonds in the taste. I scanned the room and saw Rory sitting by one of the large windows, his small frame bathed in sunlight, the tables nearest him still empty. Braben's Inn and Tavern operated under simple rules, one of them being everyone was welcome, but that didn't mean men would willingly sit near an urchin.

I paused to open the door to the corner of my mind where I'd managed to sequester Rory's memories. This rejection hurt him despite his casual demeanor, and I grieved. I slid into a chair across from him, my back to the door. Bolt sat next to the urchin, his chair angled away from us, facing the rest of the tavern.

Braben lumbered over, the smile on his face easy and natural. "Lord Dura, we haven't seen you in a while."

I returned his smile before I realized it. "I'm just Willet in here, Braben."

His eyes twinkled, and he nodded greetings to Bolt and Rory as if they were both equally welcome. "What can I get you and your friends?"

I turned to Rory. "Are you hungry?"

At his nod, I held up three fingers to Braben. "Ale for each of us, and whatever's best in the kitchen."

He nodded in approval and moved away.

"You're alone."

Most of those who ended up with the urchins mastered full use of their peripheral vision. If a merchant saw someone eyeing up his purse, he'd take steps to secure it. The fact that Rory wouldn't meet my gaze, choosing instead to fix his attention on the space between Bolt and me, brought a knot to my stomach.

"I found a witness, Willet, a night woman. She was on her way back to the poor quarter and saw the fight from the bridge."

Rory's hair hid his face, but I heard the hitch in his voice and the pat as a tear fell from his eyes and hit the table. "She was probably too close to the torches. They must have seen her."

Now he raised his head to look at me. Rory had long ago mastered control of his expression, thieves had to, but behind his large brown eyes lurked hurt and rage fighting to escape his control. "It was Constance."

Oh, Aer. Please, no.

"She's dead, Willet."

My voice ripped out of me before I could stop it. "I told you to get her someplace safe."

Rory's face twisted, tightening between grief and anger. "I tried. Don't you think I tried? She wouldn't go."

With an effort I lowered my voice. Braben's wasn't crowded this far from the noonday meal, but from opening to closing, it always had customers. "Why not?"

Rory's eyes blazed at me. "Because if she didn't work, her kids wouldn't eat, Willet. We don't work for the king and have marriages set up for us with wealthy families. We get what we take."

"It's too dangerous now," I said.

Rory laughed, his voice cracking, bitter. "If one of us gets caught stealing, we don't always end up with the city watch. Sometimes, if we're lucky, we lose a hand. Other times we die for taking something to keep us fed that some merchant or lord wouldn't notice missing for months."

His voice rose as the rage trapped behind his eyes broke free. "Constance knew what she was doing. Do you want to know the type of man that pays for a woman, Willet? Do you want to hear what men who look all clean and respectable on the outside do because they know that paying for Constance means they own her? Do you think that might be dangerous?" Rory stood up so fast his chair clattered to the floor. "It's always dangerous!"

I looked over my shoulder to see Braben coming our way with three tankards clenched in one hand—the other flexed as if he thought he might have to throw Rory out.

Bolt leaned over to put a hand on Rory's shoulder. The urchin's head whipped toward him, and one hand flashed up to twist Bolt's thumb. Bolt grabbed his wrist before Rory could dodge, but just held him there as Braben placed the tankards on the table. "He knows, boy. He can't help but know."

I took a pull from my tankard, but Braben's ale couldn't wash the taste of Constance's death from my mouth. "How did she die?"

Rory's face lost some of its anger, the fire no longer raging but banked instead, ready to flare again in an instant. "Like Nick."

I couldn't seem to think past all the memories rattling around my head that didn't belong to me. Constance was dead, poor sweet Constance, whose biggest crime was having her husband die in some stupid border skirmish. "Where are her children?"

Rory slumped in his seat. "I have them with the rest of the urchins. They don't know yet." His voice thickened. "I told them some piffle about their mother being on a trip."

Bolt shifted in his chair, breaking his surveillance of the tavern interior. "Bring the children to the lowest level of the keep before nightfall, just outside the city watch barracks. I'll have someone meet you there. I know a couple in the village of Oulsease. They lost their only child to the fever a few years back. They'll take them in."

Rory's face stiffened.

"You do the best you can by the urchins, lad, but you can't give them as good a home," Bolt said.

Rory, Aer bless him, nodded after a moment. "Who'll be there to meet me?"

Bolt nodded as if Rory had passed some sort of trial. "Her name is Manora. She's short, dark-haired, probably wearing Absold blue."

The corners of his mouth turned upward at a memory. "She'll probably have a dog with her. She likes animals."

Rory shook his head, the twist on his face bitter. "A cleric. It's too bad they couldn't have stepped in before Constance got murdered."

I watched Bolt, but he didn't respond in anger. "Nobody disagrees with you there, lad. I wish we could do something for everyone." He rubbed the thumb that Rory had tried to twist a moment earlier. "Perhaps we can do something for you, though."

Rory paused long enough to take a pull from the sweating tankard in front of him. "The church isn't interested in me, master guard."

We all leaned back in our chairs as one of Braben's serving girls brought steaming bowls of beef stew with thick slices of bread and cheese on a platter. Rory fell to it, working the spoon with one hand while the other pocketed slices of cheese in his cloak. I ate my stew but moved the bread toward Rory so he'd know I didn't want it. After a moment he pocketed that as well.

Before I was halfway through, Rory stood, his clothes bulging.

"Rory," I said, catching him before he could leave. "I can't tell you how badly I want to catch whoever is doing this. I'll pay you handsomely for a witness."

He shook his head. "You won't have to, Willet. Not now. If there are any more witnesses, I'll find them."

As he turned to leave, Bolt's hand came to rest on his shoulder. "Remember what I said, lad. The church may be able to do something for you someday."

Rory's expression conveyed his disbelief more than any words could. After the door closed behind him, Bolt flexed his fingers. "The boy's hands are quick, very quick. What's his background?"

I was too busy feeding the anger I felt at Constance's death to enter the discussion Bolt offered. "He's an urchin."

Pellin returned to his rooms at the Eclipse with Allta at his side. Two days of searching had only served to compound the mystery of Willet Dura. The men of the city watch regarded him with loyalty but a measure of fear as well. His killing of the duke's brother, the

Marquis Orlan, had cemented both of those within their mind, but Pellin had been surprised to discover that the guards' peculiar view of Dura had existed prior to his elevation to the nobility.

The depth of loyalty he inspired among most of the guard had surprised him as well. After Volsk had informed Pellin of Dura's tendency to night-walk it had still been difficult to pry the admission out of the guards who knew him. In fact, it was only after Pellin confronted a well-lubricated guard with the knowledge that he obtained confirmation of the fact.

Pellin grimaced. Worse and worse. Never before in the history of the Vigil had the gift come to any man or woman so manifestly broken. For two days, he and Allta had lived within the common room of the Sword and Shield, plying guard after guard with drink. After the first day Pellin found himself hoping to find information that would allow him to make a decision one way or the other.

He flopped into a chair close to the fire. Cold bothered him more than it used to. "What do you think, Allta, of our man Willet Dura?"

"You are better equipped to make that determination than I, Eldest."

"Am I?" Pellin sighed. Allta was a good man, his physical gift—nearly pure, like all of the Vigil guards—afforded him an astonishing mastery with weapons. Further, his talent that provided him a keen sense of space and his temperament of impulse allowed him to be unhesitatingly ruthless when the situation called for it, but Pellin desired other abilities now. Where Bolt had offered his opinion too freely, Allta hoarded it. "Dura is a soldier, Allta, not a cleric. I need a soldier's opinion of his character. Please, speak freely."

Allta's massive chest swelled with his sigh. "He inspires the loyalty of experienced fighters. He treats everyone with respect." Allta ducked his head a fraction as a shy grin played across his features. "Except, perhaps, nobles. More than one guard has mentioned Dura's charity to the poor. If what they say is true, most of his income ends up in the poor quarter."

Allta stopped.

"You've not mentioned the rest of it," Pellin said. "Those same men who praised his charity whispered of his unnatural interest in death."

His guard's face hardened. "Even if what they say is true, I've seen stranger behavior in men who've seen more fighting and death than they should."

Pellin nodded. He'd touched too many of those. Their memories fought to break free of the doors within his mind. Even locked away they took a long time to die down. "That's not what troubles me, my friend. More than one of the city watch has commented on Dura's visits to a murder scene, arriving before any messenger could have contacted him. He's not just night-walking, he's prescient."

Allta shook his head. "I would be hesitant to credit their testimony too much, Eldest. Soldiers are a superstitious lot."

Pellin grimaced. Too often the job of the Vigil required them to deny mercy to others, and he hated it. "Your humanity does you credit, Allta, but I can't afford to ignore it. Until we know what lies within the vault in Dura's mind, we must assume the worst."

"Can you not delve through it, Eldest?"

Pellin nodded. "Aye, it's been attempted before, several times, but not within the last two hundred years. More often than not, the entire mind shatters along with the vault."

"And the rest?" Allta asked.

"The few, the very few, that survive it are almost no better off—forced to relive the horror of memories they've locked away to survive." He shook his head. "No. Unlikely as it may be, I'll not jeopardize Dura in that way unless there is no alternative."

"Cesla would not have been so hesitant," his guard said in a neutral voice. "Nor Elwin."

Pellin allowed himself a smile. Perhaps Allta could be trained into blunt honesty after all. "Do you disagree with my course of action, then?"

Something bright and fierce burned within his guard's eyes at the question. "Far from it, Eldest. The idea that one should be sacrificed for many is sound, but I always thought the one to make that decision should be the one sacrificed."

Allta's simple theology coincided with Pellin's own, but a knock forestalled any reply. Allta drew his sword and opened the door just enough to reveal the thin innkeeper—a man named Lance, appropriately enough. At a nod from Pellin, Allta stepped back to allow the man enough room to speak, but not enough to enter.

"Good afternoon, Master Pellin," the innkeeper said with a bow. "There is a woman named Bronwyn asking after you in the common room."

"Bronwyn?" Pellin asked before he could hide his surprise. "Describe her, please."

Lance licked his lips, obviously afraid of giving offense. "Ah, she is of an age with yourself, with brown hair fading to gray and green eyes. She has a commanding presence, Master Padraig."

Two days. Bronwyn had returned two days after setting out for a task that should have taken her the better part of a month. "That she does, master innkeeper." Pellin forced a smile to cover his concern. "Is there a man with her?"

Lance nodded. "Yes, a great hulking fellow." The innkeeper rubbed his hands together, dry-washing them. "I do hope there won't be trouble."

"No, there'll be no trouble. Thank you, master innkeeper." He turned to Allta after Lance had departed. "Be vigilant. Something here is amiss."

"Perhaps she found Laewan."

Pellin shook his head. "No. If she'd found him alive and this close to Bunard, he would be with her."

Bronwyn sat at a table in the common room as far from the rest of the customers as placement could contrive, positioned with her back to the wall.

From ten paces away, Pellin could see she carried ill tidings. Her eyes were wide and haunted, darting as if she'd learned to fear shadows in her absence. Balean, her guard, stood with his back to the wall, his hands hidden in his cloak. Beside Pellin, Allta stiffened.

"Eldest, I must precede you."

Allta's request brought him up short. "Is there danger here?"

"I can't see Balean's hands."

At his nod, Allta loosened his sword in its scabbard, stepping around to place himself in front, and they closed to within five paces. "Be seated, Balean, and place your hands upon the table."

Balean shook his head. "I will not. This member of the Vigil is in my charge. The Eldest must approach alone."

Pellin stepped into view, prompting Allta to hiss his disapproval. "What did you find, Bronwyn, that requires such assurances?"

Her gaze bore into him, as though she could delve him without physical contact. "Death."

Fear hollowed out his middle before Pellin could halt it. "Why do you doubt me, Bronwyn?"

She shook her head, not answering.

Pellin stepped forward, stripping off the gloves he wore, offering his arm to her touch. "Delve me if you doubt."

The rasp of a sword being drawn came from his guard behind him. "I cannot protect you, Eldest, in such close quarters."

Bronwyn hesitated before removing the glove on her left hand and brushing her fingers across the back of his wrist. Pellin watched her shudder as a lifetime of images and memories flooded into her, but when she broke the touch, she seemed satisfied. Balean sat and placed his hands upon the table, his back straight and his feet placed apart.

Pellin seated himself, his heart still hammering. "What did you find?"

She glanced at the table before answering. "Balean and I took the most direct route to Owmead, thinking Laewan would have desired speed." Her breath shuddered through her. "At each village we made inquiry, asking after Laewan and Osten." Her eyes welled with anger. "We were correct in our assumption."

"You found him." Even to his own ears, Pellin's voice sounded hollow, as if he'd spoken within the rock confines of a tomb instead of the wooden interior of the Eclipse.

But to his surprise, Bronwyn shook her head. "Not Laewan. Of him, there was no sign, but at the village of Dromair the villagers' tongues still wagged with the discovery of a body none of them knew, found two weeks ago." Her lips tightened until they paled. "Thinking that would have been about the time Laewan would have arrived, I decided to investigate."

Pellin closed his eyes, nodding. "He should have been the first of us to Bunard."

"I used the letters of command to prevail upon the local clergy to disinter the body, hoping to discover my intuition was wrong."

Pellin waited.

"I'd hoped for too little," Bronwyn continued. A network of wrinkles radiated out from her mouth, a tight circle at the center of a spider's web that communicated anger and fear. She'd loved Laewan as the son of her heart, if not her womb. "When they unwrapped the heavy canvas shroud, it was Osten who lay before me."

"How did he die?" Allta's voice rumbled with threats of violence.

Balean's gaze slid past Pellin to latch on to his. "A dagger thrust to the back of the head."

The room swam in Pellin's vision as the implication of Bronwyn's discovery struck home. "Did any of the villagers recall seeing Laewan?"

Bronwyn nodded, flexing her right hand as if at the memory of their touch. "Their recall is questionable, but I delved the innkeeper and the stable hands. Laewan left Dromair by the northern road, toward here, toward Bunard."

And they hadn't seen him in the city. "Before or after Osten was killed?" Pellin asked.

"After," Allta and Balean said at the same time. Bronwyn's guard faced him at the same instant as Allta, their expressions as hard and dark as flint. Guards didn't leave their charges. Not ever.

Chapter 21

We went back to my rooms in the keep with sunset still two hours away. I had Robin's sword strapped to my side. Bolt let his gaze fall across it every now and then but never uttered anything to accompany the wistful look on his face that I assumed to be some mixture of loss and grief. The weapon fit my hand with a balance so finely wrought it could have wielded itself. I'd never seen or held its equal. Even Laidir could not boast such a blade. That in itself provided insight. The Vigil must have had access to the most gifted weaponsmith on the northern continent.

Even so, I needed more. I'd failed to retrieve the daggers from the toughs who'd pinned me in the alley, and I wanted every weapon I could get my hands on. I kept an extra brace of them in my room against such need. My intentions were simple: go out into the poor section of the city before sunset and hunt those who'd killed Constance and Nick. My stomach danced at the thought of wandering the poor quarter at night with something that could sneak up on the best thief in the city, but each time I threw images of Constance and her children at my fear until anger burned it away.

I passed through the small outer room into my quarters and stopped. I'd never been an orderly man, but there was a purpose to my rooms that I maintained. The few objects for which I held some emotional attachment were still there. My father's ficheall board with its pieces rested undisturbed on the small table opposite from the bed.

The ancient books of history on the southern continent I'd accepted at Custos's behest still gathered dust on the nightstand. But clothes were strewn everywhere, thrown from the mammoth wardrobe that dominated the wall farthest from the door, and blankets were piled in a heap at the foot of the bed. "Someone's been in here."

A whisper of sound, the hiss of steel and leather, accompanied Bolt's arm pushing me to one side. "Wait in the hallway."

I stepped back to let him precede me, but I stayed in the outer room, searching the shadows with Robin's weapon weaving in my hand. It took Bolt less than a minute to confirm our solitude.

"What were they after?" Bolt asked.

I shook my head. The only thing of value I owned, a jeweled cloak pin Gael had given me on my elevation to the nobility, still rested atop the table.

Bolt shrugged and left the room, sheathing his sword as he went. The fog in my brain that came from too little sleep wouldn't lift enough to let me see what was wrong. Something more than clothes or covers was out of place in my quarters, but I didn't have the time or patience to put it together. Sunset would be upon us in an hour.

I went back to the armoire and opened the dark wooden drawer halfway up that held my knives. The thieves hadn't bothered with them. I hefted one, sharp as a razor and balanced for throwing. At the rate I was losing them, I'd have to visit Laidir's arms maker and commission another set.

"Who made Robin's sword?" I asked as I tucked three blades in the small sheaths behind my back, on my left hip, and inside my boot.

"You can't afford him."

I patted the deflated purse that held the gold coins I'd taken from Robin. "No, but the Vigil can. If he makes throwing knives the equal of his swords, it might be worth the investment."

Bolt shook his head. "For something you're likely to lose?"

Before we departed my apartments, I took a folded scrap of parchment and wedged it between the door and the jamb two hands above eye level. An experienced thief would spot it, but anyone else would hardly notice it—and if they did, I doubted whether they could replace it at the right spot.

"Where are we going?" Bolt asked.

"We have to get to the poor quarter before sundown and there's a stop to make along the way," I said as we descended toward the cells.

His nodded his craggy face without betraying the thoughts behind it. The silence irritated me. Desperation put a reckless edge on my fatigue—one I'd seen on others too many times during the war, once on myself. People usually died shortly afterward. "You need to know why," I prompted.

The creases across his forehead and around his eyes might have shifted, slightly. "You keep tapping your sword hilt, and you've replaced the daggers you lost in the street fight. It's not exactly the same as mounting your best horse and unleashing the dogs, but it means the same thing. We're going hunting."

His matter-of-fact assessment nettled me. "You're pretty calm for someone who might be dead before morning." I felt as if I were about to head into the Darkwater all over again. Pinpricks of light accompanied disjointed images dancing inside my head. I didn't recognize them, and I shoved someone else's memories away.

"It's doubtful we'll encounter any danger." Bolt's face cracked into a grim half smile.

The cocky grin annoyed me. "These people are deadly enough to kill one of your own and quiet enough to sneak up on the city's best thief without being noticed. I'd feel better if you could summon the sense to be afraid."

"If they wanted to kill you they would have made the attempt before now, and if they're quiet enough to kill Nick, I doubt we can track them."

"We don't have to," I said. Stress made my voice harsher than I intended, and I could feel the tension in my throat, like lute strings tightened to the breaking point.

Bolt stopped and turned to face me. "I'm listening."

"There are two bridges into the poor section," I said. "Neither of them are lit that well. Unless our killers are actually making their home there, they have to cross the bridge at least once."

He watched me, his eyes cold as the winter wind that blistered through the cut each year. Without any movement I could put a name to, he'd changed from a relaxed soldier into something coiled and deadly. "Tell me why they're not in the poor quarter."

Tightness around his eyes might have been anger or fear or the intensity that comes to fighting men before they kill someone. I reconsidered my earlier opinion of his demeanor. I didn't like this one any better. "Because no one's gone missing. The people in the poor quarter are practically stacked on top of each other. If there's enough room to bed down, some urchin or lady has a makeshift home there. Even if our killers could find a place to hide, they'd never be able to leave and get back to it without being seen a dozen times or more. Rory would have known their location the night after Elwin died."

Bolt brought me to a stop with a grip on my upper arm that could have doubled as a carpenter's clamp. "No."

I didn't try to pull away this time. "You're supposed to protect me"—I shrugged—"or kill me. I still haven't figured out which of those orders Pellin thinks is the most important. But you don't have the authority to keep me from doing my job. Bunard is my city, and someone is killing my friends."

He released the arm, but his expression twisted, craggy with disgust. "Twenty years ago, I could have drawn steel and struck a fly from the air quicker than you could blink, and I was still less than Robin was a week ago. If we fight these men in the dark, we die."

"What would you have me do? They won't come out during the day." I walked away as if I felt sure of my purpose.

But his voice followed me. "You're a reeve. I expect you to use your brains. Throwing our lives away doesn't qualify. If I have to knock you out to keep you safe, it's all the same to me."

We came out on the north side of the keep and circled around. The cut, a half-mile-wide rift between the mountains, raced away from us to the north, the farthest peaks still topped with snow. The westward sun glinted against the mountaintops on the left, bathing them in warm light that faded in the valley as the purple shadows from the western ridge edged ever eastward. It hit me.

Light.

I turned to my guard. "We have to get to Gael." I set off at a run, the prison forgotten.

She stood in a corner of her workshop, alone. Events screamed for haste, but for a moment, in imitation of our eventual joining, I let our memories combine so that I saw myself as an amalgam of our two distinct histories. I saw her, part of myself, caressing a bolt of fabric with trembling fingers, her gaze looking through the cloth as if it weren't there. She turned at the sound of our footfalls, and I put her memories away, returning my mind to normal.

"Willet." She smiled, but her lips imitated the quiver in her fingers.

I hated myself for rushing her, but the light was dying outside, and I wanted desperately to make sure none of the citizens of Bunard accompanied it. "I need to get to Myle before dark."

Uncertainty drained from her like water through the sluice of a dam. With a brisk nod the cloth slipped from her fingers, forgotten, and she moved past us, lifting her cloak from a peg by the door as she left.

Bolt fell into step beside me as we left the estate of Gael's uncle by the back gate. "Who is Myle?"

I kept my voice low enough to keep it from carrying. "An alchemist. He's incredibly gifted, but his mind is damaged." Bolt's gaze sharpened into something avid. "Not in any way you'd recognize," I added, groping for words. "You have to see him to understand. Gael is one of the few people he'll talk to. Mostly, he mixes the dyes for her cloth. He won't do it for any of the other cloth merchants, and most of them don't even know he exists. But he can see into his powders and chemicals the way Pellin can see into people."

Gael led us through the broad alley that ran between the walled estates in the rich quarter until we came to one of the bridges leading into the merchants' sections. I knew the way, but as far as I knew only Gael held the key to Myle's attention. The few times I'd tried to engage Myle in conversation without Gael present, he hadn't bothered to respond. In fact, he hadn't even acknowledged my presence. His awareness of people seemed to require her presence to function.

We moved quickly, almost running, as we headed south, and the residences shifted from those nearly as affluent as the minor nobles to more simple dwellings made entirely from wood, devoid of stone in structure or ornamentation.

Yet when we circled around a broad warehouse by a deep section of the Rinwash where barges loaded and unloaded foodstuffs and other goods, we came to a small stone cottage with a slate roof. It stood apart from the warehouse on a bare patch of earth. A blackened chimney reached toward the sky, the stones at the top heavy with rivulets of soot.

Smoke floated from one of the windows whose shutters were thrown wide. I breathed a sigh of relief. I'd been in Myle's workshop during the winter, breathing the fumes of his craft when the piercing cold from the northern cut forced the windows closed.

We stepped around to the door, and Gael twisted the handle without knocking or calling greeting.

"Won't he be startled?"

I shook my head. "No. Come. You'll understand."

The interior of Myle's shop boasted the ordinary tools of the alchemist—mortars and pestles, a furnace with an attached bellows, crucibles and slag rakes, as well as a host of implements I couldn't identify. Thankfully, the furnace hadn't been lit. I saw Myle sitting by the window where we'd seen the smoke, his back to us, lank black hair shielding his face, a curtain he used to hide from the world. Bolt closed the door, forcing it shut over the threshold with a loud scrape. Myle never shifted.

My guard's face creased. "Is he deaf?"

"No," I said, "but until he hears the voice of someone who can pull him from his thoughts, he might as well be."

We followed Gael as she moved around to his left. Now we could see the object of the alchemist's concentration. In his left hand he held a piece of thread from which dangled a sliver of metal. I couldn't be sure, but it looked to be part of the sample I'd delivered to Gael. Myle held a small harp in the crook of his right arm, his fingers wrapped around the tuning peg. By an almost imperceptible amount, he turned the peg, raising the note of the highest string on the harp. He plucked it, then bent his head to the sliver, listening.

I nodded Gael forward.

"What have you found, Myle?" Her voice echoed the note of the string, perhaps two octaves lower.

Myle spun on his stool at the sound of her voice, ignoring the steel that appeared in Bolt's grip. He gave Bolt and me an owlish blink, as if our presence surprised him. Then his gaze slid from us, uncomfortable, settling on the sliver at the end of the string. "I've never worked with pure aurium before," he said. "I had to send to the library for the tests to use."

"How do you know it's pure?" Gael asked.

Behind his curtain of dark hair, he smiled. "It won't react, but it's not glass. It doesn't burn or melt, not even in the kiln. The harp was the last test. Whatever note you play, it echoes back. Only pure aurium can do that. Impurities spoil the tone."

I nodded, but inside I put Myle's discovery with all of the other pieces of the puzzle that refused to fit. Why had Elwin safeguarded a shard of aurium?

Gael rested her fingers on his shoulder. "I've brought Willet to see you, Myle. Do you think you can help him?"

He laughed softly, his gaze still avoiding anyone else's. "Is he hunting the truth again? I don't think anyone wants him for a servant now."

"I don't know what he needs, Myle," Gael said. "Is it all right if he speaks to you?"

If possible, Myle ducked his head even more toward his table. I saw him nod more by the motion of his hair than anything else.

I stepped around Gael and pitched my voice low. "You showed me something the last time I was here, Myle. It made a great flash and I saw spots for an hour afterward. I can't remember what you called it, but I need something like that now, something that makes bright light."

He sat staring at his bowl, his gaze flicking back and forth between Gael and his chemicals. A tremor began in the outer two fingers of his right hand, working its way up his arm until Gael nudged me.

"He needs the question."

I gasped. "I'm sorry, Myle. I forgot. Do you have something I can use to make bright light?"

The tremor subsided, but he sat, his lips framing the question over and over again. Only after a moment did I realize that he altered it with each repetition, placing the emphasis on a different word like a jailer trying keys in a lock until he found one that worked.

He nodded, the gesture exaggerated by his former stillness and the waving of his hair. "Solas powder. Yes. That's it." He fingered the yellow powder in his crucible. "Which color?"

I turned to Gael. "I don't understand. Is he talking about cloth?"

Myle laughed at my question. "Prisms of glass. Prisms of glass."

She shrugged. "Ask him."

"What do you mean, Myle?"

He laughed harder. "What color do you want the light to be?"

Bolt edge forward. "He can do this?"

I nodded. "He showed me the last time I was here. Scared me so bad I thought I might wet myself. The flash only lasts an instant, but even so, I saw spots for the rest of the day. Does it still explode?"

Myle bowed his head in mourning. "I still haven't figured out how to make it burn more slowly."

"That's all right," I said. "The solas powder will work fine the way it is. Can you make it the same color as sunlight?"

He tilted his head to one side, going motionless again, but Gael had explained this to me before. As brilliant and creative as Myle was within his craft, human interaction confused him. Gael had found a key. Myle only responded to questions. Any other communication would fail to unlock his mind. Even questions took him a long time to process. He repeated my query over and over to himself again, looking for the key to understanding it. When he finally put the stress on the last word, I saw him nod, and he rose from his stool and shuffled to the side of his shop farthest from the furnace.

He returned with a collection of stone jars, tightly stoppered, and a stone mixing bowl. Gael and I stepped back from his work. The scorch marks running up the walls of his workshop bore testimony that Myle's gift had given unpredictable results in the past. But after a few moments in which he measured the powders into the bowl in ever-decreasing amounts, Myle covered it with oiled cloth and handed it to me.

A shy grin played around the edges of his mouth once more. "You'll need fire, but it will blaze brighter than the sun for a moment." He ducked his head. "Give yourself some distance."

"How do we know it will work?" Bolt asked, his face pinched with doubt.

Myle didn't respond. I stepped forward but kept my hands to myself. Except for that of Gael, Myle recoiled at human touch. "Would you demonstrate how to ignite it, Myle?"

He took a thick pinch of powder from the bowl and placed it on the cracked and gouged boards of his worktable. When he touched the flaming end of his taper to it, a flash of sunlight in miniature blinded me. I took an involuntary step back. The smell of scorched metal filled the room as I blinked and rubbed a hand across my eyes to restore my vision.

Gael came forward to place a chaste kiss on Myle's forehead. "Thank you, Myle."

Outside the workshop window the orb of the sun still showed above the horizon. Counting the purple light of dusk, we had perhaps an hour to get to the poor quarter. We stepped outside and I leaned over the bowl I held to give Gael a kiss of thanks. I tried to keep anything more from it, but the thought of what would happen if we encountered Elwin's killers and the powder failed to light rose in my mind, and I let it linger.

"That was well done," she purred. Her hand found my face, as if she'd been able to see in my mind. "If you get yourself killed, I will be displeased."

I turned my head to brush the back of her hand with my lips. "I wouldn't care much for it either."

"If we're going to do this thing," Bolt said, "we best be about it."

Still, I waited until Gael set her feet toward her home before I turned away.

We backtracked to the main street leading south toward the poor quarter, but instead of heading for the bridge that would take us into the lower merchants' section, Bolt veered toward a figure in black standing at the entrance to a tavern. Volsk. At the sight of us, he retreated into the interior.

Bolt caught the question in my stare. "I have to report."

"How long has he been following us?"

"Since the beginning," Bolt said.

"Thanks for your trust." I debated losing my temper, but another part of my mind told me there was no point. Any secret I held, the Vigil could pry from me with a touch.

Bright lamps filled the tavern, a sign that the panic gripping the poor quarter had made its way closer to the tor, but Peret Volsk sat his chair loose-limbed, the picture of a man without a worry. Bolt motioned me to a seat with my back to the wall and helped himself to the chair next to it.

"The alchemist has the shard," Bolt said without preamble. "It's pure."

I tried to mimic Bolt's stoicism, but Volsk's chuckle told me I'd failed to be convincing. "Elwin wrote of his findings. We'd assumed it had been taken by those who killed him. We'll have to retrieve it, of course."

Before I could object, Bolt related our plan to confront Elwin's killers. By the time he'd finished, Peret Volsk was sitting back in his chair, shaking his head. The hint of a smile played around the edges of his mouth, but I couldn't tell if he approved of my plan or mocked me.

"Lord Dura, that is most courageously stupid thing I've ever heard."

Ah, I thought. *Both.*

"How old are you?" he asked me.

"Thirty on the next naming day," I said.

"It's a miracle you've lived this long." He lifted his tankard in a salute. "Let's hope your luck holds out." He followed through on his toast, then put the empty tankard in front of him, his face serious. "If you intend on being part of the Vigil, Lord Dura, you're going to have to learn to let people help you."

The frank advice, so far removed from what I had expected him to say, caught me off guard. "I'm not used to working with others."

Volsk nodded. "We know, and we're aware of the reasons behind it. Trust us."

Those last two words raised the hackles on my neck. I liked Volsk well enough. I'd fought with him, and it was hard not to favor someone who'd saved your skin. But I couldn't bring myself to trust his masters.

I couldn't quite keep the edge from my voice. "I'll be inclined to trust the Vigil when they make it plain they trust me."

He nodded. "Who takes the first step, Lord Dura?"

I rose, the ruddy light bathing the street telling me I needed to hurry. "The people in control do." I gave him a tight smile. "That's obviously not me."

"Be careful, Lord Dura," Volsk called after me. "I'd hate to think our efforts at the House of Passing were wasted."

CHAPTER 22

The sky above was an inky black pierced by a scattering of stars peeking through thickening clouds as we waited. A distant rumble of thunder rolled across my hearing like a drummer's knell before an execution. Hours of night, each taking as long to pass as an entire day, had slipped by—during which we'd watched the city drift deeper into slumber, its light diminishing as each household and business shuttered windows and doors, their occupants seeking rest.

The extent of my folly became apparent to me.

I would not be able to heed Myle's direction. Whatever hunted the poor quarter could see in near darkness. I would be unable to keep a lit candle or taper at hand to ignite the mixture of powders in the bowl. Flint and steel would have to suffice, but I had no idea if mere sparks would be sufficient to set the powder aflame. I huddled in the space of one of the parapet arches, the bowl in my lap tilted toward the roadway of the bridge. Bolt knelt next to me on my left.

"We could just as easily catch some footpad or urchin," he whispered. "I'm almost hoping for that," he added after a moment.

"They're scared," I said. "The best thief in the kingdom is dead. Some few of them might work tonight, but I think most of them have gone to ground, waiting until it's safe to come out." The breeze made a subtle shift in direction. "How far away is dawn?"

"Another three hours."

The muscles in my hips cramped, and I shifted my legs to a different position. Bolt squatted beside me, unmoving as one of the blocks of stone we hid behind. "I think you should have placed the twigs farther away," I whispered. "If Myle's powder doesn't light, I won't have time to draw."

"You don't have to worry about that," he said, his voice light. "If we don't get that flash, our swords won't make any difference." Even in the dark I sensed the twist of his face that accompanied his words. "I would have put out more, but if they see too many of them scattered about, they'll know we're here."

The river lapped against the corbeled arches below with a promise of sleep.

"Was Robin that good?" I asked.

"Yes." Bolt's voice held more than just appraisal—it held the strained threads of regret, even in his whisper. "He came into his gift young, and from the time he could toddle on a child's pudgy legs, he held a practice sword." A sigh ghosted through the darkness. "Did you know he could fight almost equally well with either hand? For twelve years he accompanied Elwin."

Twelve. Not ten, I noted. They'd been together even before Elwin became Eldest. "And he was still only second best?"

"No." There was quiet vehemence in Bolt's voice at my question, as if he were denying more than just me. "Robin guarded Elwin because he didn't care for Cesla. He thought the leader of the Vigil had become too abstracted in his old age, almost secretive."

During the pause that followed I imagined my guard shaking his head.

"I told him what he saw was the natural progression of the gift, but Robin was young. He didn't believe me."

My guard stopped speaking, but the cadence of his speech suggested he'd been about to say more. "And?"

"You're not part of the Vigil yet, if ever."

I laughed just loud enough for the sound to reach Bolt's ears. "I'm squeezed between the parapet arches of a stone bridge, crouching while I wait for something to sneak up on me in the dark and kill me. I'm doing the Vigil's work. I think I have the right to know anything that might help see me to the other side of the task."

Moments slipped past. Perhaps Bolt hadn't heard me, or maybe he'd decided to ignore yet another request for information he wasn't permitted to give. I wiped my sweaty hands on my cloak, trying to keep my flint and steel as dry as possible.

"Members of the Vigil often become strange toward the end of their lives," Bolt said. "They will sometimes talk to the memories of others they've delved, arguing with the choices they've made. Other times they will sit staring at nothing, their eyes open and their gaze tracking events none but them can see. Some few seem to remain themselves for their entire life."

"And was Cesla coming to the end?"

Bolt grunted. "As their time is reckoned, yes. Perhaps Robin saw more clearly than I. After he lost the challenge match to Blade, the man who became Cesla's guard, we argued. I'd trained him personally for years until the day he bested me. Then I trained him with the other guards."

I could tell by the pitch of Bolt's voice that he had turned from his sightless inspection of the bridge to face me. "I knew Robin's every move. It wasn't hard for me to see when he threw the fight, though his defeat didn't come until a few seconds later. That loss gave him another ten years. Cesla and Blade were killed two years after Robin threw the bout."

"What was Cesla like toward the end?" I pressed.

"Reclusive," Bolt replied after a moment. "Blade wasn't like Robin. Robin was more than just a sword. He had the wisdom to speak up as well. Blade would have followed Cesla into the fire without a word—the same as Elwin."

Heaviness filled the air with the threat of storms, and a few feet away I heard the soft splat of a heavy raindrop against stone.

"By your grace, Aer, Iosa, and Gaoithe,"—the whisper came from my left—"please keep the rain away and protect your servants."

Bolt's prayer startled me. In my experience, most fighting men made a habit of calling out to their god in distress, but my guard's prayer carried the tone and tenor of a churchman.

"You believe?" I asked.

"I've seen too much not to," he said.

"You go to confessional," he added after a moment. "Why would my belief surprise you?"

I digested that even as the direction of the conversation stirred discomfort in my chest. I didn't speak of my faith for the same reason I didn't parade naked through the streets of Bunard. Mostly, I talked with Ealdor because it felt good to share my struggles with someone who wouldn't—

The crunch of a twig, then another, three paces away pulled the breath from me with a gasp. I ripped the cover from the bowl, but I dropped my steel. The clank of it against the stone by my feet rang like a clarion call in the darkness. Voices erupted from all around me.

I felt a rush of displaced air as Bolt launched himself in silence toward the nearest one. Steel against steel rang in my ears as I groped for our rescue. A scream of pain accompanied the sound of feet moving back toward me before a peal of thunder swallowed everything.

My hand brushed the cold steel of the bar, and I clutched at it as I shifted, tilting the bowl toward the sound of feet. I struck flint and stone together with my trembling hands, and a spark of white flew into the bowl to die.

Footsteps veered toward me in the darkness, and a heavy drop of rain hit my neck.

"Hurry!" Bolt's voice came from my left, back toward the way we'd come, and I shifted.

I clenched the flint and steel in my hands and clashed them together as hard as I could. Three bright sparks jumped into the bowl.

Light like the noonday sun flared and burned. My cry of heat and pain joined startled screams around me. Heat scorched my legs where I held the bowl. I searched the darkness beyond for some sign of Bolt and the things he fought, but everything beyond the dying yellow flame was blacker than soot in my vision.

Cries filled the air to accompany the meaty chunk of sword strokes finding their mark. A screamed curse, frightening in its clarity, came from my right, and a fraction of a moment later, silence.

I pulled my legs from beneath the bowl and stood, pulling the fabric of my breeches away from the burns on my skin. I couldn't see, but whether because of the darkness or because of Myle's alchemy, I didn't know.

I stood, offering prayers for Bolt's life and my own. If any of the attackers remained, they could cut me down at their leisure. Afterimages of sun fire danced in my vision, but nothing else.

"I might be blind."

"Wait," Bolt said.

His voice came from my left, and I shuffled to it, groping in the dark.

"I'll light a torch," he said. The clack of flint and steel sounded a moment later, and a yellow smudge of light intruded against the night. I should have been able to make out Bolt's face clearly by it, but dancing spots blurred them.

A smudge on his left arm turned out to be blood. It increased in size as I looked at it. I fished out one of my knives and made a cut near the bottom of my cloak and ripped it the rest of the way. "The Vigil owes me a new one," I said.

"I'll buy it for you myself," Bolt said. A threnody of higher pitches carried in his voice, as if he were forcing his usual banter. "Higher up," he added as I started to wrap the arm by feel. I shifted the cloth, but out of the corner of my eye I could see a mound on the bridge. The dead called to me. Maybe I could convince one of them to come back long enough to speak. I tied off the bandage with a knot as tight as I could make it. Bolt hadn't taken the cut on his sword arm, but he'd need time to heal as well as a foot of stitches.

I turned from my guard, surrendering to the siren call of the dead. Three bodies, dirty and ragged, lay facedown on the bridge. I'd seen men skilled at killing during the war, had even held some measure of respect for their focused savagery during battle, but Bolt surpassed them. Most men I'd known held within some portion of reluctance at taking another man's life. Their moral hesitation altered the sweep of their blade.

Not so with Bolt. The cut on his victims, blinded into defenselessness by Myle's concoction, could have been placed by surgery, a sharp incision down through the left side of the neck that had severed the arteries. Nick's killer had died as he had died, by massive blood loss.

"Let's have a look at our foes," I said.

I crouched over one of the bodies, ragged and dirty, but with the muscular ranginess that spoke of deadly quickness. Each hand still held a crescent, their half-moon blades as clean as the man was dirty. Beneath the light of Bolt's torch, I rolled the man over.

His eyes held the wide stare of insanity even in death, but for once the call of eternity slid from me. Instead, my gaze swept across his face, captured by the impossibility of his features. Moles on his right cheek disfigured the skin in a perfect triangle close to an aquiline nose.

I struggled to keep from recognizing him, but somewhere in my head a door opened and a voice in my mind called his name: Ben.

Lightning flickered through the clouds overhead, casting the bridge in blue-white luminescence. Behind me, I heard Bolt saying my name, but his call was insufficient to break the bonds of recognition. My vision narrowed, closing in until only Ben's haunted eyes remained. Darkness swallowed me.

Pellin sat his chair at Braben's Inn across from yet another member of the city watch, a weathered veteran named Biller whose face showed just how difficult he found exercising his mind to be. His tongue had required considerable lubrication before it loosened. The head of the Vigil made sure to keep his sighs of frustration hidden from the thick-bodied man across from him. Even drunken guards desired a rapt audience. If extracting information about Willet Dura hadn't been so sensitive, he would have delegated the task to another of the Vigil long ago. As it was, Toria Deel hadn't returned from her investigation of the Darkwater Forest, Peret Volsk still trailed Dura, Bronwyn still searched for Laewan, and Laewan himself had yet to emerge from whatever hiding place he'd chosen.

Jorgen remained on the far side of the Caldu Mountains, trying to maintain order in the three kingdoms that bordered the eastern side of the Darkwater Forest. Too few. They'd always been too few, even at full strength. Pellin wanted to rail at Aer, to take Him to task for giving them burdens they could never hope to shoulder.

Despite his efforts he sighed, allowing his eyes to break their rapt consideration of the guard's drunken soliloquy. What happened to Laewan?

". . . since the king's reeve isn't always in the present, if you know what I mean."

Pellin jerked as the last bit of the guard's comment registered. He slapped at a nonexistent bug on his neck to cover the motion and nodded affirmation. "So I've heard."

The guard, momentarily taken aback either by Pellin's reaction or his own indiscretion, sighed, molding himself farther into his chair. "Well, no harm done then, since you already heard." He shrugged. "And nothing bad has ever come from it, but at first it spooked the guards—not me, of course, but some of the newer men—how he would appear at a killing so quickly, looking like he was still in the last war. A lot of the men muttered at first, saying the evil one had taken him." The crags in the guard's face relaxed enough to show his approval. "After we learned the kind of man Lord Dura was, we understood better."

Shoulders heavy with muscle from hours in the yard lifted, then fell. "More than once I woke to find myself by my bunk with a blade in my hand after I came back from the valley." He ducked his head. "The fighting stays with a man, it does. No one's going to fault Lord Dura if it stays with him a bit longer." The guard raised his tankard in a salute. "Lord Dura's brought more than one killer to justice, he has."

A shadow crept over Pellin's heart as he listened to the guard. Three times in the last three days, he'd been given similar information by those in a position to know Dura the best. The pieces to Dura's personality hinted at something more than just war sickness. Though the guards wouldn't say it outright, they were still unnerved by Dura's ability to appear at a murder scene so quickly after it happened. But there was a hint of something more troubling still. Pellin leaned forward in his chair, his interest no longer feigned.

"Has he ever failed to solve a murder?"

Biller's face knotted with the effort of his thoughts. "Not any most folks would care about."

Pellin had heard the comment before. "What do you mean?"

The guard's dark brows merged over his nose. "There's some has been killed that the people in Bunard won't miss, and that's the truth. Every great city has them—men who prey on others." He shook his head. "It's not Lord Dura's fault he couldn't find the killer. Men like that have more enemies than a guttersnipe has lice. If Dura didn't catch them, it wasn't for lack of trying. Why he was there before—"

Whatever the guard had been about to say was lost. Bolt burst through the door of Braben's, his gaze cutting across the patrons of the tavern like the edge of a dagger, searching.

Chapter 23

Pellin rose from his chair, placed a pair of silver half crowns on the bar to pay for the guard's thirst. "Excuse me, my friend. I have some business to attend to." He didn't bother to wait for the guard's stumbled reply at his quick departure. Allta rose from a nearby table and stepped in behind him.

Bolt waited for them by the door, but he hardly registered Allta's presence. "I've turned half the city over trying to find you," he demanded. "You were supposed to be at the Eclipse."

Pellin stifled his shock at Bolt's preemptory tone. "Those who know Dura best come here, and we were delayed. They drink ale like a desert swallows rain."

Bolt waved him to silence before he'd finished, and Pellin's shock deepened. "I have Willet at an inn close to the river. The keeper wasn't happy about me dragging a body in there, but I gave him enough silver to shut him up." He wheeled through the door of Braben's and set a pace south toward the poorer part of the city that forced Pellin to a jog that made his knees ache.

Deep in his chest, Pellin's heart struggled to maintain its rhythm. "Dura is dead? Where's Volsk?"

Bolt shook his head. "Either he missed the trail I laid down or he's been prevented from following us. I could have used his help on the bridge."

Pellin shook off his annoyance that the guard had answered the second question without addressing the first. "How did Dura die?"

"What?" Bolt shook his head. "Willet's not dead. He's tied up at the inn."

Pellin noted Bolt's use of Dura's first name even as he grabbed the guard's sleeve as they slowed for a knot of passersby in the narrow street. "You said the innkeeper didn't want the body in his inn."

Bolt nodded, the exaggerated bobs screaming his impatience. "Dura's not dead, but he might as well be. He took a look at one of the men I'd killed and—" he shook his head, searching for words—"stopped. He just stopped." His gaze found Pellin's, whites showing around the blue of his eyes. "I brought both Dura and the body to the inn. I need more silver."

He resumed his frantic walk. Pellin gulped air into his old man's lungs and tried to keep up.

Boatman's Inn sat two hundred paces upriver from the bridge that led from the lower merchants' quarter to the poor section, the hitching rail in front balanced by docks along the back where small barges loaded or unloaded goods and passengers. Bolt led the way through the door. A low-ceilinged room with a long burnished-wood bar held a few patrons who sat next to the windows overlooking the river.

The innkeeper, a swarthy man with thinning hair and thick forearms, came out from behind the bar, his face florid and his eyes darting to the patrons by the window. "Good masters, you cannot keep those men here." He jerked his head, checking the tables closest to them. "They're dead. They don't belong here."

"I told you," Bolt growled. "They're not dead."

The keeper shook his head, his grizzled jowls following the motion a split second later. "All the silver in the kingdom won't change the sword cut that went halfway through one man's neck or the pallor of his skin. I know dead when I see it. You lied to me."

Pellin turned to Bolt. The Vigil operated outside the boundaries of the church in most matters, but their independence required a price in trust. Bolt shook his head. "I told the truth. *They're* not dead. Only one of them is."

The innkeeper spluttered and took a step toward the door. "I'm calling the watch."

Allta stepped from Pellin's side to block the keeper's path.

"Good master," Pellin said in as calming a tone as he could manage, "you're quite right to be upset." In fact, he would have liked to swat Bolt himself. What was the man thinking? "The other man upstairs is in need of my assistance. With your permission, I'd like to help him."

The keeper edged away from Allta, his eyes measuring the distance as he shuffled back toward Pellin. "Are you a healer, then?"

Pellin nodded and took hold of the man's hand to press a pair of silver crowns into his meaty palm. "Of a certain type. I assure you, once my examination of our friend is complete, we will take our friend and the body and notify the proper authorities."

The innkeeper nodded as if the motion might break his neck. "I'll give you two hours, but take them down the outside stairs by the stable. Don't bring them back through here."

Pellin nodded and forced a smile over his irritation. "It shall be as you say."

They ascended the broad wooden stairs to a hall with a half-dozen doors on each side. Bolt led them to the last room on the right. "It was farthest from the keeper's ears. Willet Dura's mind is gone. I didn't know what would happen if he came back."

Bolt's wording sent a premonition racing down Pellin's back as they entered the tiny room, the familiar stench of death almost overpowering. A pair of low-slung bunks filled the walls on either side of the door opposite a dirty window overlooking the stable. At the foot of each bed was just enough room to hold a small stand with a water pitcher and a broad bowl.

Each bed held a body. Pellin spared no more than a pair of heartbeats for the soldier. Despite the ragged state of his garments, it would have been impossible to miss the military cut to the clothes. If that hadn't been enough, a pair of crescents, those wicked half-moon blades, lay next to him on the bed. A clean cut down through the neck and into the torso gaped at him, and Pellin fought to keep his stomach under control. Rain had washed most of the blood away.

No sword stroke or blood marred Dura, yet the fixed, lifeless stare spoke plainly of his death. Relief mixed with regret flooded through Pellin's chest, and a moment later he clenched his jaws against the twist of guilt that followed. "I hope Aer has seen fit to guide the gift to Volsk after all. You told me Dura was alive."

"He is, Eldest." Bolt's voice sounded as if he couldn't figure out who to fight. "I wouldn't have wasted time tying him up otherwise."

Ropes fastened Dura's wrists and ankles to each corner of the simple bed frame. Pellin knelt and placed an ear to Dura's chest. The beat was there, but half the speed he would have expected, and his breathing was so shallow he might have imagined it.

"What happened?"

Bolt's face hardened further, if possible. "Dura decided to hunt the hunters. We went to the alchemist, who gave us something to create light."

"Ingenious," Pellin murmured, "but foolish as well. If the killers were only using the dark for concealment, it would have ended badly for you both."

He looked down at the still form on the bed. There was much to admire in Willet Dura, but the man gave deeper meaning to the word *reckless*. The Vigil depended on discretion above all else, and Dura had quickly become a liability. Already, Pellin had been forced to expose himself on Dura's account. Fortunately, no one had recognized him yet, at least not that he knew.

"It nearly did anyway," Bolt growled. "We almost didn't hear them until too late. Myle's powders worked almost too well. I kept my back to Willet's bowl, but I still saw spots for an hour or so."

He paused, turning away to check the makeshift dressing on Dura's legs. With a small nod he poured a dribble of water from the chipped pitcher onto it. "The powders burned hot enough to singe Dura's legs, but he held on while I fought. They can't stand light, Eldest. It was butcher work. From the first, I tried to set my strokes so that we might question the others."

Pellin picked out the note of defeat in Bolt's voice, but it held puzzlement as well. The guards were skilled enough to come just short of a killing blow, mortal but not instantly fatal. "What happened?"

The creases across Bolt's forehead deepened. "We went to check the first body. I held the torch while Willet rolled him over." He paused to wet his lips, but his gaze no longer focused on the cheap room of the inn. "He changed, Eldest. Dura became someone different. I still held my sword in one hand, but before I could stop him, Dura had drawn his dagger and put it through the heart of the man beneath him."

Bolt's gaze, clear, despite his age, found Pellin's. "I hesitated, Eldest. I stood there gaping like a boy who's never seen blood before as Dura killed the other two men, moving with the speed of the gifted. All the while he kept saying the same thing over and over. 'Only death serves.' I put the flat of my blade against his head." Bolt's brows deepened as he related his failure. "I didn't get a word out of any of them."

Pellin stepped back, feeling behind him for the other bed. He sat, careless of the dead body pressing into his backside. Dura's sightless gaze stared upward through the roof of the inn to who knew what beyond it. Or perhaps it had turned inward so far he could no longer sense the outside world. "It's nearly noon. How hard did you hit him?"

Bolt shook his head. "Not hard enough to keep him out this long."

"Did he touch the man before he killed him?"

"No, not skin to skin."

"Bad," Pellin muttered, "but not so bad as it might have been. Dura recognized him." Perhaps Dura's foolhardy attempt to find Elwin's killer had succeeded after all. Pellin stood, rubbing his hands to dispel his nervousness. After hundreds of touches, the prospect of falling through the tunnel into another mind still made him nervous. The weight of accumulated memories he'd managed to lock away dragged at his soul like a ship's anchor dredging mud. He sighed. There was no help for it. Willet Dura's mind might hold an image of his brother's killer. "I'll have to delve him."

Bolt shifted to block his path, even going so far as to put a hand to Pellin's chest. "No, Eldest. If the vault in his mind is open, there's no knowing what you might step into. With Cesla and Elwin gone, the Vigil can't risk it." He licked his lips. "And if his vault is closed and you break it, you'll break his mind as well."

Allta stepped forward, one hand on the long-bladed dagger at his waist. "It is not for you to gainsay the Eldest. Stand aside."

Bolt's face registered irritation at Allta's command, but nothing more. "Eldest, the man who killed three bleeding men on the bridge was not Willet Dura. Please give him time to come back to himself."

Bolt's advice was sound. In all his years as a member of the Vigil, he'd never stepped into an open vault within another's mind. But a handful of times he'd witnessed the actions that went with them. He crossed his arms, focused on reinforcing the mental locks he'd placed on those memories. Men who claimed evil to be nothing more than church sophistry couldn't imagine the depravity Pellin had seen. Images leaked from his control and he thrust them back.

Pellin shook his head. "Regardless, the attempt must be made. The identity of Elwin's killer may be in his mind." He sighed. "I wish healing was possible as well."

Bolt didn't move, but he cut his eyes to Allta. "There's no need, Eldest."

Pellin lifted his hand and Allta stepped back, his hands back at his side.

"Laewan was at the bridge," Bolt said. "He fled as soon as Dura lit his powders."

Somewhere within him, Pellin wondered at his lack of surprise. The discovery of Laewan's guard had sent tremors through Pellin that he hadn't been able to dismiss. Or perhaps his anger simply left no room for anything else. "You saw him? And you chose to waste your energy on these?" He stabbed a finger toward the body on the bed behind him. "You stopped to kill pawns?"

Bolt flinched at the accusation, but a decades-familiar defiance filled his gaze. "You commanded me to protect him." He pointed at the staring man behind him. "Dura's light gave me less than a minute. To pursue Laewan meant sacrificing one of the Vigil."

Pellin struggled to control his frustration. "He's not one of the Vigil," he spat. "He's a rogue!" Pellin could hear his voice scaling upward, and he clenched his fists to bring it under control. "In all the centuries of the Vigil, how many rogues have lasted more than a year or two? You let my brother's killer escape." He stabbed a finger at Dura's body, frozen in whatever hell of memory or nothingness Aer or circumstance decreed. "Look at him. He's almost dead already."

"We don't know that Laewan killed Elwin," Bolt asserted.

"Don't play word games with me. I didn't like it when you were my guard, and I don't like it any better now."

Bolt shrugged away Pellin's command. "You wanted to know what was in Dura's mind. I just saved you a trip into the memories that made him this way. You gave me orders to protect him. You're inconsistent, Eldest," Bolt said, his voice tight. "You don't like it when I disobey orders, and you don't like it when I follow them."

Pellin pulled in a deep breath that smelled of must and cheap bedding. "I am Eldest, and I expect you to think. Something has turned one of the Vigil, and you forfeited a chance to find out what for a rogue."

"You act surprised," Bolt said. "Dura and I met with Volsk an hour before sunset. If you'd wanted to call off Dura's plan, all you had to do was send Volsk back to us. We were there all night." The guard made a show of searching the room. "Since I don't see him, I can only conclude you saw some merit to Dura's idea."

"I did not!"

"Well, Eldest, where is Volsk?"

The door opened, and Pellin watched as Allta and Bolt, both quicker than any ungifted could ever be, drew steel before a lean dark-haired figure stepped in holding a rough canvas bag. "I'm right here."

"I've never cared for eavesdroppers," Bolt said.

"You should be grateful I was out in the hall. Your voices are carrying farther than you intend, but your accusation is unjust. Your query on my whereabouts was the first thing I heard clearly."

Pellin raised his hand for silence, then tried not to let his surprise show when he got it. "You were commanded to keep a close watch on Dura."

Volsk bowed his head. "I came to report to you, Eldest. I couldn't find you. You know the city better than I, and the speed of your movements has made it difficult to keep up." He looked at Bolt. "You, however, left a trail."

Pellin nodded.

"We could have used your help at the bridge," Bolt said.

Volsk's eyes darkened at the rebuke. "Granted, but you should be grateful I came along when I did. You left a pair of bodies behind with the kind of wounds that raise questions. I had to bribe a couple of men into cleaning the blood away. You and I don't understand the burden those in the Vigil carry, but I would think with your experience as the Eldest's guard you would have learned the value of discretion."

Bolt's eyes widened at the insult. "Perhaps you wish to avail yourself of the opportunity to instruct me. I'm sure we can find someplace private."

Volsk didn't bother to answer. Instead he turned to Pellin. "Bolt's loyalty to Dura is commendable, but perhaps misplaced. I'm afraid this may explain much." He bent over the bag to pull out a worn cloak of sturdy workmanship.

"Apprentice," Pellin began, "I'm sure you mean well, but—"

"There's blood on the hem, Eldest," Volsk interrupted. "It might be Elwin's."

Bolt exhaled his disgust. "Now, that is a mystery. Imagine a reeve getting blood on his clothes as he investigates someone's murder."

Volsk's somber expression never wavered. "Except Dura wasn't wearing this during his investigation. I followed him to the House of Passing—remember? The cloak he wore there was dark gray. This one is green. I spoke with the watch on duty at the keep that night. They saw Dura returning from the city well before first light."

"That doesn't mean the blood is Elwin's," Bolt said.

Volsk nodded. "True. Eldest?"

Pellin eyed the stain on the cloak, the cloth beneath the dark blotch stiff with dried blood. "Let us see if there is anything left." He pulled at the fingers of the glove covering his right hand, beginning with the smallest and ending with the thumb until the leather came loose. Then he reached toward the cloak, his fingers extended almost in a caress as he brushed the stain.

The sensation held little in common with delving a mind, requiring more finesse. It often yielded little or no results, and Bronwyn had always been better at such scrutiny, but if the connection to the thing or place involved family or friends of long acquaintance, traces could be felt.

He closed his eyes, emptying his mind, waiting.

There—not an image, but a feeling came to him, a familiarity like the silent company of an old friend. He opened his eyes and pulled his fingers from the cloak. High in his chest, a fire began to build. "We will take Dura to the Merum cathedral and lock him in the lower cells." He turned to Volsk. "Retrieve Toria Deel and Bronwyn. I want as many of the Vigil present as possible when I delve him."

Chapter 24

A hand pulled him to a stop before he left the room. Pellin turned to find himself looking into Bolt's craggy face, the face that had been so young when they'd set out together. Age had finally taken them both, but it had been hard to watch Bolt grow old so quickly.

"He's not a killer, Eldest."

Pellin dipped his head at the use of the title. "He may not be." He rested a hand on Bolt's shoulder. "Your loyalty is a credit, but the man we're dealing with isn't the Willet Dura you know."

Bolt shook his head once in denial, trying to shed the burden of realization. "I've never believed a vault could force a man to do something he wouldn't do otherwise."

Pellin nodded, but not in agreement. "So you've said before, but I've seen what's been done to cause men and women and children to build a tomb in their mind." How many times had he watched Cesla and Elwin break a vault open without success? How many times had he tried himself? "Sometimes, my friend, people are too broken to save."

"I don't believe that."

Bolt's hand slipped from his arm, and Pellin stepped out of the room to be alone with his thoughts. A litany of names ran through his mind—old names, some of them with twists in the middle that tripped the tongue, the identity of every vault he'd tried to break: Loschka, Nzewor, Bela-aris . . .

He wiped his forehead, grateful for the ability to lock his own memories away along with those of the people he touched. "Aer have mercy," he whispered. "Not another one." He stepped through the door at the end of the hall and descended the stairs leading to the stables.

The men brought the bodies after him, Dura rigid and staring.

"What does he see, I wonder?" Bolt said as they loaded his unresponsive form into a cart.

Pellin looked at the king's reeve, the rogue, but no sign showed on the man's face that he saw anything at all.

An arrow from their volley flew by me close enough to hear the air whistling through the fletching. I lifted my shield out of reflex and took the impact of a second arrow on it a moment later, like the blow of a fist. Twelve men copied me, mercenaries from the southern continent, whose commander lay facedown in the mud a few paces away. My arrow-riddled squad of men lay close by, keeping him company.

"Back," I screamed to make myself heard above the din. "Circle around the forest."

We crabbed backward, hoping the squad of archers would turn their attention elsewhere at our retreat.

"They're flanking us," the man on my left said. His accent pushed his words together so that each syllable leaned on the previous one for support. Moles on his right cheek disfigured the skin in a perfect triangle close to an aquiline nose.

On the slope above us I saw the archers advance. "Run. Laidir's forces are retreating. If we don't break loose in the next few minutes, they'll have until sunset to pick us off." Another volley of arrows filled the air above us. "Shields up!"

The mercenaries lifted their shields with me, and we formed a turtle until the hammering of shafts ceased. Each of the southerners held a shield with one hand and a crescent with the other. I kept my distance from the gleaming blades of those wicked half moons.

We sprinted west, circling the Darkwater as the sun set like flowing honey in the sultry air of summer. The Owmead archers refused to let us go. Shouts and laughter drifted down as they sent half their squadron ahead to cut off our retreat.

"Norlander," the man on my left said, "let us escape into the forest."

Another fall of arrows interrupted my answer. "What's your name, solander?"

He shook his head. "You can't pronounce it. Call me Ben."

"It's almost night. The forest is a sure death, Ben."

"Less sure than a broadhead shaft."

A scream on my right, shrill and high, cut across my reply. One of the mercenaries, a tall man with the rangy strength of a southerner, collapsed with an arrow through his belly. He pulled at the man next to him who delivered the mercy blow. I turned away from the way his eyes emptied of life, trying to ignore the realization of just how much blood a man had.

"They're staggering their fire," the mercenary said.

"Poll your men," I said. "If they want to attempt the forest, I'll try to guide us."

We held the shield wall as we backed toward the trunks and the canopy of leaves that sucked the light from the sky. The rain of arrows dwindled even as the barks of mocking laughter increased.

"Hide behind the closest trees for a moment," I said. "Maybe they'll go away."

I counted fifty, and the mercenary sergeant and I darted a look.

"It's no use, norlander," the sergeant said, pointing to a squad of archers that approached the edge of our hiding place. "They've outguessed you."

I stood rooted to the spot, my feet refusing the command to run. The forest, the arrow, or the mercy stroke? "No one survives the Darkwater."

The sergeant smiled, the long puckered scar across his forehead dimpling with the expression. "We have a saying south of the strait, norlander. 'If there is no second, it's because the first hasn't been tried.'"

The hiss of an arrow broke the spell binding my feet. "I hope you have a saying for surviving the forest." I ducked behind a bole two paces across. The mercenaries mimicked me, and we headed deeper into the gloom.

The men gathered into a tight mass as the light faded from the thick canopy and the dying sun. "Ben, split the men into two squads of six, four to watch each point, one to watch the floor, and the last to watch overhead." Strange smells, sweet and acrid, filled my nose, and I turned westward in an attempt to make our stay in the forest as brief as possible. "I'll take the point on the lead group."

Just before night fell, we improvised torches. Darkness closed in. A hundred paces in, some instinct warned me. I turned, searching for the men behind me. Ben's squad had—

An arrow from their volley flew by me close enough to hear the air whistling through the fletching. I lifted my shield out of reflex . . .

The cart rattled to a stop. Pellin stepped down, placing his feet with care, conscious of how the other men, silent during the ride, jumped lightly to the ground. The back of the Merum cathedral boasted several large entryways for the delivery of goods and foodstuffs to quarter the brothers who lived there.

"Peret." Pellin pulled his letter of authority from inside his cloak. "Give this to the brother who answers the door. Have him take us to the lower cells." At a look from the apprentice, he went on. "I'd prefer not to be recognized, even here." He pulled up his hood.

Even the air surrounding the cathedral held a familiar smell, as if he'd come home, but there were too many of those familiar locations, too many smells for him to attach importance to any particular one.

Bolt eyed him, his face still stiff and defiant.

"Allta, bring Dura down from the cart." Keeping his face neutral, Pellin turned to his former guard and friend. "Dispose of the bodies."

Bolt's shoulders tightened. "And then?"

Pellin tried to make his voice as kind as he could, but his grief and frustration came through anyway. "Your part in this is done. Go home."

He hadn't expected the bark of laughter. "What home have I ever had except where you and the rest of the Vigil have sent me? You're making a mistake, Eldest. You and the rest of the Vigil have depended on the insights of your gift for so long, you've forgotten the ordinary ways of seeing into a man's heart."

Peret Volsk shook his head. "You think that because he shows compassion to a few pick-thieves and night women that makes him immune to the demons inside the vault of his mind? You're a guard, Bolt, and a good one, but the Eldest has seen more of humanity than you can imagine."

Misgiving tightened Pellin's chest at Volsk's defense, and again he regretted the absence of his brothers, always so sure, so confident.

As Bolt looked at him, his eyes practically demanding some defense, Pellin sifted through the memories of long-dead men and women, each with a vault in their mind smaller than the one locked within Willet Dura. In every case those with vaults, whether noble or peasant, had killed by horrific means, and each had possessed many of Dura's same characteristics in their waking lives. A man's cruelty might be amplified, but the clues were always there—he was still the same man.

Pellin pushed that train of thought away. Elwin's blood stained Dura's cloak, a different cloak, according to Volsk, than Dura had worn that morning. That meant the rogue had gotten to Elwin before the city watch had been alerted, which meant Dura might have directed the attack that killed him. *Might have*. The words echoed in Pellin's mind with Bolt's voice.

But the answers lay somewhere in Dura's head. Pellin caught the demand in Bolt's gaze and said nothing. In the highest councils of the four-part church, the Vigil was known for justice, not mercy. They certainly couldn't afford it now.

His former guard brushed past him to approach the cart where Dura lay. Allta jerked, looking to Pellin for direction, but relaxed at a nod.

Bolt turned back, his eyes daring Pellin. "May I pray over him before I go? We serve the church after all."

He tried to ignore the insult inherent in the request. "Of course."

Bolt bent, shifted the tarp covering the rogue—Pellin would not think of Dura any other way now—and bent over him. "Aer, Iosa, and Gaoithe go with you, Willet." He put his hand on the rogue's shoulder and shook him. "Wake up, man. They don't realize how much they need you."

After a moment, he shook harder. "What do you see in there?"

An arrow from their volley flew by me close enough to hear the air whistling through the fletching. I lifted my shield out of reflex and took the impact of a second arrow on it a moment later like the blow of a fist. Twelve men copied me, mercenaries from the southern continent whose commander lay facedown in the mud a few paces away. My arrow-riddled squad of men lay close by, keeping him company.

"Back," I screamed—

I couldn't breathe. The muscles in my chest and gut fought to fill my aching lungs, but they refused to expand, as if all the air in the world had simply vanished. I opened my eyes, seeking some reason for my death, but darkness blacker than the deep recesses of a cave at night met them. I blinked, squinting, straining for some glimmer to explain why I was dying. Spots of light danced in my vision—not light, but the harbingers of unconsciousness.

I struggled to raise arms as heavy as lead pipes. They might have moved. I couldn't tell.

Weight lifted from my chest and mouth, and I sucked in air—blessed, stale, musty air—in a gasp that scraped across my throat.

"If you can understand me, Dura," a voice whispered, "be quiet. I'll explain once we're free."

I must have nodded. The owner of the voice moved off from where I lay, and a moment later hands tugged the front of my tunic.

I reached out, feeling the darkness for barriers, trying to distinguish between my present darkness and the Darkwater past. Memories and emotions shrouded in pitch swirled in my head, fighting to incite panic or rage. The pulse of blood in my ears roared with the rhythmic thunder of waves on the shore, racing and then slowing, its rhythm as undefined as my sense of self.

A hand fluttered over my torso, working its way blindly toward my wrist, where it clenched the bones with a grip that could have pulped a carrot. Bolt. My mind cleared, as if his presence provided the anchor to reality I needed to force the memories of the Darkwater away.

"Where am I?"

Our shuffling progress stopped, and warm breath ghosted across my ear. "The Merum cathedral. And that's where we're likely to stay if we're heard."

"Vigil guards?" I whispered.

"No." Even as a whisper, his voice sounded impatient. I tried to make sense of my dislocation—awake at the bridge and then asleep in the cathedral without transition, but nothing of the interval between came to me. "Can't you just fight our way clear?"

The hand on my wrist tightened for an instant. "I won't kill a good man who's just doing his job, Dura. Now be quiet."

We crept in the dark, with Bolt leading me by the hand, his steps a strange cadence, where he put his right foot forward first and then brought his left to meet it. After a few moments, I understood. Bolt wasn't injured, he was measuring.

After sixty-three of those paces he stopped. "Don't move."

The grip on my wrist vanished, and I heard the scrape of skin and fabric across cut stone to my right, punctuated by whispered imprecations. To my left, a sliver of light flared, lamplight under a distant door frame. I squinted, gauging the distance, perhaps forty or fifty paces away. I blinked and it grew brighter.

"I think someone's coming."

A grunt came from behind and below me along with the scrape of stone on stone. "Of course they are." Strain corded Bolt's voice. "Where would the adventure be in sneaking past a squadron of guards, feeling our way out in the dark, and then swimming our way to freedom if we weren't also being discovered?"

"Swim?" I couldn't keep my voice from going up an octave.

Bolt grunted again before he replied. "This door hasn't been opened in years. Some people have no consideration. Yes. Swim. You're squealing like a pig. Are you entering manhood again?"

I shook my head in the dark, even though he couldn't see me or the expression of denial I wore. "I don't know how. We need to find another way out."

"There is no other way out." A long groan of wood against stone sounded, and weakly reflected moonlight silhouetted my guard. "What kind of man grows up on the banks of a river without learning how to swim?"

I could hear water lapping against the foundation stones of the cathedral, and a fist of panic knotted around my throat. The squeak of hinges sounded behind us. For a moment I thought about returning to my cell to await whatever judgment my captors intended to dole out. The more I thought about it, the better the option seemed. I was decent in a fight, and as long as I wasn't going up against Vigil guards, I had a good chance of winning. Yes, that was it. I would sneak back to my cell and—

Bolt's fist knotted in my tunic. "Take a deep breath and hold it until I find you." He pivoted in a wrestler's move, and I shot forward through the door, launched over a small threshold and into the waters of the Rinwash.

I splashed into the depths and bobbed toward the surface, my arms and legs thrashing as if I'd been taken in a seizure. A thousand needles of cold pierced my skin, and breath exploded from my lungs as my head cleared the surface of water that must have melted that morning. I inhaled, fighting for air, and sucked murky fluid into my lungs. My body bent double as I coughed and clawed at the water, but my lungs held nothing to keep me afloat, and I drifted toward the bottom of the river. I reached up, straining for a surface I couldn't see. Where, by all that was holy, was Bolt? My mind screamed for rescue.

Frantic kicks did little to propel me toward the surface. Spots that had nothing to do with stars or moonlight danced in my vision. *Oh, Aer, please, not like this.*

I knew what would happen. I'd seen it too often to deny. My body would sink toward the bottom and wash downstream in death until decay bloated my corpse, lifting it to float on the surface miles away. Some farmer might fish me from the river, if he followed the king's command, or they might just let me drift out to sea, where the carrion eaters of the deep would pick me clean.

For a moment my hand cleared the water, but I couldn't get any higher. My body refused to obey me, jerking, moving in opposition to the simplest commands. Then, by some hope or miracle, my head cleared the surface and I pulled a whooping breath into my lungs. I reached up and grasped a hand knotted in my hair.

Bolt. I tried to climb on top of him to get free of the water.

"Be still, curse you." Something hard hit me on the underside of my jaw.

I woke up on the bank of the river with spots swimming across my vision, merging and separating from the stars overhead.

I rubbed my chin. "You hit me."

Bolt sat next to me, his arms on his knees and breathing heavily. "It's probably brilliant observations like that one that persuaded Laidir to make you his reeve." After the pitch black of the prison and the murk of the Rinwash, the moonlight allowed me to discern hints of his expression. He didn't look very concerned. "If I hadn't hit you, you would have drowned us both in your panic." He would probably never look anything other than annoyed.

He pointed upstream to the Merum cathedral, where a light swayed back and forth, low over the water. "We have to move. It won't be too long before the guard gives up hope of finding you himself and goes for help."

I stood on legs as wobbly as a newborn colt's and followed each shaking step with another until the trembling subsided. "How did you get me out?"

Bolt didn't bother to turn around to answer. "Pellin made the mistake of showing me where he was taking you. I snuck into the cells when the brother guarding you went to get his relief. After that I felt my way until I found you."

Joy at being free couldn't keep my mind from spotting the holes in his explanation. "How did you know that was me?"

Laughter drifted back to me. "You were the only one down there. The Merum haven't kept prisoners since the last war between the orders. After I picked the lock on your door it was just a matter of getting the garbage door open."

His explanation seemed to wrap everything up except the most important point. "How could you possibly know your way around the cathedral so well?"

The question stopped him for a moment, and he gave a long, slow exhale before answering. "I've been here before, Dura." He sighed with a peculiar sound of surrender. "In fact, I know the inside of every order's cathedral, here and in the rest of the kingdoms of the northern continent: Owmead, Caisel, Moorclair, Aille, Elania, even Frayel." He pointed, gesturing toward the kingdom far to the east across the mountains, his motions looking oddly weary. "I've stashed clothes and horses a couple hundred more paces downstream. After that our next move is up to you."

Chapter 25

"I don't even know what happened." The skin on my legs started to throb now that we were out of the water and memories rushed back at me, my own this time, but they stopped short of revealing anything useful. It was as if Aer had pulled a curtain closed in my mind and I'd been forbidden to pull the veil aside to see what lay beyond it. "You work for them," I said, measuring my words as much in fear of what slept in my own head as out of the desire to pry information from my guard. "Why did you defy them? Why break me out?"

"They were already making one mistake, and they were about to make a bigger one. Pellin and Volsk are half convinced you killed Elwin." Bolt kept his gaze ahead, scanning the darkness for threats but never quite looking at me. "Volsk found your cloak with blood on it, Elwin's blood. Pellin was going to delve you."

The darkness kept him from seeing me gape, but it couldn't mask the spluttering sound I made. "And you stopped this? They would have known I was innocent."

"You don't understand." Bolt's voice dropped, and I had to stifle my indignation to hear him. "Pellin was prepared to force his way past the vault in your mind to try and see inside."

My stomach collapsed into a hole in my middle, pulling my breath and heartbeat with it. They knew about the night walks. Splinters of doubt broke loose from my control to accuse me. What had I done during those walks? Not once in all my years as reeve had anyone ever witnessed wrongdoing, but that wasn't the same as knowing I was innocent.

I took a deep breath to push my fear aside and shouldered my doubt. "We need to know, Bolt. I'm the king's reeve. If I did anything wrong, I should be held to account."

Bolt's growl caught me by surprise. "That's noble, but I'm not talking about your innocence. I served the Vigil as a guard for nearly four decades. I've seen Pellin force his way past a block before on people proven guilty beyond a ghost of doubt so he could know the extent of their crimes and give the families of their victims some measure of peace." He sighed. "Guilty or not, it's unpleasant to see someone's mind break. They're put to the sword afterward. Mercy demands it." He shook his head. "And it's never worked. No one has ever seen inside a vault."

We turned away from the river once we traveled far enough to put us in the merchants' district. I didn't want to talk anymore, but this wasn't some night walk we spoke of. Something had happened to me on the bridge. "Why did I black out?"

"You are guilty of murder, Dura, just not in the way Pellin thinks. You were normal right up until you saw the face of one of the men on the bridge. You turned into someone different, someone faster. You put your dagger into those men before I could stop you."

Bolt spoke the same tongue as I, but he might as well have been from the southern continent. I'd seen him move—or rather, I'd almost seen him move—and knew I wasn't capable of the kind of speed some men are gifted with. "I'm not gifted. I'm not faster than you."

The moon cast enough light for me to see him shake his head. "No, but you were fast enough to surprise me." He exhaled, and a long thread of mist ghosted from his mouth. "I haven't been surprised in a long time."

The smells of a stable and horses guided us up the next street, and we climbed a small rise while I tried to make sense of my improbable rescue. Everything Bolt had told me only confirmed why he should have left me in prison. To a reeve, my actions would be proof enough of guilt, and yet Bolt had put himself in jeopardy to free me. "You still haven't told me why you pulled me out of the Merum prison."

He reached out in the darkness and put a hand to my chest, bringing me to a stop outside the high, boarded gate to the stable yard. "I couldn't come up with a reason for you to kill Elwin. Everything makes you look guilty, Dura. You killed two men who might have held the identity of Elwin's killer. You moved quickly enough to make you a candidate for Robin's death, or at least an assistant in it. And you have a vault in your mind where you hold secrets." He sighed. "But except for the last war with Owmead, you've never left the city of Bunard, much less the kingdom of Collum. Whatever Elwin had been hunting or whatever had been hunting him, you didn't have a hand in it."

"So you think I'm innocent?"

"I hope you're innocent, but the vault in your mind means you might be the tool of someone who brought about Elwin's and Robin's death." His voice rasped like a file against wood. "If that's true, your vault won't save you from me." He turned to put his hand on the gate latch. "I'm tired of wearing cold, wet clothes. Let's go."

I didn't follow him. "No. Not until you tell me why you rescued me. You give me contradictions as if they explained everything."

The moonlight lit his face with shadows that leached any expression he might have worn. "You don't fit, Dura. Every man or woman I've seen the Vigil track down has been a killer in both parts of their mind."

I clutched his sleeve, tried to make him face me. "You know I've killed men. Every tongue at court talks about how I tricked Marquis Orlan to his own destruction."

Air burst from Bolt's mouth, dismissing my argument. "You dispensed justice to a threat to your king and kingdom. You've also impoverished yourself to help children and women forced to live and make a living on the street. Despite your vault and occasional night walk, the men of the city watch show a loyalty to you that all the free ale in Bunard can't buy."

He turned away from me again. "I don't like complimenting people. Let's go."

"Where are the bodies?"

"Pellin had me hide them." His face, always hard, became stone. "Only I know where they're at, but if you look at them again . . ." He didn't need to finish.

I nodded, but tension ran from my chest to my throat. I couldn't afford to let myself see their faces, but other possibilities existed. "I don't intend to. Does anyone else know where you've hidden them?"

When he shook his head my next breath came easier. This would be difficult enough without having to fight others in the Vigil over the corpses. "We need to get to the keep and see Gareth. There might be other people there able to put a name and a memory to those men, but he's the most likely."

"Why him?"

It might have been an effect of the people I'd touched. Perhaps seeing the men on the bridge had weakened my ability to keep memories, any memories, from taking me against my will.

Noise washed over us, thundering against the ears and skin like ocean waves pounding cliffs. Men and horses clashed in a multitude, the impact and screaming so great it became another enemy. I stepped over a fold in the land, a dip that might have hidden a child, and I resisted the impulse to burrow into it, curl into a ball and cover my ears.

Arrows raked our front line, and men who belonged back at home mending shoes or pots went down, too awestruck by the noise and chaos to remember to raise their shields. Next to me Gareth cursed, and our leader, Captain Ean, echoed him a moment later. Our irregulars were breaking, but I caught the captain gazing over our head and turned to the south. One of the band of mercenaries—no more than a dozen, but worth three times that in battle—milled about, drifting away from us toward the enemy lines.

"Their commander is down," the captain growled. "Southerners. Great fighters, but they don't think well on their own. Willet. Gareth. Get those men back in line before they get cut off completely."

We nodded and ran up the ridge toward them with trudging strides over the turf, hoisting our shields as we went to keep from taking an arrow. Gareth's legs churned ahead of me, and I fought to keep up. We crested the ridge where the southerners stood, bunched like puppies fighting for the teat. But their shields were tight against the occasional arrow.

"Form up," I screamed. "If you want to live to feel the breeze of the southern sea again, we have to rejoin the main force."

One of the southerners, his sun-darkened face grim, lifted his foot and stamped it on the ground. "Better the high ground against the horse."

I shook my head. "There's no cavalry on this end of the line. Their foot and bowman will—"

Gareth pulled me around to face southwest. "Lord help us, Willet."

From the top of the rise I could just see over the low ridge to the west. More important, I knew our captain couldn't. "Oh, Aer."

A massive phalanx of Owmead forces seethed and shifted like ants, preparing to crest the ridge and sweep down on our northern flank. Closer, light cavalry formed up. Our whole northern line was about to be shattered. We'd never withstand the charge.

"Shields," the southerner yelled.

I pulled Gareth close. "Get to Captain Ean."

"You can't stay here. The first sweep of horses will cut you to ribbons."

I shook my head. "I can't keep up with you." I gripped his forearm hard. "Hurry."

He raced down the hill as a low rumble of hooves began in the east. Behind them, a column of Owmead foot soldiers and archers moved to flank the northern end of the Collum battle line. The southerners and I were cut off.

"What now, northerner?" the same southerner asked.

Behind us the ridge sloped upward, ever more steep, cutting off our retreat west. Less than two hundred paces to the north, the ground began sloping toward the forest. I pointed. "If we hurry, we might be able to skirt the edge and rejoin our retreating forces." I didn't believe it, but the choices were to die now under the Owmead charge or die later, pinned against the Darkwater. I thought later would be better.

I pulled myself from the memories to see Bolt staring at me as if he wasn't sure rescuing me had been the right decision. But for the first time I dared to feel hope about what lay in my mind. I wasn't a fool. My night walks began just after the last war, after I'd miraculously survived a trip through the Darkwater, where everyone else had died. The fact that those memories lay beyond my grasp coupled with my reaction to seeing the face of the man on the bridge provided a clue. What had me puzzled and left me more than a little scared was how the buried memories from a war a decade ago related to the murder of the Eldest of the Vigil.

I prayed by my hope of salvation that I wouldn't regret finding the answer. "I think Gareth might recognize the men on the bridge."

Bolt stepped in front of me before I could mount up. "We have to avoid the keep and any other place you'd normally go." On one of the posts of the fence bordering the stable yard, a cock fluffed its wings before lifting its beak toward the lightening sky and crowing. "By now Pellin knows you've escaped."

I shrugged. Bunard wasn't as big as the cities to the south, but it would be impossible for a handful of the Vigil and their guards to track a pair of men through the city. And being seen wasn't the same thing as being taken. I knew routes through the city, passages through the warrens of the poor quarter that no one else did. "He can't take what he can't find."

Bolt shook his head. "In a matter of hours he'll have every guard and clergyman on the lookout for you, and probably me as well. We need to hide. Who can you send to the keep in your place without arousing suspicion?"

"Gael. She makes an appearance at court almost every day." We were in the northern end of the lower merchants' district. Gael's estate lay perhaps two miles away.

The furrows across Bolt's forehead held misgiving in the weak torchlight. "Are you sure you want to involve her? Volsk has been following you for days. He'll have her place watched as soon as he can get enough men together."

I nodded. Volsk and Bolt wouldn't be the first men to underestimate her. "Unless you hid the bodies at her place, she'll be fine. Can Gareth find the way to them without your help?"

Bolt shook his head. "I hid them in the caves beneath the keep."

I nodded. Where better to hide the dead than in the catacombs beneath the fortress of Bunard? The cold would slow their decay, and if they were never needed again, they could be left without fear of discovery. The only difficulty would be getting to the entrance without being seen. "We'll have Gareth meet us at Myle's. I hope Volsk doesn't think of the connection between the alchemist and me." The cock crowed for the third time as we crossed the river.

Chapter 26

Pellin entered the upper level of the Merum cathedral with the odd sensation of long-renewed familiarity. He'd heard others describe the same feeling upon returning to their childhood city or village after a protracted absence of years or even decades. How many times had he duplicated that experience? Every city on the northern continent, and a few on the southern as well, spawned the same reaction. Aer have mercy, he felt old.

He followed Volsk through the warren of constricting hallways that turned with precision at right angles until they came to the limestone stairs leading down to the lower lever and the ancient cells. Allta, ever the enthusiast, came behind with his sword bared against the possibility the empty prison hid an imminent attack.

Volsk turned east toward the river and stopped next to an ancient door. "He escaped through here. Though how he managed to get this far in the dark and get it open is a mystery."

Pellin shook his head. "Not much of one. He had help. Let's continue on to the cell."

Allta stiffened. Good. At least his young guard had the mental capacity to realize from whence Dura's help had come.

Volsk, standing in front of Pellin with the lantern in his naked hand held above to light the way, stood as still as if he'd been carved from the same stone as the lower level of the cathedral. Yet something flared in the apprentice's eyes before he turned away.

They made another of those precise turns the architects of the day had favored before coming to a cell whose barred door stood ajar, unlike the rest. Pellin signaled Volsk to precede him into the cell. Allta remained in the hallway, stoic, scanning the corridor for threats.

He suppressed a sigh. Bolt's familiarity had grated, but his sardonic wit had served to lighten many of the responsibilities required of the Vigil. Ah well, Allta carried less than thirty years. Perhaps he would acquire a sense of humor along the way. If nothing else, a few decades might serve to diminish his purposeful stoicism.

Volsk lifted the lantern a bit higher. "Is it possible to delve the cell, Eldest? Dura was here less than a day, and there are other memories here, surely."

Pellin nodded. They'd trained Volsk well, and he'd shown a comprehension for the nuances of the gift that few could match. "You're right of course. I doubt I would be able to pick out the residue of Dura's stay here, especially since his mind was unaware of much of it." He couldn't help or lessen the stab of regret that came. "I'm looking for someone else." He stopped, unwilling to name his suspicion. With brusque gestures he jerked the gloves off in preparation to delve the prison. Volsk stepped out of arms' reach and raised the lantern overhead.

For a moment Pellin wished the brothers of the Merum had been less fastidious in their cleaning duties. Dust on the floor would have provided physical clues to go with the spiritual ones. He bent and went on all fours, fingers splayed to cover as much stone as possible. He would have to feel his way.

The rough, unpolished texture of rock flowed across the ridges of his fingertips. His knees protested the abuse, but the sensations faded as his gift picked up wisps and tendrils of ancient misery. But those memories and emotions had faded to barest insubstantiality, and it was impossible to put a face or name to them.

Pellin shuffled forward, leading with his hands, turning left and right, like a dog on the scent. *There*. A more recent impression. War and its handmaiden, fear, came to his senses. Too ethereal to identify, but it could only be part of Dura's mind.

"Dura lay here," he said. He traced the outline of Dura's impressions, gliding his hands across the stone. Someone must have touched him. He reversed course, setting his hands on a spot imbued with memory and purpose. Almost, Pellin had missed it.

How had he broken Dura loose of his stupor?

Pellin lifted his hands from the stone, signaling Volsk to help him rise. The apprentice held the lantern with one hand and brought the other forward to assist, but it got tangled in his cloak, and Pellin was forced to clench his hand through the thick cloth.

"Bolt was here."

"What are your orders, Eldest?" Volsk asked.

Too many emotions churned in the depths of the apprentice's eyes for Pellin to put a name to any of them. Perhaps Bolt was right. Maybe he'd relied on his gift for too long. "Ride to the Darkwater and bring Toria Deel back to Bunard. We must bring Dura in." He paused to emphasize his next word. "Alive."

"What of Bolt?" Allta asked.

"Bring him in as well."

"What if he resists?"

Ah, my friend. You were always so impetuous. And I loved you for it. "Dura must be brought in alive, regardless of cost."

"Forcing the vault will break his mind, Eldest," Volsk said.

Pellin tried not to be offended and failed. "Yes. We may have to kill him. If Aer wills, his gift will pass to you." Volsk's naked hands clenched as Pellin tugged his gloves back on, stalking out of the cell. What had Bolt seen in his time with Dura that would lead him to such extravagance?

Lights burned in all of the lower windows of Count Alainn's estate, and in one upper room. Padraig, one of the many servants in the count's employ who didn't favor me, regarded us from the other side of the threshold, obviously surprised to see me at such an early hour. As a rule, nobles didn't stir before the sun was well advanced, unless they went hunting.

"Good morning, Padraig." Despite his enmity, his bushy white eyebrows always brought a smile to my lips. That single feature in an otherwise passive face managed to convey his emotions to greater effect than most players on the stage could summon. Now they quivered over his rheumy tear-filled eyes. He checked over his shoulder before answering. "Lady Gael has left for the keep."

"Why?"

Count Alainn stalked into the entrance hall, awake and dressed to present himself at court. "You are dismissed, Padraig," he announced, cutting off whatever the servant had been about to say next. Gael's uncle turned to regard me with as much favor as he might a weevil in his porridge. "You are no longer welcome at my estate, Dura."

I was accustomed to his bluff and bombast, but this was different. The count no longer hid his enmity behind crafted insults or contrived dismissals. He'd peeled away the thin veneer of respect required by the king toward his niece's future husband and thrown it away.

I found his honest hatred refreshing. "Why did Gael go to the keep?"

He hadn't bothered to use my title, so I thought it only appropriate to respond in kind, but the flare of his eyes showed he didn't agree.

"Leave. Now." He pointed over my shoulder, expecting my customary obedience, but my days of running fetch for nobles had ended with the marquis's death at my hand.

Bolt moved close to speak. "We can't tarry here, Lord Dura."

The count's expression sharpened, and his gaze cut from Bolt to me. "Trouble again, reeve?" he spat. "You bring death wherever you go." He laughed. "And now it has turned on you."

It took a moment to put the pieces together: the lights at the early hour, Gael's absence, Padraig's sorrow, and the count's honesty. *No.*

I pushed past Alainn and ran up the broad curling staircase leading to Kera's room. The count screamed for his servants, his voice shrill with indignation.

Bolt huffed behind me. "This, what you're doing now, this is a very bad idea," he said, but he drew steel and followed.

I came to Kera's door, pushed it open against resistance, and entered to see one of the maids sprawled across the rich carpet. My apology stuck in my throat when I saw the figure on the bed, thin and pale as a candle. Her skin sagged against her face like wax from the heat of her fever. Nothing disturbed the perfect stillness of her inert form save the tiniest flutter of motion in her throat that showed the diminishing beat of her heart.

Bolt shut the door, his jaws clamped.

"Where's the physician?" I asked.

The maids clustered around the bed didn't answer.

My voice rebounded from the richly paneled walls. "Where is her healer?"

Marya, who wore a smile as often as most people breathed, shook her head, scattering tears across the thick coverlet that covered Kera's form. "He left yesterday. The priest . . ." Her voice caught, but she tried again. "The priest . . ." She collapsed in on herself—some internal fortitude or support had been broken.

Serena, her face pale, finished for her. "The priest has already been and left as well." Her dark, green-eyed gaze turned from me to Kera, and she brushed her face with the tips of her fingers. "The physician said he'd never seen someone with the wasting disease fight so long or so hard."

The wasting. I fought to stay upright, as if I were a puppet and someone had cut my strings. How long had Kera known and hidden it from everyone? Her pulse fluttered again in her neck, like a small bird in the hand, struggling to be free and losing.

The pull of death called me to Kera's side, but grief sharper than a razor undercut the detached fascination I usually felt in its presence. This person, this friend, with her support and wry wit, would die, and soon. How often had she stood for me in court, taking the worst insults the other nobles had thrown at me and turning my anger into laughter with a lightning rejoinder? How often had she saved me from death with laughter, keeping me from insulting some idiot noble who kept a trained killer as his second?

Kera was dying, and whether she was about to go into eternity to meet Aer and Iosa and Gaoithe or simply cease, those left behind would mourn, relying on their imperfect memories and interpretations of her actions and motives to sustain them. I wasn't a healer or a physician, and none outside of legend had shown a supernatural power of healing. I couldn't restore her.

Sudden banging at the door couldn't distract me from my purpose. I removed my glove.

"Willet." Bolt's voice brushed my awareness as wispy and ethereal as the life that remained in Kera's body. "If she should die while . . ." He didn't finish. His oath would keep him from revealing too much in front of the maids, but I caught his warning. If Kera passed while I delved her, the shock of her death would break my mind. So the Vigil claimed. I had no reason to disbelieve them.

Her burning skin warmed my hand, an unnatural heat, before my awareness of the room narrowed to a point. Kera's eyelids fluttered open against the weight of her mortality, and I fell into their glazed depths.

Quiet. Such quiet I'd never experienced before as her memories and emotions flowed into me—then laughter and singing and my parents as seen from the perspective of a child, tall and flowing. I could see the imprint of her mother and father on the graceful features of myself and my sister, Gael. A scene floated past, at Father's bedside, debating and winning, convincing him to give his gift to my younger sister, to Gael.

Always, laughter filled life, laughter for the pure joy of living, laughter in celebration, even laughter in defeat and disappointment. A jolt ran through me, through the memories I lived, a tremor I felt as if I clung to a rope and the cords were breaking one by one. Startled, I knew myself as Willet again for a moment. I pulled myself loose from living her memories, prepared to leave before her death took me into eternity with her.

Her life flowed past me in a series of recollections and emotions I saw as a stream of colors as bright as the cloth that she and her sister used. One, luminous and bright beyond all the others, pulled at me, and I let myself fall into it like a man craving ablution.

My—Kera's—secret, kept safe from all but Gael: a passionate love for Rupert, uncle's handpicked suitor. I laughed at the joke. Oh, brilliant! By fighting uncle, the marriage long desired had been secured. My pretending forced resignation to a match made for money had granted my greatest desire. Memories of Rupert flowed through, past, and over me, a benison of warmth that sheltered me from the cold.

A tremor shook me, and the images of life faded, growing gray and indistinct, but one last recollection came forth, hidden from all: awareness of the wasting disease and impending death, and my attempt to keep it at bay until I could be married. Sorrow as deep as an ocean when the realization hit that all efforts to live that long would fail.

I pulled out of the delving as Kera breathed her last, the barest whisper of sound that pulled the final vestige of a luminous spirit from her body. The pulse in her neck gave one last flutter like the final effort of a dying dove and stopped.

The weeping of Serena and the other maids intruded on my awareness, accompanied by the pounding of the count at the door. I looked to Bolt, who met my gaze, searching my eyes for madness or abstraction. I swallowed against my grief. "I'm fine, but we should leave."

Bolt slow-blinked his frustration. "I think I may have suggested that earlier." He unlocked the door and stepped aside, allowing the count to enter with a pair of guards who were trying very hard to look intimidating.

"You will leave!" Alainn yelled.

"That's hardly the way to address your future kin, uncle," I said quietly. "Of course I will."

I saw his gut tighten as he laughed, his gleeful malice distilled by the presence of Kera's still form, and his servants looked upon him in shock. "You stupid, untutored peasant. You really don't know what her death means." He drew himself up, his dark eyes glittering in his imagined victory.

"Don't be coy, uncle," I said. "What does it mean?"

He smiled. "Oh no. The king made you a lord. Let him explain the requirements of nobility to you." He turned to his guards. "Put away your weapons. I wouldn't have it said I treated the newest member of the aristocracy roughly in my house."

Chapter 27

I left with my heart bouncing between my throat and chest. The stupid thing couldn't seem to make up its mind. Despite his diligent avoidance of me in public, I knew Gael's uncle well enough to know he wasn't bluffing. Men gifted with the opportunistic fortitude of Alainn never bluffed. They didn't have the stomach for it. Which meant what? He hadn't said, but I wouldn't have to wait long to find out. Gael would be at the keep, trying to bring the king's healer back to cure someone who'd already passed.

Bolt and I pushed our horses up the hill, pounding through the switchbacks until we arrived at the tor. My thoughts ranged out ahead of me, but beside me, Bolt's head swiveled back and forth, looking for signs of pursuit from the Vigil. We dismounted at the south end of the keep and ascended broad steps cut into the rock before entering the interior. Dawn light hit us as we climbed, and the spring sunshine warmed everything but the knot of dread that filled my heart.

The ride had served to crystallize my thinking. I knew of only one thing that could give Gael's uncle such cause for glee, but I couldn't fathom how he meant to accomplish it. King Laidir had given that grasping little excuse for a human the bride-price for Gael to marry me. And he'd given me his word that I would retain my title and claim to Gael's hand. How did Alainn intend to countermand the king?

Servants walked the broad corridor leading to Galen's apartments, but no guards or nobles could be seen or would be for some time yet.

When I pounded on Galen's door, no one replied. I'd expected Galen or Gael to open it almost immediately.

It was only after I started using the hilt of my dagger as a knocker that I heard muffled curses from within. Several of them seemed to be calling my heritage into question. Beside me Bolt snickered, and the clench in his eyes softened.

"Are you sure he's an educated man?" Bolt asked. "Most of what he just accused your ancestors of isn't even possible."

The door opened just enough for Galen to stick his egg-shaped head into the opening. Not young, he now appeared at least ten years older. Dark circles marred the flesh beneath his bloodshot eyes, extending down almost to his cheekbones, and his skin shone with the livid pallor of exhaustion.

"I said I'm tired, you lousy get of a cur and a—" He bit off the rest of his curse involving dogs upon seeing me. Grief pulled the anger from his countenance, replaced it with defeat, and he gripped my forearm. "I'm sorry, Willet, there's nothing more I can do."

I squeezed back, conscious of the glove I wore to keep the gift at bay. "Kera's passed, Galen. I'm trying to find Gael."

He shook his head as if he couldn't make sense of my question.

"The servants at the count's home told me Gael had left for the keep," I said. "I assumed she was coming to you."

"No, lad. I didn't leave Kera's side until all hope was gone."

I pulled a deep breath into my lungs. It didn't make sense. Nothing would have been able to force Gael from her dying sister's side except a chance to save her. So why had she left?

I hated the powerlessness of my ignorance. I didn't expect Galen to know the answer to my next question, but I had nothing to lose. "Count Alainn told me I didn't know what Kera's death meant, that I didn't understand the responsibility of the nobility. Something drove Gael to the keep, Master Healer. Do you know what it might be?"

Galen's face lost expression until only lines of fatigue and an unblinking stare remained. "The king will know." The door narrowed, but just before it closed I heard him whisper, "I'm so sorry, Willet."

I knew in my gut he wasn't talking about Kera's death.

Bolt and I ascended to the height of the keep, climbing the rest of the interminable stairs that led up to the throne room and the king's apartments. Court wouldn't be open for several hours, but the king's habits were known to me. Laidir and his guards would be in his offices. We skirted the throne room, our boots echoing against the stones in the emptiness until we came to the entrance.

"Lady Gael?" I asked.

They nodded, their expressions inscrutable.

I didn't bother arguing with Adair and Carrick about my weapons. I stopped long enough to unbuckle Robin's sword and divest myself of the daggers I carried. Laidir's guards smirked as a small pile of weaponry grew, but their expressions flattened as they looked at Bolt. To his credit, my guard didn't bait the king's protectors but deposited his weapons next to mine and remained still while Adair checked him.

I'm not sure what I expected when I came into Laidir's presence, but stony silence between him and Gael while the guards stared straight ahead, their faces impassive, wasn't it.

Gael turned to me, and my eyes savored the wealth of black hair and the way her profile, strong and sensuous even in the midst of quiet anger, revealed itself. Her brows, always expressive, held an arch of tension, even rebellion, though I could detect no animosity toward her from Laidir or his guards.

Bolt turned his back to the king and his guards and murmured past my ear. "Whatever happens here, remember we don't have much time. The Eldest will have this entire city looking for you in a matter of hours."

I nodded, but inside I quailed. Events were stacking up on me, and I didn't know how to get out from underneath any of them. The king's gaze flickered across mine, refusing to hold. Gael's deep blue eyes held me. If mortal man could be allowed a glimpse of heaven, it had to be found in the depths of a lover's eyes.

"My lady." For once, I didn't bother to keep the yearning out of my voice. "Kera has passed and your uncle said something about the responsibilities of the nobility."

I turned to Laidir, willing him to look me in the eye. "Your Majesty, he refused to explain. He said you would tell me."

Gael came toward me, and I thought for a moment she would throw herself into the aching emptiness of my arms, but she proved stronger than that. From a half a pace away she laid one hand on my chest, casting a glance back at the king before speaking. "The laws of Collum do not extend beyond its borders."

To my surprise, Laidir nodded his approval. "Count Alainn, as the head of a noble family possessing a gift, has the authority to arrange an advantageous marriage for the eldest daughter. Kera's death means Lady Gael will be required to fulfill her duties to Lord Rupert, if Count Alainn so decides."

I couldn't help but laugh my shock and bitterness. "If he so decides? He despises me. I'm the peasant lord. My king, you will allow this, after you promised me?"

Laidir nodded. "Lord Dura, I do not have the authority to overturn any portion of the *Legis Noblas*. Three-fourths of the nobles would have to agree to any contravention of the law."

I knew better than to even ask that the question be put to a vote. The aristocracy would never agree to diminish their own power. My face flushed at the memory of the count's mocking laughter. If I could goad him into challenging me in court, I could use the pointed end of a sword to force him to renounce his claim to Gael.

There were only two things wrong with that plan. First, the count wasn't nearly stupid enough to allow himself to be manipulated in such a way. Second, Pellin would have the court watched. Showing up there would land me back in a cell with the Eldest waiting to split my mind open like an overripe melon.

King Laidir's voice broke into my despair. "You have forgotten Lady Gael's counsel."

I hadn't. As if my hand had anticipated my heart, I brushed my fingers along the high cheekbones of Gael's face and across the parted lips that always stole my breath, accepting her most recent memories. "If you leave Collum, he will seek you out. First out of spite because you dared to defy him, but also because he covets your gift."

She smiled, and her fingertips traced a delicious curve up my neck before knotting in my hair, tight, defiant. "I will pass the gift to Uncle, and we will marry. He will have no reason to seek me out."

I shook my head, both in denial and wonderment. "You would impoverish yourself to live as my wife?"

Her lips found mine, and we melted into each other for a brief glimpse of eternity. As we parted, she laughed. "Oh, Willet, don't you know I have a different way of measuring wealth?"

I made one last attempt to be noble, hoping with every ounce of my heart's blood that I would be unsuccessful. "You will be one of the giftless, *gnath*, and I will be nothing more than a joke, the peasant lord driven from his home."

"No," Laidir said. I turned to see him rise from his seat on the dais. "Other kingdoms may not honor your title without a gift to exploit, but I can give you letters of introduction to the monarchs south of here. You're the best reeve I've ever had, Willet. King Sylvest of Aille is a friend and good man, he could use you." Laidir gave me a tight-lipped grin. "Considering the viper's nest that masquerades as his court, he's also likely to pay you enough to make you resent me."

"Thank you, Your Majesty." I bowed my head, overwhelmed by Gael and my king. Bolt cleared his throat, and the sense of urgency I'd been carrying as a knot in my gut returned. True love and royal favors wouldn't do me any good if I couldn't keep myself free long enough to find Elwin's killer.

I knelt before my king and then took my leave with Gael and Bolt in tow. Once we were alone I stopped, taking Gael's hands in mine, longing to remove my gloves. "I need your help."

She gave me a sad smile, and her hand came up to cup the side of my face. "Anything, Willet. You know that."

I tried to ignore the more intimate interpretations of what "anything" might mean. "Find Gareth and send him to Myle's workshop as quickly as you can."

Her brows clouded, but she nodded assent.

Bolt and I retrieved our horses and rode as quickly as we could without attracting attention back through the streets. While I basked in the favor of my king and the love of my betrothed, Bolt sat his horse, withdrawn and radiating discomfort. We rode in the tension of that odd mix of silence until we came to the small stone shack of Myle's workshop.

We tied the horses and entered without bothering to knock. No smoke rose from the unadorned chimney or billowed from the windows. Myle wasn't there. I took the opportunity to seat myself on one of the stools and considered the enigma that constituted my guard.

"Something troubles you," I said.

He eyed me as if I'd commented on the color of the sky. "It's my job to be troubled. I find it avoids surprises later on."

"You're a dour sort of fellow," I said. "Do you always expect the worst?"

He shrugged. "I have reasons. First, I'm hardly ever wrong. Second, if I am, it's a nice surprise."

I acknowledged his banter with a brief smile but wasn't deterred. "Something about Laidir and Gael bothers you."

"It's my job to be bothered."

"No," I averred. "This was different. This isn't a threat. Even if I live and Gael had refused me, my life would have changed."

He nodded, hopped from his stool, and paced the cramped interior of Myle's workshop. "The members of the Vigil don't have homes as most people do, Willet. They move around a lot." He looked at me and the crags of his lined face almost hinted at pleading. "Is that the life you would wish for Gael?"

I smiled past the foreboding this unaccustomed side of Bolt awoke in me. "You saw her. Do you think she would accept any life away from me?"

Instead of responding, he changed subjects. "You delved Kera. What did that tell you of Rupert?"

I didn't understand. "He's a good man—kind, attentive. Kera loved him."

"And do you think a marriage between Gael and Rupert would be unpleasant for either of them?"

I cut the air with one hand. "It's beside the point. It's not what Gael or I want."

Bolt faced me squarely at long last, as if he were finally speaking plainly. "We don't always get what we want."

Pellin sat at his table next to the oversized window, sipping from a glass that he occasionally refilled from a dusty bottle of dark red wine. Outside, sounds of frenzied construction rose from Criers' Square, like greetings in a crowded tavern meant for someone else. He tried to ignore them.

The Eclipse, an upscale affair down the street from the Merum library, boasted clear windows, soft beds, well-crafted furniture, and a solicitous staff. None of which could rescue the vintage before him. He shook his head. Why were northerners so adept at ale and so clumsy with wine? The bottle in front of him should have been uncorked a decade ago. He sighed. It was just as well. If it were enjoyable he would have been tempted to actually drink it instead of sipping it as a way to pass the time. Outside, an old man, passing by with a shuffling gait, stopped to peer at him.

Memory tugged at Pellin. He froze, his glass halfway to his lips, when Toria Deel, dusty and travel-worn, came through the door with her guard, Elory. The fire-haired islander, so different than the quick-tempered ancestors that sired him, scanned the interior of the inn before allowing Toria Deel to approach. She paused to undo the strip of black cloth that bound her hair behind her before approaching. The mercurial Elanian, with her dark, flashing eyes made Pellin uncomfortable. Young in the ways of the Vigil, she attempted to place demands upon him as Eldest that unnerved him. Elwin had been more to her liking. Pellin's older brother had seen nothing wrong in one of the Vigil being wooed by an apprentice.

Pellin gritted his teeth, but there was little to gain in gnawing the same old bone. Elwin was dead, and his decisions had been bequeathed to Pellin with the sword stroke that had severed him from life. At least Volsk wasn't here. The apprentice would be out for some time yet, gathering Bronwyn and the rest of the Vigil.

"You're late," Pellin said and then winced at the sound of impatience in his voice. He held up a hand in apology. "I'm sorry, sister. Events here have not proceeded according to plan."

"'If you want to make Aer laugh, tell Him your plans,'" she quoted. But her face held no trace of amusement to accompany the age-old jest. If anything, she became even more somber, the usual fire of emotions she wore on her skin banked and hidden from sight.

She sat down without preamble, pulling an oak leaf from her pocket. It was dark green at the center and at the base, fading to a lighter green around the edges. "Delve it," she said in response to his questioning look.

He shrugged, removed the glove on his right hand, and placed them lightly on the veins that ran its length. Disgust wreathed his features as he opened his mind and spiritual corruption oozed into his senses. For all intents, the leaf appeared normal, if a bit dark, but beyond eyesight it seethed with malice, its surface infused with corruption that fought against the sunlight. Pellin resisted the urge to break the contact. He slid his fingers closer to the stem, his touch confirming that the sickness had originated from the roots, evil drawn from the very earth and fed into every root, branch, and leaf. The oily feel carried the stench of death in his mind.

And it held something else as well, a hint of familiarity he couldn't place. He sought it, but the leaf's link with life, however twisted, had been broken for too long to reveal. With reluctance, Pellin broke the contact.

"How far past the boundary stone was it?"

Toria Deel shook her head. "No farther than the last check. The oak tree I took this from sits on the northwestern border of the ancient corruption. Some of the branches are still unaffected, their leaves hale and healthy to the touch."

She paused as the barmaid approached their table and waited until a glass twin to Pellin's was placed in front of her. Toria Deel filled it from the bottle and drained half of it before leaning back in her chair with her eyes closed, her face to the ceiling. "That's dreadful. You should have ordered ale."

The tremble in her fingers didn't subside until she drained the rest of the glass, but she didn't bother to refill it.

"Why were you so late in coming, Toria Deel?" Pellin asked. "The Darkwater is two days' ride from here." He flicked at the leaf still before them on the table. "This takes a moment."

She opened her eyes and tilted her head to meet his question. "Maybe I imagined it. I know what you think of me, Pellin. You delved me when I completed my apprenticeship, but I can read your tone and your eyes. I'm young. I'm impetuous." She gave a small laugh. "I'm Elanian."

Taking a deep breath, she asked, "Did you feel it?"

He nodded. "There was something, a hint of a memory besides the Darkwater and the presence of other plants and forest creatures, but the link has been severed for too long. I couldn't pick it out."

"Human," Toria Deel said. "It was stronger while the leaf was still attached."

Pellin's chest seemed too small to hold his panic. Collum and Owmead were at peace, free from drought and the wars that went with it. "Who would be foolish enough?" he spluttered. Aer help them, they didn't have the manpower to chase down a corrupted and find Elwin's killer at the same time.

Now she availed herself of the bottle again, pouring herself another glass, drinking, so scared she didn't bother to grimace at the hint of vinegar in the taste. "It was more than one, Eldest."

He stared at the leaf where it lay, mocking him and his gift.

Chapter 28

"Creation groans," Pellin whispered.

"Eldest?" Toria Deel asked.

Pellin jerked as if her presence surprised him. "It's a quote from the liturgy I say to myself whenever I'm surprised by the presence of evil. 'Creation groans beneath the curse.'"

Toria Deel searched the upscale inn, scanning each face before moving on. "Where is everyone? If people are returning from the Darkwater, we have a disaster on our hands. Everyone will have to be delved. We need every member of the Vigil here, gloves off."

He could feel his eyes trying to start from his head. "In a city of this size? Do you have any idea how long that would take? You can delve what, perhaps half a dozen souls a day before your mind shuts down?"

He should have chosen his words with more care. Her chin came forward at his tone. "What of you, *Eldest*? You keep reminding me how young I am."

He looked down, breaking away from the heat of her indignation. "Ten. Perhaps a dozen, but I would need to rest for several days afterward."

"But you're stronger than any of us." She shook her head. "I've seen you touch the reverence of an abandoned church and the grief from a decades-old grave cloth. How can that be?"

His lungs couldn't pull enough air. He wasn't meant to be Eldest. Curse Cesla and Elwin for getting themselves killed. "The gift exacts a toll, Toria Deel. We become more sensitive, yes, but that sensitivity means the memories of those we delve strike us deeper, come closer to the core of who we are. The difficulty of keeping the essence of the self intact increases over time."

Pellin cut his eyes to Toria Deel's guard, foreboding cutting through his self-pity and defeat. "Where are Peret and Bronwyn?"

She looked at him as if his question didn't make any sense. "He's here keeping watch over that rogue you're enamored with."

Pellin was shaking his head before she'd finished. "I sent him to bring you back from the Darkwater."

Toria Deel's eyes caught fire, as if Pellin were somehow to blame for Volsk's absence and possible jeopardy. "Bronwyn is delving the road to Bunard, tracking the path of those returning from the forest."

Horror filled Pellin at the extremity of Bronwyn's task, and a moment later, anger. "She's going to burn herself out."

Toria Deel shook her head. Her face still held the blush of youth so far removed from Pellin. "Go easy, Eldest. Laewan was her apprentice, almost a son to her."

Pellin clenched his teeth against his response, but it broke free anyway. "Cesla and Elwin permitted their attachment. And yours," he added. "I never approved of it."

Toria Deel straightened. "Your pardon, Eldest, if we are not made of stone. Perhaps when we have lived as long as you have our humanity will leave us as well. Then we will be the Vigil you desire—cold and calculating, without the inconveniences of personal attachments."

Pellin didn't respond to Toria Deel's rebuke. He'd gone too far.

"What of Dura?" Toria Deel asked.

It couldn't be avoided. He would just have to tell the tale again when Bronwyn reached Bunard. "Dura's vault opened and he killed three of the men working for Laewan. I had him imprisoned."

She shook her head, uncomprehending.

"The men were helpless," Pellin said. "Dura killed them to keep them from being questioned."

"Rogue," she spat. "You should have broken his vault when we first took him, Pellin."

"Perhaps," he sighed. "But Elwin's gift was freely given."

"And when has a rogue ever lived long enough to become one of the Vigil?" Toria Deel pressed.

"Never," Pellin conceded. "But just because a thing has never happened doesn't mean it never will."

She sat back, folding her arms across her chest, obviously unconvinced. "And did you find anything when you forced his vault, Eldest?"

He forced himself to meet that gaze, braced himself for the fire that would fill it. "I never got the chance. Bolt broke Dura from his prison before the attempt could be made."

Perhaps it was a blessing that she didn't erupt with accusations at the missed opportunity, that she sat in shock, her head shaking with little jerks as she considered and rejected the courses of action open to them. "You'll have to bring the orders of the church and the king into it now. Secrecy avails us nothing if we can't find Elwin's killer. It's folly to believe his death and the reach of the Darkwater aren't connected."

He nodded. "I know. Retrieve Bronwyn. If I'm going to browbeat the church and the nobility, I want to present as large a show of force as I can."

I waited, measuring time by the movement of shadows creeping across the walls of Myle's shop. Bolt stood by the door, his hand on the sword he wore like an extension of himself, content to wait.

How do you withhold trust from someone who saved your life? Yet, questions rattled around my brain, fighting for my attention, taking on a life of their own. They refused to be shunted to the side so easily as others' lives and memories. That's how I knew they were mine.

Every time I tried to think through Elwin's death I ended up in my own past. I imagined his body in my mind, the way he lay crumpled on the grass, collapsed in on himself, with Robin a few paces behind him, dead from blood loss against the floodwall. The former Eldest had been felled by a sword stroke to the head, a single blow that had failed to kill him immediately. I stood and wondered if I would come to regret that it hadn't. Robin, his sworn defender, had been cut down by weapons that hadn't been used since the last war, crescents.

The image of those weapons made my mind itch to think about

something else. Not one crescent wound marred Elwin's body. I didn't have a nice, neat trail of clues, but I had something nearly as convincing: a certainty in my gut that the facts of Elwin's death were linked to my memories of the last war. I shivered. No wonder the Vigil wanted to break the vault in my mind.

"I'm going to have to look at them again."

Bolt turned, his craggy face inscrutable. One day I was going to have to learn to read the furrows and wrinkles in his expression. "If you're thinking of trying to break your own vault, you're wasting your time."

Frustration at my ignorance and his reluctance combined to make me testy. "Are you ever going to tell me what you know? Because if you are, I'm going to mark the day on parchment. It will give me something to look forward to if I live that long. But if you're not, then you broke me out of prison so I could die somewhere else, which seems like a waste of time and effort."

His face didn't change much, but I got the impression of amusement. "If I told you everything now, things would be worse, much worse. I believe the Vigil needs you to live."

"Why?"

He almost smiled. "You spent a night in the Darkwater and came out alive and you're still alive."

I shrugged his explanation away. "I can't explain it. Ealdor's spent the last ten years trying to understand how, but the memories won't come."

"Why won't they?"

Even now, just thinking about trying to remember what happened set me to pacing, and I longed to run away from Myle's workshop. "Because something happened."

"What?"

I threw my hands up. "I don't know! Don't you understand? I've been over it and over it. I've been to see Ealdor nearly every week for ten years. If I tell you what I remember, it won't matter. It's not true!"

Now I had his attention. "What's not true?"

"My memories are a lie." I turned away, looking for something on Myle's shelves to distract me. "Everything I tell Ealdor stays the same up until I enter the Darkwater. After that it changes, but I never realize it. Do you want to know what Ealdor told me? I've told him a score of different versions of what happened before I managed to stumble my way out of the forest." I pointed north toward the caves of the tor and the bodies hidden there. "In my memories, those men died."

His eyes became as still as the rest of him. "There's something evil there."

I laughed, short and bitter. "You don't have to convince anyone. Everyone knows better than to go into the Darkwater. No one comes out alive."

I wasn't facing him, so he called me by name. "Willet." He paused. "Some do."

The furrows across his brow and the nest of crow's feet around his eyes showed not a trace of jest. "I live here, Bolt. I know better."

"Not often," he continued as if I hadn't said anything. "It's what the Vigil does. It's how they got their name. They guard the Darkwater, tracking any who blunder in and out during times of peace or who get driven in and escape during war."

I shook my head. "No one came after me."

Now he smiled. "You wouldn't have known it, but someone did. They must have thought you were lying, or that you'd managed to skirt the edge without entering the true Darkwater. It doesn't begin at the edge. That's a belief they've encouraged to keep people safe."

Cold, like the point of a dagger in winter, traced its way through my middle. They'd known about me. "But the night walks."

He shook his head at me. "Willet, any number of veterans wander in their sleep, trying to find healing for the horror of war."

"Why did they think I was lying?"

If it were possible for stone to grow still, that would have described his face. "You weren't killing people. Every man or woman who has survived the Darkwater at night has come back with a vault in their mind, perfectly normal, perfectly sane. Until the vault opens. Then they kill those around them, loved ones or friends, without discrimination or remorse."

I'd been a reeve for ten years. The memories garnered since the end of the last war remained with the clarity of an artist's brushstrokes in crimson. I picked out one more lurid than the rest. "There was a man. Gravin. He worked as a farrier. Everyone called him a gentle giant. He wouldn't even kill the mice in his shop. He'd trap them and take them out to the field." His bearded face with his sweet lopsided smile rose in my mind's eye. "He killed his wife and children one night, snapped their necks. The neighbors found him with his hands still around his wife's throat."

I looked at Bolt, his gaze giving me all the confirmation I needed. "He never went before the magistrate," I finished. "He just disappeared. We were told the king took care of it."

"The Vigil took him," Bolt said.

"They broke his vault."

He nodded. "Yes. Most likely they took him someplace away from the city. Then they delved him."

I shook my head. "You told me that's never worked. Why do they keep trying?"

"Because they don't know what's in the Darkwater that drives people insane." Bolt's hands lifted from his sides, mimicking the helplessness of the men and women he served. "They've never been able to heal anyone or find the cause. And when they're done, nothing's left—just emptiness where thoughts and love and compassion should be. But they keep trying."

The sound of hooves announced Gareth's arrival, but Bolt hadn't finished. "It won't do you any good to open your vault, Willet. Whatever is in there consumes you. You won't remember what you become."

I believed him, but deep inside something rebelled, refusing to cooperate. Something had happened to me in the Darkwater. "Memories don't just disappear."

He nodded his agreement. "No. They don't."

Chapter 29

Gareth stood by his horse. His face knotted at seeing Bolt before relaxing a fraction when I emerged from the shadows of Myle's workshop behind him. He cut his eyes to my guard before giving me a slight bow, as if he were concerned about giving offense. "Lord Dura."

I dismissed the title with a wave of my hand at the same time Bolt made a sound in his throat like he'd swallowed his laughter. "I don't think I'm going to be a lord much longer, Gareth—if I ever was."

The corners of his mouth tilted upward. "It never did fit you very well." He paused with his head tilted to one side. "Or maybe it was the other way around. You never seemed of a mind to play the part."

I thought about that, and an unexpected thread of joy bloomed in my chest. "No, I didn't, but I got what I wanted out of it."

Gareth nodded and smiled. "Lady Gael. You're a lucky man."

Bolt shifted his feet. "The longer we delay the more likely we are to run into trouble."

"What's this about?" Gareth asked.

I moved past him to my horse. "I'll tell you on the way." I decided to keep things simple. "Three men attacked us two days ago. We killed them, but I can't identify the bodies. We thought you might."

The hooves of our mounts clattered against the cobblestones, drawing attention, as if our horses conspired to surrender us to the Vigil. Bolt searched the crowd, but no one approached us or even appeared to take note.

Gareth knew the streets of Bunard as well as or better than I did. My request wouldn't be considered unusual, but the manner of its delivery and execution stuck out worse than a drunken libertine in a church pew. "You're in trouble, aren't you, my lord?"

Bolt shot me a look, his expression telling me not to betray the Vigil's existence. "You have no idea, Gareth. The less I tell you, the less people can hold against you."

His plain face knotted, and he actually looked angry. "Don't you worry about that. I owe you, Willet. You sent me back to alert Captain Ean while you stayed with the mercenaries."

I searched for the memory and found it, but hundreds of conversations with Ealdor had taught me to doubt myself. "I did?"

He shook his head at me. "How could you not remember?"

I stammered for a moment, relieved that at least that much of what I held in my head was true. "That was a long time ago."

Gareth rolled his shoulders. "It might as well have been yesterday for me."

On my right, I heard Bolt mutter under his breath. "Hold on to that thought."

We approached the keep from the southeast, weaving through alleys as we came closer to the religious section. We stopped at the last inn before the cathedrals and paid the stable hand a silver piece too many to keep our horses against our return. Bolt pulled a trio of unlit torches from behind his saddle and handed one to each of us.

"Keep it hidden," he warned. "We'll pretend we're visiting a grave." He cast a sour glance at the sky. A thin layer of clouds covered the sun, barely enough to cool the air. "Rain would have been nice. I don't fancy walking this close to the cathedrals with my face uncovered."

There were entrances to the caves on every quarter of the tor, but the ones on the north side didn't connect with the other three. As with every entrance, the access lay within the ancient graveyards surrounding the king's keep. This one lay adjacent to the Merum cathedral.

"You hid them there?" I asked Bolt. "Why, in the name of all that's holy, would you do that?"

He scowled at me. "It needed to be close and it needed to be cold.

If you'll remember, I had an errand at the cathedral I needed to take care of."

I pointed to the square where the criers for the four orders plied their trade. Workmen for each order busied themselves setting up wooden stages for the spring festival, Bas-solas. I shook my head in wonder. I'd almost forgotten. In the strangeness of my own life it seemed easy to forget that everyone else's kept going.

A crowd filled the square, but every eye was fastened on the man standing just outside the boundary, the speaker for the Clast. Red-faced and gesturing wildly, he hurled imprecations at the other criers and the crowd. "The gifts are a lie." Spittle flew from his mouth. "A man can choose to be whatever he wants to be. Who's to say I can't be a smith or a musician or a healer?" Half the crowd nodded with him, the other half looked confused. "We do not aggrandize ourselves with hoarded gifts like nobles. All men and women are one, none better than the others."

"Every organization needs a leader!" the Merum crier yelled. "Those with the gift to lead should do so."

I stood in shock that the crier had surrendered the daily office to confront the Clast.

"Not so," a voice cut in. Next to the screamer, another man stood, his face covered by a hood. "A man should lead because he has the vision and will, not because of some mythical gift for it."

The first speaker for the Clast inclined his head—more than a nod, but less than a bow. "I have the honor of introducing you to one of the Icons of the Clast, a man who leads because of his vision and labor, not because of some gift. A man who so steadfastly refuses recognition that he will not deign to show his face. A man who is one of us."

The criers tried to rebut, but when the men from the Clast descended the scaffold, the people began to disperse.

Bolt nudged Gareth and me out of our transfixion. "Come. The crowd will shield us as we make our way."

We kept our heads down and stepped in line behind a knot of men and women, pretending to be part of their group. They tracked along the high stone wall that formed the boundary of the graveyard and ducked into the entrance as they passed. Bolt led us to the right, away from any prying eyes that might have noticed, and we waited, watching the entrance for signs of pursuit.

Bolt pointed across the grounds toward a mausoleum set against the base of the cliff. “The entrance is just past there.”

We moved in a random pattern, pretending to search for a name among the stones until we could see the opening to the caves just beyond the molded white marker of some forgotten duke’s final resting place.

We cast one last glance back to make sure the graveyard remained empty and then darted into the cave as one. Bolt stopped to light his torch, and the yellow light threw lurid shadows against the rock walls.

Bodies filled hand-hewn ledges in the rock walls, compressed and stacked over time as Bunard had tried to accommodate the inexorable tide of the dying through the centuries. Most were nothing but collections of bones. Some wore the mummified grins of skin stretched like black parchment over their skulls. We shuffled our feet as we moved deeper into the catacomb to keep from tripping on the bones.

Ten paces into the cave the temperature dropped enough that wisps of mist from our breath floated against the light, gossamer on the breeze. I didn’t care for enclosed spaces, and the cave reminded me too much of the prison in the Merum cathedral. “How far?”

Bolt took a right turn that led us north. “Not far. I didn’t have enough time to take them any deeper.” He stopped, turning to Gareth and me. “We’re here. I found a niche in the rock a few paces up ahead on the left where I could lay them.”

I picked up on his cue and turned to Gareth. “See if you recognize the men. Tell us anything you can remember.”

His features danced in the torchlight, casting the question framed on his face in a dozen angles that danced and flowed into each other. “You’re not coming?”

I shook my head. “You don’t need me for this.” I reached forward to guide the torch he held into the flame of Bolt’s. “Make sure you get a good look.”

He nodded, and in a matter of heartbeats they disappeared behind a jagged wall of rock. Their voices echoed from the stone, giving them a richness they lacked in the open air.

"Crescents?" Gareth asked. "Haven't seen those in quite a while."

"Help me roll them over," Bolt said.

Grunts bounced from the walls, then silence.

Gareth's voice drifted to me through the chill damp, as ephemeral as the mist from our breath. "That's not possible."

"Why isn't it possible?" Bolt asked.

I could imagine Gareth's troubled expression, his head moving slowly from side to side in denial. "They're older, maybe a bit older than they should be," Gareth said, "but I know them. The last time I saw them was on the far side of a wedge of Owmead soldiers, huddled under shields."

Even from where I stood, I could hear Gareth's sigh. "These men have been dead for the last ten years."

"Obviously not," Bolt said.

"Then Willet was lying," Gareth's voice carried confusion and judgment. "He said they died."

"Did he say how?" Bolt asked.

Anger welled up through my middle, spreading to my arms and legs until the chill from the air faded and my face burned with shame and anger. The memory of the Darkwater set my feet itching to run from the cave, but I fought it off. I wanted to catch Elwin's killer as much as ever, but right now, more than anything, I wanted to know what had been done to me.

And I wanted recompense. With interest.

I stepped around the ledge of rock and waited for my eyes to adjust, but I didn't look at the faces of the dead. Not yet. Bolt looked at me as if I'd gone mad, and I saw him searching my eyes with his sword in his hand. I hadn't seen him draw it.

"I'm still me," I said. Gareth's expression said plainly he thought we were both insane. I nodded to him while I removed my sword belt and daggers. "We're going to need his help."

"You are an idiot," Bolt said, enunciating each word as if there were some chance I might not hear him from four feet away. "The last time you saw their faces"—he glanced at Gareth—"you blacked out for two days."

"And how long can we stay ahead of Pellin and the rest?" I shot back. "You've told me how the people with vaults end up, sitting, staring at nothing. Idiocy is exactly what I'm trying to avoid." I licked my lips and concentrated on not looking down at the three dead men at our feet. "You can bring me back if you have to. Just do what you did before."

Bolt's voice went flat. "I almost killed you."

"Thanks for not doing that," I said, but no one laughed.

"What are you planning on doing?" Gareth asked.

How much could I tell him? "The memory of these men causes something to break in my mind," I said. "I don't know why or how, but they're connected with Elwin's death."

Gareth nodded. Night walks and dream terrors were something every soldier knew about. "And you mean to look at them to see if there's a clue there," he said.

I nodded, ignoring Bolt's stony-faced disapproval.

"What do you need me to do?" Gareth asked. But instead of answering, I looked to Bolt.

"Help me hold him," he said finally.

Gareth nodded, and the two of them wedged their torches into crevices in the rock wall. I closed my eyes and knelt on the floor of the cave at the head of the three bodies. Bolt knelt next to me, his arms circling my chest, and Gareth grasped my ankles, ready to yank my legs out from beneath me if needed.

I took a deep breath and waited for the flood of memories that didn't agree. Then I opened my eyes.

Chapter 30

Firelight flicked across the man's face, weaving tongues of shadows against dead features beginning to purple. A scraggly beard of coarse black hairs hardly disguised the cleft chin or the prominent cheekbones that I'd seen ten years earlier on the other side of Collum. Recognition shattered my thoughts like glass, splintering them like thin pottery against heavy flagstones to the distant sound of laughter, mocking and cruel.

I blinked and the wall of the cave came into focus—Bolt with his arms wrapped around me, pinning my arms to my sides, and Gareth standing over the bodies that all lay facedown. My chest heaved, and my breath rushed in and out of my lungs with the high wheezing sounds of the desperate.

"How long?"

Bolt's arms dropped away, and he stepped around into view. "Only a few minutes. We turned the bodies facedown, but you just stood there with your fingers twitching. We waited for a while and then I closed off your wind. I didn't uncover your mouth and nose until you went limp." He shook his head at me. "This is foolishness."

"I can't fault you there." I turned to Gareth. "Can you check to see how much daylight remains? I want to be out of here as soon as we have enough darkness to cover our exit."

He looked happy to have an excuse to be somewhere else. As soon as he was out of earshot, I faced my guard. "I heard laughter, mocking me just before my mind left."

Bolt shook his head. "That could mean anything. How many sets of memories have you absorbed?"

I sifted through the past few days, trying to account for the accidental touches that had confounded me before I discovered the truth of Elwin's gift. "Maybe as many as twenty."

"Too many," Bolt said. "You're lucky to be sane at all. Most members of the Vigil can't take more than eight a day."

I looked at the bodies. "How can I be sure I'm sane?" I asked myself. My guard answered me anyway.

Bolt's smile held none of its usual mocking. "I've seen insane. You're still yourself, mostly."

I wanted to believe him, but I stepped back and slumped against the wall of the cave, fighting to keep my feet and my determination, but I was beaten. I had nothing to work with, and if there were any clues hidden within my mind, I couldn't get to them. In truth, I couldn't be sure of anything. The memories of what happened in the Darkwater seemed as real to me as any others.

"Nothing," I said to myself, though Bolt might have thought I addressed him. "There's nothing to work with."

"You're giving up too easy," Bolt said. "I'd heard you were better than this. I heard that Willet Dura could see past the façades men use to hide the truth."

I jabbed a finger at the bodies. "You think this is easy?" When he didn't answer, I went on. "I need something to work with, guard, and neither you nor your masters have given it to me. Despite almost getting killed by men who should be a decade's worth of dead by now, we've got no way to—"

I stopped, unwilling to breathe lest I scatter the thread that drifted through my mind. I grasped it, holding it gently with my thoughts, as if it were the filmiest wisp of spider's web. "I'm not the first." I shook my finger at Bolt. "You said so."

He nodded, but I hardly noticed as I tried to trace the strand of thought back to the next clue. The men on the bridge. I'd been focused on the wrong ones. The southerners had lived in the Darkwater, no matter what my mind had said, for the last ten years, but the man commanding them hadn't.

"Before they called you back to protect me," I said, my excitement growing, "how long had it been since you'd served the Vigil?"

Bolt's eyes narrowed. "Five years come Long Day this summer."

"Tell me about Laewan," I commanded.

He shrugged. "I didn't know him well. I saw him a few times around Owmead and Collum in the years before I left the Vigil's service. Despite what you might think, Willet, the members of the Vigil can go a year or more without seeing each other."

I nodded, smiling. "But not five, and certainly not ten."

A light flared in his eyes, and I spoke to it. "Laewan commanded those men on the bridge, but they'd been in the Darkwater for the last decade, waiting."

"Waiting for what?"

I shook my head as a cold certainty lodged itself in my gut. It was like a game of ficheall. I'd been worried about pawns while knights and kings were after my head. "What is the Vigil's primary purpose?"

Bolt's eyes narrowed, but he answered my question anyway. "To track down the killers among us that people without their gift can't find."

He hadn't gone far enough. "And what if the killer was one of their own?"

Bolt stared at me for a handful of heartbeats before he nodded. "We told you it was possible, warned you against it. Sometimes one of the Vigil will drive themselves past the point. The walls they erect in their minds to keep the memories separated can fail. The mind can't withstand it."

I nodded. "And that's the other reason every member of the Vigil has a guard. To put them down if they go insane."

Bolt shook his head. "It's not insanity, not the way most people think of it. It's the price of service."

"Tell me how that looks." My heart banged against my ribs. I wanted to be wrong, but I'd felt the struggle in my head.

"They're totally incoherent. The memories of dozens or even hundreds of people come crashing together, and the mind can't sort them. Their speech becomes garbled and their actions are worse. They lose control of their limbs, jerking and twitching. They can't walk more than a few steps without falling down." His voice trailed off at the end.

An image of Bolt standing over me, his sword bright and sharp, poised for the mercy stroke, came to me, and I shuddered. "How many times in the history of the Vigil has a guard taken the life of his charge?"

He squinted. Maybe he searched for some reason to avoid answering me. "Four. But all of those were at least a dozen centuries ago."

The way he clipped his words at the end practically screamed "Half truth!" but I ignored it. "And how many times has a member of the Vigil taken his guard by surprise and killed him?"

His blue eyes narrowed. "Never."

"Until Laewan," I said.

"He lost himself," Bolt said. "Nothing more."

But his expression told me he didn't believe it. "The ability to surprise his guard and kill him doesn't sound like he lost himself." I shook my head. "No. It's something else—and what's more, you know it."

The curtain I'd seen so often on Bolt fell across his eyes again, like a sudden darkness that takes a man unaware, like the shock of night. A muscle in his cheek jumped just before he spoke.

"Laewan delved you," he said.

Of course. Foolish, I should have seen it earlier. "When?"

Bolt shook his head. "That's not the right question."

"How can that not be . . ." I stopped. *Aer have mercy.* "How often?"

"Often enough. Members of the Vigil keep a written record of their contacts," he said. "In case something happens. You're in them, of course."

I closed my eyes, hardly needing to ask the question. "And when was the last time Laewan delved me?"

To his credit, he didn't try to duck the question or shade his answer. "Just before he disappeared. By all rights he should have broken your vault and been done with it, or at least advised the rest of the Vigil about you, but he kept the knowledge of you secret."

I threw my hands up in surrender. "Why?"

He shrugged. "It might have been nothing more than curiosity."

"Pellin doesn't believe that. I don't even know what Laewan looks like." Bitter laughter escaped me. "No wonder Pellin suspects me. I have the good fortune of having survived the Darkwater, and his man goes missing after he last delves me."

"I guarded him for years, Willet," Bolt said. "He's a good man."

"I tend not to bother with those distinctions when someone is trying to kill me. You said it yourself—the Vigil has never gotten anything useful from delving the mind of those broken by the Darkwater. So why would Pellin agree to delve me?"

I let the question and the weight of silence work on my guard, refusing to speak, forcing him to come to the realization he steadfastly wanted to avoid.

"He thinks you've stolen Elwin's gift," he said at last. "And he thinks you've somehow managed to turn Laewan as well." He rubbed his forehead. "But I don't know how he came to that."

I laughed. "Does the Eldest tell you everything?"

He shook his head. "He's only been Eldest for a few days."

I shrugged away his objection. "Elwin had been planning to relinquish his gift for years. Pellin knew he would be Eldest as soon as he did so."

I tried to remember the face of the man at the bridge, the one who'd driven the southerners before him, but nothing came. I needed confirmation, but I knew without a doubt I'd seen Laewan before, and often.

Gareth walked into the chamber with torch in hand. "The sun has set, Lord Dura, Master Bolt. And it's started to rain."

"Where do we go?" Bolt asked.

That knot in my gut tightened. I knew better than to make a decision in anger—they rarely turned out well—but I wasn't in the mood to be sensible. Sensible would have been to run and not stop running until my feet hit the sands of the southern continent. No. Pellin and the rest of the Vigil held knowledge I wanted. Why did I night-walk? Why did the stares of the dead hold so much fascination for me? Why did the faces of men I'd fought with a decade ago, men who should be dead, break my thoughts?

"We're going back to court."

"What on earth do you hope to accomplish there?"

I looked at the man who'd rescued me, who might kill me. "There are too many holes in my head. I need information, and I know how to get it."

The rain allowed us to keep our hoods up and our faces hidden from the eyes of any of the Vigil who might be looking for us. I still wasn't convinced they'd be searching. Custos had impressed me with their need for secrecy. I didn't see them breaking cover for the likes of me. If everything he'd told me about the abilities of the Vigil was true, they only needed to exercise a little patience and they could run me to ground at their leisure.

I didn't bother to stop by my meager quarters for a change of clothes. Dirt matted my tunic, mud from my swim in the river spattered my cloak, and it all smelled of earth and sweat. The nobles in Laidir's throne room were always insulted by my presence. My disdain for the niceties of court would be deeply offensive.

Every eye would be watching me, which was exactly what I wanted.

We came into the keep by the western side, the smallest of the main entrances and the least used, and climbed the dark stone steps toward the upper level and the king's throne room. We'd missed the evening meal. That was usually concluded by sunset, but the real entertainment would have only just begun. Under bright candlelight, the nobles would dance, drink, and laugh into the hours of the evening.

We came to the entrance, and the guards balked at my appearance. "The court might take exception to your dress, Lord Dura," the one on the right said.

I knew both of them as solid men. We'd laughed over a tankard or two. "I'm counting on it, Sevin."

The guard on the left, a crusty sergeant named Ren, laughed. "Are you picking another fight, then, Lord Dura?"

I laughed and let a twinkle shine in my eye. I needed the guards to let me through. They had the power to turn me back if they suspected I meant disrespect to the king. I'm pretty sure my appearance qualified. "You never can tell, gentlemen. You never can tell."

Sevin's eyes gleamed. "That would be something to see. I missed the last one. As the king's guard, I'm honor bound to ask you if you mean him any disrespect."

I shook my head, sober and earnest once more. "I do not. You know how I feel about King Laidir."

"Aye," Ren said. "That we do."

"But," I added, "the rest of the nobles are another matter."

"Well then," Sevin said, "I think we should step inside to make sure you don't insult the king with your dress." He winked. "We'll be watching you very carefully, Lord Dura."

I nodded. "I thought you might."

We stepped inside the court to the sound of music. Once through the doors, Bolt pulled me to a stop while he closed his eyes, swaying in time to the beat of the drum. I saw the care lines on his face ease, and in that moment I realized my guard had the soul of a poet, even if he didn't possess the gift.

"You're not really planning on starting a fight, are you?" he asked when he opened his eyes once more.

I shook my head. "No, but I'm hoping one of the Vigil will be here. I'm counting on their need for secrecy, and I need the information they have. If I threaten to expose them, I think they'll surrender the knowledge I want."

The creases in his face came back, the music forgotten. "You know it's my duty to prevent you. Such a thing is considered tantamount to an attack."

I nodded. "I suspected as much, but you're on the run with me. Sooner or later you will have to choose your allegiance."

He shook his head. "You and the Vigil only think you're fighting each other. There's nothing for me to choose."

"And you think Pellin will accept that explanation?"

His mouth compressed into a line. "Probably not." A crowd of nobles moved before us, rotating in counterpoint in a pair of large circles to the strains of the music. "There might not even be any members of the Vigil here."

I smiled and pointed to various members of the four orders decorating the outskirts of the room in the colored robes of their sects. "That's okay. If what you say is true, at least one of those is here watching for me. They'll send word." I turned to face Bolt. "When the Vigil comes, I'll threaten to expose them to the entire court. All we have to do now is wait."

Bolt shook his head, pointing toward a man standing at the right of Laidir's dais. "No you don't."

Volsk, attired in a well-cut tunic and hose of understated blue, stood to one side, his head working back and forth as he scanned the room. I waited until his gaze latched on to me and he pushed himself away from the wall, drifting in our direction. A pair of church functionaries followed him, their red and brown robes marking their allegiance to the Merum and Servant orders.

Clever man, I thought. Bolt might fight Volsk, but he wouldn't attack members of the church who were just following orders.

"There . . ." I began.

"I see him," Bolt said. "You know I won't fight them for you, and I won't let you attack them."

I smiled. "I'm not planning on using my sword."

Without waiting for his objection, I entered a gap in the outer circle. I held up my hand as the men moved in the opposite direction from the women. I hadn't bothered to remove my gloves, and I couldn't help but notice the dirt caked onto the leather from the day's adventures. The countess opposite me noticed it as well when our palms smacked together. When she caught sight of me she gasped, but I held her fast. Unwilling to make a scene, she completed our promenade. I laughed as she scrubbed the hand against her dress before raising it again.

I processed with the rest of the men, moving around in a slow circle as the musicians played through the refrain. Mutters built around me, and stares gathered to me as a flame draws moths.

Perfect. Soon, every noble in the room would have their gaze fastened on me. Out of the corner of my eye, I saw Volsk approaching, his face a mask of confusion as he took in the state of my clothes, a splash of mud against the rainbow backdrop of court. Even the least of nobles could bring an accusation in court, and if the accused party were present, they were obligated to respond. Volsk was walking right into my trap.

I saw women jockeying with each other, exchanging places in their effort to avoid contact with me. The notes of the refrain cascaded into the next verse, and I raised my hand. When a woman of middle years, dressed in deep shades of red that accented the sable wealth of her hair, clenched my hand, I gulped, cursing myself for my stupidity. *Oh, Aer, how could I have been so foolish?*

"Lord Dura," the voice purred at me, the nails digging through the leather of my glove and into the back of my hand.

"Duchess," I murmured, trying discreetly to pull my hand away. She gripped me fast. "I pray you pardon my indiscretion."

Her eyes gleamed with triumph. "I will not," she whispered. "But more to the point, neither will my husband."

Better than any player or storyteller, she donned the horrified look of the affronted and stepped back as the music switched, and in the same fluid motion she struck me across the face. "You dare!" Her screech filled the hall.

I looked left and right, saw that the lords and ladies closest to the duchess were allies of the duke. Only then did the magnitude of my blunder become apparent. I'd given the duke the insult he craved at last. It was no surprise when unseen hands spun me around and I saw a closed fist streaking toward my face, the opening salvo that would lead to a challenge, a fight with the duke's hired sword, and my death.

Chapter 31

I didn't see the point of letting the duke hit me since I was about to die anyway, so I caught his hand just short of my face. Dark like his brother, with the touch of gray at his temples that the women at court seemed to favor, his eyes widened in fury. I tried to focus, but I could feel the skin of his hand through a tear in my glove.

No, not now, I thought. But the gift didn't listen to me. I fell through the tunnel into the duke's eyes, and a wash of memories spilled over me. I tried to pull away, but the pull of my hand was as feeble as the dying twitch of a fish in the bottom of a boat. His memories flooded through my mind as his hand held me fast. Time slowed, and my heart took an eternity to fill and a longer one to squeeze the flow of blood through my veins. A life of power and the desire to increase its reach and exercise took root in my mind.

I relived what the duke would never admit, not even to himself: a silent satisfaction that his brother had died, removing a threat to his title and all that went with it. And I saw something else. . . .

My cheek stung, and I stumbled back, tripped over something soft, and ended up on my backside. His professed hatred of me was a sham, an appearance he donned like a rich red cape that completed his façade.

"You mock us, Lord Dura, with your presence and your disdain. Until now I have refrained from challenging you out of respect for my king. This, despite the fact you murdered my brother." The duke looked to his wife as the entire court gathered into a broad circle around us. On the dais, I saw Laidir rise from his throne and begin the descent to the floor, his face stricken.

"My lady," the duke said with a bow. "Though it pains you, I pray, would you please recount the insult this, this lord, so impudently assaulted you with."

I couldn't help myself. I started clapping. Titters from the crowd deepened the duke's color, and he swept his eyes across the assembled nobles, silencing them.

The duchess curtsied to her husband, her eyes mere slits, raking across me with the venomous stare of an asp. "When I commented on Lord Dura's dress, he replied that filth may be worn on the outside, but in court it usually adorned the inside, and he cited you and your brother as examples."

The crowd gasped in concert, as if the cue caller at a play had held up the sign.

Nobles parted, and Laidir strode into the circle. "I trust you have witnesses to verify your accusation, Duchess?"

The duchess curtsied again, not quite as low as she had for her husband, but low enough so that the king could find no fault with it. "Of course." She rose and swept her hand behind her. "Duchess Prevar and Countess Caite were next to me in the promenade."

The women stepped forward and curtsied in tandem. I found myself admiring the coordination with which my duel and death were being orchestrated. How long had the duke been waiting for me to slip up and give him the opportunity to issue his challenge?

"It is as the duchess says, Your Majesty," the countess said. The duchess nodded her affirmation.

I pitied Laidir in that moment and wished it had been possible to spare him the coming spectacle. My death would serve to diminish his prestige for some time. I would have liked to avoid that. Over his shoulder, I caught sight of Volsk, his unblinking stare impossible to interpret. Angry? Avid? I couldn't tell.

"Very well," he said, turning to the duke. "I take it, Duke, that you will wish satisfaction."

The duke's smile showed all his perfect teeth. "Of course, Your

Majesty." He turned to fix his gaze on mine. "Since Lord Dura has established the precedent of exacting justice here in court, I demand satisfaction immediately."

"Of course you do," the king said with a sigh. "And will you be engaging Lord Dura yourself?" The king's tone became pointed, and I heard more than one lord and lady gasp at the implied insult.

A muscle jumped along the duke's jawline. "There is no need, Your Majesty. I think honor will be served by allowing our seconds to duel. Lord Baine will stand for me."

The crowd and the king cut their eyes to the whippet-like man in his late twenties standing to one side of the duke. Baine smiled as if I'd given him a gift and raised both arms above his head, stretching before turning to one side and flowing into a lunge with the smooth fluidity of honey pouring from a jar.

The duke favored me with an oily smile. "Do you have a second within the king's court willing to stand for you, Lord Dura?" He took an exaggerated look at the crowd to the sound of laughter. "It appears not. It seems you will have to fight."

I could see two possible outcomes to a duel with Baine. He could toy with me to make an example of anyone who dared to insult the duke. Or he could make an example of me by killing me as soon as our swords crossed. I couldn't figure out which I preferred.

Laidir turned to me, his gaze asking me to find some way to extricate my life and his prestige from the duke's trap. "What say you, Lord Dura? Is there some reason you've favored the court with your attire? Would you gainsay the duchess's account?"

I saw the invitation in the king's offer, but this part of court protocol I knew as well as any man. The duchess had closed the trap with the inclusion of two witnesses. The king might delay the duel if I denied the charge, but in the end the duel would happen, and the longer we put it off, the greater the loss of the king's prestige would be.

Of course, I could always take the opportunity to try to run away, but the duke had enough resources to ensure I appeared for the duel, even if his men had to drag me there.

I bowed. "I will not bother to deny the charge, Your Majesty, but I will not confess to it either. The duke means to have my blood."

I cast about for some means to defeat Baine. I moved over to him, removing the gloves with the tear that had betrayed me. "That was well played," I murmured, offering my hand.

He eyed my right hand and with a smile extended his left. I nodded, though in truth I doubted I could have hurt him enough to affect his grip. I took his left hand in mine and let myself tunnel through into his eyes.

Memories of hunger and discipline washed over me, countless strokes of the sword and a soaring exultation at each victory. I unclenched and stepped back, sorting through his memories, struggling to use what I needed and wall off the rest. I knew two things with certainty: No amount of death would ever satisfy Baine's hunger. And I had no chance of defeating him. He had mercilessly eliminated every weakness in his form and technique just as ruthlessly as he would dispatch with me. And he was gifted. True, it wasn't pure, but in a few seconds my body wouldn't know the difference.

Laidir scanned the crowd. "Is there anyone here who would stand as Lord Dura's second?" Laughter filled the throne room, and the flush that crept above my collar mirrored the king's.

I heard a sigh, and Bolt shouldered his way through the press. "I will stand."

The duke laughed. "Here is sport indeed. The peasant lord will have a peasant do his fighting for him." He shook his head, his eyes glittering colder and harder than agates. "But no, I think not. It is Lord Dura's blood I want, and it is his blood I will have. Only the nobility may issue or accept a challenge here."

Bolt looked at me, his face puckered as if he'd eaten a bushel of persimmons. "You're a nuisance."

"On that we agree, peasant," Lord Baine said. "One that I intend to eliminate."

Bolt dismissed him with a brief shake of his head and turned to address Laidir, reaching within the recesses of his tunic to tug on a leather cord around his neck. "Will this satisfy the dictates of your court, Your Majesty?"

He held a silver medallion worked in flowing lines that surrounded a miniature sword. Tarnish had blackened the metal until only the broadest outline could be seen.

Laidir took it in his hands, a lopsided grin showing his bemusement. "I haven't seen one of these since I was a boy." The crowd quieted, sensing the king's surprise. "Are you really an Errant?"

Bolt nodded. "Retired mostly, but once given, the title remains." He turned to the duke. "And it's a designation all of the kingdoms of the old empire must honor. Collum is bound to recognize the title."

The duke laughed, but his eyes held the glitter and frustration of rage. "Do you think your death will save him, Grandfather? Once you are dead, Lord Dura will find some other means of insulting his betters—be it a week or month or even a year from now—and the peasant lord will have to stand for himself eventually." He laughed. "Why not take your medallion to the tavern and spend your final years selling tales of errantry to the guards in return for ale?" The duke shrugged. "Dura brings death wherever he goes. Why die for him?"

Bolt's craggy face never shifted expression. "Be quiet. I don't like it when men I despise say things I agree with."

I would have laughed at Orlan's splutters if I hadn't been preoccupied with Bolt's danger. He didn't know that he was about to duel someone with a physical gift.

Orlan turned to Baine. "Finish him quickly," he snarled.

Laidir turned to the duke, his eyes hooded in the candlelight overhead. "Duke Orlan, is there anything I can do to dissuade you from this?"

The duke's expression, too avid to be called a smile, stretched his lips tight against his skull. "Nay, Your Majesty, I have awaited this day since your reeve brought shame upon my family."

The king nodded. "If it is blood you demand, Duke, it is blood you will have. But I will remind you that your brother stood convicted by his own actions."

The duke didn't bother to respond. I jerked at the tug on my sleeve and turned to see Bolt standing at my elbow. "Swap swords with me," he said. The craggy wrinkles in his face were set in concentration. "Robin's is a bit better than mine."

I nodded, tried to speak, but two sets of memories and the realization that Bolt's history was far different than I'd suspected contrived to muzzle me. I unbuckled the sword and managed to unhinge my jaws as we traded. "Lord Baine is a gifted killer," I whispered. "The sword is his life."

"'A blade has two edges,'" Bolt quoted. "But thanks for the warning."

The king motioned the crowd back to the walls, an order they were loath to follow. I saw Sevin and Ren pushing them back, their faces lit with the avid attention of onlookers at a spectacle. Sevin gave me a smile, as if I'd arranged the entire event for his pleasure. *Idiot*.

Baine shed his cloak and stretched again, bending double before stretching his arms behind him. Bolt unlaced the knot at his throat and folded his soiled cloak. He drew Robin's sword and extended his arm, waggling it, testing the balance. I saw him adjust his grip the merest fraction and repeat the process before nodding to Laidir.

The king backed away, and the two men drew within three paces of each other before stopping, swords ready, their free hand raised behind them.

"Begin."

Baine darted, less than a lunge, but more than a swordsman's step. His blade whistled toward Bolt's throat.

I heard the parry, but I must have blinked, because I didn't see it. Bolt stepped back two paces and sheathed his sword while Baine swayed in astonishment as a thin line of red appeared on his neck.

The assembled nobles watched in horror as the line separated and became a trio of rivulets that flowed down toward his tunic. Baine lifted his free hand to his throat, stared at it in shock when it came away painted crimson. I heard him try to draw breath, his mouth working and his free hand groping the air. His knees buckled, the stunned look still on his face. Then he fell forward, the sound of his sword loud as it clattered against the stones. Blood spread into the joints of the floor.

Even Laidir looked shocked, but he recovered. He turned to Duke Orlan, who stared at his hired sword as if he expected someone to wake him from a bad dream. "You're having an inauspicious day, Duke Orlan. Replacing a swordsman of Baine's value will be difficult, I'm sure." He smirked. "Of course, if you find it necessary to take offense with Lord Dura in the future, you have the right to challenge Lord

Dura and fight yourself." He paused to glance at Bolt, who stood at my side, his face craggy with irritation. "Of course, you may want to give some thought to that since Lord Dura can refer your grievance to his second."

The duke turned his attention to the king, his eyes blinking in the candlelight, trying to focus. "No. I'll not give him the opportunity."

Laidir's brows drew together over his hazel eyes, taking the duke and duchess in the sweep of his gaze and his voice filled with displeasure. "Then I would suggest, my lords and ladies, that we dispense with such trumped-up challenges in the future."

I checked the crowd surrounding us, their expressions a mix of horror and loathing I'd become accustomed to. At some point, Volsk must have left. I grabbed Bolt by the arm and tried to leave. "We need to get out of here."

He looked at me with a mixture of annoyance and surprise. "Get out? We should never have come here in the first place. First you want to come here, then you want to leave. Do you have to learn everything the hard way?"

I shook my head. "No. I saw something when I touched the duke."

His eyes narrowed until I could barely see their color. "What does he have to do with you?"

"Nothing," I said. "That's just it. He—"

"Too late," Bolt said, his voice dead. He nodded toward a pair of figures heading toward us—Pellin and Allta.

CHAPTER 32

Pellin and his guard were still twenty paces away when a commotion at the door to the throne room put a stop to Sevin and Ren's open-mouthed gaping at Bolt. Gareth, bearing a cut along one shoulder that bled freely, came running in.

"Sire, we've been attacked!" He stood, chest heaving, and I watched as his color lightened another shade.

Laidir strode toward the bleeding reeve, his quartet of guards shadowing him with their swords drawn. More than once they steered the king away from Bolt. Laidir tapped one of his guards, Carrick, on the shoulder. "Bind his wound before he passes out on us."

Without hesitating, the guard ripped Gareth's cloak into strips, folded one into a tight bundle and used the rest to press it into his wound. He gasped and paled before he steadied, and I saw a bit of color return to his face.

Pellin and Allta stood close enough for me to feel their breath, but they waited.

"Speak, man," the king commanded Gareth. "Who attacked?"

Gareth cut his eyes to me, waiting for me to grant him permission to speak, before he bent double. "Southerners, Your Majesty. Half a dozen men with crescents forced their way into the guardroom." He stepped toward the king, found his way blocked with a pair of sword points at his chest. Gareth raised his hands above his head. "Your Majesty, I've alerted the keep guards."

Laidir's brows rose. "You roused five score men to fight a handful?"

Gareth nodded, neither shamed nor apologetic. "They're gifted, Your Majesty."

Laidir's face paled, and his gaze took in Bolt's presence at my side. "Do you have knowledge of what their goal might be, Lord Dura?"

I nodded. "By your leave, my king, may I depart to investigate?"

Laidir nodded his permission, but his voice held enough steel for a dozen swords. "You will give me your report directly after, Lord Dura." He turned to a pair of his guards. "Get every guard not already on duty into the halls." He looked around the room at the nobles adorned in their garish finery. "And commandeer as many of these fops who wear blades as you have to. It's about time they lived up to the oath they swore."

I'd moved to follow Gareth back down to the prisons, when Laidir's voice cracked like a whip in my direction. "Not you."

I turned to see him staring down Pellin and Allta. "You will remain with me."

Pellin's blue eyes widened, and I saw his expression flash between refusal and indignation before settling into stiff resignation. He bowed like a piece of parchment being folded in half. "I am at your service, Majesty."

"Willet is still my subject," Laidir said. "He will return."

I nodded and turned on my heel to follow Gareth out of the throne room.

"Out with it," I said to Gareth as soon as we'd passed from hearing.

His color paled again, but the bleeding from his shoulder had mostly stopped. "It's the men we saw in the caves. Not the dead ones—their comrades," he added, as if one of us needed reassurance. Under the circumstances, I was just as happy he'd taken a moment to clarify. "I didn't want to say anything in front of the king."

"At least somebody around here thinks before they speak," Bolt muttered.

We descended the countless stairs to get to the bottom of the king's tor, passing through the Hall of Remembrance with its weapons and then by the offices of the king's administrators and Galen's quarters before Gareth took us outside the halls of the keep to get to the prison level at the bottom. We entered the hallway to the guardroom from the south side to the sounds of men shouting, but without the clang of weapons.

Bolt's chest relaxed, and I saw him exhale in relief through pursed lips. "It's over. The southerners wouldn't bother to yell, dying or not."

We strode into a bees' nest of activity filled with screams and moans of the injured, guardsmen and servants running everywhere. And bodies.

"Aer have mercy." Gareth raised his hand and traced the sign of the arcs on his forehead.

I counted twenty dead guards, men I'd known for years, before we saw the first southerner. For once, the eyes of the dead held no allure for me. My revulsion ran too deep. Blood covered everything, as if buckets of crimson paint had been tossed into the cavernous guardroom.

On the far wall by the door leading to the cells, I saw four bodies in tattered battle dress, their skin a deep olive, each man holding a razor-sharp crescent. I pulled my gaze away before I could recognize any of them but then noticed a body different from the rest—soft, without the muscle, padded or otherwise, that came with the exertions of the sword or other honest labor.

Andler.

Death had hardly changed his color, but the haughty expression was gone, replaced by the surprised look of a man whom eternity has taken unaware. Arrows and crossbow bolts riddled his body. For a moment, a strange anger burned in my chest that men who'd served my king with honor should somehow be grouped with Andler in death. The keys to the cells were still in his hand.

I grabbed Gareth by the arm, pointing to the dead merchant. "What is he doing here?"

We stepped carefully to avoid slipping on the blood of friends and foes mixing at our feet and came to the open door leading to the cells. Shouts beyond it testified to the frightened state of the prisoners. At the entrance, a guardsman's body, Ordal, lay crumpled, his throat cut and his hands resting against the door.

I pulled my sword and stepped through the doorway and over another of the dead southerners. Two more of the former mercenaries, riddled by bowshot until they resembled overgrown prickle-hogs, sprawled amidst the broken furniture on the floor. Prisoners cowered in the corner of their cells or clamored at the bars, depending on their disposition.

"They're all still here," Gareth said. "If they meant to free any of them, it failed."

I might have nodded, but I doubted Gareth's assumption. Something else was at play here, and my gut, where I usually kept my intuition, screamed the answer at me. I ignored it. I'd been wrong before, not often, but even if I was right about Andler and the southerners being here, I would need a very convincing argument to keep Pellin from cracking my mind open like a hen's egg.

I waved Gareth forward, breaking the trance the sheer amount of blood and bodies seemed to be weaving on him. "Gareth, how well do you remember that last day of the war?"

His stare went past and through me until it saw ten years into the past. "Like it was yesterday."

I nodded. Perfect. I couldn't afford to be wrong. "How many of the southern mercenaries were there?"

He shrugged as if the question were inconsequential. "Twelve. You know that, Lord Dura."

"I know," I said. "I just wanted to be sure. We lost one to bow fire after you returned to the captain, and the signs indicated one of their number was killed during the murder of Elwin and Robin, bringing their number to ten." I gestured at the bodies of men littering the floor around us. "How many of those men are here?"

Gareth went back to the entrance to the cells, high-stepping over the limbs of the fallen. When he got back, surprise lit his face. "There are seven." He shook his head. "With the three we saw in the caves, that's all of them."

Bolt looked at me as if he wanted to pry open my skull and read my thoughts for himself. I turned and walked to the last cell, the one I'd never reached days earlier when I'd almost driven myself insane absorbing memories that weren't mine. None of the doors to the cells were open and none of the prisoners had been freed, despite the fact that the keys were in Andler's chubby fist. I looked inside. Empty. Closed and empty. I signaled to Bolt and we went back to the guardroom, the coppery smell of blood somehow worse now than it had been before.

I searched the faces of the men standing, wounded or otherwise, looking for someone who could give me an account of what happened. A tall man who wielded a scowl the way a farrier would a hammer stood to one side, barking orders.

I waded through the press of bodies and noise until Jeb saw me. The scowl deepened. "Dura."

I nodded. "Aer must have a plan for you, Jeb," I said. "If you'd been here when the attack started, somebody would be fitting you for an oversized box."

He barked a laugh that didn't have any humor in it, then laced the air with a tapestry of curses, most of them involving me.

"Impressive," Bolt murmured.

I knew better than to take offense. Jeb might decide to hit me, title or not. "Most of those things aren't really possible, you know."

His eyebrow, as thick over his nose as it was over his eyes, lowered some more. "Where have you been, Dura? The poor quarter is boiling like a pot over a fire, and people are disappearing from the lower merchants' section every day."

Jeb didn't know it, but he'd just answered a question and confirmed one of my suspicions. He shook his head. "Dura, you've got to do something about the poor quarter. The urchins are armed to the teeth, and they won't listen to anyone in the city watch. It's gotten so honest people can't go through there at all."

That had Rory's signature all over it. If the watch couldn't protect the people in the poor quarter, he wouldn't hesitate to put a sword or a dagger into every hand. "Has anyone else been killed?"

Jeb looked at me as if I'd lost one of my minds. "How should I know? Do you know how easy it is for a pickpocket to hide in the shadows, even in the daytime? The little toughs have organized their own militia. They're not letting anyone in or out of the poor quarter without permission." His face softened from openly hostile to merely threatening. "You've got to do something, Dura. The king wants the poor quarter brought under control."

I didn't have time, but I nodded. The trick would be getting word to Rory without getting killed, but if my suspicions were correct, the poor quarter wasn't in danger anymore. "I'm going to report to King Laidir now," I said.

"Good," Jeb muttered. "Make yourself useful, Dura." He looked around the room. "Aer have mercy, what happened?"

I'd never heard Jeb sound reverential about anything before, and for some reason that scared me. I walked out of the guardroom and back through the entrance tunnel, letting the cool air cleanse the scent of death from my nose. Bolt walked at my shoulder. I stopped, gathering myself before beginning the ascent to the top of the keep. "Tell me," I said. "In your years with the Vigil, did you ever see anything this bad?"

For a moment he just stood as still as the rock of the tor. "Things with the Vigil are always bad—that's why they're there—but never anything on this scale."

I hated being right, but Bolt had given me another clue. I turned toward the stairs and began the long climb. "Laidir and Pellin will be waiting on us."

Bolt fell in beside me. "How are you going to keep the Eldest from breaking your vault?"

"With your help, I'm hoping to convince him that he's got bigger things to worry about."

Soft laughter came from beside me. "Just how do you intend to do that?"

I tried to ignore the feeling that I was walking to my own execution. "I'm going to tell him what's happening."

We passed soldiers everywhere on the way up. And every noble who thought he had the right to command the king's men—which meant most of them—stalked the hallways with bared steel barking nonsensical orders. Fortunately, Laidir had trained his men well. They followed their own chain of command, and when some fop with a rapier shouted orders at them, they nodded and pretended to obey.

Bolt gave an approving nod to the organization of soldiers as we ascended. "Your king has a good head on his shoulders."

"He's not just gifted, he's wise," I said. "And unlike most nobles with a gift, he's not content to sit on it. The books in his library aren't for show. He's read the writings of the best minds in history about how to rule." I sighed, longing for something impossible. "If he'd been born into a different time and family, he would have been the standard by which all other rulers were measured."

"Would you really wish that on him?" Bolt asked.

The question took me off guard until I thought of the burden of ruling Collum multiplied a dozen times over. "No. He seems content."

I trudged up the steps at the east end of the Hall of Remembrance and came out into the hallway leading to the throne room and the king's audience chamber. Men in king's livery lined both sides, standing at ease but wearing the tension that comes from waiting in ignorance. As we came within a few paces of the door, a runner padded up to the officer in charge, his weapons jangling with each step.

I knew the captain, though not well, a stump of a man named Draig, who didn't tolerate fools. He said something to the runner I couldn't make out that sent the man padding away again before turning to me. "The king and the rest of that crowd in there are expecting you, Lord Dura."

I nodded.

He closed the gap between us until I could smell his chain mail. "What happened down there?"

I didn't see any point to keeping Draig in the dark. "Someone tried to break into the prison cells."

His brows made half circles of surprise over his dark brown eyes. "There's something you don't see every day. Bad?"

I nodded. "Aye, but I think the king's guard put everyone down. I think the worst you have to deal with now is nobles running around shouting orders and looking for someone to prick with their swords."

He made a grunting sound that was probably equal parts agreement and disgust before he nodded to the man at the door.

Bolt and I stepped into the king's audience chamber. I stopped just inside, halted by the crowd of people in front of the king's dais. The door banged shut behind me.

Chapter 33

"The fat's in the fire now," Bolt muttered beside me. "Things are never so bad that they can't get a little bit worse."

The Chief of Servants stood on the king's dais next to a hooded figure on his right. I couldn't see into the shadows, but Allta stood to one side, so I assumed it was Pellin. The Vigil guard still wore his sword, which explained the looks Laidir's guards gave him, like terriers eyeing a mastiff. As we entered, a pair of them gave those same looks to Bolt.

Arrayed along the right side of the room were other figures, all hooded, each with a guard behind them. Every one of those guards looked at me as if I were some disease-raddled leper intent on infecting their charge before I died. I noted Volsk's absence with regret. We'd fought together. And from what I could tell, we shared a mutual respect and similar view of the world. I had no illusions about his allegiance, but he seemed to possess a fair share of common sense.

Bolt kept up a steady stream of muttered comments beside me. Most of them seemed to fall into one of two categories: frank assessments of my stupidity or probabilities of our survival.

The Chief of Servants cleared her throat as she bowed to the king. "Your Majesty, since the tidings we are about to discuss are of a sensitive nature, I would advise that we clear the room." Her tone twisted her request into a command, and her pointed glance made it clear she meant the king's guards.

For a moment I thought Laidir would refuse. Over the past year I'd seen him act against his self-interest more than once when his principles became involved, and he hated being bullied. King Rymark of Owmead had attempted it before the last war. Fighting between the two kingdoms had started shortly thereafter.

When he finally nodded, it was more of a jerk. "Very well." He turned to his guards. "Escort *everyone* out with the exception of my hooded guests, Lord Dura and his guard, and the Chief of Servants."

Allta's face went stiff, and he leaned forward to have a whispered conversation with Pellin. The Eldest nodded but then shook his head. The rest of the Vigil guards didn't seem any more inclined to comply with the king's command than Allta.

I stepped forward. "Your Majesty, if it will help matters, we will surrender our weapons."

Laidir's expression twisted as he glanced at his guests. "I may not be able to guarantee their return."

"That's describing a mountain as a molehill," Bolt muttered. "Laidir has quite a gift for understatement."

I tried to ignore him. "I understand, Your Majesty."

We piled our weapons in front of us, which the king's guards scooped up on their way out. When every armed man had left the room, Pellin and the rest of the Vigil pulled their hoods, and I looked on the collective faces of my accusers for the first time.

Laidir didn't bother to stand or offer anyone a seat. "As you can see, Eldest, Lord Dura has honored my command to return. Until I revoke his title, he owes his allegiance to me."

Pellin's blue eyes glittered at the king's tone. "His gift supersedes any title or oath he holds." He paused and then gave the smallest of bows. "Your Majesty. Dura has within his mind a vault, a hiding place which not even he can see into, and that makes him a threat to everyone around him. This vault falls under the authority of the Vigil to address."

"You mean to *break*," Laidir shot back.

Pellin and the rest of the Vigil stiffened. "What I *mean* is that Willet Dura is the province of the Vigil alone."

I saw Laidir flush. What Pellin didn't understand was just how far

Laidir would go if pushed. The king rose from his seat on the dais and descended the steps to approach me. When he drew near, I went to one knee, gratified that Bolt copied me.

But Laidir went past us. With one fluid motion, he shot the massive bolt of the door home. He turned, throwing his cloak back over his shoulders to reveal the plain and quite functional sword at his waist. The king stood, prolonging eye contact with each of the Vigil, letting the implication take hold: Laidir held the only weapon in the room. He wasn't above using sword-point diplomacy.

He moved back toward the dais, circling around Bolt until he stood a few paces from Pellin again. "It's interesting how two men will see a situation or a man in different ways. You see something dangerous in Lord Dura that needs to be eliminated." Laidir smiled without humor. "But I see something dangerous to my enemies." He tapped his sword. "I can see a time and a possibility when Lord Dura might be Eldest."

"You dare?" Toria Deel spat. "You threaten the Vigil? You are nothing. Your reign is the barest blink of an eye."

Pellin winced as Laidir's eyes flashed.

He pointed at Bolt. "I'm sure each of your guards is his equal, but if I give the word, they will die and each of you will spend the rest of your days in the cells."

Pellin stepped from the dais. "It is ever the strategy of the enemy to get us to fight ourselves. Your Majesty, the kings and queens of the continent along with the head of each order alone know the responsibility the Vigil carries. It is within your power to imprison us, but at what price? Would you take your enemy to your bosom?"

Laidir's face still showed the mottling I knew to be a sign of temper. "I do not suffer insults. Perhaps it is time for new blood in the Vigil."

Pellin cut off Toria Deel's hiss. "Silence!"

Laidir pointed. "That one will beg for my forgiveness."

Bolt leaned over to whisper in my ear. "Are you planning on saying anything soon? We're going to have a brawl on our hands any moment."

"I don't think so," I murmured. "The gift of kings includes some measure of physical power, and everyone in here knows it. Besides," I added, "Toria Deel and the rest could use a little humbling."

Bolt's laughter rumbled deep in his throat. "No argument there, but I can't allow any real harm to come to them. I vowed to protect them, even if it means attacking the king unarmed."

As he said this, I noted the glances the Vigil sent his way whenever Laidir's attention strayed. I stepped forward to speak, but Pellin's voice broke the silence first.

"Toria Deel, you will apologize now."

Her eyes flashed hot enough to light tinder. "I will—"

"Else you will surrender your gift to another," Pellin added softly.

His words quenched the fire in her eyes. She jerked into a curtsy as if her back were breaking. "Your humble servant craves pardon, Your Majesty."

"We have very different definitions of humble, my lady. However, I accept your apology."

I didn't bother to hide my smile. Laidir turned from Toria Deel with a dismissive wave of his hand. Her eyes flashed daggers at him behind his back, but the king's smile answered mine. "What tidings do you bring us, Lord Dura?"

I bowed, careful to show the king all the respect his title deserved and a bit more as well. "Your Majesty, the assault on your prison was carried out by southern mercenaries from the last war, men we thought long dead. Bolt and I first encountered them two nights ago on the bridge leading to the poor quarter."

Pellin spoke. "Your Majesty, it should be noted that Willet Dura's guard mortally injured two of those three men, but your vassal killed them before they could be questioned."

Laidir eyed Pellin, the flush creeping up his neck once more. "In this room he will be addressed by his rightfully earned title. The proper form of address is *Lord Dura*. I don't repeat myself." He turned from the Eldest to me. "Is this true?"

Bolt took a half step forward and answered for me. "It is, Your Majesty, but there are many reasons a man may kill another."

Laidir almost smiled. "True enough, and I've seen most of them: justice, revenge, even mercy. But the question must be answered, Lord Dura. Why would you kill a man who was already dying?"

I shook my head. "I don't know, Your Majesty."

"Lord Dura"—Pellin drawled my title—"couldn't know, Your Majesty. According to his guard, when he saw the face of one of the attackers, his vault opened. And then, just as everyone who has survived nightfall in the Darkwater has, he killed those nearest him."

Laidir stood, his eyes hooded in thought while I stewed under the glares of the people who wanted nothing more than to crack my mind open like an overripe nut.

"You." The king pointed at Bolt. "What do you have to say about this quandary? You're one of the Vigil guards and an eyewitness to Lord Dura's behavior." He pointed at Pellin and the rest of the Vigil. "The looks they give you hold equal parts expectation and anger. Given half an opportunity, you come to his defense. Why?"

Bolt didn't bother to acknowledge the unspoken commands the members of the Vigil tried to send him. "Because he doesn't fit the pattern, Your Majesty. Lord Dura emerged from the Darkwater ten years ago. The member of the Vigil assigned to Collum's portion of the Darkwater never saw fit to break his vault."

"Well," Laidir said, turning to the figures arrayed opposite him. "Let us hear from that member."

"Not possible, Your Majesty," Pellin said. "Communication from him ceased. It was that silence that pulled the former Eldest, Elwin, north—to find the reason. And he was killed here, Your Majesty, silenced before he could tell the rest of us what he suspected."

Toria Deel raised her arm, straight as a tent pole, to point at me. "Elwin's blood was on Lord Dura's cloak, Your Majesty. Not the cloak he was seen wearing as he investigated his death, a different one." She pressed on as if she were pushing a dagger. "In some way, your Lord Dura has managed to suborn one of the Vigil and kill the Eldest."

"He seems sane enough to me," Laidir said, but the certitude present in his voice just a few moments ago had faded.

"No one contests that Lord Dura appears to be a decent man in his right mind," Bronwyn said, her voice all the more intense for its quiet. "But that is ever the way with the offspring of the Darkwater. We must know if the threat we face is of Lord Dura's making or whether he is merely a vassal."

"And how would you determine this?" Laidir asked.

"We must delve Lord Dura and force the vault open," Pellin said. "We have been loath to do this because he carries the gift, and who can say why Aer chose him as a vessel."

He sighed, shaking his head. I actually believed he regretted what he proposed.

"But we can no longer delay," Bronwyn said. "The tidings from the Darkwater are frightening. I have tracked people from the cursed forest back to Bunard, Your Majesty. After the gates of the city, the trails disperse."

Laidir chewed one side of his lower lip at this, his fingers tapping the hilt of his sword. "And what of Lord Dura? Will forcing the vault in his mind heal him?"

"No, Your Majesty," Pellin said.

"Tell him the rest, Eldest," Bolt said, but Pellin shook his head.

My guard faced the king. "In all the years the Vigil has guarded the Darkwater, Your Majesty, they've never learned anything from the minds they've broken. There is nothing to be gleaned from the vault, and when they are done, there is nothing in the rest of the mind either. Those who have been delved in that way die shortly thereafter, their minds so broken they no longer possess the will to eat or drink, even when food and water are placed before them."

"No," Laidir said, his voice flat. "I forbid it."

I let out the breath I hadn't realized I'd been holding.

"It is our only chance," Bronwyn said.

"It is no chance at all," Laidir snapped.

"If it does not succeed, then at least we have removed a threat," Toria Deel said. "There's no other alternative."

"Perhaps there is," I said. "Your Majesty, I'm not Elwin's killer, but I can find him."

"How?" Pellin asked. The challenge in his voice was unmistakable.

"I'm the king's reeve," I said. "It's what I do. In attacking the prison, our enemy has shown himself to be desperate. Why else would he sacrifice so many men?"

Laidir nodded, his eyes thoughtful. "Go on, Lord Dura."

I bowed my thanks. "The southern mercenaries from ten years ago are all dead, Your Majesty. Eleven of them entered the Darkwater with me, and one was killed during Elwin's murder."

Pellin moved to speak, but I cut him off. "The number has been verified. Three died at the bridge."

"Murdered by you," Toria Deel said.

I ignored her. "The other seven were all spent in a single attack on your prison after killing everyone in the poor quarter who might have witnessed Elwin's death. Your Majesty, this attack is both a blessing and a curse. The blessing is that we have a means of determining the enemy's intent."

"And the curse?" Laidir asked.

I pointed to one of the Vigil. "Lady Bronwyn has already hinted at it. It's the only reason I can think of to sacrifice all of your men on an attack that might fail."

Laidir's breath whispered from him. "Because you've already arranged for reinforcements."

Chapter 34

The glare Laidir turned on Pellin and the rest of the Vigil held nothing of mercy or forgiveness in it. "The keeping of the Darkwater is your charge. In your presumption you have tried to issue commands to me in my keep, but you've yet to tell me how you're going to meet this threat."

He pointed a stubby finger at Bronwyn. "You say you've tracked people from the cursed forest to my city. How many?"

She shook her head. "I don't know, Your Majesty. The gift is an ill tool for such work."

Laidir snorted his disgust. "Allow me to summarize your position, Eldest. The members of the Vigil are being hunted and killed by an enemy you've been unable to find. You don't know how many of those the Darkwater has corrupted have invaded my city. You wish to break the mind of my best reeve in an attempt to gain information you've never gained from anyone in all the centuries your order has guarded the Darkwater."

The king laughed his scorn at Pellin and the rest. "I can only conclude your real purpose in delving one of my nobility is to eliminate a possible threat. You think Lord Dura killed your brother Elwin. Have I left anything out?"

Pellin's face turned to stone, but his blue eyes glittered. "What would you propose, O king?"

Instead of answering, he turned to me. "Why did they attack the prisons, Lord Dura?"

Inside I winced. *Oh, my king, what have you done?* With that one question Laidir had delivered me into the hands of the Vigil as surely as if he'd bound my feet and hands. If I confessed to the knowledge of a witness, the Vigil would take me at the earliest opportunity and pry the information from my mind. Dissembling was out of the question. Despite their conviction of my guilt, they weren't stupid, and the village idiot could piece the reason for the attack together.

Bolt inched closer until our shoulders touched. "Courage, Willet."

Courage? I almost laughed. It was easy enough to come by when you didn't have any choice. "I believe there is something in Elwin's death, Your Majesty, that the enemy is desperate to keep hidden. I think there was a witness to Elwin's murder in the prison."

Toria Deel stepped forward. "Your Majesty, Laewan was already seen at the bridge. Our knowledge of him leaves no reason to kill this mythical 'last witness.' But if, as I've said, as the blood on the cloak proclaims, Willet Dura killed the previous Eldest, then the attack on the prison makes perfect sense. If you let Willet Dura leave this room without our touch, you're a fool."

Laidir laughed at the outburst, raking Pellin and Bronwyn with the sound. "So convinced you've found your killer that you've stopped thinking. Just how was Lord Dura supposed to orchestrate the attack while he was in the Merum prison?"

Toria Deel threw the king's scorn back at him. "He didn't need to. The corruption in your precious reeve has taken Laewan."

"And there your argument fails to convince me," Laidir said. "Eldest, as a member of the church, you are bound to the truth. In the Vigil's long history, has anyone ever fallen to the vault in another's mind?"

A flicker of doubt could have clouded Pellin's gaze before he answered. I might have imagined it. "No, never. But there is something different about Willet Dura. You've said so yourself."

The king shook his head. "Perhaps I have judged your order too harshly, Eldest. Perhaps you've spent so much time in the presence of evil you can see little else. Lord Dura entered the Darkwater ten years ago. Has anyone ever kept its influence at bay for so long?"

"'Evil slumbers, never sleeps, ever into your mind it creeps,'" Bronwyn said in a singsong.

Laidir looked to be on the verge of rolling his eyes. "I would have thought someone of your station would quote something a bit more substantial, perhaps a warning from the *Collection of Admonitions* within the liturgy. Instead you throw ancient children's rhymes to me."

"They survive to this day for a reason," Pellin said. "In any war there are sacrifices to be made. You know this. We are at war, just as you have been."

Laidir bristled at the comparison but didn't bother to respond. Instead he went to one of the desks scattered around the room to scribble a few lines across a piece of parchment before stamping it with his seal. His gaze found mine as he poured the fine sand across the script to dry the ink. "I'm more sorry than I can say, Willet, that you've fallen in with these people." He crossed the space between us and I found myself clenched in his embrace.

"This won't protect you from them," he whispered. "I have no power over them outside of Collum and precious little in it." He gave my arm one last squeeze. "But they don't know how far I'm willing to go."

He turned from me to face down the Vigil again. "Lord Dura holds in his possession a signed writ of Ymbren."

Pellin crossed his arms over his chest. "Your Majesty must realize the writ holds no power or authority over us. Why would you do such a thing?"

Laidir nodded once, slowly. "You have proven yourselves impotent against this threat. For all the power your gift bestows, you are unable to find Elwin's killer, one of your own has fallen under the influence of the Darkwater, and you intend to break the mind of the man best able to help you."

"And once the three days of the writ of Ymbren have run, Your Majesty, what would you have us do then?"

Laidir glanced at me, his gaze somber. "You may do whatever seems best, but I would ask that you give Lord Dura a free hand until then. I owe him my life because of his ability to see where others cannot. The enemies of Collum underestimated him, much to their sorrow. I simply ask that you allow your enemies time to make the same mistake."

He approached Pellin with his right hand extended. "Will you do this, Eldest?"

Pellin, gloved and protected, stared at the king's hand for a moment before taking it in his own. "We will allow Lord Dura to proceed unless we uncover additional compelling evidence against him."

Toria Deel shook her head, mouth gaping in her disbelief. "You would agree to this?" She stabbed a finger at me like a poniard. "Is it not enough that he's killed the Eldest and corrupted one of the Vigil? You would allow him to finish off the witnesses to his crimes?"

Whatever softness or indecision clouded Pellin's expression vanished. He turned a face made of flint on his subordinate. "Our arguments have failed to persuade His Majesty. And in this he is correct—we have no proof. Can you provide it?"

Toria Deel extended her right hand, jerked the glove off with her left. "Aye, I can."

I took a step back and reached for a sword I no longer wore. Bolt placed himself in my path.

"No!" Pellin's voice crackled through the air.

Toria Deel shook her head. "I do not mean to break his vault. I only wish to see what the enemy sought in King Laidir's prison."

Pellin shook his head. "And do you think Lord Dura would trust us enough to allow our touch now?"

"No," I said. I swept Pellin, Bronwyn, and Toria Deel into my gaze. "Understand this—I will take any attempt to touch me as an attack. And I will do my best to kill you."

Even Bolt looked a little startled, but Pellin just tilted his head to one side and gazed at me in mild surprise. He turned to the king. "Three days from this hour."

With relief and terror fighting each other for room in my throat, I watched them shake hands. As king, Laidir had the right to issue a writ of Ymbren to stay an execution for three days, allowing time to search for new evidence. Named after the man Iosa had raised from the dead, it offered me a chance to prove my innocence. Of course,

Ymbren had been killed by Iosa's enemies a week after his revival. I tried not to think about the possible parallels. I had three days.

Bolt and I waited until the Vigil left the room before taking our leave as well. The panicked bustle in the halls of the keep continued, but it no longer held any concern for me. The attack on the prison had failed. The Absold believed Aer watched over fools and the ignorant, and I made a mental note to drop an offering in their coffers if I survived past the next three days.

The two of us made for the southern exit of the keep. At the return of our weapons, I felt dressed again, relieved of my nakedness. Bolt looked only slightly more dangerous than he had in Laidir's audience chamber.

"Where did you put her?" he asked.

He only smiled when I looked at him.

"I was with you when you scrambled your mind trying to prove their innocence, remember? She was in the last cell on the left, the girl you knew was innocent. That's your last witness."

"She's safe, but I can't tell you where she is," I said. We walked in the quiet of his unvoiced recriminations while I struggled to come up with some reason for my silence other than the distrust I still harbored.

We exited the keep, entering the cool night air of Bunard in the spring. As always, I thought of the fertile vale that lay between Collum and Owmead and said a silent prayer for a plentiful harvest. "We killed each other over food, just as we've done for hundreds of years whenever the wind came from the west, carrying drought." I sighed. "They swore not to delve me for the next three days. They said nothing about delving you," I said as we turned the corner into a nest of naked sword points.

"Quite right." Toria Deel smiled from behind her blade. Her guard, Elory, flanked her right, and Volsk stood on her left, both hands gloved and holding steel as well as an expression that held regret and resolution. The presence of Bronwyn and her guard, Balean, did surprise me.

I didn't bother wasting words on Toria Deel. "Does Pellin know you're here?" I asked Bronwyn. "Is this how the Vigil keeps its word?"

At least she had the decency to look ashamed, but the sword in her hand never retreated from its bead on my chest. "Laewan was like a son to me." She shrugged. "The Eldest's intentions are laudable, but—"

"Let me guess," I interrupted. "You can't afford them just now." My laughter surprised them. "It's always the same. You're prepared to be moral and noble right up until it becomes inconvenient, and then it's about what's necessary."

"Cleverly spoken—" Toria Deel laughed—"but 'evil wears many guises.'"

"Adages to soothe your conscience must be nice," I said to Bronwyn.

She looked at me as if her lifetime couldn't hold the burdens she bore. Aer and Iosa help them. What did the Vigil have to sacrifice for their service? For a moment, I regretted my words. In their place I might have done the same.

I nudged Bolt forward. With five swords against two, I didn't fancy our chances. There was nothing to do except hope he had no memory of Branna. Her face would avail them little. Had her name ever been mentioned in Bolt's presence? I couldn't remember.

Toria Deel and Bronwyn came forward, naked hands extended toward Bolt's arm. I'd never seen anyone else delve another, and despite the duress of our situation I watched with interest as their fingertips came to rest on his flesh.

The darks of their eyes might have grown—the dim torchlight outside the keep made it difficult to tell—but their expressions went vacant. A moment later they withdrew, Toria Deel's face hard as steel and etched with disappointment. But Bronwyn's face held a note of surprise, and the look she gave me carried a hint of speculation it had never held before.

Toria Deel's steel found its way into her hand again. "Nothing. He's hidden it even from you."

Bolt tugged his sleeve back down to cover his arm without reply.

"Take them," Toria Deel said, looking at me the way a cat eyed the prey she'd wounded. "We will keep Dura safely locked away until his writ expires, and then we will delve him."

Bronwyn sheathed her sword, nodding for her guard to do the

same. "That will not satisfy the command of the Eldest. If you wish to continue, Toria Deel, neither I nor my guard will assist you."

"If I must," Toria Deel said.

As she turned to reply, I took two steps back to pull the throwing knives from my boot and hip.

Bronwyn turned her back and faded into the darkness, her guard following.

"You may wish to rethink your strategy," Bolt said. "While Lord Dura is not the equal of a Vigil guard, he is quite handy with those knives. If I engage Elory, he will be too busy to keep those blades from your throat. At this range he won't miss."

"And I can throw with either hand," I added.

Volsk's eyes narrowed, his loyalties for the moment no longer divided. "I do not fear him or his knives, Toria Deel."

I met his gaze with as much cold indifference as I could muster and cocked one hand over my head, holding the knife by the blade. "But I won't be aiming for you. I'll be aiming for that pretty white throat of hers. I think I have a better chance of surviving your sword stroke than her touch."

I smiled, showing teeth. "I'm sure you understand my position." My heartbeat shook me where I stood, and I prayed Volsk and Toria Deel wouldn't call my bluff. Killing a woman was beyond me, even in self-defense.

"No," Toria Deel said, stepping back to sheath her sword. "We will do as the Eldest has commanded. In three days you will be unmasked, Dura."

CHAPTER 35

"They're going to be following us," Bolt muttered as we set off from the keep.

I nodded. "For now, it's all right. I have no intention of leading them to the girl. I can't. I don't even know where she is."

The streets of Bunard this close to the keep usually thronged with people as they came and went on their way to the better inns and taverns to drink and continue the business they'd started in the street markets earlier in the day. News of the attack must have spread. The sound of footsteps, which should have been as thick as raindrops against the cobblestones, shrank to intermittent patters as people left the streets.

Which made my guard and me easier to follow. "Will she try to take us?" I kept to the most crowded well-lit streets as I could, striving to keep us in the light.

Bolt shook his head. "I don't think so. Volsk is her intended. There's too much for her to lose. Their only hope of being together is if the gift somehow comes to him, either from you or someone else." Something warped his tone, creating a slight twist, as if he were dodging a certain admission.

"Why should it matter who someone in the Vigil marries?"

The ward in Bolt's tone grew. "The weight of their gift makes it difficult for the Vigil to take a spouse who does not also hold the talent. The marriage always ends in mourning." His voice fell back into its normal cadence. "You're dealing with desperate people, Dura. Good or bad, desperate people will make desperate choices. When Cesla died ten years ago, his gift vanished, went free. They're still looking for it, which is why Jorgen's not here."

I shook my head. I hadn't heard the name before. "Who's he?"

"The member of the Vigil assigned to Frayel." He sighed. "It seems as though the Vigil has been battling poor chance for the last ten years just as you have. If the gift lands on a man or woman who has little contact with others, it becomes hard to find." He rubbed his chin. "There are trappers and prospectors in the far north of Collum and Frayel, men who go for years without seeing another. Jorgen has spent the last five years running down every rumor coming out of the frozen wastes, but so far he hasn't been able to find it. Now, with Laewan's corruption, the Vigil of the northern continent has been reduced from seven to five."

Something shifted in my thoughts at this, a possibility I couldn't name, and my mind worked like the gears on a portcullis winch that had just started to turn but hadn't quite meshed. We crossed the bridge that took us from the nobles' quarter into the upper merchants' section, hugging the right hand rail, where the torches cast guttering light across the arch.

I turned right at the main road, following the bend of the river. Merchants who customarily filled the streets enjoying the profits of their labors were nowhere to be seen. Link boys, the torch-bearer lads who escorted the merchants on their rounds at night for a copper, stood on the corners waiting. Everything Bolt had said made perfect sense, but none of it rang true. His tone had been filled with the deliberate rhythms of a man trying very hard not to say something.

We passed a large three-story house of stone and wood, the windows dark. I kept going until we got to the next alley and held my breath as we turned right down it and right two more times until we came back to its front. Not the faintest hint of light showed in the windows.

"We'll need torches," I said, walking to the nearest corner. The jingle of my purse had been reduced to a forlorn clink, and the two coins remaining hardly weighted the cloth. I pulled one and held it out to the boy of nine or ten, who eyed me with curiosity.

"I want to buy a couple of torches," I said, handing him the coin. His eyes grew wide, the whites reflecting the yellow light as he touched the silver penny with trembling fingers. Without taking his eyes from it, he reached back and handed me a pair of torches wrapped in cotton tow and soaked in pitch. After being lit, they guttered and smoked thickly for a moment before the flame steadied, and we walked back to the house we'd circled.

Bolt checked over his shoulder, but if we were being followed they were far enough away to give the impression we stood alone on the street. Of course, the torches would have acted like a lighthouse to anyone within half a mile, but if Toria Deel and Volsk had followed me here in hopes of finding the girl, they'd be disappointed.

Four paces off the street and three steps up brought us to the door of Andler's home. I didn't need Bolt's warning to enter sword first, but the inside of the house held the sound and feel of emptiness. Our footsteps made hollow echoes against the wooden floor, uninterrupted by the presence of flesh or breath within. No servants or maids with lit tapers waited to greet their master back from his errand.

Bolt scanned the room, searching for something he might need to kill, but I could see questions building in the set of his shoulders and the squint of his eyes. Andler's empty house went a long way toward confirming my suspicions. At the same time I could no longer afford my distrust of Bolt, however grounded in my realistic assessment of his loyalty. What I suspected—most of it, anyway—needed to be shared, even with Pellin and the rest of the Vigil.

"We're in the house of Master Andler, a merchant who also happened to trade in people," I said. "He turned a profit selling comely young women dressed up as nobles for the amusements of other merchants and some of our members of court." I shrugged. "Of course, many of the girls preferred not to participate in his business venture. Master Andler would then use his considerable wealth against the family business in order to persuade the girls to change their mind."

Bolt's knuckles whitened on his hilt. "You said 'turned.' He's dead?"

I nodded. "The merchant in the prison guardroom. He died from arrows and crossbow bolts, not crescents."

I watched him make the connection, chewing the inside of one cheek in thought. "What's his connection to Laewan and the Darkwater?"

I moved through the entry hall, lighting candles as I went until the darkness receded enough to make Andler's home feel almost normal. "That's what I'm hoping to find."

Bolt shook his head. "Why not just delve the girl?"

A pair of quick heartbeats passed before I replied. "I told you, I don't know where she is."

"You're afraid, aren't you?" Bolt said quietly. "You think it's just possible you killed Elwin."

I found myself wishing his last statement had been more of a question. The candle flames licked up toward the ceiling, casting steady shadows as we regarded each other, not moving. "Yes," I said, "I think it possible."

Taking a deep breath, I faced him, letting my sword point drop toward the floor. "Have you ever been a killer in your dreams?" I surveyed Andler's furnishings, the rich woods, the thick carpets, hoping they might offer some clue, but mostly I didn't want to meet Bolt's gaze. I looked anyway, but he stood before me, neither affirming nor condemning. Yet.

I took a deep breath of the house's scented air into my lungs. "At night, I fight in my dreams, sometimes with a sword, sometimes with my hands, raging and unthinking until I've killed my enemy. Then I wake, panting and sweating, unsure if the dream really happened or if it's the night terrors other soldiers talk about." I couldn't keep my gaze from his any longer. "And sometimes when I wake there's blood on my cloak."

Bolt gave his head a small shake. "In ten years no one has seen you do anything other than talk to the dead. I don't think there's any power in hell that can make a man what he's not."

I nodded my thanks, but his assurance said nothing about me, really. "I used to think so too. Sometimes, when my nights are untroubled by dreams, I still think that."

I put my foot on the first stair leading up to Andler's bedroom suite. "And sometimes the reeves will catch a man whose been secretly killing for years, driven by something no one wants to name." I took another step. "If I'm Elwin's killer, I would prefer not to have my mind broken. The sword would be better."

He came along beside me, his sword pointed forward. "If I have anything to do with it, you'll have it."

We turned, checking the doors leading off the hallway until we found one that opened onto an oversized sitting room filled with couches and rugs done in shades of green and rose. Paintings filled the space above the wainscoting to the high ceiling, depicting pastoral scenes from the seven kingdoms of the northern continent, their colors more real and vibrant than the actuality.

Bolt moved to the nearest one. "These are brilliant, but I don't recognize the artist."

We stepped to the wide, heavy door leading to Andler's bedroom, and I held my breath as I turned the handle. Years of working as a reeve had almost inured me to the strange tastes men or women such as Andler exercised in the privacy of their bedrooms—almost, but not quite.

The bedroom occupied the entire west end of the house, big enough to have its own echo. On the far wall a large grated fireplace heavy with ash sat cold and unused. A few paces away, an oversized four-poster bed filled the southern wall, the heavy curtains closed against the chill.

I started toward it, but Bolt put an arm across my chest and shook his head. "Get out of the line of fire."

I positioned myself next to the armoire. The burnished wood would offer some protection against a thrown dagger, less for a short bow, and almost none from the bolt of a crossbow. Then again, the emptiness of the room told me there wasn't anything living behind Andler's curtains, but there was no reason the curtains should be drawn closed if no one slept on the bed. Customarily they were left open.

Using the bulk of one of the posts to shield himself, Bolt flung the curtain at the foot of the bed open with the tip of his sword. The thick blue fabric fluttered and opened to reveal nothing more than an ordinary bed. I stepped across the room, drawn by his disappointment and my own, knowing there had to be something there.

But there wasn't. It was just the ornate bed of a self-indulgent merchant. "This doesn't make sense. Where are the servants?"

"Maybe he didn't expect to come back," Bolt said. He picked at the pillows with his sword, skewering them one at a time and tossing them to the floor.

I started the process of emptying out the massive dresser and the armoire. A small red pillow fluttered past my head. "I touched him before I knew what Elwin had given me," I said. "Andler wasn't the type to sacrifice himself. If someone sent him on a suicide mission, he would have run the opposite direction until he dropped." I stepped away from the bed to take my frustration out on one of the pillows, kicking it into the fireplace, but it was too small to offer any satisfaction.

We left the bedroom to search the servants' quarters on the third floor, but the thin layer of dust on the stairs and the landing confirmed our earlier assessment: Andler hadn't used his house in days. So where had he been?

"Is there a cellar?" Bolt asked.

My sigh couldn't fully capture my disgust. "It's Bunard—there's always a cellar." I looked at the high ceiling. "Andler's not going to have any use for it anymore. We can probably pick up a nice bottle or two of wine."

Bolt gave a derisive snort. "In Collum? The whole kingdom should stick to ale."

We descended back to the first floor and made our way to the rear of the house, searching for the door or steps leading to the cellar. Even small houses in Bunard took advantage of the cool the rock of the city offered against the spring and summer warmth by maintaining a root cellar. Larger ones, like Andler's, expanded it to include space for wines and casks of ale as well. Even a momentary touch on the merchant had revealed his appetite for drink.

A broad door off the kitchen revealed heavy oak steps leading down. A draft of air, cool as the earth from a grave, washed over us, and the flames of our torches guttered and hissed in protest. Despite the cold, sweat managed to trickle down my back, and I pulled my sword.

We stopped at the bottom of the stairs. I stood there with my ears straining, but the chaotic dance of torch flames confused me. While the house above had held the dull, dusty sense of abandonment, here in the basement, I felt something else. The darkness made me uneasy in a way the lightless prison cell of the Merum cathedral hadn't.

We raised our torches, the flames licking the rock of the ceiling and revealing a long arched tunnel of native stones held together with thick mortar joints. Along the wall to our left, a rack that could hold hundreds of bottles of wine stood about half full. Where the rack ended, small wooden casks marked in charcoal with their contents and vintage year filled the rest of the space. On the opposite wall, larger ale barrels competed for space with bins holding vegetables and dried fruits.

"Stay by the stairs," Bolt said as he moved toward the containers, his sword point forward. "If anything happens to me, don't try to be a hero. Get to the Vigil." He sniffed the air. "I've never cared for turnips." He raised the lid on the first bin, his gaze darting from its interior to the space around him as he sifted through the contents. When he finished, he lowered the cover so that it settled back with a barely audible click.

When he opened the next lid, I saw him jerk, his sword flicking almost faster than my eye could follow before he exhaled. Stepping back, he stood on the balls of his feet and motioned me forward. "Take a look."

I knew there couldn't be any real danger, but that knowledge seemed weak beside the certainty of fear that sent my heart pounding so that I couldn't hear my own footfalls. My fingers groped forward across the grain of the lid, seeking purchase while holding my torch at the same time. Despite Bolt's silent assurances, I kept my sword arm free.

The shadows of the bin's contents receded as I opened the lid to reveal the purpled flesh of a man's hand, and my reaction mimicked Bolt's. I jerked backward, then lunged forward again to catch the falling lid before it could clatter back into place. Gripping it lower, closer to the hinges, I opened it all the way until it settled against the wall behind.

Stuffed into the small space and smelling of onions and decay lay one of the city watch facedown, the arms flung outward, in a last gesture of pleading. I tucked the man's arms by his sides, the joints bending without protest, but stiffness through the chest and neck prevented me from rolling the body over. As gently and with as much respect as I could, I put my hands beneath the dead man's chest and lifted until I could make out his face by Bolt's torchlight.

I let him settle on his back, reciting the antidon I'd learned as an acolyte, even as I noted the deep gouging wound on the left of his chest. A dagger thrust, not the mark of a crescent.

"Do you know him?"

Ahden's stare caught me, his eyes staring through me to whatever fate he'd met on the other side of the infinite. He'd been a minor part of the city guard, and I'd never had occasion to speak to him at length. Now I wished I had.

"What's out there, Ahden? What's waiting for us?" I whispered. He didn't answer. I wanted to cry, I felt so bereft.

"Dura!"

I started, blinking and squinting against the light of Bolt's torch, my thoughts a mixture of memories I hoped belonged to me. Closing the lid, I stepped back.

"Do you know him?"

"Yes." I nodded. "He's one of the city guards. Ahden." A memory nagged at me, trying to surface, but nearness of death called the others, the ones I'd taken so much trouble to lock away, and I struggled to keep them from coming out. Nothing more than his name would come to me.

Bolt moved to the far end of the room where a pair of ale casks as big around as I was tall filled the space between the floor and the ceiling. Ahden's face as it might have been, hale and in the flush of life, filled my thoughts. Bolt held his torch forward, illuminating the area between the larger barrels before peering behind them.

"Here."

The memory wouldn't come. I shook myself like a dog in the rain and stepped behind the barrel. The far wall disappeared into shadow, our light too weak to illuminate the distance, but jagged teeth of dark gray stone showed where the final wall should have been and chunks of mortar and heavy stones, some half my height, littered the floor around the opening.

Air poured from the darkness, carrying hints of sound and scent.

I stood by the ragged opening, silent and unmoving, but the draft mocked me—its whispers incomprehensible, uttered in a language I couldn't comprehend.

I put the point of my sword into the inky black shadow that filled the hole and struggled against the fear washing over me. "This alone might have sent Andler to the headsman." My voice came out in a whisper, even though we had spent the last half hour clomping around in our heavy boots on the floors above, sending our thumping echoes into the cellar.

"Why's that?" Bolt asked. He didn't bother to look at me. The sudden change in my posture had put him on his guard as well, and his head swiveled, searching the shadows beyond Andler's cellar for threats.

"Bunard sits atop caves upon caves. The reason the city's never been taken is because every king with a thimble's worth of sense has made sure to keep them blocked off. That's another reason every section of the city has a branch of the Rinwash flowing through it. It's been used to flood the caves connecting one quarter of the city to the next." I shook my head. "But it's impossible to get to them all. What good is the height advantage of the tor if your enemy can climb through the caves and attack you from within? Stonemasons make a good living in Bunard keeping the underground walls in good repair."

I turned from the opening, my sense of caution finally outweighing my impatience. Three days or not, I couldn't let a threat to Bunard go unreported. "We can't go in there until we notify the king."

Bolt nodded toward the opening. "Sense. It leads back toward the keep."

I turned my back to the gaping maw behind us. A whisper of warning, a scrape of cloth against stone, was all I heard before a weight crashed against the back of my head.

My torch bounced against the rocks of the cellar and went out. I struggled to my hands and knees as figures poured from the hole into Andler's cellar. Then Bolt's torch went out.

Chapter 36

Pellin eyed Allta with a mixture of frustration and wonder. In all his years in the Vigil he'd never worked with a man so resolutely silent or adamantly humorless. It made him want to climb a table in the nearest inn and sing bawdy poetry just to see if Allta's expression would change.

It probably wouldn't.

He sighed. The position of Eldest had come to him before he was ready, which was the same thing as saying the position of Eldest had come to him. Cesla's death had upended the smooth operation of an organization that had run for centuries with hardly a change.

He turned his attention back to the scrying stone in front of him. It remained a blank canvas, just as it had for the past two months. The shard, one of seven identical pieces fashioned from the same diamond, held resonance with its kin, allowing him to communicate at need with the rest of the Vigil. But the process required him to use the stone at the same time as the other members of the Vigil.

Once again his call had gone east over the snow-capped mountains that walled Collum from Frayel, its sister kingdom of the north. But again there had been no response. Jorgen, the Vigil's man who guarded the Darkwater for that kingdom, had fallen silent.

He lifted the pointed shard from its base and examined it for nicks or other damage that would explain the silence. There were none. Perhaps it was Jorgen's that had sustained damage. The clear yellow crystal, while durable, wasn't immune to damage. That would explain the silence.

Pellin shook his head at his foolish optimism. The silence of the scrying stone he could understand, but on his arrival to Bunard he'd sent a flock of colm, the swift carrier birds. None of them had returned, and no answer had come.

The northern continent's Vigil was now reduced to himself, Bronwyn, and Toria Deel—less than half the strength it should have been. He pointed to the empty seat across the small table. "Allta, please sit. I wish to ask your opinion."

His guard nodded once with the stiff gesture of a man surprised by a sudden discomfort, like a servant invited to sup with the king.

Pellin smiled, hoping to set Allta at ease, but the gesture seemed only to heighten his guard's apprehension. He let the expression slide from his face. It didn't match how he felt in any case. "Dark times."

Allta nodded.

Pellin sighed, again. "Tell me, Allta, who did you train under?"

His guard blinked. "Eldest, you were there for much of it. I began my training under Bolt and completed it under Robin."

Pellin listened to the answer, doing his best to keep from gritting his teeth. "Allta, I'll speak plainly. I need as much counsel as I can gather. The Vigil sits on the edge of a blade. Cesla and Elwin are dead. In some way Laewan has been corrupted, which has never happened before, and Jorgen's stone and carrier birds have gone silent."

"The reeve's doing," Allta said.

Hearing his guard repeat the accusation from Toria Deel filled Pellin with misgiving. "Do we know this?"

"Eldest?" Allta asked. "You and Toria Deel brought the charge yourselves."

Pellin nodded, reaching for the stone, his hands suddenly uncomfortable in repose. "Tell me about Bolt."

Allta didn't settle into his chair exactly, but the tension in his neck and shoulders eased a fraction, and the wariness around his eyes and mouth receded back to their normal watchfulness. "The people in my village said the gift ran strong in my family. During summer I would catch flies in midflight, capturing one in each hand. But he beat me black-and-blue for years during training."

Allta's green eyes sparkled at the memory. "I was a different person then, Eldest, young and cocksure, so sure of my superiority." He shook his head. "I still remember what Bolt said to me when he offered to make me one of the best swordsmen in the world."

Pellin cocked his head. Along with the rest of the members, he had delved each new recruit to make sure there were no potential problems among them. Quite a few were rejected, but after that the Vigil left the training of new recruits to the existing guards.

"'Black and blue are the colors of humility,'" Allta quoted.

Pellin shook his head. Bolt had a limitless supply of quotes, most of which he tended to make up on the spot. "I don't know that one."

Allta smiled, a gesture that accentuated his youth. "I doubt you would, Eldest, but after the first day of training, I did. I hadn't been touched by anyone in my village since I was fifteen, but I carried more bruises after that first training session than I care to remember."

Surprised laughter bubbled up from Pellin's chest, and for a moment he lost himself in the unexpected joy, letting it wash through him as if it could cleanse him of his doubt. But the moment passed and responsibility settled back on his shoulders like a lead cloak. "He thinks Dura is innocent, you know."

Allta's face showed the clash of opposing thoughts, but he offered no resolution to the conflict Pellin proposed.

"Tell me, Allta, did Bolt seem himself when you've seen him the past few days?"

Released from having to consider mutually exclusive ideas, his visage relaxed once more. "Yes, Eldest."

Pellin nodded. "Agreed. He seems as sarcastic and disagreeable as ever. So why would a Vigil guard put himself in danger to free a threat like Willet Dura?"

Allta stared at him, waiting for the answer to the rhetorical question. And that, he thought, was the difference between Bolt and every other guard in the Vigil. Bolt didn't believe in the existence of rhetorical questions.

Pellin rose from his chair. "The only answer I can come up with is he wouldn't. And that leaves me with an uncomfortable prospect."

"Eldest?"

"It is possible Elwin's death and Laewan's turning have nothing to do with Willet Dura at all."

He turned to Allta. "Did Bolt ever offer a saying about broken swords?"

Allta smiled. "Eldest, he had sayings about everything."

Pellin grunted at the admission. "I think he made most of them up, but for some reason I remember this one. 'Better a broken sword than nothing at all.'"

Allta shook his head, signaling unfamiliarity, and Pellin shrugged. "Not exactly poetry, but it's true, nonetheless." He retrieved the scrying stone from the table to wrap it in its protective cloth and placed it back in his pack. "Dura is a broken sword. I need to know whose hand is wielding him."

I heard the voices first, whispers with inflections that I couldn't quite sort out. I blinked but still couldn't see anything, the darkness so complete it was as if I'd been submerged in a vat of pitch. I stretched my face to make sure my eyes were open, but the scenery didn't change. A knot on the back of my head throbbed with the motion, and a sticky layer of dried blood clung to my neck.

My hands and feet were tied, though it seemed unnecessary. No one could have found their way out of darkness that came from the inside of a rock. To keep myself from panic, I tried to imagine Gael's response to my carrying another scar. She thought they made me look rugged, but at a certain point a man started to look too much like a quilt. At least this one would be hidden by my hair.

It might have been the thought or my attempt to dispel the darkness, but I chuckled. The tenor of the whispers around me changed, but not enough so that they could be understood.

"You find amusement in your situation?" a cultured voice said.

I turned toward the sound. My captives could see in the dark. Their reaction to movement without sound told me as much. "If I lose my hair, my wife is going to be cross with you for putting another scar on my head."

"You threaten me?"

I heard the crack of flesh but never saw the open-handed blow that whipped my face to one side. Fire blossomed in my right cheek, and the part of my mind that could still think, the part that earned me the title of reeve, noted that my interrogator was probably left-handed. The other part noted the stars in my vision were totally useless, since the cave remained shrouded in black.

"By no means," I said as politely as I could. "I'm merely concerned that my betrothed might find the addition of yet another scar on my head less than attractive."

My head whipped to the other side, the blow as strong as the one before, and I amended my theory—perhaps he was dual-handed. For a certainty, he was devoid of humor. "Where is the girl?" the voice asked.

I closed my eyes to concentrate. Having them open had proved useless against people who could see in the dark. *Breathing.* I could hear it, not just once but perhaps half a dozen times, placed around me at varying distances, but no laughter, not even the hint that any of the observers found my predicament amusing.

For a moment I couldn't hear anything except the frightened pounding of my own heart. I'd met men without emotion before, servants or toughs so devoid of feeling they existed only to follow their next command. Even a cruel man who delights in the pain of others could be manipulated. When all else fails, the reward of an even greater harvest of misery often enticed them to bargain or at least wait.

The men or women around me didn't possess enough humanity to note my suffering in any way, good or bad, which meant negotiating would be a waste of time. I had to play dumb.

The sigh of displaced air warned me, and I threw my head back, causing my captor to miss his blow. I hoped he would believe I could see in the dark as well.

"What girl?" I asked.

"Better." The voice came closer then veered left to walk a tight circle around me as it spoke. "The one you imprisoned, the merchant's plaything."

I shook my head, my eyes open now, but still useless. "She should have been there. I don't know where she is." I tracked my interrogator as well as I could. "Why is she important?"

If I thought to throw him off by pretending ignorance, I was mistaken. "Your belief that this is an exchange of information is in error. I ask—you answer. That is all."

He continued to pace around me. Judging by the bend in my legs and the direction of his voice, I judged him to be about my height, perhaps a bit shorter. Casting back, I replayed the scene at the bridge, sifting through my memories until I saw Laewan illumined by the fire of solas powder. Tall and gangly, he would have overtopped me by almost a hand.

So who was this?

The brush of fingers traced a light touch, almost a caress, across my chest, shoulder, and back as the voice's owner continued walking the circle around me. "Being able to see in the dark has a number of advantages," he said. "Used in conjunction with more traditional techniques of persuasion, it can prove quite effective."

The hand stopped, resting just over my heart, warm with its owner's blood. Why had I expected it to be cold?

"You see," the voice continued, the breath warm across my ear, "the suspense of not knowing from which direction the pain will come heightens its effectiveness. I've seen men who could withstand the rack or even the irons crumble once the lights went out." The timbre of his voice strengthened from the sibilant whisper until it sounded almost normal. "Over the years I've made a study of the human body, learning its workings, how it responds."

"Sounds like you would have made a fine healer," I said.

Soft laughter echoed around me. "What makes you think I'm not?"

The clink of metal conjured images from history that made me sweat: thumbscrews, brazen statues, branding irons designed to fit the curves of the human body. My breaths came short and quick. Torture had been outlawed since the four orders had made peace hundreds of years before. "What about your oath?"

The fingers traced a final gentle arc along my neck, his touch dissipating as he withdrew until it disappeared. "That's for—" the voice hesitated—"daylight. For the poor, simple man obsessed with flights of fancy he tries so hard to dismiss as he tends the sick and injured."

Cold air settled into the cave and my stomach. It took me a moment to piece together the fact that my torturer spoke of himself. "When did you go to the Darkwater?"

In the silence that followed, the breathing quickened among those who watched, the echoes of their panting mixing until it sounded as if the cave itself had come to life. My captor never answered, but I could sense movement and the sounds of metal, like someone fiddling with a blacksmith's puzzle, continued. The sound circled around me and dipped in height until it came from just beside my hands.

"The secret to pain," the voice said, "is to start small. Thumbscrews are a simple device, really, but exquisitely painful."

The ropes prevented movement, but I balled my hands into fists. This only served to amuse him. Soft whispers of mirth floated across the back of my neck just before a crushing pressure on the tendons along the back of my left hand forced it open. Cold iron slipped over my thumb.

"Let's start here," the voice said.

The rusty squeak of the screw being turned brought sharp metallic teeth into contact with the knuckle. I tried to jerk my hands away, tip the chair over, anything, but I remained fixed to the spot. "What if I agreed to talk?" I panted. I wouldn't—giving up the girl was putting the knife to slit my throat in their hands, but in the dark, with Bolt dead or captured, I could only play for time.

"Of course you will." The smallest whine of the screw buried the teeth into the joint, compressing the bone against the metal bar. Red, the color of pain, flashed and cascaded through my mind as bolts of agony shot up my arms. They hadn't bothered to gag me and I didn't see the point of being noble, so I inhaled, prepared to scream. The entire city of Bunard sat atop the caves. Someone would have to hear me.

Cloth filled my mouth at the last moment. My tormentor chuckled again. "Hope denied is its own torture. Used in conjunction with the unknown of the darkness and real pain, it also can be quite effective. As for talking, you have been given to me and I don't care whether you talk or not. I've waited for another opportunity such as this for too long, biding my time until I could learn more of what the body can endure. It would be a shame to forgo such an educational experience."

The pain hadn't receded, but I fought the shock, striving to breathe without gasping. *Oh, Aer.* I needed to speak. Without speech I had no means of even attempting to manipulate my torturer.

The screw tightened again, and lightning flashed behind my eyes. I struggled, working my tongue to push the cloth out of my mouth, flinging my head back and forth to loosen it. Something broke loose at the back of my chair, forcing my captor to hold it in place.

That gave me the time I needed to push the wool out of my mouth, but I didn't scream. "If you break my mind, Laewan will never find the girl," I snarled. "You'll end up in your own thumbscrews."

I screamed, striving to fill the caves of Bunard until my lungs burst. But I'd only begun when lights exploded in the back of my head. I fell from consciousness until it receded to nothing in the distance.

Chapter 37

Memories from every touch of Elwin's gift flooded through my mind. Somewhere in the hints of identity that the rest of the world named Willet Dura, I knew I was unconscious. But those fragments held no more power or permanence than all the recollections of nobles or felons I'd absorbed. A dozen lives flashed past me, as ethereal as mist, as substantial as gossamer.

Pain came to me, physical agony that pierced my semiconscious state, flashing from my hands and feet. I didn't know if I sat, stood, hung, or floated. Agony struck with lightning bolts of intensity that burned away all memories and identities for an instant before they returned.

They merged with me, and somewhere in my soul, where Aer had spoken and left his mark, I convulsed in an agony of revulsion. Pride and violence, pettiness and cruelty, all of them on a scale both large and small, filled me as I lived through the duke's lifetime, and then Oberd's and Erich's from the prison cells. Jealousy and hatred I could handle. In the depths of my heart I'd wrestled with the unique experiences that were universal to every man or woman. But Erich's memories claimed me, stained my soul as indelibly as if I'd committed each act of violence, each rape, each murder myself.

The fragile walls I'd erected in my mind to keep myself sane, to retain my identity among all the others, came crashing down, and I walked through a dozen lifetimes that blended with each other until all sense of my self disappeared.

"Where is the girl?" A voice threaded through the torrent of memories that washed me away. *Girl?* I hadn't been a girl in decades. A memory opened of myself, basking in the sunshine of Collum's summer, my face turned toward the light, a scattering of freckles greeting the warmth. But that was long ago, when dreams of love and other girlish notions seemed real, before grief and age turned me into a crone.

"Tell me about the girl," the voice ordered. I might have shaken my head. *Admit nothing, Erich,* I told myself. *They'll never find her. Her bones are buried deep in the earth of Bunard. No one saw you, no one knows. The only witness who can betray you is you. Say nothing.*

"Enough," a new voice ordered to the accompaniment of boots on stone. "Remove the devices. I will delve him."

I screamed as blood and pain flooded back into my thumbs and toes and the wash of identities receded for a blessed instant filled with torture. Then the last words I'd heard registered. *Delve.* I convulsed, gorge plowing through the clench of my throat, and I vomited. *Hide it,* my mind screamed at me as Branna's face, young and scared, rose in front of me.

"I don't know how," I answered.

Custos, not young but less aged than his true self, floated past in the recesses of my mind. I reached for the memory, thrusting myself into it, willing myself to be Custos with the last of my strength.

Case after case filled with parchments, scrolls, and codices surrounded me, stretching away until they grew small with distance. I gazed at them with the easy familiarity any other man would regard his best friends. Only then did I notice that my arms were filled to overflowing with scrolls, the writing on them flowing, blocky, or spidery, depending on the author.

The scratchy, spidery text of the one on top drew my attention, and I craned my neck to read the title—*The Acts of Erich of Bunard.*

With a shudder I thrust it from me, putting it on the nearest case among other scrolls whose writing remained indistinct and undecipherable. I sighed, safe from its contents. I held up a hand in forbidding, and the case, scroll and all, disappeared behind a door, taken from view as if it had never been. With a mental twist I locked the heavy oak panels of the door within my mind, hiding the key within my own memories.

I gasped in shock and relief, but then shook my head at my own surprise. Was I not Custos, Keeper of the Library? I nodded even as hints of doubt threaded their way through me, but I pushed them away. Instead I looked at the next scroll, noted the title of a minor character from history, Oberd, and likewise placed it upon a case.

Raising my hand, I commanded the case to disappear as I'd done with Erich's, no longer surprised when it did so. The room around me grew smaller, the walls no longer hazy with distance but visible. I shifted the pile of scrolls in my arms, moving from case to case, putting a single scroll in each one. I didn't know why it was so important that I keep them separate, only that I must do so. With each banishing the room emptied and shrank until my arms were empty except for a single rolled parchment.

Time and urgency pressed upon me, though the reason lay beyond recollecting. I studied the last one even so, examining the script of its simple two-word title, thinking it held some meaning for me beyond the others—*Willet Dura*.

I hesitated, my fingers tracing the writing that seemed somehow more familiar to me than the others, as if I'd read it so often that I could recite it from memory. But that was ridiculous. I was Custos, I held every document in the library within my mind.

I walked to the last case in the emptiness of the domed room and place it on the shelf. I held up my hand to banish it . . .

And stopped.

Fear rippled through me like the disturbance of a pebble dropped in a reflecting pool, not urgent but insistent. I was forgetting something. Foolish. How could I forget—I who had never forgotten anything?

I looked in my hand, shocked to find a book—*Custos.*

This also? With a shrug I placed it next to the scroll of Dura's life and they touched. I staggered, my mind blank and confused. Who was I?

My hand lifted to banish this last piece, the final scroll and book and shelf. But I paused, a tremor of foreboding gnawing at me, as if I contemplated something more than the banishment of memories. The emptiness of the room, my own mind, struck me then as I surveyed the doors leading from it, doors locked with no way to open them except for the last scroll I was about to banish.

I stared at it in vain, trying to pull some measure of knowledge from it, some answer. Any key I kept would be accessible to the enemy as well. They would appear, force the scroll that was Custos's knowledge from me, and use it to open the doors. I no longer remembered why this could not be allowed to happen, but I was certain of the imperative.

Yet if I banished the last piece of knowledge within my mind, how would I return to myself? How would I reclaim the memories that were my right? Pressure built against the room, and the trickle of my remaining intuition told me that if I woke I would find myself in agony.

I needed to live, but I couldn't afford to leave my enemy a means to open the doors. I sat upon the dusty stones of the floor, regarding the last shelf and the room. Time had no meaning here, but my thoughts drifted, meandering like a stream born in the mountains, taking whatever path the lay of the land designated until many miles away it became something more.

I studied the walls of the domed room, seeing the thick stone that offered surety for my memories for the first time. They were my walls, the thick impregnable walls of the sanctum in the Merum library. The pressure of an idea formed in my mind, and I trembled. I was just a librarian. Where had I learned to contemplate such risks? I looked at the book with the name *Custos* on it once more. My name?

I shook the question away. It didn't matter. With a thought I put my plan in place and then placed the knowledge of it within the scroll holding the last scrap of identity I might claim. Raising my hand in the same gesture of will as before, I drove the last shelf from the now empty room—taking memory, knowledge, and light with it.

Noise in the hallway, the sounds of surprise and indignation, woke Pellin from his slumber. The window outside his room in the Hall of Servants showed the first tinge of coming dawn, still too early to lend any color to the sky other than the first charcoal shade of gray.

More commotion came, the pitched voices of a man and a woman seeped through the heavy wood of the door, crept in the crevices of the threshold before three staccato raps silenced the discussion.

He donned his cloak and paused long enough to fetch a taper from the fireplace and light a candle before answering. Crowded at the doorway stood five figures—Allta, Bolt, Toria Deel, Elory, and Volsk. Bolt was the only one of the five not holding steel, but he wielded his disdain for the others—and Pellin himself—like a weapon, his eyes flashing insults and imprecations.

"They took him, Eldest," Bolt said without preamble.

Pellin didn't bother with obvious questions of who had taken whom. He'd always considered such dissembling beneath him. "Bronwyn and her guard are in the next hallway," he said to Allta. "Bring them."

His guard padded off, and Pellin motioned to the rest of them. "Come in. The room has almost enough seats to accommodate us all."

He turned a well-cushioned chair that faced the fireplace toward the couch and seated himself, signaling his visitors to do the same. "Please," he said when they made no move to comply. "I can listen better when my neck doesn't hurt from craning to see who is speaking. It only takes a moment to stand. I think we can afford that much time."

"Can we?" Bolt said. He opened his mouth to say something more but stopped when Bronwyn and her guard entered the room.

The second-most-senior member of the Vigil left to the northern continent noted the gathering and looked around the room with alarm. "Where is Dura?"

"Taken by Laewan's men," Bolt said.

"So he says," Toria Deel added.

Bolt rounded on her. "Proof." He thrust out his arm behind him while he kept his glare on her for a moment longer. "I will not leave this to chance or belief, Eldest. Delve me."

Pellin restrained a sigh. His erstwhile guard would insist, and he would be right to do so. Fractured not just in opinion but in truth, they could no longer act in faith. He stepped forward and placed his hand on the corded surface of Bolt's forearm, felt the hardened muscle of countless sword strokes through the hair and skin before the tunnel swallowed him and a flood of memories flashed along the contact.

Most of them he knew. Pellin allowed the torrent of images to flow past him, ignoring them until they became unfamiliar. Then he stepped into the waters of memory, accepting it unto himself, beginning five years ago when Bolt left the duties of guarding the Vigil to the younger men he'd trained for so long.

The stream of images came to an end as Pellin broke the contact, still surprised after so many years that so little time had passed. He stepped back with a nod toward the seats. "I understand your need for haste," he said to Bolt, "but I will not rush into a trap that might extinguish the Vigil from the northern continent."

He turned to address Bronwyn and Toria Deel. "Delve him. Before I start issuing commands some of you may be tempted to bend"—he eyed Toria Deel—"I would have you know what I know."

Bolt huffed his displeasure but held out his arm for their touch. A moment later they stepped back from him, their brows creased in worry or doubt. Pellin couldn't tell which.

"Please sit," he said again.

Toria Deel and Volsk took the seats on the couch, sitting close enough to touch despite the room on either side. Bronwyn took a seat in a chair that was a duplicate of his own. Bolt perched on the edge of a small table, his face stiff with disapproval.

"I fail to see the need for counsel, Eldest," he said. "Torches and solas powder are sufficient to cleanse the caves beneath the city and take Dura back."

"Cleanse, yes," Bronwyn said. "But probably at the cost of Dura's life. If I were the enemy I wouldn't leave a sword behind me for the enemy to use."

"You can't afford to leave him there," Bolt said. "If Laewan delves him, you will lose whatever information he has to offer—and you will lose him as well. Once they have his memories, Dura is useless to them." He turned to Bronwyn. "They'll break the sword that threatens them."

Pellin shook his head, not in denial of Bolt's logic but in addition. "Agreed, but that's assuming Laewan can still delve."

"And why could he not?" Bolt challenged.

"The gift is Aer's," Bronwyn said. "If Laewan has fallen into corruption, the gift may no longer work for him, or it may have left him altogether to become free. Even now, some man or woman may hold within them the gift of domere, and Aer may be calling another to join our ranks."

Bolt's eyes blazed with outrage. "Now you talk of your gift and Aer? After you threatened to break Dura's mind?"

"When you have sifted through the vile memories of those like Dura who carry a vault within their mind," Toria Deel said, "then you can speak. Until then do not presume to interpret Aer's intention to us."

Though it was not directed at him, Pellin flinched beneath the scorn in her voice, but Bolt was undeterred.

"I know *good* when I see it," Bolt said, his voice almost too quiet to be heard. "Just as I know self-interest." His leisurely gaze swept back and forth between Volsk and Toria Deel, insinuating.

Toria Deel at least had the decency to blush. Volsk's eyes burned. "The guard is right," he said. "Dura must be rescued, whatever the cost."

Bolt's scorn filled the short bark of laughter that erupted from him. "Why do I mistrust your support, apprentice?"

Volsk shook his head. "I have no answer to your doubt except that I have fought side-by-side with Dura, as an ally. Believe what you will."

Bolt pushed himself from the table, took a step toward Peret Volsk. "I will tell you exactly what I believe."

Pellin clapped his hands, the noise cracking through the confines of the room, silencing the contention between its occupants. "I will speak. Questions of intent are best left to Aer. For now we and our enemy have one thing in common. We both need the information Dura holds. We must devise some means to enter the caves and fight a foe that can see in the dark or else surrender Dura to them."

He raised a hand to maintain their silence. "If Laewan has not delved him already."

I stood or floated in darkness, unable to tell which for an instant or eternity, denied knowledge of the passage of time that comes with conscious thought. Sound came first.

"Suitable," the voice said, "but a bit of light will serve me better."

A glow filled the space around me, revealing a man in a domed room. I moved to inspect him and only then did I realize that I was there as well.

The man looked down at me, his face a moue of disdain. "Show me the girl."

I looked at him in surprise. Couldn't he see the room? "There's nothing here."

His narrow unlined face twisted, and he crossed the space between us without moving. A spidery hand filled with strength clenched my throat. "You'll find my touch less gentle than that of those cattle you've experienced before." His fingers tightened. "Show me the girl."

I strained for breath, grappling with his arm to pull enough air to answer. My voice came out in a croak. "There's no one here."

For the first time since he'd appeared, the gangly stranger seemed to take note of the domed room, the light a simple presence without source. He turned a slow circle, searching, his eyes widening at the emptiness. "It's not possible," he growled. "No human can empty their mind so completely."

He disappeared from in front of me to reappear at one of the doors leading from the room, trying the handle, striving to open it, but it refused to move. Setting both hands on the lever, he strained until his neck corded and curses poured from him in a high keening language.

Moving with violent jerks, he tried each door in turn, struggling to open them. With a wordless cry of frustration, he turned from the surrounding wall to face me once more. "You have no idea what you've done. You've locked everything in your mind away. It's all gone, every last vestige of yourself."

His demeanor changed as quickly as the snuff of a candle, and he smiled, but I couldn't tell if his expression was cruel or amused. His hands gripped my head, and his thumbs forced my eyelids back. "Untutored fool. When you locked the doors, you didn't leave yourself a key. You've cut yourself off from the knowledge of your past and yourself as surely as if I had done it for you."

The stranger paused to laugh. "There's no way back for you, nameless one. It would be a mercy to kill you." He came forward, a smith's hammer appearing in his hand. "This, too, is beyond their power, but not mine. Not ours." His long arm lifted the heavy weight high overhead, the knuckles white with tension, tightening in preparation. The hammer started down.

"No." He stepped back at the last moment and the hammer disappeared. "It will be better to leave you this way, I think. Driven by compassion and desperation, they will tend you, spending their time and energy trying to bring you back to yourself while their destruction marches upon them unaware." He laughed again. "Yes, your life will serve me. They'll feed you gruel and change your clothes when you soil them, and they'll come here to fight the emptiness you've made of your mind. You'll spend the rest of your days in this room, without a single memory to comfort you or bring you back."

The stranger lifted one arm and disappeared, taking the light and awareness with him.

Chapter 38

They waited just long enough for the sun to crest the mountains to the east, bathing Bunard in a daffodil-yellow of morning light. Then Pellin, with his chosen company, entered Andler's sprawling multistory house and made for the cellar. Of the Vigil, only Bronwyn and her guard remained outside, safeguarded by the light of the sun against the worst possible outcome. Toria Deel, accompanied by her guard, Elory, and Volsk trailed just behind him. Allta and Bolt led with torches, their armed presence bolstered by a pair of Servants who each carried large bowls of Myle's solas powder, ready to create phos-fire at a moment.

A squad of Laidir's guards followed just behind the four men in front, their arms clanking enough to warn anyone within a quarter mile of their approach. Pellin held mixed feelings about that, but none whatsoever about the final member of their squad.

Gael.

Bolt had suggested the solas powder, but when they'd sought out the alchemist, the former Vigil guard had related Dura's predicament to Lady Alainn with uncharacteristic forthrightness. Pellin's eyebrows crept upward at the memory. The girl, she was hardly more than twenty, hadn't even tried to bargain her way into the company. She'd simply strapped on a light rapier and announced she would be coming, her, a lady of the nobility.

Things had obviously changed since Pellin's last stay in Bunard. It had taken all the real and implied authority he could muster to force her to the rear of the company.

He sighed. Even if they emerged victorious from Laewan's threat, it would take months to disguise the presence of the Vigil in Collum.

They descended into the cellar, the temperature dropping with each step into the cool of the earth, and stepped through the broken stone and into the caves beneath the city. The scent of blood hung in the cool air and brought gorge to Pellin's throat. A dozen times a dozen memories tried to break loose from behind their walls, and he thrust them away with a mental push that made him wince. Behind him he could hear Lady Gael uttering oaths against any who might have harmed Dura. Toria Deel's face, kissed by the light and shadows of the torches, bore creases of confusion.

The cave made slight bends but meandered northwest toward the keep. Pellin sighed. They would have to alert Laidir and likely the entire populace would hear of the threat beneath them. Perhaps the resulting flood of rumor would serve to disguise the Vigil's existence.

When they turned the next corner, the passage opened into a broad cavern, the space filled with blunt stone daggers hanging from the ceiling, resembling mythological dragon's teeth, and the smell of blood intensified. In the center of the wet pitted floor lay Dura.

Pellin's breath hissed from him. No one living would stay in such a position. Even unconscious victims of torture would curl, trying to protect their wounds.

Gael pushed her way through Vigil and soldier alike to run to his side. She didn't clutch him but stopped just short to touch her fingers lightly to his throat before probing his head and neck for injuries. Pellin's estimation of her, and Dura's taste in women, rose at the display. "Clever girl," he murmured.

Bolt nodded. "Aye. If she'd clutched at him, she might have made his injuries worse."

"He's alive," Gael said without taking her eyes from Dura's face. Her hands worked their way down his torso, her touch featherlight, to his legs. She stopped to call his name, but Dura's chest rose and fell with uninterrupted rhythm. "His eyes are open, but he's not seeing me."

Pellin's chest constricted. With his left hand he pulled off his right glove, and cool air ghosted across his fingertips before he became conscious of his motion or intent.

Toria Deel's hand, also uncovered, pressed against his chest. "Allow me, Eldest," she said. Her eyes, dark even in the light of day, wore unaccustomed shadows of doubt. "If there is a threat in his mind, I am the most expendable of the Vigil."

Distrust, pointed like the tapered blade of a *kiri* dagger, stabbed through him. Toria Deel had shown herself willing to bend his commands to her own ends and desires. "You swear not to try to break his vault?" Pellin whispered.

She nodded, the full lips of her mouth flattening at the implied accusation and its validity. "I swear, Eldest, not to break his vault until you've given permission." Behind her, Volsk's eyes, shadowed by a stone dragon's tooth, were unreadable.

"Take care," Pellin said.

She turned and went to kneel with her hands folded in her lap on the far side of Dura's body, across from Gael as the woman continued to call to him.

"His injuries may be more than physical," Toria Deel said, her voice halting. "Sometimes people hide within their mind to escape. I have some experience with such." She lifted her bare hand. "May I?"

Pellin noted Gael's nod showed nothing of the distrust that crept up his neck. Toria Deel placed her naked fingertips on Dura's brow. Her face went slack in the torchlight, and the touch lingered beyond Pellin's expectations. Volsk had just started forward when Toria Deel pulled her hand away, ignoring him and Pellin to address Gael once more.

"He's gravely injured in spirit, my lady." She reached across to offer comfort, her bared hand taking hold of Gael's. "There is a healer within the Hall of Servants who possesses more skill with this type of injury than any other," she said after a pause.

Gael's face hardened into determination. "We will take him there, but Galen will tend his physical injuries."

When Gael turned to give orders to the soldiers, Toria Deel caught Pellin's gaze and shook her head.

Willet Dura's body lay on one of the large four-poster beds reserved for visiting dignitaries within the midst of the Hall of Servants. Not so grand as those within the Merum, it still boasted heavy velvet curtains and a broad fireplace to ward off the chill of winter. While the accoutrements would never be considered fine or grand, the pitcher, bowl, towels, and the rest boasted a quality of craftsmanship that appealed to Pellin. Each had been made to be functional yet pleasant to the touch, their beauty captured by the balance within the hand instead of the ornamentation to the eye.

He turned to the bed. Dura, he learned, might have been much the same. "His shell," Pellin said pointing at the bed. "His physical presence without personality is evidence our enemy is elsewhere."

Volsk, who stood as always next to Toria Deel, nodded—but not in agreement. "Evidence, Eldest, but not proof. Scripture tells us it is ever the way of the enemy to break his tools once he is done with them."

Bolt shook his head, eyeing Volsk as if he were a bug that needed to be squashed. "Contemptible."

Volsk, instead of becoming defensive, peered at the guard, appearing to consider the charge. "Is it contemptible to be on guard against deception? If so, I will gladly wear the accusation. But allow me, Eldest, to elucidate. Willet Dura is a good man." He turned to Bolt. "Are you surprised to hear me admit it? From the moment we stood together in the House of Passing against the attack, I knew it. It has been my job to trail you, but I was also tasked to gather what information I could and relay it to the Eldest. I've heard how he tends the dying, gives money to the urchins running the streets of Bunard, and gives women of the night respect they receive from no other."

Volsk turned again, the gaze he turned on Pellin holding resolution and demand. "But all of that is beside the point. By some means unknown to us, he is one of those who survived a night in the Darkwater."

"Us?" Bolt snorted. "Do you carry the gift already?"

Volsk refused to rise to the challenge. "No, but I am the apprentice until it comes to me or I become too old. I know what the vault in his mind means."

"Meant," Toria Deel said.

When Pellin and the rest turned to her, she turned dark eyes etched with sorrow and doubt to each of them. "Meant," she repeated, breaking eye contact to look at the floor. "There's nothing left within his mind that can bring him back. Even the vault is gone."

"Yes," Volsk said. "Nothing that we could name as Willet Dura remains, good or bad."

Pellin nodded, knowing what would come next, what had come next every time the Vigil had forced their way into the vaults of those broken souls who'd survived the Darkwater.

Bolt must have seen it as well. He shoved himself away from the wall, his posture coiled, like a spring. "You're forgetting one thing. Aer chose him to carry the gift."

Bronwyn sighed. "But we don't know why. And while it is tempting to try to ascertain Aer's design, in the end we will be right back here. The Vigil itself is under assault, the gifts that define it are missing." She lifted her head to Pellin. "Can we afford not to free his gift?"

Some instinct or warning drew Pellin's gaze to Toria Deel, and deep within he hoped she might offer him some means to avoid this thing they were all talking about but taking pains to keep from naming. "What did you see when you touched Lady Gael?"

Toria Deel's eyes welled as her lips parted to speak, but her throat constricted, and her gaze found the floor once more. "Something beautiful and fierce," she whispered.

"If it must be done," Bronwyn said, "let it be done quickly."

"And how long will it take you to find his gift once it has gone free?" Bolt demanded. "To train the one who receives it to be a functional member of the Vigil? Has Jorgen managed to find Cesla's gift somewhere in the trackless wastes of the north?"

"All the more reason to do it quickly," Bronwyn said. "And for mercy's sake," she said to Bolt. "Would you leave him there, trapped alone in his mind, without even the consolation of his memories to keep him company?"

Bolt's craggy, weather-worn face closed as completely as a door. "Here you are in the midst of any number of circumstances you've never seen before—a member of the Vigil has been corrupted, and a man carries both the gift and a vault—and you stand here facing your uncertain future with the same notions you've used in the past." Bolt shook his head. "Fine. Kill him. Free his gift—as if that could help you with Laewan's treachery, as if his death will help you lift the veil on what's happening here."

He paused, raking each of them with his glare. "Which one of you will tell Lady Gael he has to die? Don't bother looking to me—because that's one task I won't do for you."

Silence filled the room, a quiet physical immobility shot through with discomfort and guilt that Pellin knew meant the duty would fall to him—the price of age, the consequence of failure.

Toria Deel stood. "I will."

Relief alloyed with guilt washed over him, touching a hundred similar memories he'd locked away, his and others, before he pushed it aside. He stood, crossed to Toria Deel where she sat with her head bowed. He couldn't see her eyes, but a tear fell from behind her thick curtain of lustrous black hair to wet the dark green fabric of her cloak, the moisture turning it almost black.

This was the Toria Deel he loved best, the empathetic bearer of Aer's gift, the member of their number who strove to see past the burdens of life to the good. He took her hands in his own, her smooth, dark skin contrasting to the creased, age-worn flesh he extended with its blotched covering. Their memories merged, and he saw how her love for Volsk, with all its fire and commitment, enabled her to understand the cost Lady Gael would bear.

"No, daughter," he said, using the term of endearment he'd adopted for the much younger Vigil member the day she received her gift. "This is a burden you do not have to take. The task is mine."

She released his hands and raised her head, her eyelashes clinging to unshed tears. One of them fell when she shook her head. "He's not a task—he's her love." Her jaw came forward in defiance. "She should hear it from a woman, from someone who understands."

He turned from her to see Volsk waiting impassively for instruction and sighed. "Bring Lady Gael and the apothecary. Spilling blood isn't required. Tell him we'll need somnal powder and poppy sap." The two together, even in relatively small quantities, created a lethal dose. Physicians and apothecaries often provided it as the final solution for those in the last agonizing stages of the wasting disease. Upon taking it, patients quickly lost consciousness, their breathing and heartbeat slowing until they drifted into death. The entire process took less than two hours.

The click of the door closing behind Volsk brought Pellin back to himself. "I don't doubt you, Toria Deel, but I wish to see the state of Dura's mind for myself." He turned to Bronwyn. "And I would like for you to see it as well."

He indicated Bolt with a nod. "In this respect my old friend is correct. We are in unfamiliar waters on a strange ship." He held out his arm toward the bed and Dura's body. "Lady Bronwyn?"

With a nod of resignation, she stood.

Light came into the domed room, and I ceased floating, anchored by the vision of the floor, the walls, the curve of the ceiling, though I didn't know why. That the darkness receded surprised me. That there would be someone else in the room provided an explanation for the light, and I settled in the center.

She had streaks of gray in chestnut hair held back in a bun above green eyes that seemed old even for the worn skin of her face. She spared a glance for me and then circled the room, peering at the floor and the walls.

"I know this place," she said to herself. "This is the sanctum within the library of the Merum cathedral, though the shelves and cases are gone. Not one scroll or codex remains, but the room itself is the same."

She turned to me. "Why are you here, Dura?"

I looked at the room, illuminated by the pale yellow glow of light that came with her, that came from everywhere. "There's nowhere else."

Her brows lowered, and a vertical line appeared between her eyes as she shook her head. "Do you understand that you made this place, the repository of all your memories before they were banished?" She shook her head again. "But why here?" she said in a softer voice. "What is it about the library's sanctum that's so important to you?"

Her footsteps, carrying her around the edge of the domed room, scattered a bit of dust by one section of the circular wall before she stopped and closed to within an arm's length. "Do you know who you are? Do you remember anything?"

I shook my head. The questions seemed the same as the one before. "There's nothing here."

She pulled her lower lip between her teeth. "I see that. Tell me, who emptied the room?"

I looked around. The room was the room. It didn't change. "I don't know."

More lines appeared in her face. "Oh, Willet, there's nothing we can do for you."

She vanished, and the pale yellow light winked out.

Bronwyn pulled her hand away from the pale skin of Dura's slack face, but her expression held more than just the grief Pellin expected. Her furrowed brows held confusion as well as resignation.

"What did you see?" Pellin asked. He couldn't have put a name to the hope within his chest that guttered like a dying candle that refused to go out.

Her breath sounded loud in the still room. "Nothing we can use, but something strange, nevertheless." She turned to Toria Deel. "What did you see when you delved him in the cave?"

Toria Deel tilted her head the way she did whenever curiosity took hold of her. "Nothing too unusual, a round room with a stone floor and locked doors. I think there was a window in the roof."

Bronwyn nodded, turning to Pellin. "I know that room, Eldest, as do you. It's the sanctum of the Merum library."

Surprise threaded its way into Pellin's thoughts, and his own memories of that room, crowded with scrolls and parchments, arose in his mind. He turned to the bed and the inert form of Dura on it, searching for explanation there, but only the shallow rise and fall of his chest replied.

Toria Deel's voice firmed. "What is the sanctum, Eldest?"

Pellin sat in the chair opposite Toria Deel, leaning forward with his elbows on his knees. "It's the part of the Merum library where they store the oldest and rarest manuscripts. I've visited it several times over the years to make sure there are no references to the Vigil there. I haven't found anything in ages, but I make it a habit to check every so often just in case."

"Why would Dura put himself there?" Toria Deel asked.

"Exactly." Pellin nodded. "It's not his home or the home of his betrothed or even the keep of Laidir, where he's lived for so long." He shook his head. "I've never seen someone place themselves in such an odd place."

"Dura is a reeve, Eldest," Bolt said. "Above all he would try to leave a path for you to follow. Don't you think you should understand this before he dies?"

Pellin caught the shift in language, almost let it slip by but decided not to. "You mean before we kill him?"

His former guard didn't flinch. "Yes. I mean that."

Instead of returning to the argument they'd had before, Pellin sought Bronwyn. "Was there anything there?"

She shook her head, darted a glance at Bolt. "No, Eldest. Not one memory remains that might guide him back."

He nodded. "Still, we have time before Volsk returns with the apothecary and Lady Gael. Visit the library, by stealth if it can be arranged, but now at any rate. See if there is anything there that might help us—" he nodded toward the bed—"or him."

Pellin sighed, weary as only very old men could be, and flexed his hand. "In the meantime, I will delve him."

Chapter 39

My floating ceased and bright light lit the domed room. I stood facing an old man with crystal blue eyes surrounded by a dense network of wrinkles. A fringe of cropped gray hair circled his head, leaving the front and the crown bare. He didn't bother to speak to me—simply inspected the room without stepping from his spot.

When he turned to me, his eyes were mere slits. "Why are you here?"

I didn't understand the question. Why wouldn't I be here? There were doors in the domed room, but they were all locked, and I could see them only when someone brought light. "There's nowhere else."

The old man's squint changed character, and he stepped away from me to circle the room, trying each door as he went. "So many," he said softly. "It usually takes years to amass this many."

He stopped between doors, his feet spraying a cloud of dust between one footstep and the next. "The sanctum was never so dirty as this." He knelt to finger the powder, sifting it between his thumb and forefinger. With a jerk, he straightened to try the doors on either side. They didn't move. "I wonder what you put behind these."

He sighed and turned to me. "Has anyone else been here?"

I shook my head. "There's no one here. It's empty."

He looked at me, and the squint in his eyes wavered in the bright light that came from everywhere. "I'm afraid you're right, Willet."

The name held no meaning. "Who?"

"You," the stranger answered. "Willet Dura."

The words were unfamiliar.

"What about Lady Gael?" the stranger asked, his voice pleading. "She's tall, with hair the color of midnight and a smile brighter than a thousand candles. And she loves you, Willet. Her blue eyes dance whenever she comes into your presence."

I looked around the room. "There's not anything else."

Instead of replying, the stranger lifted a hand in farewell, and the light vanished.

Pellin opened his eyes and stepped back from the bed. "It's as you said, Toria Deel." He shrugged. "A little dustier than I remember the sanctum, but undoubtedly the same."

He didn't want to look at Bolt, but there would be no escaping it. He faced his old friend. "There's nothing left of him. It's all gone. Laewan has already broken his vault."

Anger, tight and coiled, built in Bolt's eyes. "Why would he do such a thing if Dura was already in their camp?"

When Pellin didn't answer, Bolt faced Toria Deel, his posture stiff, demanding. "If you had trusted him with the gift, you would have had the ally you needed."

She stood, her eyes rimmed in crimson but her expression passive as a rock while Bolt fumed. "It's possible," she said after a moment. "But it's also possible he might have behaved like every other survivor of the Darkwater." She tilted her head, questioning. "How fast was he on the bridge? As fast as you, Bolt? Faster? What if we'd taken him to our bosom and his vault had opened in our midst? How many of the Vigil might he have killed?"

She shook her head. "I will not accept the guilt that comes from prudence. As you say, we've never seen this before. We are old, but not infallible."

Bolt didn't answer, choosing instead to walk to the bed and seat himself. Dura's head lolled with the motion, the slit of his eyes open without seeing, his mouth agape.

Drawn by Bolt's loyalty, Pellin went to stand next to his old friend, to wait.

Several hours later, Bronwyn was the first to return with her guard, which Pellin found surprising. What was keeping Volsk?

She pointed to her guard. "I sent Balean to distract the librarian while I entered the sanctum." Her lips tightened. "I think I know why Dura chose it."

Pellin's heart skipped like a calf, but before the expression of hope could completely form on his face, Bronwyn waved it away.

"It's one of the old gift texts by Tiochus."

Pellin let his annoyance show. "I thought we'd gotten rid of those long ago."

Bronwyn shrugged. "Evidently not. On a certain level I've always admired him. Of all the early historians, he's the one who came closest to fully cataloging our gift. I still don't know how he managed to do it."

"That would explain how Dura managed to exert some measure of control." He turned to Bolt, a sudden thought occurring to him. "Did you know about this?"

The guard shook his head. "No. He must have gone there after he left me in the poor quarter."

"That," Pellin said slowly, "means we'll have to do something about the librarian. It's likely he knows about us. We'll have to clean the sanctum again."

Toria Deel stood and paced the room, her steps short and harsh against the floor, shooting glances at the door. "That can wait. How do we find Laewan? And what does he intend?"

The questions couldn't be denied, but neither could they be answered, at least not yet. "The three of us will have to quarter the city until we find some place that holds a memory of him. Then we'll have to follow his trail."

A sharp exhalation burst from Toria Deel at this. "In a city this size? Eldest, you're asking us to find an acorn in a wheat field."

Pellin didn't have an alternative for her. Lord have mercy, his bones ached with fatigue just considering his own suggestion. Bolt, still seated next to Dura's motionless body, no longer took note of the conversation. Toria Deel resumed her measured steps back and forth across the room.

An hour later, Volsk opened the door, holding it for Lady Gael, who stormed in, her eyes flashing. He entered after muttering something to the squat apothecary who waited in the hallway outside.

"You lied to me," Gael spat at Toria Deel. "You're no healer." She flung a hand at Volsk. "And this oaf refused to bring me here unless I came in secret."

Pellin stood. "That was at my direction, Lady. Those who damaged your betrothed mean us harm as well."

Fire burned in Gael's gaze. "Damaged? Is he a piece of property to you? They tortured him!"

Toria Deel approached Gael as she would an injured fawn, her feet no longer clacking against the floor. "I am a healer, Lady, though not in the way you or anyone else in the city would reckon." She pointed first to Pellin and then to Bronwyn.

Pellin drew breath to speak, but Toria Deel shook him off.

"Lady," she said softly, "may I have your oath on a matter of secrecy?"

Gael shook her head. "And why would I consent to bind myself in such a way?"

Toria Deel nodded. "Because our survival depends on it. The same men who have broken Lord Dura hunt us as well. If they know of us, they will hunt us down and kill us too."

Gael tore her gaze from Toria Deel and ran to Dura's bedside, the embrace giving way to a quick examination a trained physician might have done. After she'd satisfied herself, she turned to glare at Toria Deel and the rest of them once more. "Explain yourself. He is unconscious but hardly dead. His heart is strong and his breathing is regular. Even the burns on his leg are not as serious as they might have been."

Pellin stepped forward to address her, his stomach knotting. He had never been good with people, not like Cesla, who could inspire such fierce loyalty, or even Elwin, who had a way of speaking encouragement when it was most needed. "The damage, Lady Gael, is in his mind. Our enemy has broken Lord Dura's mind, emptying it. The memories that define each of us, that make us who we are, are gone in him."

Gael darted a look toward the bed before her spine stiffened. "I don't believe that. There's no power or gift that can do such a thing. I have seen fits before."

"Not like this," Toria Deel said. "And there is a power that can do such a thing. Ten years ago Willet Dura spent a night and a day in the Darkwater and emerged."

"That's impossible," Gael said, brushing aside Toria Deel's words as she would a fly. "No one survives the forest."

"Almost no one," Bronwyn said. "That's our task—to find those few who do and safeguard those around them from their insanity. Some few, a very few, are not caught, and those are the men or women you hear about, who seem perfectly normal until they go on a rampage, killing all around them until they are cut down themselves."

Gael's mouth firmed in denial. "Willet couldn't have been in the Darkwater. He never did such a thing."

Bronwyn nodded. "Nevertheless, his mind bore the evidence of it."

"How could you know that?"

Pellin felt Toria Deel's and Bronwyn's gaze like a physical touch. At least they left it to him to decide. "That is our gift, Lady. Aer has gifted some few of us so that we can see into the mind of others."

"*Fayit* tales," Gael said, flatly looking around the room. "Here I thought you were possessed of greater wit. You could have invented something better."

Toria Deel stepped toward her. "Your disbelief is understandable, and in its way is one of our greatest accomplishments. But I will offer you proof. Will you consent to be convinced?"

Gael nodded. "I warn you, I am no child to be swayed by some sleight of hand or magician's diversion."

Toria Deel's mouth turned upward in a smile that looked sad at the edges. "I don't doubt it. I want you to think of a special memory you have, one that no one but you would know—not your uncle, not your sister, not even Lord Dura. I want you to hold it in your mind."

Gael's eyes grew distant for a moment before she nodded. "Very well. Now what?"

Toria Deel reached forward. "Now give me your hand."

Lady Gael, calm and assured, clasped hands with Toria Deel, who closed her eyes, her head bowed before opening them once more. Pellin watched her step back, her eyes unreadable.

"Is it true?" Toria Deel asked.

Gael shook her head. "I will not be taken in by a teller's trick."

Toria Deel nodded as she turned away. "This is the memory Lady Gael held in her mind. I saw a young girl, perhaps ten or eleven years, well-dressed, having the semblance of Lady Gael walking with another during winter who bore some resemblance to her. In the memory they were walking the streets of Bunard. They passed by another girl, ragged and dirty and thin, who begged alms from them."

Toria Deel licked her lips. "Lady Gael and the other girl passed by, slowing, and the other girl tried to give the poor girl some money. Lady Gael pulled her away, citing haste, and the two of them moved on, the poor girl's face showing her dashed hope. The memory shifts in time to the next day. Lady Gael returns to the same spot alone, searching, but she can't find the girl. The spot where she begged was empty."

"That's the end of the memory," Toria Deel said.

Pellin looked to see Gael's face, pale as wax.

"I never found her." Her voice ghosted across his hearing.

"Perhaps—" Toria Deel began, but Gael's raised hand cut her off.

"Don't comfort me," she rasped. "Bunard is big, but not that big. I know what happened." She looked toward the bed, toward Dura, tremors building across her face. "Is there nothing left of him?"

"No," Toria Deel said softly.

With a wail, Gael buried her face in Toria Deel's shoulder, her cry a guttural mixture of loss and rage. Pushing Toria Deel away, she turned to face Pellin, somehow sensing his position. "I will tend him. For as long as he lives, I will ensure he is fed and cared for," she said, "and loved. I've lost my sister. I will not lose him as well."

Toria Deel lifted her head, her gaze locking with Pellin's. It should never have come to this. In all the years of dealing with the Darkwater's broken, he had dealt with the shock of unexpected and unexplained violence, but he'd never had to rip someone's beloved from them. With a silent curse for the circumstances that cornered him and another for himself, he nodded to Toria Deel. That one simple gesture made him feel dirty, as though he'd fallen into the foulest midden and couldn't wash.

Toria Deel—bless her for this, as well—only nodded. Her eyes held nothing of the condemnation Pellin reserved for himself. Gently, she turned Gael to face the bed. "Would you have him spend the rest of his days trapped in an empty shell, his soul bound to a mind that no longer carries any spark of life?" Toria Deel swallowed thickly, her throat working at the familiar motion. "Is that what he would want?"

Gael took one quick step away from Toria Deel, her mouth agape in shock at the suggestion before it melted and she slumped, the steel leaving her spine. "No," she whispered. "It's not."

As if he were dousing himself in filth once more, Pellin turned to Volsk and motioned toward the door. The apothecary entered, his hands cradling the somnal powder and poppy sap.

Gael turned at the sound. "So soon?"

Because he couldn't bear his defilement any longer, Pellin put aside his discomfort and went forward to take Gael's hands in his own, taking ownership of the responsibilities as Eldest again. "How long would you have him wait?"

At the question a hint of iron crept back into her stance, and she shook her head the barest amount. "Not one second longer. But I would like to say good-bye first." Without waiting for permission, she crossed to the bed and seated herself, bending low to touch her forehead to Dura's, speaking.

Pellin couldn't hear them, but he felt no desire to move closer. That she might say something the Vigil would find useful occurred to him, but there were lines he wouldn't cross. If Aer demanded Willet's death of them, of him, then Aer would have to find a way to help them besides having him eavesdrop while love died. Pellin clenched his jaws until his teeth ached. If Aer spoke to him right now, he wasn't sure he would listen.

Lady Gael spoke to him for the better part of an hour, the cadence of her voice shifting from warm to pleading to angry over and over, each sound its own torture for Pellin. When she stopped talking, she stayed, her head touching Dura's, her hands cradling each side of his face for long moments. Then she kissed him.

But nothing happened, no movement, no sound, no awakening as from the tale of Loch and Loriel rescued them from their duty. He'd hoped, but he'd stopped believing in tales so long ago.

Gael stood and turned toward them, away from Dura, and walked past to the door. When her hand found the latch she paused to speak over her shoulder. "Willet is gone. I won't diminish his memory by staying for this." She closed the door behind her on the way out.

Pellin wanted to flee with her, but duty nailed his boots to the floor. He motioned the apothecary forward. "You know what to do?" The man nodded, his face appropriately somber, and Pellin wondered if the expression was genuine or practiced.

"I'll require help getting him to a sitting position. It will make it easier to get the mixture into him."

Bolt muttered something caustic under his breath. When they turned to him, his gaze found Pellin's alone. "Poison. It's not a mixture—it's poison."

"He's gone," Volsk said. "Your condemnation is unfair. I'll help you," he said to the apothecary.

Bolt stepped in front of the apprentice before he could take a second step. "You will not touch him."

Pellin raised his voice, assuming the full weight of his responsibility. "Yes. He will. Volsk is our apprentice and the Vigil needs him. If Aer desires him to receive the gift, we will make it possible. If not, then Aer can make the gift free."

For a moment, he thought Bolt would refuse, but after the space of a dozen heartbeats, he stepped aside. "The lot of you, you're no longer human. You've absorbed the memories and feelings of so many others, you've banished all of your own."

The rebuke sent a dagger through Pellin's heart. "Perhaps you should wait outside."

Bolt nodded. "Probably, but I think a man should have at least one friend with him when he dies."

Pellin turned from Bolt's second stroke and nodded to the apothecary. Together he and Volsk levered Dura to a sitting position on the bed, leaning him against the headboard. Volsk took Dura's left hand and placed it on his head.

The apothecary poured a dose of somnal powder into the vial of poppy sap and swirled the contents, studying the mixture. After a moment, he nodded in satisfaction. "Much of it he'll cough out," he said to Volsk.

"Will it be enough?" Volsk asked.

The apothecary nodded. "Aye. After the first cough, I'll pour some more into his mouth and he'll swallow by reflex."

He tilted Dura's head up and poured from the vial. Dura sprayed the thick liquid across the bed, but the apothecary tipped his vial again, and Pellin saw Dura's throat work, swallowing. Pellin sat on the couch next to Toria Deel to wait.

Chapter 40

I floated or stood without knowledge or the passage of time, alone, as I had always been and ever would be in that place. Then a glimmer of light appeared, a point so small that I might have imagined it if I could have imagined anything there. It grew, offering enough illumination for me to realize I no longer floated, but stood, yet not enough for me to see my surroundings.

With nothing else to do, I waited, watching the point of light expand, though whether it did so quickly or slowly I had no way of knowing. Then it occurred to me that instead of growing, it might be moving toward me, or I toward it.

The brightness grew enough for me to see by, and I found myself in a circular domed room with a single window overhead and doors spaced at intervals along the wall. I stepped toward the light and stopped. At my feet a pile of gritty dust scattered with my steps. Another dozen steps brought me to the source of light.

A hole in the wall.

I touched it and the mortar holding the stones together disintegrated into powder and more light streamed in. The hole grew more rapidly now, spreading out to encompass the two doors on each side, eating away at the stone that held the frames and hinges in place. I stepped back as the doors and their frames fell toward me with a crash and a billow of dust.

A bookcase appeared in the room holding a white scroll and book, and a black scroll as well. I reached out to the single book on my right, the cover thin and soft to the touch. It disappeared.

Memory flooded into me.

I was Custos once more.

The hole stopped spreading, the rest of the walls intact, as obdurate and indomitable as the stone they resembled. I looked at the other two scrolls, two opposites. They pulled at me. Was I really Custos? I reached for the white, ignoring its dark twin. At my touch, both of them disappeared and I reeled, knowing myself, my true self.

Willet Dura.

I looked around the room, saw the hole in the wall, and laughed with the surprised delight of a child. "I can't believe that worked." I knew that voice, and for a moment I stood in the light, reveling in the memories that made me. Good and bad, joyful and sorrowful, mundane or important, I basked in them all.

Laughing with the knowledge of myself, I walked the perimeter of the room on light feet, scattering the sawdust I'd used to create the wall around the two doors of memory that defined me.

But then I stumbled, fighting to get my legs under me, but they wouldn't respond. I tried to lift my arms, but invisible weights held them to my sides. I fell. Not understanding. I'd built this place for my mind, a place of safety from Laewan. I willed myself to stand, but lethargy gripped me, holding me to the floor. Why? This room was mine.

My body. What was happening to me? Had Laewan changed his mind, deciding to kill me after all? If I woke myself, he would know I'd tricked him. Everything I knew would be his to take.

I curled, drawing myself into a ball, fighting to keep despair and disappointment at bay. My ploy had almost succeeded. Almost. "Well, at least it doesn't hurt." I mustered a smile. "And now I'll know what's on the other side."

Pellin stood next to the apothecary, who held Dura's wrist in his hand. "It's close."

At Pellin's order, Volsk had knelt, holding Dura's hand atop his head, his eyes desperate and pleading. The temptation to verify the apothecary's assessment came to him, to take hold of Dura's wrist and feel the waning flutter of his pulse for himself. He pushed it aside. The Servants knew their business. "Thank you," Pellin said softly, "for your service."

With a nod, the apothecary laid Dura's hand across his lap and bowed to Pellin, his face still wearing the same mask of commiseration people donned at death. "I can send for the gravesman for you, if you wish."

Pellin shook his head. "No. That won't be necessary. We will take care of him." The apothecary turned sideways to slide by him, and Pellin edged forward toward Dura to give the thick-bodied man room to wedge by.

The apothecary nodded his thanks. Half turning, his hand knocked into the standing candelabra, pushing the earthenware jar from his hand. Pellin saw it tumbling toward the floor, saw the look of surprise on the apothecary's face as he grasped for it. Reflexively, Pellin jerked his bare hands away from the contact, but his legs hit the edge of the bed and he sprawled across it.

And touched Willet Dura's hand.

Memories cascaded into him, thousands upon thousands of remembrances of pain and sorrow and love. Gaël's face, more luminous in Dura's mind than in real life, shone. Pellin watched in shock as portions of Willet Dura's life cascaded through him just as it had before.

How? It wasn't possible. Dura's mind lived.

But as Pellin watched, joy turned to ashes. Darkness shadowed Dura's memories, the edge of each vision blurring. With a jerk, Pellin straightened, pulling his awareness from Dura's mind, and spun to grab the apothecary by the arms. "Wake him!"

The apothecary shook his head in incomprehension, his mouth gaping.

They didn't have time for explanations. Pellin slapped him across the face. "How do we undo the poison?"

He licked his lips. "Distilled chiccor root, but there's too much somnal and poppy in his stomach."

Bolt appeared next to him. Pellin hadn't seen him move. "Get it!" the guard grated. "And run as if your life depended on it."

The apothecary lumbered from the room, picking up speed. Bolt pushed Pellin aside and hauled Dura up, throwing the reeve over one shoulder, his head hanging down. "Put your fingers down his throat."

Pellin wedged Dura's mouth open and jammed two gloved fingers in as far as they would go, but Dura remained inert. Volsk moved to step away, but at Bronwyn's direction he circled the bed, kneeling to replace Dura's hand on his head once more.

"Nothing's happening," Pellin said.

Bolt spewed a stream of curses. "Wiggle them, Eldest. You're old, haven't you ever had a friend poisoned before?"

Pellin fluttered his fingers, working to move them in the confines of Dura's throat. "No."

Dura twitched and thick purplish liquid ran from his mouth. "That's it, man," Bolt said. "Fight."

He bounced up and down on his feet, shaking Dura's body while Pellin struggled to keep his fingers in his mouth. More liquid came, as thick as syrup and smelling of bile. Still Bolt bounced him. "Where's that accursed apothecary?"

I watched as my memories blurred before me, growing indistinct at the edges. Would there be anything left of me after I died? I didn't want to lose the images of my life. After a moment I laughed at myself. It wasn't as if I had any choice in the matter.

The thought of ceasing to be pained me, but I set that aside also, enjoying the freedom of my powerlessness. Nothing else would be required of me. There was literally nothing more I could do.

That comforted me for a moment before I realized my error. As my memories blurred like wet paint in the rain, I prayed, stumbling through the words of the redeemer's prayer like a man fumbling for light in the dark.

I finished it and started again, the words coming easier the second time, but after I'd finished, a sense of incompleteness remained. What more could I say? An ache in my chest gave me the answer. Pulling her image from the rest, I thanked Aer for Gael and then prayed for her, that she might find love again.

A final contentment suffused me, and I relaxed, expecting my memories to blur until they faded completely. To my surprise they remained, neither growing sharper nor more indistinct. Wonder and questions accompanied them. What was happening in the waking world? The temptation to open my eyes and wake filled me. I drifted toward consciousness.

A blow, almost physical, shook me, and memories I didn't recognize bombarded my mind.

Allta supported one of Dura's arms, Bolt the other, as the two guards held him upright and the apothecary poured more of the black chiccor root syrup down Dura's throat, working the muscles of his neck to make him swallow. A spoonful at a time, the mixture disappeared.

Pellin stood close, watching, taking each involuntary twitch of Dura's fingers or face as a sign of hope. The rest of the Vigil circled them, Volsk standing behind them, retreating from Dura at the first sign of his resurrection.

"A bit more," the apothecary murmured. He looked at Pellin out of the corner of his eyes. "Your pardon, sir, but never before now have I been asked to administer the final draught and then provide the antidote. My teacher at the college always said I had a good memory for the arcane. If not, I doubt I would have been able to help you."

Pellin nodded. "My thanks. Your intervention is much appreciated. I will inform the Chief of Servants of your service and see to it that you are rewarded."

The apothecary smiled as he placed another spoonful in Dura's mouth. This time the reeve, whom Pellin had thought of as a rogue, swallowed weakly on his own.

"Honesty compels me to admit that I merely undid what I had already done," the apothecary said with a deep chuckle. "I don't think she will see much to be rewarded in my actions."

Pellin smiled. "Leave that to me."

Dura's arms twitched, and his legs jerked as his eyes fluttered open.

His head lolled on his neck and Pellin watched as he tried to bring his gaze into focus. After another moment of struggle that wrung pity from Pellin's heart, he hung limp in the guards' grasp, as if he'd been nailed there.

"I feel awful."

The muscle in Bolt's jaw jumped and wetness filled the deep wrinkles around his eyes. "Aye," he said, "but you feel, praise Aer. You feel."

The apothecary stepped back, handing the rest of the chiccor root potion to Pellin. "Get the rest of this in him, and don't let him sleep until next sundown." He looked around the room. "My teachers at the college also said I had an unhealthy curiosity. I think this is my chance to prove them wrong. You have my utmost discretion and silence."

Pellin nodded, not speaking until the door had closed behind him. Allta and Bolt half-walked, half-carried Dura to the couch, where they put him in a sitting position. Pellin crossed to him, flanked by Toria Deel and Bronwyn, and handed him the vial. "You're supposed to drink this. It's to counteract the somnal powder and poppy sap you have in your system." He wrinkled his nose. "If it tastes as bad as it smells, you probably won't like it."

With a glance to Bolt, who nodded his approval, Dura upended the vial and drained it. He stuck out his tongue. "It's worse." He shifted and winced. "Everything hurts."

Pellin nodded. "We've dressed your wounds, but you'll carry some scars." He stopped, aware of a crippling fatigue in his own limbs as the rush of Dura's plight wore off. Allta, sensing his need, brought him a chair and he sat. The rest of the Vigil followed his example, arraying themselves around Dura in a semicircle.

"I caught a glimpse of your memories, Lord Dura, but not enough to see how you managed to survive. You'll have to forgive my curiosity, but all three of us delved you and there was nothing there. Your mind had been emptied of every memory, all of them locked away. We've only seen such emptiness in the minds of those whose vaults we've forced." He couldn't help but shake his head in wonder. "The fact that you are here among us is incredible. If I had not delved you myself, I wouldn't believe it."

Dura nodded but didn't speak, his eyes wary.

"How did you do it?" Pellin prompted.

"Why should I tell you?"

Bolt's face split into a craggy grin. "Good question."

Pellin sat back in his chair considering. Cesla or Elwin would have done this better. They'd been good with people. Not him. Even as a young man, he'd been better with books. He still preferred them, but he had learned two things about the vagaries of men and women during the course of his long life that he could use. First, never underestimate the power of a question. Second, humility was strength. He employed both of them now. "What can I do to earn your trust?"

Dura's eyebrows lifted, his surprise mirrored by Bolt and everyone else in the room. "Let me delve you."

Pellin sighed. "Agreed, but I would ask you to wait. You've read the scroll by Tiochus. Most of it is true. Too many delvings in too short a time will break your mind." He lifted one hand, palm up. "And I'm old. I have a great many memories."

Dura turned to Pellin's former guard. "Bolt?"

A nod. "You can trust him on this."

"At a time of my choosing, then?" Dura asked.

"Agreed," Pellin said. He breathed a soft sigh of mourning. Dura would regret his bargain.

"You all delved me while my mind was empty," Dura began. "Did you notice the doors?"

Pellin nodded. "It's the mind's way of keeping all the memories we've absorbed separate from each other, a protection against insanity." He shook his head. "All your doors were locked."

Dura smiled as if enjoying a joke. "I put all my memories away. There was something Laewan wanted from me that I needed to protect—the identity of the last witness to Elwin's murder." He turned to Pellin. "Did you see it?"

Pellin shook his head. He hadn't. Dura's memories had already started to fade with the onset of death. "No. In my shock at your survival, I forgot to look for it. Most of what I saw centered around Lady Gael."

Dura essayed a weak smile. "I'm not surprised. She's worth my best and more."

Pellin leaned forward, drawn by his curiosity. "Who is your witness?"

But Dura shook his head. "The more people who know the identity, the greater the risk. No. Once we catch Laewan, we'll trade delve for delve."

"But if you're killed," Bronwyn said, "the witness's identity will be lost."

The reeve smiled weakly. "Then I would suggest you help me stay alive."

Bolt laughed. For once, Pellin was tempted to join in. "Then tell us how you managed to restore your mind."

"The walls," Dura said. "They appeared to be solid stone, but one was nothing more than sawdust held with mortar, and in the middle of it I placed a block of ice. My hope was that Laewan would see the emptiness of my mind and let me live. Once the ice melted, the sawdust and mortar crumbled. The door, frame and all, collapsed, restoring my memory." He smiled. "I thought it had worked until I felt myself starting to die. I guess Laewan decided to kill me after all."

"Oof," Bolt said.

Pellin raised a hand, commanding silence. "Tell him, but later. Who taught you to do such a thing?"

But Dura shook his head. "A friend provided the clues. I was desperate enough to try anything." He dropped his gaze to his shaking hands, which he held out before him.

"A side effect of the chiccor the apothecary used to force you to wake," Pellin said. He doubted Dura's explanation of the mind trick he'd used to deceive Laewan. The words rang true, but incomplete, as if he'd held his breath when he finished speaking. With a mental shrug, he took that topic and placed it in the corner of his mind where he could satisfy his curiosity another day. He sighed. After all this time, there were still so many things he wanted to know and learn and do. A dozen lifetimes wouldn't be enough.

Chapter 41

I fought to keep from shaking and lost. Pellin and the rest of the Vigil didn't seem to notice the battles I waged with my body. An aching need for sleep pulled at me and made the room swim in my vision, but every time I closed my eyes, my lids popped open, and I struggled to keep my teeth from chattering whenever I opened my mouth.

The root explained half of it. Soldiers in the last war had often chewed chiccor sticks to ward off the fatigue from days of fighting. A few of them had dropped dead in midbattle, their hearts bursting from the twin strain of sleeplessness and drug-induced wakefulness. How much of that stuff had they poured into me?

"How will we find Laewan?" Toria Deel asked.

She looked first at Pellin, then at Bronwyn. I stifled a tremor of surprise when she included me with a quick glance that seemed almost neutral. That added a tally mark to the number of questions piling up in my head.

"And," Bronwyn said, "what does he intend?"

"How was he turned?" Pellin added.

I tried to ignore the fact that most of the room looked at me at that point. I failed. "I never met Laewan until his men caught me and tortured me." The heat of anger served to burn away a little more of the chiccor root and whatever else was wrong with me, and the tremors in my legs subsided. "In my experience, people don't usually torture their allies."

"If you live long enough, you'll find just how limited your experience is," Volsk said from behind Toria Deel's chair.

Words that would have constituted a threat from any other man held only amusement from the Vigil's apprentice. His words held a hint of something I'd been trying to piece together, but this latest piece of the puzzle failed to bring the picture into focus. "What do you mean?"

Something—a door or a window into his thoughts—closed at the question. "Nothing more than an observation that your experience is as limited as mine was when I first apprenticed." The smile tilted, and his face wore the confident assuredness it always held in my presence, but the fingers of his free hand moved, shaping random patterns, jerking without his knowledge.

I didn't understand him, but the look on Pellin's face I knew all too well, a desire to change the subject.

"The questions of Laewan's corruption and intentions can wait," he said. "We must find him first. Absent any other ideas, we'll have to delve the city, searching for his traces until we can run him down."

Toria Deel shook her head. "Eldest, is there no other way? Of the three of us—"

"Four," Pellin interrupted with a nod to me.

Breath hissed from her. "Regardless. Of the four of us, only you and Bronwyn have the experience to delve the inanimate."

For a moment I saw the briefest flare of anger in the old man's eyes.

"Then you will have to learn." He regarded each of us, his gaze as blue and cold and brittle as the northern ice. "Lord Dura, you will accompany Bronwyn. Toria Deel, you will come with me. We will teach you the rudiments of what you need to know."

"Eldest," Bronwyn began, her objection plain with a single word. "It takes years of practice to acquire such skill. Lord Dura can hardly be expected to—"

Pellin's voice cracked with frustration. "Dura has been delved by Laewan. Extensively. If he has any skill at all, he should be able to sense his presence. Now"—he stood—"Toria Deel and I will take the eastern part of the city, working outward from the keep. You and Lord Dura will do the same to the south."

I looked at Toria Deel and Bronwyn as I forced wobbly legs to support me. Their faces plainly said Pellin's plan wouldn't work.

In the end—after I'd stumbled and almost pitched over the ledge of one of the bridges and into the river—we wound up on horseback. Bolt retrieved Dest from the stables and put me on his back. An idea occurred to me. "Is it possible to delve animals?"

Bronwyn, riding next to me on a pale gelding, nodded. "It is, but there's nothing more to an animal's mind than the basic instincts you would expect." She made a vague gesture of permission or invitation toward my mount. "Try it. There's not enough information there to endanger you in any way."

I removed a glove and rested my hand on Dest's head. The overcast sky and the keep faded from my awareness as I became suffused with horsey thoughts. There were images, but they were overshadowed by the impressions of scents. Above all, Dest seemed to live almost entirely in the present. Memories were few, and those that existed were tied to basic emotions—food, comfort, pain. But there were hints of personality there as well. Deeper in his mind I saw his familiarity and affection for me, mostly as a source of treats and companionship, but those impressions were untainted by any of the more negative emotions I'd seen in humans.

I blinked to clear my vision and saw Bronwyn looking at me.

"Well, Lord Dura, what does your horse think about?"

I couldn't help myself. "He feels sorry for your gelding, and he'd rather be accompanied by a mare."

Bolt guffawed.

"He does not," Bronwyn said. "Try not to be crude." Bronwyn's face narrowed in disapproval, which I suppose was the whole point.

Despite her assurance, the link made me dizzy. Bolt grabbed the reins from the other side where he walked between Bronwyn and me. "Try not to ride him over a cliff. That's the sort of thing that puts Pellin in a bad mood."

"As if he needed help," I muttered.

Bronwyn's face pinched. It didn't need much encouragement. "He is Eldest, Lord Dura," she said in frosty tones. "He knows far more than you can imagine, and while he would never consider his blood to be noble, nearly any title in the six kingdoms short of king is his for the asking. You should treat him with a measure of respect."

"Probably," I agreed. "But if he knows so much, why did he insist on a plan he knows wouldn't work?"

"I don't know what you mean," Bronwyn said in clipped tones.

"I think you do," I said. "Since it will take years to train me to sense Laewan's passing, Pellin must have some other motive for his plan. He placed me with you and Toria Deel with himself. Why do it that way?"

She looked away from me to stare ahead. "If you become part of the Vigil, you will have to learn obedience."

"You mean unquestioning obedience." I gave my head an exaggerated shake and almost fell because of it. "I don't even give Laidir that. If everyone but the fellow in charge stops thinking, then one mistake can undo you all."

"Well said," Bolt murmured. "I may want to borrow that one."

Even Bronwyn's guard, Balean, gave a slight nod.

We came to the bottom of the keep, and Bronwyn dismounted next to the entrance. People moved in and out looking almost normal, but their furtive glances gave evidence to the rumors running through the city.

Bronwyn moved off to the side, near the left hand of the broad, heavy arch, where traffic was thinner. I poured myself from Dest's back like water from a pitcher and almost ended up on my backside when my feet touched the ground. Bolt's laughter didn't help matters, but I managed to totter childlike to Bronwyn's side without putting my face to the cobblestones.

She removed her glove, her movements casual, pretending to survey the sky to check the weather. Putting her bare hand to the stone, she stilled, small changes in her expression showing the impressions she received.

She stepped back. "Place your hand where I put mine and tell me what you feel."

Despite what I'd said earlier, I wanted whatever training the Vigil had to offer. I'd been close to death before, but never so near or for so long as I'd been since Elwin's passing. Only a fool turned away from knowledge that might keep him alive.

But the touch of the rock only echoed the noise and traffic of the people around us, and the sound of their clatter and commotion departed to return a moment later. I strained, trying to pick out a single thread from the tapestry of transient memories lodged in the stones.

"Relax," Bronwyn said. "You can't force it."

I tried, but nothing stood out. It was like delving Dest except a thousand times more ephemeral, as if the rock refused to absorb the thoughts and feelings of those around it deeply enough to retain their individuality.

With a sigh, I lifted my hand away and opened my eyes. "It's just noise. I can't pick out anything." I turned, waving an arm at the carts and foot traffic proceeding in and out of the gate. "It's all just an echo of this."

Bronwyn nodded. "Nothing more?"

I shook my head.

Her face mirrored my disappointment. "It was much the same for me when I began many years ago." She turned away from the keep. "Come. We will depart from the Eldest's command long enough to see if you can sense Laewan's presence in places we know he has been."

Later our horses brought us to the bridge over the Rinwash where Bolt and I had been attacked days before. Heedless of the farmers and merchants who streamed back and forth over the corbeled arches, Bronwyn dismounted. But before she turned her attention to delving, a young lord passed by, his horse's coat glossy, reflecting the ruddy light of the fading sun.

Her eyes, a dewy green, settled on the rider and she sighed. I followed her gaze, surprised to recognize him. I knew Kaelan from court, or rather, I knew of him. The son of a minor noble, he seldom called attention to himself and seemed to be one of the few men who didn't seem to mind my low birth. For this reason I liked him well enough, even though he had a face and build any sculptor would have wanted to use as a model.

Bronwyn watched him go, and in that look I saw the thousand little cuts time had inflicted on her.

"Would you believe I was young once?" Bronwyn said. Her face held a self-mocking twist, as if she chided herself for admiring the flower of Kaelan's youth.

I don't jest when someone drops their armor, I don't care who they are. It is possible I might have something less than kind to say, depending on the circumstances, but I don't mock their honesty. "Why would I doubt it?" I said. Behind the wrinkles and gray hair, I could imagine she had been a beauty in her youth, with eyes the color of the sea close to shore, fine features, and rich chestnut hair.

She shook her head. "Sometimes I do . . . so long ago." She gave herself a little shake. "I don't regret my choices, Lord Dura, but even the best decisions beget thorns of regret that will pierce you later." Her gaze was direct, and she spoke with the earnestness of a fortune teller.

Half-turning from me, she pointed at the massive stones of the bridge. "Where did you see him?"

Bolt and I pointed to the left railing on the far side of the bridge. Leaving her horse with her guard, she moved to the railing with us trailing in her wake like baby ducks following their mother. Casually, she removed a glove and let her fingers trace the contours of the stone, the image of a woman stopping for a moment to admire the view. Her eyes closed, and I saw movement behind the lids.

She stopped, her mouth and fingers trembling. "It's here. What happened to you, my apprentice? What happened?"

I went forward and rested my hand where hers had been, the stone warmed by her skin, but it was the same as before. Echoes of remembrances flooded into me, but they were so transient I couldn't discern details to any of them. It was as if I hung suspended over a fast-flowing river composed of thousands upon thousands of different currents, each a different color, winking in and out of sight too quickly for me to follow. Each time I tried to reach for one, it darted away from me like a corfish in a pool.

Undaunted, I put both of my hands on the stone and let myself drop into the echoes of memory. Impressions swept past me faster than starlings, darting around my mind with hints of sight, sound, or emotion. One flew through me and I saw a merchant, felt his desperation as he hauled the last goods of a risky venture over the bridge. I waited, but the rest of the memories dodged me.

"This is useless," I said, letting go of the stone.

"What did you see?" Bronwyn asked.

"A desperate merchant. That's all."

Disappointment added a few years to her face. "Just the one memory, nothing else?"

I nodded.

She sighed, her shoulders slumping as if more than her lungs had deflated. "I had hoped Pellin saw some innate talent in you that I did not, but it seems as though your education will progress much as anyone else's."

"Meaning," I said, "that it will take years for me to acquire a skill that I need right now."

She nodded.

The sun drifted toward the western horizon, and around us the traffic on the streets thinned as merchants made their way toward inns and farmers began the trek to their homes in the outlying villages. "I don't fancy giving Laewan an invitation by staying out on the streets after dark."

I stumbled for a moment, trying to remember if the woman in front of me held a title. I couldn't remember any, but I'd hardly spoken more than a word or two at a time with her. I smiled over my embarrassment. "I'm sorry. How am I supposed to address you?"

She gave me a surprised grin, and I saw a glimpse of the woman she would have been in her youth—not a great beauty, but one whose smile would be counted precious to some certain man. Maybe more than one. "Technically, Lord Dura, I don't have a title."

I gave a low chuckle. "We almost have something in common, then. Most of the nobles here would say my title is a mere technicality."

The smile deepened, touching her eyes. "Lady Bronwyn is the term most people use to cover the discomfort they feel at submitting to the authority of an untitled merchant's daughter."

I nodded. "Then, Lady Bronwyn, I offer you the hospitality of my home. It is the humblest house in the nobles' district, but whatever I have, you're welcome to. It's likely to be a bit dusty. I rarely use it."

She bowed her head. "We know, Lord Dura, and it is nobly offered, but risk or no, I must trace Laewan's passage through the city." She paused to give a conspiratorial duck of her head. "Pellin knows that in this, I am the most skilled in the Vigil. Perhaps that is why he put us together."

I shook my head. "The streets aren't safe for you, Lady Bronwyn."

"They aren't safe for anyone, Lord Dura."

I'd argued with Gael often enough to recognize a losing position when I owned it, but I had one final move I could make. "Then I will commandeer a pair of the watch to accompany you. Four make a far less appealing target than two."

She smiled again, and I could imagine how suitors might have tried to make her laugh. "As you wish. We will wait for them here."

Bolt and I crossed the bridge back toward the nobles' quarter and the keep. I ordered the first pair of the city watch from their usual stations and sent them back toward Bronwyn. I would rather have sent a squad, but most of the watch was still patrolling close to the keep, and many more were guarding the caves.

"What happened?" I asked Bolt.

To his credit, he didn't try to play dumb, though I didn't doubt he could do an admirable job of it. His face was half stone already. "I was close enough to the stairs in Andler's basement to feel my way back up them in the dark and out into the street. Laewan's men didn't try to follow."

I listened as he related the sequence of events in his plain soldier's language, not trying to steer my opinion, merely giving me the facts. Still, I could sense his gaze on me as he related the Vigil's decision to use somnal powder and poppy sap. It was the only time I caught anything more in his tone. When he finished, two facts stuck out in my mind like the quills of a prickle-hog. "Volsk put my hand on his head?"

Bolt nodded, his voice tight. "Pellin commanded it."

My guard's explanation relieved me. I'd fought with Volsk. I didn't wish to contemplate the fact that he might betray me. Bolt's explanation explained the rush of unfamiliar memories that hit me as I regained consciousness. I had them locked away but made a note to go through them if we ever ran Laewan to ground. I needed to know more about the Vigil, and those memories might serve me, but at the moment the inside of my head felt like the jumble of Myle's workroom with tools and liquids and powders strewn about in a fashion that defied order. I didn't know whether the fits of dizziness came from the drugs or the effort to keep all those other selves locked away.

At the moment, the other quill concerned me more. "They brought Gael in to say good-bye?"

"Toria Deel's idea," Bolt said.

That surprised me. "Really?" I laughed. "How did Gael react when they told her I was alive after all?"

Bolt reined his horse in without answering and I turned to him in shock and anger. "Someone told her, didn't they?"

In the fading light, his craggy face might have been embarrassed.

I fought to keep my voice low. "It would serve the lot of you right if I let Gael know where she could find you. What is wrong with all of you?" I didn't really expect an answer.

"You're dealing with people who don't associate with others in the usual way very often," Bolt said. His voice had that subdued aspect to it again, as if he had to choose his words with caution. "Remember, something as simple as shaking hands is denied to them. To minimize the chance that they might inadvertently tap someone's memories, the Vigil lead reclusive lives. After a while, I think they forget how normal people relate to each other."

I patted Dest on the shoulder and twitched the reins, changing destinations. I didn't relish another confrontation with Count Alainn, but it couldn't be avoided. "We'll have to make a quick detour."

Bolt looked at me, his expression speculative. "You never intended on going home tonight." He wasn't asking.

I shook my head. "No. Though I would have if Lady Bronwyn had taken me up on my offer. I'm not sure what Pellin intended when he threw us together, but I'm pretty sure he knew I wasn't going to be able to delve the places of the city to help track Laewan." I had a vision in my head of the tall, spindly man by the bridge. "But there are other ways to track a man."

Bolt nodded. "There aren't that many places in the city where you can hide the kind of force he's amassing. Bronwyn couldn't have followed their traces unless there were a lot of them."

I caught something in his tone that warned me I'd made a horrible mistake. "How many?"

"Scores, at least."

Something more than fear ate its way across my gut. *Oh, Aer,* I prayed, remembering a child's prayer, *keep us this night*.

"I'm going to ask some questions," I said, my voice hard, "and I need real answers." He nodded and I went on. "How long does it usually take for someone who survives the Darkwater to snap?"

To his credit, he took a moment to think about the answer. "A few days, perhaps as much as a week in some cases. It's quick."

I shook my head, fighting the terror in my gut. "Laewan has no need to hide anyone."

Chapter 42

Bolt shook his head. "I don't understand."

I stared at him. "The members of the Vigil don't associate with people, you say? Then I'll wager they don't join in a game of bones very often."

His eyes narrowed at the mention of the universal game of chance played on both continents. It consisted of a pair of four-sided dice, each face a perfect triangle. Some cultures painted a glyph on each side and wagered on the possible combinations, but the most common game consisted of numbering the face of each die from one to four. The minimum roll was two and the maximum was eight. Glyphs or numbers, the game had a thousand different ways of being played, but every variation was built on the chances of rolling the different combinations.

"The survivors of the Darkwater are like a game of bones," I said.

Bolt gave me a lopsided smile. "I've played a few times. Soldiers are notorious cheats."

I nodded. "Exactly. How long has it been since Bronwyn returned from the Darkwater?"

Even in the fading light of day, I could see the blood drop from his face.

"What would you think," I asked, "if you were in a game of bones and every roll was over four?" I shrugged. "At first you wouldn't think anything of it. After all, six is just as common as four, and five happens even more often."

Bolt's eyes were wide. "But you should see a two, three, or four eventually. Aer help us, Dura. One of the survivors should have snapped by now."

I nodded. "Which means the time of their breaking is determined by Laewan. He doesn't need to hide them. The survivors can go right back to their lives here in the city until he calls for them."

Bolt turned his horse. "We have to get back to Bronwyn. If Laewan controls them, any passerby could be his, and they're expendable. Vigil guards are trained to see danger everywhere, but even I don't suspect every man or woman on the street of the killing rage."

I nodded. "I'm not going with you. There's not enough time to find Bronwyn and get to Gael before dark. You've got more experience at this than I, but if I suspected someone was hunting me, I know what I would do."

"Hunt them."

"When you find Bronwyn," I said, "commandeer as many men from the city watch as you need. Put a ring of steel around her and wait for me at Braben's. Send someone to Pellin. I'll come as soon as I can."

I thought myself adept at hiding my thoughts, but Bolt's gaze shifted, not so much looking at me as looking through me. I wondered if perhaps he had some gift I didn't know about. I turned Dest toward the nobles' quarter and dug my heels into his flanks. Ten minutes later, after galloping the streets with my sword pulled in suspicion, I pulled up to my destination. Half the sun had dipped below the horizon, and the half that remained glowed a dull red, an omen of bloodshed.

None of the peasants or merchants I flew past had offered even a hint of violence, but try as I might, I couldn't find any comfort in the fact. If I could have stretched out my hand and lifted the sun into the sky to extend the day, I would have. *Aer help us,* I breathed. What was coming?

I banged the knocker on the count's door and waited. A moment later it opened to reveal Marya, and I breathed a sigh of relief.

"Marya," I breathed, "thank heaven. I need to speak to Gael."

Her eyes grew wide and she gaped for a moment before answering. "You're dead."

I shook my head. "Just mostly. It was boring. I need to see Gael."

I heard a sound in the background and Marya straightened, her voice pitched to carry. "I'm sorry, Lord Dura." She cut her eyes to the left. "You are no longer welcome on these premises."

She began to mouth something to me, but before I could make sense of it a man's hand came around the edge of the door, pulling it from her grasp. Count Alainn stood in the doorway, his smile gleaming and feral. "Ah, Lord Dura. What a surprise. You're just in time."

He turned to Marya. "We mustn't be rude to our guest, Marya. Lord Dura is an old friend of the house."

He turned back to me, his voice dripping with venomous hospitality. "Come, Lord Dura. I'm sure you wish to speak to Lady Gael. We've been enjoying a quiet chat in the sitting room."

Alainn showed me his back as he spun on his heel, heading toward the south wing of the estate and the high-ceilinged room that served as the formal greeting area for guests. Oil lamps that gave the room a soft amber glow illuminated rich carpets and paintings of Gael's ancestors. I stepped into the room a step behind Alainn. His façade of hospitality didn't run deep enough to allow me to precede him.

Gael sat on one of the richly decorated couches to one side, her hands folded in her lap. Across from her sat a pair of men, the one on the left a younger version of the tall, gray-haired man on the right. They filled the couch with the effortless grace of those born to the aristocracy.

Count Alainn's hand found my elbow. "Allow me to introduce you, Lord Dura." Gentle pressure urged me forward.

"This is Baron Corrin of Aille." He indicated the older man who stood to take my hand. "And his son," he said with glee before donning an expression of mild surprise. "Pardon me. You've never met Lord Rupert Corrin, have you, Lord Dura?"

Rupert. Kera's betrothed. I'd barged in on Alainn's attempt to substitute Gael's hand for Kera's. An invisible knife seemed to be twisting its way through my guts. Why was she just sitting there? The Gael I knew would have launched herself from the couch in anger and relief. She would have thrown herself into my arms or slapped my face. Perhaps both.

I already knew about the power her uncle wielded over her. He had the right to arrange her marriage or force the gift from her, but those were insufficient to explain Gael's sudden lack of spirit.

"Tell us, Lord Dura," Count Alainn spoke by my ear. "To what do we owe this unexpected pleasure?"

Even after almost a year among them, the ways of the nobility still confused me. There was obviously a proper, expected response, and it was just as obvious I didn't know it. I opted for honesty. Men such as Alainn often failed to understand it.

"I came to relieve Lady Gael's mind on my behalf," I said, bowing. "I'd heard she had been informed that I was dead, killed in the king's service."

Baron Corrin and his son, Rupert, stood, their eyes unclouded by any suspicion of the subtext of our conversation. "Word came to us as well, Lord Dura," Baron Corrin said, "but I am glad to see you are well."

I couldn't hear anything other than plain honesty in his speech. Rupert met my gaze for the barest instant, using his father's speech to avoid looking at me. He, at least, had been aware of Gael's betrothal to me. Gael sat. Suspicion gnawed at me. I stepped around Alainn, before he could block my way, and over to her. A teacup sat in front of her. The contents half gone. Alainn's hand closed around my arm as I moved to pick it up. After being manhandled by my guard, I enjoyed the feel of breaking his grip with a sudden twist and pull of my wrist.

Gael stared ahead, her eyes glassy. I picked up her teacup and smelled it, then touched the liquid to my tongue. The scent of rose petals and cloves drifted upward, but beneath it I caught the taint of belladonna syrup. I turned to Alainn. "You drugged her."

"Perhaps we should withdraw," Baron Corrin said. His bow took in the count and me. "Come, Rupert, it is plain the count and Lord Dura have matters to discuss."

Alainn's smile turned oily at their departure. "Lady Gael mourns the death of her sister acutely but desired to greet Lord Rupert and his father."

Kreppa. "I know your niece better than you count. She would mourn, yes, but she has a strength you do not possess and cannot begin to fathom, and it doesn't include belladonna tea."

He laughed. "I can't decide which I shall enjoy more, Lord Dura, the wealth her marriage will bring me or knowing it came at your expense." His grin widened. "I'm really in no rush to decide. I intend on spending the rest of my years weighing those two joys against each other."

I shook my head. "Why, Count? She's more than willing to surrender the gift on you."

His eyes danced. "Because the gift is secondary to the marriage, fool." The count wagged his head at me. "Such a peasant. Baron Corrin desires the alliance as much as I." He straightened, pretending surprise. "I find myself unexpectedly in your debt. There is a certain joy to your unthinking honesty I'd never appropriated before."

I clamped my teeth shut over a thousand rejoinders. Any of them would serve to alert the count to our plan. On his own he would never conceive that Gael and I might voluntarily surrender our nobility in order to be together. I couldn't chance his suspicion.

"*Kreppa*," I spat at him.

His laughter warmed me. "Oh no, Lord Dura. You'll not trick me into challenging you or your hired sword."

I spun on my heel, and thankfully, he didn't attempt to follow me. I caught Marya at the door. "Keep the belladonna away from her. If she doesn't remember my visit, let her know I'm alive."

At her nod I stepped out into the dying light of Bunard.

Out by the count's small gatehouse, Dest greeted me, whickering and nosing me as I stood in my amazement. I let myself take the moment it required to put my arms around his neck. I told myself I was being foolish, but Gael's lack of response stabbed me with bereaving, as if I'd managed to cheat death only to find it had taken her instead.

I shook my head, trying to deny that emotion its power. If she was willing to flee with me to the south and be the wife of a reeve, then I would be only too happy to let her. In my ten years working the city, I'd seen too many loveless marriages to condemn either of us to one.

I mounted and turned Dest away from the nobles' quarter toward the boundary between the upper and lower merchants' sections of the city. After five minutes the sky darkened from slate to pitch, and the lamplighters and link boys appeared at the corners, looking hopeful as I passed, but I avoided them. Laewan's men would appear perfectly ordinary right up until the time he opened their vault. If I were within sword's reach, I'd be hard-pressed to defend myself.

Shadows stretched caricatures of Dest and me as we passed one corner, moving across the fading light. Memories taunted me like the pieces of a blacksmith's puzzle that I knew went together but refused to without knowledge of the trick. I approached the bridge leading to the lower merchants' quarter and passed the last link boy standing on the corner next to a tavern. The boy's torchlight would reveal me to any of those within and make me an easy target for a well-thrown dagger. With a twitch of the reins, I crossed over to the deeper shadows on the other side of the street.

I was rounding a corner, the lights of the bridge beckoning, when I heard the whistle of an arrow. I snapped the reins, knowing even as I did that I was too late. A meaty *thunk* sounded just behind me, and Dest reared and twisted, screaming. I clutched the reins and clung to his neck as the world pitched. The hiss of arrows sounded all around me as Dest bucked and darted, trying to rid himself of the broadhead in his hindquarters. Arrows drew sparks from the cobblestones.

A glance over his head showed me the tor. We were facing the wrong way. Sawing the reins, I managed to turn him back toward the bridge. Dest lurched forward. The world tilted as I nearly pitched from the saddle. I dug my heels into his flanks, praying the archers weren't good enough to hit a moving target in the dark.

I cursed myself for a stupid fool. Of course. The darkness didn't hide me—it revealed me. Laewan's minions had already proved they could see in the dark, and without the means to make phos-fire I was helpless.

Whistles and sparks followed me as I galloped away, and I sampled some of Jeb's vocabulary. How many men were up on the rooftops? The arrows trailed off, and I fought to get Dest under control as we crossed the bridge. In the torchlight his eyes rolled, and air whistled in and out of his nose as he champed the bit.

"Easy, boy," I said. "We're safe. I'm sorry, Dest. I should have brought Myle's powder." I would have laughed at myself for apologizing to my horse if I hadn't almost been killed. "When we get to Braben's I'll give you a real apology." We crossed the merchants' bridge at a gallop, and I steered him through the streets on a winding course away from Braben's. After half an hour without being attacked, I steered him toward the tavern at a walk, trying to appear to be nothing more than a bored reeve on his rounds. My shoulders twitched, and I jerked at every unfamiliar sound, but no more arrows came.

Braben's stable boasted a couple of decent hands, small wizened men more comfortable in the company of horses than people. I couldn't fault them. Timmis came forward, his eyes wide.

"What have they done to you, Dest?" he said.

I dismounted and turned to see a second arrow lodged in the leather of my saddle. "Can you pull the arrow, Timmis?"

He nodded without looking at me, his hands already probing the area around the wound. "It's deep." He led Dest into a stall and positioned him where the horse could lean against the wall before turning to an oat pail and a stoppered jar from one of the shelves at the back. "I'll have to give him some sedalin paste, won't I, boy?" He patted Dest's shoulder, and the horse nuzzled him.

"Thank you, Timmis," I said.

"Don't you worry none, Lord Dura. He'll be right ways soon enough."

I turned to leave, then remembered my word. "Give him lots of your best oats when he's ready, Timmis," I said. "I promised."

Timmis smiled, showing the gap where his front teeth used to be. "I would have anyway, my lord."

"And keep the torches well-lit tonight. Understand?"

He looked at the arrow and gave me a solemn nod. "Aye."

I went in through the back, threading my way through the empty kitchen before coming out into the equally deserted gathering room behind the large fireplace. When I saw Pellin and the rest of the Vigil at a side table, I let go of a breath I didn't know I'd been holding. Bronwyn sat to his left, her eyes a little wide, and Toria Deel and Volsk sat across from them. The four guards stood around them, leaning against the nearby tables but looking as casual as taut bowstrings.

Chapter 43

"Were you followed?" I asked as I pulled up a chair. Bolt moved to stand behind me, making his loyalty plain. I could have hugged him.

Pellin shook his head. "Are you sure this is necessary?"

I shrugged, trying not to let my irritation show. "You can go ask Dest."

The Eldest looked to Bolt with a lift of his eyebrows.

"Dura's horse."

I pointed to the stable with my chin. "Timmis is pulling an arrow from his hindquarters now. A hairsbreadth either way and he'd be pulling a second one from me. I may need a new saddle."

The ride through the night air and the panic in my chest had burned through a bit more of the drug-induced fog filling my mind. I gathered thoughts and memories that wandered around my head and started to plait them together into something that might make sense. Holes in the weave made me gnash my teeth at what I might be missing. After a second I amended that. I was definitely missing something, probably several somethings. I just hoped they wouldn't get me killed.

"Eldest," Toria Deel said, "we must find Laewan quickly. The longer we delay, the more people we'll have to delve. Survivors of the Darkwater will fill the city."

It would have been easy to pity the Eldest in that moment. The authority of the Vigil didn't fit Pellin. He sat like a man trying not to squirm, but no one else could shoulder it. "Delving to find his passage takes time, and we're limited to daylight."

He looked to Bronwyn, who sat back in her chair, her arms crossed in denial though nothing had been asked.

I shook my head. "If he moves each night, you'll never catch up to him. He could lead you through the streets of Bunard by the nose for months and you'd never find him. If his path crosses over itself, you're as helpless as a hound with too many scents."

"Do you have anything to offer?" Toria Deel demanded. No sarcasm or haughtiness alloyed her speech, only impatience.

I ignored her or tried to until Pellin added his voice to hers. "Lord Dura, you know the city better than any of us. Where might he hide?"

"Bunard is ancient," I said. "The alleys between streets contain thousands of nooks and crannies that can hide a man. There are stretches of the city that haven't housed tenants since the last war. The lower merchants' and poor quarters are a warren. The only people . . ."

I stopped, waiting for an idea to take root. If I could get Pellin to agree to it, I'd be able to repay a debt. I waited, not wanting to be the first to speak.

"Yes?" Pellin asked.

Perfect. "We need a net," I said. "If Laewan knows you can track him through the city, he'll move each night, to stay hidden, until he is ready to strike. His people can see in the dark, so they'll be watching to see if he's followed." I paused, fleshing out the idea. "What we need are people who can hide without being seen, whose night vision is nearly as good as theirs and can watch for his passing, enough people to make a living net so that they don't have to follow him."

I could almost feel Bolt smiling behind me.

Pellin nodded. "Who are these people?"

"People small enough to be overlooked," I said. "The urchins."

Volsk's voice cracked across the table. "The what?"

But Pellin put up a hand. "Street thieves. Can you trust them?"

I nodded. "They've lost a few of their own to Laewan and his men. Plus, you'll be buying their loyalty and more."

The Eldest's eyes narrowed. "And more?"

"That's my price," I said without blinking. "I want them off the street. If you can find homes for them, fine. If not, I want the church to house them and care for them as if they were Aer's gift."

"Or . . . ?" Pellin asked.

I shook my head. "There is no *or*. I'm not going to ask children to put themselves at risk for nothing more than the goodwill of Aer and king."

"Well said," Bolt murmured. I saw the other guards nod in agreement.

Volsk shook his head. "You would entrust the safety of the Vigil to children?"

Bolt spoke before anyone else. "'Better a willing knife than—'"

"There's no need to throw quotes at me," Pellin said, raising his hand. "I've already agreed. But," he said, cutting Volsk's next protest off as well, "we will use every weapon that we can bring to hand. The four of us will track Laewan during the daylight so that we can narrow the search."

Toria Deel leaned forward, her face tight with embarrassment. "Eldest, you know I'm not equipped for that."

"No," Pellin said with a nod toward me. "Neither of you are. But there is a way to shortcut your training." He turned in his chair toward Bronwyn, who sat still and pale with her hands clenching each other on the table.

Her head moved back and forth in small jerks of denial. "Please. Let them learn on their own."

The nest of lines around Pellin's blue eyes deepened, and he blinked away tears. "I'm sorry, Bronwyn. You're the most skilled of us, and there's no time to do it any other way."

A wisp of graying hair fell across her cheek as she ducked her head in quiet sobs whose sound didn't carry past our table. Pellin turned to Toria Deel. "Delve her. With her memories as your guide, your skill at tracking will approach hers."

"I don't understand," I said to Pellin. "Why can't she just hide the memories that trouble her and reveal the ones that will show us how to delve the city?"

Pellin looked at me with something that might have been pity or sorrow or some mix of both. "Our strengths are much like anyone else's, Lord Dura. They derive from our experience and pain. Lady Bronwyn could show you every delve she's ever made to train you, but it's her background of loss and shame that enables her to sift with such skill the impressions and emotions of others within the stones of the city." He sighed. "There's no other way."

"'In pain and loss will you triumph,'" Toria Deel quoted softly.

Bronwyn continued to sob, scattering tears, her withered body shaking with small mewing sounds. She showed no sign of having heard Pellin until she stretched her right arm out on the table toward Toria Deel. She tugged at her sleeve until she bared her frail, age-thinned skin.

"Promise," Bronwyn whispered. When Toria Deel didn't respond she spoke again. "Swear not to speak of what you see."

Toria Deel nodded, her dark eyes moist as she removed the glove from her left hand and laid her fingertips on Bronwyn's skin like a caress. Fresh sobs came from her, and I watched Toria Deel's gaze widen as the store of Bronwyn's memories flashed across their touch.

Toria Deel's hand lifted, and for a moment her posture mirrored that of her older counterpart, hands folded and head down. Blots of crimson stained Bronwyn's cheeks, and she yanked her sleeve back into place with the haste of a woman caught exposed in her bath.

"A man?" she asked, throwing the question at Pellin like a spear. "Knowing, you would have me delved by a man?"

Pellin nodded, his face closed to any emotion, but his fingers trembled. More than anything, I wanted to crawl away from Bronwyn's shame. But measured against the lives already lost and those that yet would be, I couldn't refuse.

She sat on my right. When I leaned toward her to speak, she jerked as if I'd slapped her. "We are all acquainted with shame, milady. Though I was denied the orders of the Merum priesthood, I am intimately familiar with the rite of confession."

Dismissive laughter mixed with her sobs. "Even in the confessional, a penitent is allowed to choose their words or skip the horrors of their past too potent to reveal. The priest cannot compel it. No wife or husband or child will know another as you will see me, Lord Dura."

"You've delved me," I offered. "You know the people I associate with. Is your past so grim?" I asked.

Breath gushed from her, leaving her wilted. She offered me her left arm, the dark green cloth of her sleeve pulled to reveal her veined skin. "You must see for yourself."

I put my hand on her arm, enfolding her wrist, trying with touch to offer her comfort. She gazed at me, intent, waiting for some sign of judgment or revulsion.

I tunneled through the green of her eyes, and memories flashed by. Down through the long years of her life I sank, like the wreckage from a ship that finally yields to the waves, fluttering slowly through the trackless depths of the ocean until it comes to rest on the bottom. After what seemed centuries where I watched and absorbed the delicate changes in wood and stone that would allow me to track a man through a city, I came to Bronwyn's youth.

I was King Laidir's reeve. I knew the patina of civilization, the veneer of humanity, to be far thinner than most would believe. Years of enforcing the laws of Aer and king had taught me as much. Even so, Bronwyn's memories caught me off guard.

Yet as they flooded through the touch of our skin and I lived and felt them as my own, admiration swelled within the small part of my mind I retained as Willet Dura. Few women or men would have been able to rise above such circumstances as she had, or as quickly. How had she done it? Then it came. In the midst of her debasement at the hands of another, the gift came, given by the unexpected blessing of one who'd witnessed her courage. Yet that too had carried a cost. Her own memories could have broken her, much less the ones she'd absorbed in her first days within the Vigil.

When I lifted my hand, Bronwyn no longer faced me. Toria Deel had promised never to speak of it, and I intended to keep that promise as well, with this one exception. "I only thought I'd seen courage before today."

Pellin and Toria Deel pulled their scrutiny from Bronwyn to me. They both nodded their thanks—Pellin's gesture grateful, uncluttered by any other emotion that I could see, but Toria Deel's head dipped as if unwilling, her expression unreadable.

I didn't have the time or means to decipher it. Pellin said something to Allta I didn't quite catch, and his guard reached into his cloak to pull a piece of folded parchment. The Eldest spread it on the table and Bunard stretched before me in detail.

Pellin gave the map an approving look. "One of the things I've always admired about the priests in Collum, they have an attention to accuracy you don't find in the kingdoms on the southern end of the continent. The maps of Aille and Elania are practically works of art, but the cartographers won't hesitate to sacrifice precision for artistic expression. It can make navigating their cities something of an adventure."

As Pellin pored over the parchment, I saw him relax. The similarities to Custos became obvious. Both men were more comfortable in the presence of books, of facts and words, than in proximity to the capricious natures of men. I doubted Pellin had ever lived a day under the ambition to be Eldest.

"Lord Dura," Pellin said, "how long will it take you to enlist the aid of the urchins?"

"I'll have to find them first, but no more than a couple of hours." Rory would be the key. If he accepted the offer, the rest of the urchins would follow.

Pellin appeared to only half hear me, his attention on the map. We referred to different portions of the city as the poor quarter or the merchants' quarter, but the Rinwash had actually been engineered over the years to divide the city into fifths. Laidir's keep formed the first portion set against the hills to the northwest with a large branch dividing it from the nobles' quarter. After that, other branches cut the city into sections occupied by the upper merchants', lower merchants', and the poor.

The Eldest tapped the image of the keep with his index finger. "Laidir has already stationed men in the caves beneath the keep and has masons working to inspect and rebuild any of the walls beneath the city. It's unlikely Laewan would hide there."

He paused, stilling except for the rise and fall of his chest. "Toria Deel, you will take the lower merchants' quarter; I, the nobles'; Bronwyn, the upper merchants'. Lord Dura, since you will already be in the poor quarter, you can search it. Let us meet back here two hours before sunset to decide where to place your net."

Outside Braben's brightly lit taproom the sounds of the city settling to sleep came to us, the clop of a horse's shoes on the cobblestones, the call of the link boys offering light and torches to passersby, the hoot of an owl.

"We'll have to take rooms here," Pellin said gazing out the window.

Moments later, I ascended the stairs, following Bronwyn, Toria Deel, and their guards, with Bolt just behind me. I'd had occasion to stay at Braben's several times over the years. While the accommodations would never be called luxurious, the sleeping rooms mirrored the taproom. Simple, clean furnishings exuded warmth and welcome.

A bed large enough for two filled the space of one wall opposite a closet. A clear-paned window, one of Braben's few indulgences, looked out over the Rinwash, and a stand held a large pitcher of water and a basin with a linen towel just beside. I locked the door. After I splashed water on my face, I moved to turn down the lamp.

"Don't," Bolt said. He'd drawn the curtains over the window as soon as we entered. Now he stood by the door, sword in hand. "You'll have to sleep with the light on."

The precaution made sense. "What about you?"

"I'll sleep some other time." He pulled a small piece of chiccor root from his pocket and bit a sliver from it, the smell of anise strong in the air.

I didn't bother to undress, but I didn't want to soil Braben's sheets with my dirty clothes, so I lay on the top blanket and blocked the light with one of the pillows.

Sleep took me, dragging me down into unconsciousness. I tried to order my thoughts on the way, working to understand the sense of unease in my gut, but I ran out of time. Too much had happened. The fight to shake off the effects of the drugs had taken everything I had.

Chapter 44

Sound came first, the distant thunder of Bolt's voice as it merged with a blissfully ordinary dream, then the smell, an acrid stab of smoke. I struggled toward waking, fighting my way through a delirium of fatigue. Something cracked across my face, and I blinked away tears to see Bolt standing over me shaking the sting from his left hand.

I rubbed my cheek. "You could have used the water pitcher."

Bolt's voice crackled. "We may need it. The inn's on fire."

"What?"

He shook his head at me as I stumbled, pulling my sword with one hand and catching myself on the bed with the other. "Try not to hurt yourself."

I scowled with the effort of corralling my uncooperative thoughts together. My mind kept splitting, running into different directions. "Where's the fire?"

Bolt nodded. "Better. It's in the taproom. Braben has it under control, but we've got more arrows coming."

The window outside showed the inky black of night. Sticking close to the outside wall, I edged along until I could glance out the window, but the view showed nothing. The link boys had long ago turned in.

"They found us," I said. "If we go outside, they'll pick us off in the darkness." Lantern light cast a network of shadows across Bolt's face.

"It's still two hours until dawn," he said.

I doused the lantern. "It's just a target now." I looked out of the window again, but nothing moved across the street. With a longbow our attackers could be several streets away. As I watched, a line of light and fire streaked from a building to my right toward the inn. A second later I heard the crash of glass and alarmed yells.

Bolt swore. "Those aren't the voices of any of the Vigil." Footsteps pounded on the stairs with calls for water. "Where's the city watch?"

I shook my head. "Probably dead."

Another arrow streaked from the darkness, the light arcing in from street level off to my left like a yellow stab of lightning. I listened but didn't hear the sound of glass, and I breathed a prayer of thanks for Braben's slate roof and the wet weather. I closed the curtains. "The back of the inn butts up against the Rinwash. We could circle around."

Refusal etched his face. "That might be exactly what they want you to think, and it may not be necessary. Most of the arrows are missing their mark."

I shook my head. "How could they miss at this distance?" The crash of breaking glass and another panicked scream came from beneath us. "We have to help. They'll burn Braben's Inn down."

"Maybe," Bolt said. "But if they don't like the light, the blaze will keep them at bay. There are only five of the Vigil left. Four of them are here in this inn." He stepped close so that his face came within inches of mine. "Do you understand, Dura? In the six kingdoms that border the Darkwater, we have exactly five people left who can fight against it. Did Laidir ride at the front of the charge?"

He made perfect sense, but Braben had shown me hospitality and more. He'd given me aid when I needed a place to hide a body and a friend from the clutches of the Orlan family. "I have a debt here," I said.

I tried to step around Bolt to the door, but I wasn't anywhere close to fast enough. Before I'd taken a step he stood in front of it, sword drawn, as implacable as stone.

"Pellin won't appreciate it if you kill me to keep me safe," I said.

He shrugged. "I won't kill you—I'll hit you on the head with the flat of my blade. You can't go anywhere if you're unconscious."

I didn't doubt it. "Marquis Orlan, the man I killed in court, had men in Laidir's employ and even in the Merum cathedral loyal to him." I shrugged. "Orlan was very thorough. He'd bought loyalty throughout the city." I looked at Bolt, daring him to deny me. "But I had a friend he didn't know about, a portly innkeeper with a gift of hospitality."

Bolt's face wrinkled in disgust. "Blast it, you're reckless. How did you manage to survive to adulthood?"

"Friends."

He shook his head then sheathed his sword. "Better a death with honor than a life with shame," he said.

I nodded my thanks. "I like that one."

He grunted as he turned to open the door. "I hope it's not prophetic."

We descended the broad wooden staircase, met Braben on the way up with a bucket of sand, his face clouded with anger and incomprehension. "Blast it, what do they want?"

I gripped his forearm. "Me—but I'm going to do something about that now."

His gaze found mine, and for an instant some of his anger redirected toward me, eyes blazing at the danger I'd subjected him to. A moment later, I saw him shove it aside. "Well and good, Lord Dura."

We found Pellin and the rest of the Vigil in the taproom, well away from the windows. The guards had placed their charges behind the heavy bar, and they stood on the opposite side, swords bared. One of Braben's daughters, Ryanne, stood armed with a bucket of sand and a blanket, waiting for the next arrow to come through the broken window.

Glass exploded inward as a flaming arrow lit the interior of Braben's, the smell of naphtha and spirits strong in the air as flames splashed the wood. Ryanne darted forward, parceling out the gritty sand in her bucket as if it were precious. Allta and the rest of the guards crouched, waiting for an attack that never came.

I didn't bother to hide my disgust. "Is it the habit of the Vigil to let girls take the brunt of danger?" I asked Pellin.

Spots of color might have lit his cheeks. "This attack is aimed at the gift, Lord Dura. Would you have us hand Laewan the very thing he seeks?"

"I can help," Volsk said from the other end of the bar, where he stood over Toria Deel like a second guard. "Give me a bucket," he said to Ryanne. Even in the dim light, I could see Toria Deel's pride at his simple act of service.

Bolt preceded me through the kitchen door into the closed yard of the stable ground. A couple of arrows smoked in the damp earth, but so far nothing had hit the stables. Timmis and Nobb stood in the protective overhang of the roof, armed with anger and buckets of dirt.

Timmis set his bucket down and moved toward the collection of tack hanging on the wall, but I waved him off. "I'll be walking. Take care of Dest."

We passed through the stables and scurried to the wall overlooking the Rinwash. The current moved south, toward our left, the opposite way I wanted to go. I hopped into the murky water with my knees bent, praying to hit bottom before I went in over my head.

I stopped dropping when the water hit hip level, my boots sinking into soft mud. I grabbed for the stones of the wall on my right and pulled until my feet came free of the sucking ooze. Ahead of me, Bolt sheathed his sword and used the outcropping of the granite wall lining the river to help pull himself along. Needles of cold pricked my skin from the waist down as the wet steadily soaked its way up my garments.

"Ever been to the southern continent?" Bolt asked. I wondered how he kept his teeth from chattering. Mine sounded louder than the mistimed beats of a drummer's tabor. "I went with Pellin once. It's always warm," he said, "except when it's blazing hot."

"Sounds awful," I stuttered through my shivers.

"It is, but I like to think about it when I get cold."

We pulled ourselves along for nearly two hundred paces before we found a spot on the bank shallow enough to grasp the top of the flood wall and pull ourselves up. We stood, squeezing out our cloaks and letting the water drain from out boots, searching the sky back toward Braben's for the telltale flight of an arrow.

We didn't have to wait long. I headed for the closest alleyway with my sword in one hand and a throwing knife in the other. I crept forward with Bolt on my left, feeling for each step. An idea started to nag at me, one even I thought foolish, but it wouldn't leave me alone. "How many times has the Vigil delved someone from the Darkwater?"

Bolt might have shrugged in the darkness. "Six times in my lifetime," he said with that catch in his voice. "It doesn't happen often. Most of the time the men and women are killed, cut down before the Vigil can get there."

"Have they ever managed to delve someone while their vault was open?"

We groped our way to the end of the alley before cutting our way to the left down a street crowded with overhangs of merchant shops.

"No," Bolt said. "And you're insane."

"So I've been told." I remembered the dark scroll in my mind I hadn't been able to open and tried to ignore the fact that Bolt and the rest of the Vigil might be right. "Do we even know who we're fighting?"

"Laewan."

"Laewan's a pawn," I said. "Unless you expect me to believe that one of the Vigil can suddenly just decide one day to become evil. And what about the men and women who've been to the Darkwater? Laewan seems to have some control over when their vaults open without even touching them. Is that a power the Vigil has?"

"No."

The part of my brain where I kept my common sense rebelled at the idea. As usual it lost almost immediately. "It's worth trying."

Bolt touched his sword, his expression serious. "You know my duty."

We paused before the last turn. At the end of the next alley, one of Laewan's men stood, shooting flaming arrows toward Braben's Inn. Bolt came close enough that I could feel him speak as well as hear him. "Whatever is in these men makes them dangerously quick. Common mercenaries took out the best of the Vigil. I may not have time to protect you."

"I might be able to see where Laewan is hiding."

After a moment I heard him sigh. "'Desperate times call for desperate measures.'"

I nodded, even though he couldn't see me and sheathed my sword, leaving just my dagger. "I like that one too."

"It's not mine. If we're going to do this, let's be about it. Best to be foolish quickly and get it over with."

We inched down the alley, rolling each step to keep from being heard. I could hear the flight of each arrow now, the hiss of traveling fire as his arrows left the bow. A moment later I could better see the archer as he stood by a pot of naphtha. I shifted closer to the wall and prayed to avoid knocking into anything that would give me away. At the end of the alley, I peeked around the corner and saw his face. *Oh, Aer.*

I hadn't expected to recognize any of them. Why would a butcher go to the Darkwater? Barl, his eyes blindfolded against the light, dipped an arrow wound with cloth into a black pot before lighting it from a candle. Then he nocked and let it fly at Braben's across the street. Now I knew why some of the arrows had failed to find their mark, but from such a distance he wouldn't miss many.

I didn't have time for pity. Any second he might hear or sense me behind him. Holding my breath, I grasped the edge of the wall and stretched forward, my fingertips straining for Barl's neck.

Some sound or instinct must have warned him, and everything happened at once.

Barl whirled, impossibly fast for a man that big, his hand darting to his belt. I leapt forward, striving to touch him before he saw me. I heard the whisper of a throwing knife, saw the dim flash of steel by candlelight as my hand and Bolt's dirk made contact at the same instant. I tunneled into Barl's mind, falling through the gaping surprise of his stare as a dagger buried itself in his throat.

I'd seen images of life before, had felt the thousand different emotions that make a man. I floated through the darkness of the past as Barl, searching for the thing that had twisted my life from what it had been. Memories floated through me of life, work, marriage, and children, each carrying the taint of envy, a layer of rot that I wouldn't remove. Images of the rich colored each recollection, and jealousy seeped its way into the good until every memory became gangrenous, poisoned beyond redemption.

A thread of life touched the rage I knew as Barl, and I followed it, grasping it with my mind, and images opened before me, pictures I knew too well, the presence of the Darkwater.

I paused, the part of me that was still Willet Dura holding my spot on the thread, unsure. As quick as my touch was, I had only seconds before Barl died. Even now, the colored threads that were his memories carried a labored pulse in time to his failing heart.

To go forward in time in Barl's memory meant learning more about the evil that had taken him, me, but if I went back, I would know how Laidir's subjects had been suborned into evil and by whom.

I looked forward on Barl's memory to his time in the Darkwater, but blackness covered it—not the empty dark of night, but rather an obsidian murk that swallowed every attempt at light without a ripple. While I watched, it moved toward me, creeping slowly, like a virulent infection, consuming more of the thread I touched.

Something waited in Barl's mind.

I spun away. Horror and fear of being watched from the dark awoke in me, and I fled backward in Barl's memory, away from that sentient darkness, searching for the reason he'd gone to the cursed forest. Who had planted the idea in his mind? The thread of memory I tracked pulsed, growing dimmer, and I raced along it, images running backward from the edge of the forest back through the frantic horseback ride from the city of Bunard, to the stables where I'd stolen the best horse I could find. The memory took me to the shop I'd left at noon, back through the morning customers he hardly noticed, to the morning, to dawn.

I relived anticipation, the expected culmination of years of growing envy as I walked in the early light toward my butcher's business, my plan in place. I tracked back, sensing the answer, racing toward it even as memories and emotions faded, the pulses growing weaker.

I slowed, my progress lurching to a halt despite my panic for haste. I looked back along the thread of memory I clutched, and I knew horror.

Threads of darkness reached for me, wrapping themselves around me like thousands upon thousands of strands of a spider's web. Each filament stuck to me, binding me to this place in Barl's mind. I struggled to move forward, to reach the answer I saw just ahead of me, but for every midnight strand I broke, two more shot from the darkness, pinning me.

The thread of Barl's memory frayed, unraveling in my hands, dissipating into nothingness. With everything I had, I willed myself forward, managed to move a fraction of time closer to the answer before more of the dark threads stopped me. I turned, saw the blackness of the Darkwater coming for me.

Barl's thread fell from me and there was nothing left but black filaments that anchored me to his dying mind and the creeping night that came for me. I had to tear free from Barl's mind before he died. With a wrench, I tore the threads loose and fled.

But darkness faster than thought caught me, pinned me beneath a thousand strands. Pain flared, and my mind went black.

Water splashed over me and I jerked, gasping and shaking, cries of desperation working free of my chest. I sat on cobblestones. *Praise Aer.* I reached up with shaking hands to rub a knot on the side of my head. I winced, but gratitude for the pain washed over me, and I managed to pull a shuddering breath into my lungs.

Bolt stood over me, lit by the light of a flaming arrow. "Don't you have any idea of caution?"

I probed my head, pulled my hand away, surprised by the absence of blood. "I couldn't get out." My voice sounded like the plaintive cry of a child. I didn't care.

Bolt dropped a few of Jeb's more imaginative phrases on me before he said anything that made sense. "I noticed. You were locked with him for almost five minutes. I kept waiting for you to pull out of the delve, but you stayed. When I saw Barl's eyes lose focus, I hit you with the hilt of my dagger."

I shuddered, remembering the last moments within Barl's mind. "Thank you."

"What did you see?" Bolt asked.

Dizzy, I shifted to lean against the edge of the building, pulling my knees up against memories I needed to lock away. "A small man who hated his life. Someone sold him on the idea that going to the Darkwater would give him the revenge he wanted."

"Who?"

I shook my head. "I almost saw it, but there was something else in Barl's mind." Bolt watched me, and I saw doubt flicker across his eyes in time to the dance of his improvised torch. "It pinned me there. I couldn't move back in his memories to see who talked him into going to the Darkwater, and I couldn't move forward to see what happened to him there. If you hadn't knocked me out when you did, my mind would have died with Barl's."

"Or worse," Bolt said. "Would you have died? No one's ever delved an open vault before."

A different horror, one that made death in Barl's mind appear trivial by comparison, engulfed me. "We have to tell the rest of the Vigil not to touch them." As if saying it opened a door in my mind, the last puzzle piece to Elwin's death dropped into place, and I knew without the smallest grain of doubt the identity of his killer.

And it didn't matter.

Chapter 45

I unfolded from my sitting position, my motions jerky and uncoordinated, my limbs refusing to obey the simplest commands. I clutched Bolt's shoulder as I tried to get my legs underneath me. He'd been generous with that blow to my head, but wobbles or not, I was just happy to be alive.

"The attack stopped as soon as you delved him," Bolt said.

I stepped into the empty street. "That pretty much confirms Laewan has control of everyone who's been to the Darkwater." I hated being right.

Bolt didn't bother to look at me. "Except you."

The nod I attempted only made me dizzy again. "Yes. Sooner or later I'm going to have to answer that question or Pellin will never trust me."

If I could have slowed my steps to Braben's, I would have, but the crow of a rooster told me I didn't have time. Laewan had eyes in the city at night. The fight between him and the Vigil came down to a simple proposition: Could the Vigil find and kill him during the day before he found and killed the Vigil at night?

The whole thing was a toss of the bones without a way to tell which glyphs would end facedown on the table. We stepped into Braben's. The inn had taken a few more arrows, and scorch marks stained some of the walls, but the place seemed largely intact. Pellin and the rest of the Vigil sat away from the windows, their guards ever vigilant, waiting for dawn.

The rest of the guests were nowhere to be seen. I didn't know if they had returned to their rooms voluntarily or if Pellin had once again paid for privacy. It didn't matter. For a moment I considered keeping my mouth closed. Finding Laewan trumped all other concerns. The identity of Elwin's killer no longer mattered. I checked that thought. Or did it? The rest of the Vigil believed that knowledge to be of paramount importance. So long as they believed that, it would be difficult for them to focus on anything else.

Pellin, Bronwyn, and Toria Deel sat at a large round table of plain smoothed boards, nothing fancy, but the workmanship made you want to run your fingers over the grain. I made it a point to sit across from Pellin. Bolt took his position behind me. I offered a silent prayer, asking his forgiveness.

Now that I'd come to the moment, I didn't know where to begin. The Vigil looked at me with that silent expectation of a group that has carried on unnecessary conversation while they waited.

"We managed to sneak up on one of the attackers." I didn't want to look at any of them, especially Pellin. I found myself staring over his shoulder toward the back of the inn. "I got a look into his mind before he died. His vault was open." The Vigil stared at me without moving, their eyes wide, but unreadable nevertheless. I took a deep breath. "I understand why you don't trust me." I tapped my head. "I can't tell you what's in my vault, but for some reason Laewan has no hold over me."

"So you say," Toria Deel said, but her voice lacked its usual heat.

Instead of getting angry, I merely nodded. "So I say. But if I were working for him, I wouldn't have bothered to risk my neck against the attack."

"What did you find in the attacker's mind?" Pellin asked.

"Envy." I sighed. "Jealousy. A lust for revenge on the world he believed made him less than others. All the stuff you'd expect to see in the soul of a man who's given himself over to his resentments."

I paused, took a deep breath. "And the identity of Elwin's killer."

The rest of the table looked at me as if lightning had found Braben's and struck our midst.

"Who?" Pellin demanded. When I didn't answer, he leaned forward, his expression bloodless and angry. "Give me the name, Dura!"

I shook my head. "I need to explain. The vault in Barl's mind held more than just a storehouse of hidden memories. There was consciousness. It came after me." Even the memory of the strands pinning me made me want to vomit. "If Bolt hadn't knocked me out, it would have had me." I paused to look at all of them. "Something has gotten free of the Darkwater."

"Impossible," Volsk said. But the rest of the Vigil didn't seem as surprised.

I shrugged off his denial. "Barl's mind wasn't just broken. Something else was in it, and I was helpless against it. If it had always had that control over the gift, would any of you be here?"

Pellin looked at me, his crystal blue eyes weighing, sifting what I'd said as if searching for a flaw. "Bolt?" he asked without taking his gaze from me.

"True," my guard said. "Even as he was dying, Barl kept him locked in the delve until I knocked him out."

"What does this have to do with Elwin's killer?" Toria Deel asked.

The dawning of knowledge or intuition might have been the reason Pellin's eyes widened.

"It's the only explanation," I said. "Robin was cut to pieces by crescents. They didn't just kill him, they reveled in his death, but Elwin died from a single blow to the head." I looked at each of the Vigil in turn, ending with Pellin. "A sword stroke. The people who killed Robin didn't just take his life, they took his dignity. His body was a mess."

Pellin nodded. "Robin deprived them of what they wanted."

"They weren't trying to *kill* Elwin," I said. "They were trying to turn him."

"Ridiculous," Toria Deel said. "You're basing the skill and capabilities of the Eldest on your own meager experience." Bronwyn mirrored her doubt.

I stood, turning to my guard. "I'm sorry."

"He was my son." Bolt's face closed, and I watched as he fell into grief.

Oh, Aer. I resolved to speak to him later when we were alone, after

I had time to come up with something to say that didn't sound trite. There might never be enough time.

I turned to Pellin. "Would it be possible to delve Robin's sword and know?" I asked.

The look on his face told me he already believed me, but I wanted confirmation. I didn't say it out loud, but all I really had was a theory that fit most of the pieces.

There were still too many unanswered questions for my liking. Robin had killed Elwin to keep the Darkwater in Laewan's mind from taking him. Fine. But how had Laewan been corrupted? Something about the Darkwater had changed. Minds weren't just being broken by evil anymore, they were being inhabited by it.

Pellin gave a small shake of his head. "The . . . " He swallowed, and I saw a muscle in his jaw clench before he forced himself to go on. "The sword is just a thing. It would verify Robin's hold on it, but the . . . contact with Elwin would have been too brief to permit delving." His tone left little doubt, but he looked to Bronwyn anyway.

She nodded. "Such recognition surpasses the capabilities of our gift."

Silence fell, covering the table while the men and women of the Vigil found small reasons not to look me in the eye. With the possible exception of Pellin, their disbelief was apparent. I cursed myself for speaking. My explanation of Elwin's death must have seemed nothing more to them than the contortions of an animal trying to escape from its trap.

A cock crowed outside, and I turned in my chair to see that the charcoal silhouettes of night had given way to the muted grays of the coming dawn. The sun would crest the mountains to the east inside the hour.

My chair scraped against the floor as I pushed myself away from the table. "Iosa willing, I'll have the urchins come to each of you as you search."

I gave Pellin a bow, the first. "Eldest, I'll meet you back here two hours before sunset and you may decide how to cast your net."

I departed Braben's by way of the kitchen door and came to the stables. Timmis stood at the entrance, an old pike from the last war in his hands. Dark smudges of fatigue lay beneath each eye, but his gaze was alert.

"How do they fare, Timmis?" I nodded toward the stable.

"Well enough," he rasped through the gap in his front teeth. "But they don't like the smell of smoke. No, they don't." He shook his head. "Nobody's ever attacked Master Braben before, Lord Dura. I don't know what to make of it."

Timmis's need for comfort wove threads throughout his words, and I wanted more than anything to give it to him, to say there would be no more attacks. He stood before me, one of those men or women more at home with their animals than the people around them. Deep in the depths of his brown eyes I could see memories he'd put behind himself start to surface, memories of fighting and death.

Something in my expression made him flinch. "Stay watchful, Timmis. Horses are important. Keep them safe."

He nodded thanks that I'd given him the job he would have taken anyway. "Aye, Lord Dura. Dest should be good to ride if you don't push him too hard."

"Thank you, Timmis. Dest has been a faithful friend." I grasped his forearm as one soldier would another, a grip of equals. He straightened, and I saw his free hand grip the pike a bit tighter.

"Bless you, Lord Dura. It's a pleasure servin' a man who knows the value of his mount."

Bolt rode beside me as we moved along the arcing roads that mirrored the four man-made branches of the Rinwash and defined the crescent of Bunard. Braben's sat at the junction between the upper merchants' quarter and the lower, and we left the water behind to enter the domain of those poorer merchants that defined the cramped housing and street market of every city.

The craftsmen and women who occupied this section already moved about their tasks, readying wares and tools and food for the day ahead. Streetfront shutters creaked and stall doors protested as their owners moved about in the lightening dawn.

Bolt hadn't spoken since the Vigil's meeting, not a single word, his face as closed and inscrutable as the cover of an untitled book. The silence between us grew in weight, accented by each echoing clop of a hoof or the shallow call of a merchant. I wasn't good with people—too honest, too impatient to display the truth. What had I accomplished by revealing Elwin's killer? Nothing. The rest of the Vigil might decide not to believe me. There were enough gaps in my assertion for them to squirm away from the truth if they wished. Honesty compelled me to admit Toria Deel might be right, though something in me twisted at the admission.

"I might be wrong," I said to the air in front of my horse. We rode for another ten paces before I heard Bolt reply.

"No."

When we rounded another bend in the street I darted a look at my guard, but nothing in his visage or demeanor acknowledged my presence.

"Robin was the best," Bolt said. His voice deepened until his words came out as a growl, and I could only guess what price this admission must be taking.

"Guards have a gift, Dura. Free or bestowed, every one of us who watches over the Vigil has a physical gift from Aer that we shape to our calling to protect those with your gift. Once upon a time, I had a son whose mother died. When I traveled, I took him with me. The life of a Vigil guard is usually more stable than this. We tend to move to a new kingdom every ten years, but the heads of the orders ensure we are well financed.

"Robin was three when he came into his gift one morning, looking at me over his porridge, his eyes wide with surprise." He sighed. "His gift must have been pure, Dura, or as close to it as this world can be. I still wonder who first received it, how it passed from father to daughter or mother to son, what change it made on their lives, and how the gift came to be lost to them."

He turned to look at me then, as if desperate to make me understand what Robin meant to him. "It wasn't just the gift that made Robin the best. A gifted fool can swing a sword. Robin had something more. He had an intuition, a knowing about him. Do you know he almost never had to fight? He could sense danger and avoid it. He would see the set of a man's eyes or the way a woman managed to casually keep one hand hidden, a hand that might hold a dagger, and see the threat behind it."

Bolt shook his head. "The members of the Vigil and their counterparts on the southern continent bear godlike burdens and power, but they're just men and women, with all the frailties and misjudgments common to flesh. Elwin was no different. He, like Cesla before him, thought his judgment to be infallible, but my son loved him." Bolt's voice broke and his jaws clenched. "Dear Aer in heaven, what did it cost Robin to kill him?"

He stopped, still staring ahead. With his admission, Bolt shared the onus for my theory, but I didn't see the need. "I could be wrong."

"No. The ability to put a man's motives to his actions—this is your talent." He shrugged. "It might even be a gift. Just because the church hasn't catalogued it doesn't mean it isn't."

He shook his head. "But I can't figure out how Laewan could have deceived Elwin so completely. The Vigil rarely delve each other. There are almost too many memories to hold."

"Perhaps they forced the touch upon him. They could have stripped Elwin's gloves from him, forced him into the touch."

Bolt saw the flaw in my reasoning as quickly as I did. "To do that they would have had to kill Robin first. No. Somehow Laewan deceived the Eldest. Elwin was struck down first, by Robin's hand." He turned to me as we crossed the bridge over the Rinwash to the poor quarter. "And Aer brought you to the Vigil." He stilled further. "It may be that you are the result of Robin's last and best act of courage."

I bowed in my saddle at the compliment. "I will do my best to honor his memory."

Bolt nodded. "From almost anyone else that would sound trite. I choose to believe you."

He shook himself, casting the topic away. "How will we find the urchins?"

Inside, I breathed a sigh of relief at the change in topic. "We won't have to. They'll find us. Jeb says they've got the poor quarter bottled up to keep their own safe."

Chapter 46

They met us almost as soon as we came across the bridge. I'd been watching for them, but they still surprised me, melting out of shadows at the edge of a building that shouldn't have been large enough to conceal them. With mismatched clothes and the remains of someone's castoffs for shoes tied together with twine, two urchins sauntered toward us with the bored air of aged sentries.

"Mornin', milord," one of the boys said as he ducked his head. His hair might have been blond, but spots of dirt dyed it a piebald brown. "We don't usually get visitors to the poor quarter before sunup."

The other urchin, looking bored and casual, meandered around to the back of our horses. Bolt's gaze didn't shift, but I saw him yawn and stretch so that his right hand found the inside of his cloak.

"You don't get visitors at all," I said. "Not since the urchins decided to safeguard the streets yourselves. But there hasn't been an attack here in days, has there?" I looked at the grime-streaked buildings that made the poor quarter. The dilapidated structures created a warren of alleys and dead ends only a fool would enter.

The urchin shook his head. "No, milord, not since we started keeping vigil."

I smiled at his accidental pun. "I need to see Rory."

He shrugged his shoulders. "I don't know anyone by that name. You talk to me. I'm Bounder."

I didn't have time for the usual runaround the urchins gave the city watch to amuse themselves. I reached into my cloak for the token Rory had given me. "Bounder, let me give you some advice. First, don't try to sneak an urchin behind the horse of a man who's trained it to kick on command." I pointed to my chin. "Second, if you see me, don't annoy me by making me wait." I pulled the round wooden medallion from my cloak and thrust it forward. Out of the corner of my eye I saw the other urchin back away from the horses before reappearing at Bounder's side.

A small nod was all the concession the urchin gave me before he spoke. "I'll take you in." He pointed at the mounts. "You'll probably want to leave your horses here."

I turned to the urchin at Bounder's side, a girl, perhaps eleven or twelve, with hints of bright red along the tips of her hair. "What's your name?"

A cool green gaze that was too old for her face met mine. "My friends call me Flame."

I dug into my pocket for a pair of silver pennies, enough to buy Flame two decent meals. "Well, Flame, I'd like to be your friend. Will you stay here and mind our horses until we return?"

She looked at the two pennies I placed in her palm in wonder. "It feels different."

"What does?"

Her smile erased some of the years she shouldn't have had in her gaze. "The money. I've never held coin I've earned before."

It was hard to breathe, as if the air in the poor quarter had suddenly turned thick. I debated telling her and Bounder of the deal I'd struck with Pellin but decided against it. As much as I wanted to give them hope for a future, I didn't want to raise their expectations only to have them dashed if Pellin and the rest of the Vigil, including me, ended up dead. "Do you like that feeling, Flame?"

When she nodded, I forced a small laugh. "Then I hope you have the pleasure of encountering it again soon."

We followed Bounder into the warrens of the poor quarter, the light hardly breaking through the crowded overhangs of the buildings. I looked forward to each struggling smudge of light on the garbage-strewn cobblestones. Bounder navigated his way through the maze with the skill of a woodsman negotiating a forest trail no one else could see.

After fifteen minutes we came to a building so dilapidated it leaned against its neighbor for support. Bolt eyed the lintel with a jaundiced gaze as we passed beneath it. "We could meet in the alley," he said. "At least that way we'd have a chance to jump clear when this thing finally decides to give way."

The rotting post at the corner of the hovel didn't inspire confidence. "Just don't lean against anything."

He snorted. "Are you kidding? I'm not even going to take a deep breath."

Whatever floor the building had once had was long gone, rotted or removed to be replaced by hard-packed earth. A hearth still remained in the center of the far wall, standing straight but looking tilted because of the slanted structure around it. A few sticks and pieces of old boards still burned with a desultory flame, giving more smoke than light or heat. Rory stood in front of it, but most of the other urchins were curled on top of makeshift pallets around the room, sleeping until nightfall.

Bounder tugged at one of Rory's sleeves, pointing toward Bolt and me as we approached. Rory broke his conversation and came to me.

"Another day in the midst of heaven, yah?" he said in his fake accent. Doubt clouded his gaze. I couldn't help but sigh. No matter how many times I sought Rory out, I always had to establish trust with him, had to prove my intentions.

"I don't have time for this, Rory," I said. "I need your help." I met each gaze pointed my way. "I need all of you."

Rory laughed. "That's a lot of coin, Willet, and not to be insulting, I know how much you get paid. You've already surrendered everything this month."

"I'm not talking about money, Rory," I said, but I looked at all of them, awake or otherwise. "I'm talking about homes."

All expression, genuine or feigned, dropped from Rory's face to be replaced by a stoic intensity that could only presage anger. He stared at me for a moment before his mouth tightened and he stepped close enough to pick my pocket, though he kept his hands at his sides. "That's going to cost you, yah? There are some things you don't jest about."

I lowered my voice to match his whisper. "I'm not joking, Rory. The church is desperate, and we need help. They've promised a home to every urchin who wants one."

He shook his head. "I don't believe you. If people wanted to help us, they would have done it. As soon as your danger is over, they'll throw us back on the street, and I'll have to gather everyone up all over again."

I could see the pain in his gaze at the thought of surrendering the urchins. "Homes, Rory," I whispered. "I'm talking about real homes, where they'll have people who love them and learn a trade that's not thieving or whoring. They'll always have the streets. Do you have the right to take that opportunity from them?"

I looked into his eyes. "And you, Rory. Don't you want a home?"

He shook his head. "The entire poor quarter is my home. And it's theirs too." He laughed, but the gaze he turned to me held a hopeless longing so intense I had to look away. "Can you picture any merchant or priest having me, Willet?"

"None of them are going to take you," Bolt said.

I jerked at the wound my guard had just laid on Rory's soul, but before I could respond, he went on.

"Come with me, lad, out into the light," he ordered. And before Rory could respond, he turned his back on us and went back to the alley.

Rory watched as Bolt left without looking back, a kaleidoscope of all possible shades of hurt and anger flashing across his face before he followed, his hands balled into tight fists. I didn't suspect Bolt of casual cruelty, but the death of a loved one, son or spouse or daughter, could twist a man.

I fell in behind and stepped into the alley where Bolt had positioned himself in the largest pool of light he could find.

When he saw us he beckoned me forward. I stepped around Rory, my curiosity keeping me silent. Bolt fished into the pocket of his cloak and took out a silver penny, handing it to me.

Then he said to Rory, "Willet's going to rest the coin on his palm between us. I want to see if you can grab it before I can. We'll do it twice."

Rory laughed, but the injury Bolt had given him lurked behind the sound. "I'm not interested in your penny, growler. Now, if you make it a half crown, you might have my attention."

Bolt smiled as he fished into his cloak again. "I'm just a guard, but if you take the penny we'll up the second wage." He showed the larger coin, enough to feed all of the urchins for a week, before putting it back.

Rory's eyes narrowed to slits, his face pinched in suspicion, but the lure of Bolt's silver drew him in. I put my hand with the coin resting on the palm halfway between them, and Rory drew within a span, his feet braced but otherwise relaxed.

Bolt stood opposite. "When Dura gives the word, we'll both go for the coin."

Rory nodded, his focus not on the coin but on Bolt. Silence dropped over the three of us like a blanket, stretching.

"Now!"

Twin blows struck the palm of my hand from each side, but the movement that accompanied them blurred. I struggled to sort who had won, trying to figure out whose touch I'd felt first. Rory, not smiling, held up the silver penny, taunting Bolt with it.

"Now the half crown, if you please."

Instead, Bolt reached into the folds of his cloak and retrieved a full crown, the coin looking all the bigger in comparison to the penny Rory had won. The silver felt warm and heavy against my palm.

"As before," Bolt said, "but this time you'll have to wait for me to move."

Rory's face tightened at the change in the rules of the game. "When did a noble or a merchant ever play square with those from the poor quarter?"

Bolt shrugged. "My money, my rules."

Silence stretched as the urchin and the guard mirrored each other on either side, so different in build, yet each standing with the same odd mixture of tension and calm. My own heartbeat surged in my ears, a steady push of noise that defined their strange duel.

Motion without sound erupted from both, and again I fought to determine who'd won. I looked down at my palm to see the coin still resting there.

Rory shook his hand, muttering curses. "I knew you would cheat, growler, but I had you beat anyway."

Bolt nodded. "Almost inhumanly quick, and intuitive as well. You beat me fair, Rory. If I hadn't struck your knuckles you'd have the crown as well." Slowly, he lifted the coin from my palm and gave it to him. "You're needed."

"No." I shook my head. "I won't allow it."

Bolt lifted an eyebrow at me. "There are things you don't know about us, Willet. One of them is how we pick our replacements. Robin was mine." Something too complex for me to unravel showed in his face. "Do you have any conception of the honor it was to train my son? It had never happened before in our history. Now it's my responsibility to find my replacement again." Bolt turned, shutting me out of the conversation.

"You're gifted, Rory. There are perhaps a score of men who could have taken both coins."

Rory, standing in the pool of light in his worn-out shoes and ragged clothes, wore his refusal like a shield. "What do you want from me, growler?"

"I want to give you a home away from the poor quarter," Bolt said. "Willet's going to need a guard." His face creased into a smile that showed deep lines around his eyes. "I'm too old to do it for very long. I want you to take over for me."

"Why would I want to guard him?" Rory asked.

"Because what he's doing is important. It's hard to say just how important. The training is hard, Rory, and it's quite likely you'll hate me before it's over."

Rory laughed, his face still closed in refusal. "You're not much of a barker, yah?"

"I can't sell you this," Bolt said. "You have to volunteer for it." He looked over my shoulder to the hovel where the rest of the urchins waited or slept. "But you're already acquainted with need. Now you're needed for something bigger. There are two things that make the job worthwhile. First, you'd be helping with one of the most important tasks in the world. Second . . ." Bolt smiled. "You'll be one of the most dangerous men in the world."

"And all I have to do is protect Willet?" Rory asked.

Bolt shrugged. "I won't lie. The job is more difficult than it sounds. For a grown man, he shows remarkably little sense."

I saw Rory stiffen. "He's the only growler who ever helped us. By Haedes, he's practically the only person who ever helped us."

Bolt smiled. "You're loyal. Hang on to that. You'll need it."

"I won't put the urchins in danger," Rory said to me. "Home or no."

I shook my head. "I just want them to hide." Then I explained our plan to put a net around the places in the city where we thought Laewan might be hiding.

"Tricky," Rory said. "But we can put them up on the rooftops. Your killer might be quick, but unless he has some magical way to shed weight, he won't dare to follow." He gave a grim chuckle. "Not unless he wants to chance breaking through the slate on the rooftops."

Rory looked over his shoulder. "We'll meet you at Braben's."

"You could come with us now," I said.

He shook his head, looking uncomfortable. "I have to take your offer to the urchins, and a lot of them are still coming in from the streets." He darted a look at Bolt. "And I'll need to appoint a new leader for them from those who stay behind."

I felt the twist of regret in my stomach. "Why would any of them stay behind?"

Rory gave me a sad look, but whether it was due to my incomprehension or not, I couldn't say. "Some of the urchins won't take the chance, Willet. My story doesn't exactly read like a tale from the legends, but some of these have a history that makes mine look positively pampered. They won't risk that kind of trust ever again."

Far, far down, where I'd never be able to quench it, anger burned at what had been done to the boys and girls that comprised the urchins. "If they refuse, I'll make sure the church finds a way to help them, even if I have to confront the heads of the four orders myself. They won't have to risk their trust again if they don't want to."

Rory looked at Bolt with a lopsided smile. "I would imagine that kind of attitude is the reason he needs a guard."

Bolt nodded. "In part, but it's also why he's worth the trouble."

CHAPTER 47

"When did you decide to do that?" I asked Bolt as we left the poor quarter.

He didn't offer any pithy soldiers' quotes, which I took as a sign of progress. "From the first time we met. He grabbed my thumb before I could stop him. It would be interesting to know the history of his gift. It seems Aer has a purpose for him."

"Or you do," I said.

He nodded. "When the fight is going against you, grab the weapon that comes to hand."

I sighed. It had probably been too much to hope for. We had time before returning to Braben's, and there was something that needed doing, so I turned Dest's head toward the nobles' quarter and urged him into a trot.

"Gael?" Bolt asked.

I nodded. "If we come out the other side of this, my time in Bunard will be done." The buildings and streets of the city, tracing their arcs along the branches of the Rinwash, were as familiar to me as my own skin. I'd never known any other city, and leaving it would be like abandoning a part of me. I berated myself for resisting. If Rory could pick up the reins to a new life with more questions than answers, so could I.

"Gael will have to surrender her gift and we'll still have to sneak away." I caught Bolt's eye. "Alainn lusts after the money her marriage would bring with every pulse of his heart. He won't want to let her go, gift or not."

It happened again, as it always did whenever I spoke of a life with her—Bolt's face closed, which for him meant moving from wooden to stony.

I steered Dest across his horse's path and pulled to a stop. "I don't know what the Vigil intends to do with me if we survive this, but I'm not giving up my life with Gael. Do you know how many people have a chance at real love?"

My voice came thick and loud in the street. "Nobles give each other away in marriage for power or advantage, binding themselves to people they can hardly stand just to grub for a little bit more." I laughed. "Then they die. And here's the funny thing—the ones they leave behind never send that power or money or influence with them. The graves, the barrows, or the pyres get only us. I may be a fool, but I want something different for myself."

Bolt shook his head, and I saw him draw breath.

"No!" I held up a hand. "I don't want to hear it. If I have to, I'll surrender the gift to Volsk. Then you and the rest of the precious Vigil can go on your merry way and you can leave me out of it."

I wheeled Dest around and dug my heels into his flanks until he broke into an easy canter. When I came to Gael's estate, Bolt reined his horse to a stop behind me and dismounted, his movements quick enough to block me from approaching the servant at their gate.

"Do you trust me?" he asked. He sidestepped to block me as I tried to go around.

Old anger twisted my guts. "Of course not. I don't trust anybody."

I stopped trying to go around him and walked straight ahead, hoping he would surrender and move. I ran into a hand that might have been cast of iron. "Think, Willet. When did you stop trusting people who were trying to help you?"

I laughed at him without trying to pull the memory into focus. "About the time I got raised to the nobility and everyone started trying to kill me."

"No." Bolt shook his head. "That's not true. Think."

His demand pushed me back into older memories, despite my

efforts, and my head started to hurt again. "There's no point." There were too many doors in my mind that were too new for me to keep them straight. Bits of other people's lives leaked free, and I put a hand out to Bolt's shoulder to steady myself, hating the show of weakness.

"The Darkwater," Bolt said.

"Of course," I snarled back. "Do you think I'm an idiot?"

I waited for him to smile at the obvious opening, but his face grew somber instead. "No, Willet. I think you're a survivor."

"Then let me have her." I had no idea if I spoke to Bolt or Aer, but I would have gone to my knees and begged if I thought it would have helped.

Bolt's face hardly changed, but his eyes filled with more sorrow and regret than a human should be able to hold. "I'm not saying you can't, Willet. I'm saying you won't. I'm your friend. Fight through the poison the war and the forest put in your mind and trust me. Wait."

"Wait for what?" I tried not to scream, but sorrow and pain broke over me like a wave, threatening to drown me. Since Laidir had stepped in to force Alainn to grant permission for us to marry nearly a year ago, I'd lived each day in fear that something would take away what I prized more than anything.

The creak of the gate, a squall of hinges protesting movement, pulled us out of our argument. Gael stood, looking pale and wan in the light of Bunard's spring. But then she brightened, as if she'd discovered an unexpected source of strength.

Then she was in my arms. I buried my face in the scented wealth of her hair and held her fast, like a drowning sailor holding a spar.

"I thought I dreamed you," she told me. "Then when Marya told me you lived, I spent every hour searching for you."

She ran her fingertips over my face, as if she doubted the vision of her eyes, first touching my nose, then my cheeks and chin before starting over again.

"I'll call the priests to witness," she said. "Alainn can have his gift." She smiled.

"What of Rupert?" I asked.

Gael smiled and her fingertips left a trail of warmth as they ghosted down my jawline before her hand came to her side. "Without the gift, his father has no incentive for the marriage."

I pulled her close, giving Bolt a look of triumph, ignoring the way he shook his head. "The sooner we leave Bunard, the better. How quickly can you gather your belongings?"

Her brows drew together, and I chiseled the look of her into my memory. I'd won. Despite everything circumstance had conspired to throw at me, I'd beaten it and wrested victory and happiness from it.

"Four days," she said.

I patted Laidir's writ, calculating. I'd begun to think the Vigil might accept me as one of their own, but they'd yet to give me any guarantees. "Can you make it two and a half?"

She nodded. "Tomorrow, I'll transfer the gift to Alainn. Anything that won't travel, I will sell to him or a competitor." Her lips parted in a smile. "My last gift to him will be an education in business. I'll pit him against the other houses. His first lesson will be expensive, I think."

Her face turned serious as she turned to Bolt. "Do not think I've forgotten your friends' deception. Before I surrender my house and my name, I will ensure you are all called to account in front of the king for Willet's 'death.'"

I put my hands on her shoulders and turned her to me, exulting in the knowledge I would have this face to look upon for the rest of my life. "No."

Her brows lifted, and I went on. "In this, they are blameless. They thought my mind was dead because of my doing. I hadn't counted on them coming for me as quickly as they did, or else they never would have called the apothecary."

The flare of anger and pain dimmed a bit in Gael's gaze without leaving. I loved her with everything I was or ever would be, but I knew this—once roused, her anger was difficult to extinguish. I wouldn't be surprised if she tried to call the Vigil to account regardless of what I said, but after a moment she gave her head a little shake as if she were casting off that train of thought and came into my arms again.

"Don't go out after dark," I told her. "Not for any reason."

Questions filled her eyes that I didn't have time to answer, but she nodded, and I loved her for that trust.

She tilted her head to look at me beneath her lashes, and her full lips curved upward in a little bow of a smile. "The summers are warm in the south, Willet. I understand the fashions are quite daring by our standards. Alainn will have the gift, but for the next day I'll still be able to create designs as before. Some of them will be for you alone." Her voice dipped to a sultry register. "I think you'll be surprised."

I pulled her into an embrace, tilting her head and falling into a kiss. My gloved hands kept me from delving her while my lips roved over hers, but my imagination conjured uses for the gift besides tracking criminals. "I will have a surprise or two for you as well."

We parted and she turned, giving me a last glance over her shoulder before walking back past the gatehouse. I mounted Dest and turned his head toward Braben's without looking at Bolt. I didn't want to see whatever disapproval or sorrow he wore on his face.

The sound of distant hammering behind me drew my attention. Alainn's estate lay within half a mile of the northernmost channel of the Rinwash and then the cathedrals of the four orders and Laidir's keep. A chorus of hammers brought me to attention, and needles of dread pierced my heart.

The sound of hammering itself wasn't unusual in Bunard. Gallows were sometimes constructed near the prison to execute those few caught in murder or treason. But the swell of sound I heard, like a storm bank rolling over the horizon, didn't belong to anything as small as a single gallows.

Bolt rode close beside me, and I reached out to grab his sleeve, trying to think, to render some sense of the past two weeks. "What day is it?"

He looked at me, curious and uncomprehending of my alarm. "I'm not sure."

I shook my head, working to keep from screaming in frustration. "Well then, what week, man? What week?"

"The fifteenth."

With a curse, I spurred Dest toward the sound, praying to Aer that Bolt was wrong, that we hadn't made a blunder that would unleash horror in Bunard. I pounded through the streets yelling at nobles, merchants, and peasants alike to get out of my way, until I rode into the square framed by the massive cathedrals of the four orders.

I jumped from Dest's back, staring in sick fascination at the stages being built in the broad street in front of each cathedral, massive raised platforms for the ceremony of Bas-solas.

Bolt thundered up behind me, but I was already moving, running across the square to grab the dirty cassock of a Merum priest directing sweating workmen.

"The festival, when is it?" He didn't know me, and I saw him draw back in startlement and confusion. "Curse you, man. When is Bas-solas?"

The priest tried to yank his cassock from my grip. "Tomorrow. Let go of me."

I didn't *know* anything. But every instinct I carried with me, every experience that had taught me to imagine the worst and then expect it, screamed that Laewan would attack during Bas-solas, the festival of the death and rebirth of light.

A hand clamped onto the upper part of my arm and spun me around. Bolt stood on the verge of slapping me across the face. "What's so important about the festival? Every order in every kingdom on the northern continent celebrates it."

I nodded, groping for words to explain. "But it's not really Aer's feast day. The liturgy says nothing about it. When the priests first came to the northern continent centuries and centuries ago, they co-opted Bas-solas to teach the story of Aer to the people."

"How do you know this?" Bolt asked.

I touched an old memory, one I thought I'd put far enough away so that it no longer pained me. "I was a postulate in the Merum order. Two weeks from taking my vows, war broke out." I rolled my shoulders, trying to shed a burden that existed only in my mind. "It's a long story, but I got conscripted. In the first campaign across the southern border, I killed five men. And that was the end of the priesthood."

Thankfully, his eyes showed nothing of pity or anger, nothing I would need to respond to. "What about Bas-solas?"

"Before the priests came, it was called Bas-fuil. It means blood death. Every kingdom celebrated it. The people would wear masks and pretend to be evil spirits roaming the streets, but the northern kingdoms took things a bit further. Everyone would engage in mock battles between good and evil with wooden daggers and animal blood during the dark."

"What does that have to do with Laewan?"

I shook my head. "Tomorrow, just after noon, the entire city is going to be caught up in a game that looks like a series of brutal fights between good and evil, complete with fake weapons and blood you can't tell from the real thing. Every few years, someone gets the idea to engage in a real murder along with all the fake ones."

I looked toward Laidir's keep. "Someone has to get to the king. If we can't find Laewan before noon, Bunard will be a bloodbath."

"Why?" Bolt asked.

He still didn't understand me. "Haven't you ever been in Bunard for Bas-solas?"

"No."

I looked up at the western sky, where the sun shone all yellow and warm, as if it could do nothing else. "The sun doesn't just dim a little the way it does in the south. It goes out. For two hours, the streets of Bunard are going to be as dark as a moonless night."

Bolt looked at me, his mouth agape. "Dear Aer in heaven."

My mouth had gone dry. "Exactly."

Chapter 48

Voices yammered in the back of my head, but I couldn't lock them away—they were all mine. I tried to sort through a hundred different scenarios, all of them worse than the previous one, trying in vain to come up with some kind of plan. A buzzing noise kept breaking my concentration, and after a moment I looked up to see Bolt talking to me. I pulled myself out of the chaos of my thoughts long enough to hear him.

"You have to leave the city," he said. "I can't protect you here."

I shook my head as if he'd started spouting the language of the sand people in the southern continent. "Leave? Are you mad? We're the only chance Bunard has."

"Bunard is lost." His tone carried all the finality of judge and executioner. "We can't fight heaven knows how many people who've been infected by the Darkwater." He paused to take a breath, and a bit of his stoicism reasserted itself. "I can't protect you from people who can see in the dark. I'm supposed to keep you alive."

"I have my own vows to keep, and one of those is to protect King Laidir and his people."

Bolt had it within his power to force my cooperation. He could have a sword or dagger in hand before I could blink. With a simple rap on the head, he could toss me over the back of my horse and cart me out of town like a sack of onions. "Please. If we leave now there's no one else who can stop this."

I saw his fingers twitch, and I flinched, but he merely stood, regarding me while his expression continued to sour. Then he sighed. "Pellin never played my loyalties against me this way. You know the people of Bunard might not even need protecting. The whole purpose of this might be to get you and the Vigil in one place so that they can kill you."

I caught his gaze and held it. "Do you want me to turn my back on people I've sworn to protect for 'might' and 'maybe'?" I asked.

Instead of answering, Bolt mounted his horse and twitched the reins so that it faced south. "We have to get to the others."

I put one foot in the stirrup and mounted Dest. "I have to warn Laidir."

Bolt ground his teeth. "Send one of the city watch."

"No. He won't believe anyone else but me."

"Have you forgotten the plan, Willet?"

I held up a hand as if I were asking for alms. "Pellin and Rory can put the urchins in place tonight without me. There's nothing I can do until dawn tomorrow, but Laidir will have to pull his men together tonight."

"How is he going to protect the city?" Bolt demanded. "He doesn't even know who he's fighting."

"He holds the gift of kings. He'll figure it out," I said, hoping it was true. Bolt had yet to show any sign of agreement. "If I go now, I can be back at Braben's before nightfall."

Bolt shook his head. "No. Meet us at the Merum cathedral. That place is a fortress. Even if they find us, a few flaming arrows will hardly scratch the stone." He grimaced in disgust. "Pellin is going to tear my ears off for letting you go off on your own."

I smiled, forcing my face to don an expression that belied the fear churning in my gut. "Just give him one of your quotes."

Bolt didn't return the grin. "Yah. He hates those."

I rode Dest as fast as the crowded streets would allow. Priests and merchants with their coteries streamed to and from the keep. My horse brushed more than a few.

"*Kreppa!*" one dowager screamed at me. I clucked my tongue in mock surprise. Laidir's court often played host to language that would make a seaman blush. I gave my horse a pat on the shoulder. "Dest, it's positively shameful how some people let their tongue run loose. Seriously, you would think a lady of her years would have learned how to control her temper by now."

Dest flicked one ear back toward the sound of my voice before he ignored me. I dug my heels in when the crowd thinned. The sun started to redden. If I didn't hurry, nightfall would catch me on the street.

I left Dest at the stable next to the prison and ran through the triple guard Laidir had posted at the entrance to the keep. The guards went for their weapons before they recognized me, but then they closed ranks anyway, cutting me off from the entrance.

I came to a stop just short of sword reach. "Where's the king, Sevin? I have to see him."

He shook his head. "No one in or out except by token."

I ground my teeth in frustration. I didn't have time for this. "By whose command?"

"Queen Cailin."

Suspicion bloomed in my chest. "When did she issue the order?"

Sevin looked at me as if my question didn't make any sense. "Two days ago."

Shaking my head, I beckoned him closer until he blocked the view from the rest of the gate watch. I might get Sevin to look the other way and let me pass, but the other guards would have to think I really had the token. "No. What time of day did the order come down?"

He blinked and I could see doubt begin to sprout in his mind. "Two hours after midnight. Lieutenant Kayle reported it."

I kept my face neutral. "Did none of you think to confirm her command with the king?"

Sevin drew back, his back stiffening. "She's the queen, Lord Dura."

Edging closer, I dropped my voice. "What we're fighting comes in the dark, Sevin. If you don't trust me, come with me to the king. Put the point of your spear in my back, and if I make one wrong move, you can run me through, but I have to warn him. There's going to be an attack during Bas-solas tomorrow."

Sevin looked over his shoulder toward the guards who watched us, brows drawn or lifted, as temperament dictated. "Dig in your cloak," he whispered.

Inwardly I sighed. "Thank you." I pulled Rory's token from my cloak, the simple wooden coin, and held it out for Sevin's inspection, shielding it from the other guards with my hand.

He gave me an officious nod before doing a crisp soldier's pivot that allowed me to pass. "I will accompany Lord Dura to King Laidir's court," he said to the mass of guards at the gate. He stopped the sweep of his gaze on a red-haired giant of a man with a beard as thick as a horse brush. "Sergeant Phyle, you have command until I return."

As soon as we were out of sight of the guard, I walked as fast as I dared without raising Sevin's suspicions. If I broke into a run he just might have used his weapon on me. Even so, I set a pace toward the top of the keep that had us both panting by the time we arrived. Outside the western wall I could feel the sun racing toward the horizon, mocking my circumstances and haste.

We entered through the wide double doors of the throne room, the noise and bustle filling the space from wall to wall and floor to ceiling, as if nothing untoward had ever happened or ever would, but underneath the costumed gaiety of Laidir's court hung an edge of nervousness. Laughter burst from knots of Collum's ruling class quicker than bolts of lightning, forced and unexpected, and the dancers on the floor, moving in their contrary circles, jerked through their prescribed steps to keep time to the unnaturally fast music.

Laidir's court seethed with fear so great none of them bothered to bait me as I made my way to the king's throne. From a distance I could see Cailin eyeing me with her usual distaste, but I could detect nothing unnatural about it. She just didn't like peasants, and that included me.

I drifted from the entrance to the side, searching for Gael, but neither she nor her uncle were among the dancers who weaved their circles on the floor or the knots of gossips and plotters around the periphery of Laidir's throne room. The king sat on his high-backed throne, watching the festivities of his court as if nothing but peace filled his kingdom. I admired his ability to exude such calm strength in the midst of turmoil. Again I grieved that he hadn't been born to a different time and family. What an emperor he would have made!

Several minor lords and ladies, most of them from the extensive

Daliagh family, clustered around the throne, but one of them saw my approach, and magically they made their bows or curtsies to the throne and melted away. I tried to suppress a smile—being a pariah had at least one advantage.

Queen Cailin saw my approach, and for a moment her vapid gaze sharpened into something more, something I'd never witnessed in her before. Calculation, focused as the point of a dagger, crackled across the distance between us, and I stumbled. Doubt came in waves, crashing into assumptions I'd spent years building. I knew the look of knowledge and intelligence, and as surely as I breathed, Cailin's glance held it.

"Lord Dura?" Laidir's voice broke through my shock. "Are you well?"

I went to one knee, staring at the floor as I tried to devise some plan that would allow me to discern the truth. Laidir had always regarded his wife with as much affection as he could, but though he'd never spoken of it, I knew he would have loved a woman with less beauty and more intellect.

"Lord Dura?" the king called again.

I stood, placing my hands behind my back and removed my gloves. My mind rebelled, and fatigue washed over me again, as if I'd asked war-weary legs to carry Jeb up the uncounted steps of the keep. "Your Majesty, as much as I hate to take you from the pleasures of your court, I have tidings that I would deliver in private."

Laidir regarded me with relief. He hated overseeing the court dinner each evening, and I knew he would appreciate the opportunity to escape it, even under the guise of receiving bad news.

"But first," I said, stepping forward, "I would offer my obeisance and farewell to Queen Cailin. It is doubtful I will ever return to your court after tonight. Those circumstances that we spoke of earlier have come to pass. I will have to renounce my title."

Cailin smiled at me, and again I saw intelligence glittering in her eyes where none had ever been revealed before.

But she took the bait, praise Aer, extending the back of her hand for me to kiss. I knelt over the pale, pristine flesh that had never seen work or hardship, wanting nothing more than to run away, but I forced my mind to build another doorway where I could store her memories. I fought down a wave of nausea and took her hand in mine.

I plunged into a thousand memories of court and accompanying emotions where I saw friends and enemies whose handclasps and enmity were known to me. In the dim portion where I retained some knowledge of myself as Willet Dura, I noted that I saw everything I had expected to see in Cailin's mind, but all of her recollections were flat, her memories and emotions mere paintings, things witnessed instead of experienced.

Then I delved deeper in time, and the tor and streets of Bunard faded and a shining city on the coast rose before me, a temperate city of cool summers and mild winters: Loklallin. A man, broad chested and resplendent on his throne, looked at me in pity, his gaze filled with regret.

"You will never rule," the man said.

Rage, hot and consuming, filled the memory. "Shouldn't the throne go to most capable? Aren't you the king, Father?"

The man shook his head. "Even a king rules by the consent of his subjects, and to do that he must be willing to be bound by law just as any other. The throne and the gift will go to your elder brother, Wynton, but there is a place for you, Cailin, by his side as advisor. I hope you will take it."

I shook my head. "I will not consent to stay here, and if I cannot use my mind for myself, I will not use it for another. I should rule. I have worked to develop every talent Aer or circumstance has given me while Wynton has lived the life of a libertine, bent on deflowering an entire field of maidens. No."

The king's face hardened. "So be it. Your marriage will be arranged."

I slipped further into the past, skimming back to witness her tutors' amazement and approval. Talent, they said, on a level to almost qualify as gifted. Wonder and excitement defined me, the thrill of my mind awakening to its own ability.

I prepared to sever the link. Outside of Cailin's mind I stood, bowing over her hand while the king and court watched. Just before I left, I saw it, shrouded in darkness and glee. Floating to it I saw a dark scroll, black as night, without any means to open it.

I'd never seen one but my own, but I knew without confirmation that I gazed upon a vault within Cailin's mind.

I straightened, releasing the queen's hand and staggered back a step. Laidir and Cailin eyed me, curious. How long had I been in her mind?

"Lord Dura, are you well?" Laidir asked.

I nodded, then regretted the motion as dizziness and nausea threatened to dump me on the polished floor at their feet. "Yes, Your Majesty," I said, swallowing bile. "But time weighs heavily on me."

Laidir rose, bowed to his queen, and led the way with his four guards to the side entrance. Inside, I quailed. How could I ever explain to Laidir that his wife had practiced a deception for years—worse, that Queen Cailin had been to the Darkwater?

In the king's private audience chamber, I knelt, touching one knee to the stones, and waited for Laidir to give me permission to speak.

"Your face is as pale as winter, Willet," Laidir said with a sigh. "Every time I see you like that, my guts turn over. Someday I want you to bring me glad tidings."

I nodded without rising. What I was about to tell the king wouldn't just distress him, it might very well anger him. I kept my eyes on the floor, even though I hadn't observed strict protocol with the king since the first day I'd been raised to the nobility. I heard another long exhale above me.

"Rise and speak, Lord Dura. If your news is dire, I think it best we get to it directly."

Laidir had dozens of sycophants who specialized in the style of court speak, a method of using a lot of words to say practically nothing. One of the things he appreciated about our interaction was the fact that we dispensed with such idiocy. "We believe Laewan is going to attack the city tomorrow, during the festival of Bas-solas." The guards on either side of Laidir started.

Chapter 49

I saw Laidir turn the idea over in a focused gaze before he gave one slow nod. "Clever. By attacking during the midday darkness, while everyone is costumed for the reenactment, he extends the element of surprise." His already deep voice had dipped, a familiar precursor to anger. So far, it wasn't directed at me. "But I will ask of you the same that I asked of the Vigil. Where is your evidence?"

"I have none that I can present, Your Majesty, only an instinct that tells me that an enemy that uses darkness as this one does will use Bas-solas to attack."

Laidir nodded, his eyes narrowed in thought but noncommittal. "And what will this enemy use for soldiers?"

"Lady Bronwyn has found evidence of a large number of people returning from the Darkwater."

"So she said. And how does she know this, Willet?"

Despite our friendship, I chose my next words with care, attempting to guide Laidir to the conclusion of his own accord. "The Darkwater leaves a mark on them that the Vigil can see, but there are too many for us to track down and delve."

He almost smiled, but his eyes tightened as if at an unexpected hurt. "Us? Do you count yourself among them now, Willet?"

He was almost there. "Yes, my liege. In this I do. The gift allows me to know who carries the mark of the Darkwater in their mind."

My words struck him, leading, I hoped, to the next right question.

"How?"

I held up a gloved hand, hoping that Laidir's memory for detail wouldn't fail him. "By touch, Your Majesty. If I remove my glove, I can see whether they've been to the cursed forest." I swallowed. Almost I said, *"Many have been that one would not suspect."*

I waited, knowing he couldn't help but catch the shift in my tone.

When he spoke, his voice was a quiet rumble, like the rare shaking of the earth. "You're wearing both your gloves now, Lord Dura."

I tried not to wince at the use of my title.

"Yet in the throne room, you bid Queen Cailin farewell with a bare hand." He leaned forward, his elbow on one knee. "Tell me, Lord Dura, what led you to suspect my wife."

Only a fool tried to lie to Laidir—everyone knew that. Most importantly, Laidir knew that, which would make my accusation all the more difficult for him to deny. "A glance, my king. Nothing more."

His lips compressed to a line when I paused, and his right hand curled into a fist. "If you continue to require prompting, Lord Dura, I shall become cross."

I took a deep breath, then launched. "The queen's glance toward me before now has always been vague and disinterested, Your Majesty."

"Not you alone," Laidir said. "I know my wife, Lord Dura."

I nodded. "Yet today, Your Majesty, I saw something more. When she looked at me, for a moment I saw the keen edge of intelligence. You've known brilliant men and women, Your Majesty. Is there not something within their glance that is different? There is a sharpness to their gaze, a way of observing their surroundings that speaks of the intelligence of their mind. In the exordium of the liturgy, it is referred to as—"

Laidir slapped his hand on the arm of his throne. "I know what it's called, Lord Dura!" Now he looked faintly hurt. I'd just told him that the wife he'd always wanted and never had, had been at his side all along, unwilling to love him enough to reveal her true nature. "Why?"

"She wanted to rule. When she could not, she vowed never to serve another with her mind." I paused. "But that has changed."

Laidir leaned back on his throne, a virtual copy of the one in the court, his face pulled to one side in a self-mocking expression. "Well, glad tidings, then. After my first wife dies childless and Cailin has sat at my side like a lump of dough, she has now decided to join me as a near equal so that we can rule together in love and harmony."

Laidir's sarcasm cut like the flicking tail of a whip, but I had no choice but to answer his words instead of his intent. "No, Your Majesty. Queen Cailin has been to the Darkwater. I've seen it in her mind. Just after noon tomorrow, during Bas-solas, she and all those who've embraced the cursed forest will become something else."

I raised my head and held Laidir's gaze, hoping I could compel him to ignore five years' experience and his own insight and believe me. "Your Majesty, you must do whatever you can to protect the city during Bas-solas. And yourself."

Solitary laughter bounced from the books and instruments that filled his shelves and tables before the carpets and tapestries absorbed it, but it held no mirth, no joy. "Even if Cailin had journeyed to the Darkwater, I'm not the one who would be in danger. If she has managed to deceive me for half a decade, I present no threat of discovery."

Rage and hurt flickered in the depths of his eyes and he stood, dismissing me. "Look to yourself and your companions, Lord Dura. If the cursed forest has infected the people of Bunard, it is you they are hunting." He took the first step down the dais. "I must call my captains."

He walked past me with his guards in tow. I grabbed the last one by the arm, ignoring the hand that flew to his hilt. "Laidir is your king. Don't leave him alone with anyone. Remember your duty."

His face closed against me. "We know the meaning of loyalty."

I left the keep and raced the encroaching sunset to the Merum cathedral, making tally marks in my head of each threat coming against us. Inside I raged. There was no way to meet them all. And my king had seen to the heart of the threat—all of Laewan's machinations were nothing more than a means to wipe out the Vigil.

I shook my head as I slowed Dest to a trot in the press. It didn't fit. If one of the gifted was killed, the gift merely resurfaced elsewhere, given by Aer to whomever he chose. Killing any of the Vigil would mean time was lost while new members were trained, but . . .

I pulled Dest to a stop. Unless Laewan could kill all of us. Who would be there to train or even seek those who came into the gift?

I stepped through the gatehouse of the Merum cathedral as a fair spring sky shifted from blue to crimson. Any other time I would have stopped to admire the color streaking the sky with wispy pink clouds. Now they only reminded me of bloodshed I would be unable to prevent. A few urchins raced past me, running to their appointed spots in the city as I dismounted to walk the paved flagstones. A handful of dirty, unshod peasant children with dirty faces, abandoned by relatives and circumstances, constituted our army. A stricture from my days of training as an acolyte drifted across my mind. *Aer will use the weak to confound the strong.* What better place to gather such an army than the cathedral?

I almost believed He might intervene. Almost.

I presented myself to the guards at the entrance, and a functionary escorted me through the massive iron-bound doors to one of the smaller rooms in the cathedral—a room that dwarfed Braben's entire taproom.

Bolt saw me first, and I could see tension flow out of him in the set of his shoulders and the uncurling of his fingers. Pellin turned from a map of Bunard spread across a polished rosewood table that gleamed like blood in the lamplight of the windowless room.

"Were you successful?"

Was I? I shook my head. "I've spoken with the king, but the queen has been to the Darkwater. There's a vault in her mind. I tried to warn him, but I don't know if he believed me."

"You should have broken it," Toria Deel said. Her voice came out flat, with as much emotion as I'd use about killing a rat.

"You'll pardon me if I don't share your eagerness in this regard," I shot back. "Besides, I don't know how."

The edges of my anger slipped from her countenance, failing to find purchase. "Simply reach out with your mind and tear it to pieces." She shrugged. "I hope you do not find opportunity to regret your inaction."

"You mean your own," I snapped.

"The king may not be in danger," Lady Bronwyn said, speaking before Toria Deel could reply. "If the queen hasn't harmed him before now, she may not." She looked at me with eyes that were too hard to read. "Perhaps her vault is as quiescent as yours."

"No." I sifted through the queen's memories like a baker working flour. "She's been regarded lightly all her life, and she's dangerously intelligent."

"Ha, not like you at all." Bolt, standing guard behind me as I looked at the map where portions of the city had been marked, cleared his throat. "But if she kills the king at the beginning of Bas-solas, the entire city could fall. The guards will pull back to the keep while those tainted by the Darkwater run rampant."

His warning twisted my guts. How many levels of powerlessness were there? "You have to do something," I said to Pellin.

He nodded, but nothing in his gaze spoke of confidence. "I will ask the Chief of Servants to see him tomorrow morning. She is always escorted by at least two attendants, but now I will suggest that they be armed." Pellin turned his attention back to the map. "This is where we've stationed your friends, Lord Dura."

Ice pierced me at the thought of using children to track Laewan during the night. "Do they know what Laewan looks like? Did you tell them to stay hidden at all costs?" My words tumbled out of my mouth.

Bronwyn nodded. "Despite what you may think, Lord Dura, we do care what happens to them."

"And we have used some of our more prosaic resources," Pellin said, nodding to Toria Deel. She clasped her hands, and I could see they were smudged with charcoal. "Toria Deel is a skilled artist. Each group of urchins has a likeness of Laewan in their possession." He looked at her with pride shimmering in his gaze. "She's quite good, actually, almost gifted."

Toria Deel blushed, ducking her head as her dark skin suffused with warmth that suddenly made her seem girlish. "Not even close to gifted," she said, "but there was a painter who lived near me when I was young. I used to watch him work. It took me a very long time to learn." She stopped and looked away from me, appearing uncomfortable.

I ignored the map with its placements and impossible demands, setting my hands on the table so that I could see each of the Vigil. "We have to find Laewan before Bas-solas."

Pellin nodded, resolute but not confident. I'd seen men like him before—men who disliked the burden of command no matter how well-equipped for it they were. "We know, Lord Dura," he said. "Bolt has informed us, and this is not my first time to be in Bunard for the festival."

"Didn't you realize what would happen?" Had he known?

He shrugged. "In my time the city didn't fall into complete darkness. Even had I known, there would be little point in borrowing trouble from the future."

I could feel the flush of anger flooding upward through my face like water filling a bucket. "Little point? With enough warning Laidir could have called off the festival altogether. Farmers and merchants come from all over the countryside to the festival. It's several market days crammed into one, and when the sun goes dark tomorrow, those people are going to be in danger."

Pellin had started shaking his head even before I was through. "The threat is aimed at us, Lord Dura."

I took a pair of deep breaths before I spoke. "That's what Laidir said when I told him Cailin had a vault in her mind. If you're wrong, the entire kingdom of Collum will fall. The dukes will fight for the throne and Owmead will come in to scoop up the pieces."

Bronwyn nodded. "Civil wars are an unfortunate part of history, Lord Dura."

"Unfortunate? What's wrong with you people? This is my home. King Laidir is my friend, and I don't have so many of those that I can afford to throw one of them away like an undersized fish."

"Then listen to your king," Pellin said.

"Fine," I snarled, "but what do we do during Bas-solas if we can't find Laewan?"

Pellin looked to the rest of the Vigil as if checking to see how much support he had, a gesture of doubt. "We gather here. The bishops of the four orders have promised us all the guards they have. If we let ourselves be seen and Laewan attacks us here, it will save us months, perhaps even years, of work in Bunard."

I shook my head. "What?"

Bronwyn, standing at my right, spoke into the pause. "We cannot let those stained by the Darkwater remain in Bunard, Lord Dura. They're a threat to all those around them. If we tempt Laewan with a prize, the entire Vigil gathered in one spot, he cannot help but attack. But we will have every guard the entire church has at its command hidden here, waiting."

I gaped at her as the horror of what she intended became apparent, and I looked at the thick walls of the cathedral in revulsion. "It will be a killing field," I said. "You're going to use Bas-solas to cleanse Bunard." I wanted to puke.

Toria Deel's gaze, hot and indignant, found mine. "We can't cure them," she spat. "If we could, we would have cleansed *you* of the taint."

Coarse laughter rasped its way out of my throat, and I jabbed a finger at Volsk standing behind her. "You mean instead of poisoning me in the hopes that my gift would go to him?"

Bronwyn took a step forward. "That is unjust, Lord Dura. You ask us to trust you when every experience tells us otherwise. Do you not understand how vast that experience is? From the time the gift first came to me during—"

"Stop!" Pellin slammed his palms on the table, the crack of sound startling Bronwyn into silence. For a moment something blazed in his eyes at her, an assertion of power and authority that carried hints I couldn't decipher. Again, the feeling nagged me, tugged at my experience as reeve, that there were pieces to the puzzle that was the Vigil that I had missed, but I had no way of putting them together.

"We have a plan," Pellin said after a moment. "If Aer wills it, we will find Laewan before Bas-solas, but if we do not, we will gather here." His gaze found mine. "I'm sorry, Lord Dura. If we cannot find the master, we will have to kill the servants."

I rolled my eyes. "Did you borrow that from Bolt, or is it your own?" I turned on my heel.

"Where are you going, Lord Dura?" Bronwyn asked.

"To get some parchment and ink." My voice dripped with scorn. "I want to commit Pellin's brilliant strategy to memory so I don't forget it." Someone behind me gasped at my disrespect, but I was too angry to care, much less apologize. I left the meeting room. A few seconds later Bolt came out the door, three paces behind me, probably with orders not to let me leave.

Chapter 50

"That was unfair," Bolt said as he fell into step beside me.

I wasn't in the mood to be charitable, magnanimous, or least of all, fair. I'd failed to convince the man who was the closest thing I had to a father of his danger, and now I would be part of a massive slaughter, presuming I lived, of men and women whose only crime was being stupid enough to go to the Darkwater. Turning right at the end of the corridor, I pulled in a lungful of the stuffy air of the Merum compound and let it out in a long whispering sigh.

"I'd be more inclined to be fair if the people back in that room hadn't tried to put me out of my misery. I have a vault in my mind, but I'm not some slavering dog that needs to be put down. What if it's the same for some of those people?" I took another right with the realization of my destination dawning on me at last.

"That may be," Bolt said, "but in all my years with the Vigil I've never seen it. Willet, they never got to any of those the Darkwater infected before they went mad and you're the first to delve a man while his vault was open." He paused, gathering his words. "You speak of losing Collum to Owmead—the Vigil must safeguard against losing the entire continent to the Darkwater."

I took another turn, and at the end of a long hallway I could see the high paneled doors that led to the library. A hint of the musty smell of old parchment drifted to my nose, and I calmed. Perhaps Custos would forgive me for not bringing him any sweets.

When we entered the door, an acolyte in white with ink smudges on his fingers met us, his eyes straining to focus on objects more than ten inches away from his face. "How may I serve you, sirs?"

I nodded with a smile, taking comfort in this small piece of normalcy from my past. But it was accompanied by a small rebuke. Until a moment ago I hadn't even thought of saying good-bye to my friend, the master of the library. "Is Custos about?"

The acolyte nodded. "He's just returned from the city."

That took me aback. Custos never left his books and scrolls except for the occasional trip to the market for his sweets. Even then, he usually counted on visitors or acolytes to fetch them for him. "Would you tell him Willet Dura is here to see him?"

The acolyte nodded. Misgiving clouded my thoughts, like the threat of a storm, but I drifted to the nearest shelf to pick a codex at random anyway. Too much of my life had changed and would change. If I had to leave my city, at least I could engage in our game once more before I left. Finding a page at random, I selected a paragraph to test my friend.

Custos rounded a row of bookshelves ahead of me almost at a run, driving the alarmed acolyte before him.

"Willet," he said, coming close and squeezing my arms over and again as if to convince himself of my presence. His breath came in ragged gasps, testimony to his haste, and his hands continued to roam up and down my arms. "You must come with me. I've discovered something." He turned, heading deeper into his domain, speaking so that I had no choice but to follow.

"Can you imagine it?" he said. "I went out into the city and I learned something, something that wasn't in a scroll or a book. I've written it down." He shook his head and looked around, spotting Bolt and pointing. "Do you trust him?" he asked almost in accusation.

I gave the question serious consideration before answering. Custos might be placing his life in my hands. With the librarian I could never tell. "Yes."

He nodded as if that decided the matter. "As I've said, I've written it down. Many times. But I waited before sending it to the other libraries until I could see you."

He shook his head, and his pace quickened until we came to his sanctum, the place where he kept the oldest and most fragile works of the library's ancient collection. He closed the door behind us, and the stale odor of old parchment intensified. Bemused, I took in the room. A pair of large candles on the center table illuminated recent, handwritten works. But other than that, the construct I'd built in my mind matched it exactly.

I picked up one of the sheets of crisp new parchment that lay on the table, eyeing Custos's neat blocky handwriting. "Is this what you want me to see?"

The shake of his head was almost violent. "No, no, no. That is only the record." He eyed Bolt, his dark eyes squinting until they almost disappeared. "Does he know about you?"

Bolt started, turning to me, his eyes wide in accusation, but I held up a hand. "I'll explain later." To Custos I said, "Yes, he knows."

Custos nodded. "Good, good, good." He thrust out an arm, pulling up a sleeve. "Look."

I smiled, shaking my head. "There is too much in that precious brain of yours for me to hold, old friend. And my mind is very tired now."

He frowned. "I will put everything away except for a pair of memories. Come, I have been searching the city for you for days." Then he smiled again, and his face lit like the sun burning through a weak mist. "Imagine it, me learning something that doesn't come from the library."

I removed the protective glove from my right hand, noting idly that the gift felt more natural when I used it with my sword arm. Someday I vowed to take the time to consider that.

Bolt stood next to me, my Vigil-appointed protector. How many times had I almost died since he'd assumed the task? And yet he'd done nothing in its execution I could fault.

"Come," Custos said, almost dancing on his feet where he stood. "I think you will be as amazed as I."

Just before I put my hand on his arm, he pulled back, and I saw him blink several times in quick succession. "The order is important," he said, squinting. "You must look at the older scroll first. I will make sure you know which is which."

He offered his arm once more. Touching it, I fell through his gaze into his mind, losing myself as I merged with the librarian. I blinked, wondering for a moment if the delving had failed. I stood in the center of the sanctum exactly as before, but a moment later, I relaxed. No one and nothing were here with the exception of the large trestle table in the center with a pair of scrolls upon it, one slightly yellowed with age.

I marveled again at his ability to organize his mind to such a degree. With any other delving I fell into an instant procession of sight and sound and moving memories, losing most of myself as I sorted through them backward in time until I found what I needed. Here Custos had preserved the two memories he wanted me to see, eliminating the burden I would feel with any other person.

I grasped the yellowed scroll, and it flashed into light and nothingness, and I fell into memory.

A man walks ahead of me. Nothing about him looks remarkable. Judging from the thinning hair going to gray and the rounded shoulders that would eventually become a stoop, I deem him to be perhaps sixty years or more of age.

I know this place. The man in front of me walks along the merchants' way, preparing to cross north over the bridge toward the cathedrals and the keep. *Bunard*. I look at my surroundings, each building infinitely familiar and yet somehow wrong.

The man in front of me turns, showing sharp crystal-blue eyes surrounded by a nest of wrinkles. *Pellin*.

I stayed within the memory, taking in the details, but the second viewing failed to reveal any more importance to the memory than the first. Custos had left his sanctuary of scrolls and books to follow the leader of the Vigil. But why?

I pulled out of the memory, but stayed within the room Custos had constructed in his mind. Once more two scrolls lay on the table before me. Curious, I took the second scroll, the parchment still new, supple. My last thought of myself was to wonder what calamity lay captured within the memory I held. Taking a deep breath, I watched and waited as it flashed into pure, white light.

I walk as Custos on the streets of Bunard once more, moving north toward the Merum cathedral in the distance, my pockets filled with almond-encrusted dates that guarantee happiness for the day. Across the street a man sits by the clear window of the high merchants' tavern. His face turns to me, and I see Pellin once more. I stop, knowing the tug in my mind that constitutes recognition and begin sifting through the library within my mind.

The memory and the delve ceased, and I found myself without transition back in the sanctum with Custos and Bolt standing near me. Nothing untoward had occurred in Custos's memories.

"Why?" I asked the librarian as his gaze danced. "What did he do that made those memories so important?"

Custos's glee almost overwhelmed him. He stood before me, his weight shifting from foot to foot. "No, no, no. It's not what he did, young Willet. He did nothing at all that I could tell. It's when he did it."

Despite the fact that only the three of us occupied the storehouse of the Merum's most precious records, he looked around to ensure we wouldn't be overheard and leaned forward to whisper to me. "Those memories are forty years apart."

I stared at him as if he'd spouted some foreign tongue at me. That couldn't be right, but I knew Custos. Even before I'd delved him I'd spent years trying to trick his memory into making a mistake, selecting scrolls or books at random from the contents of the prodigious Merum library.

"No gift does that," I said. I breathed, but the air failed to satisfy. A giant hand had hollowed out my middle, leaving naught but a shell of skin and bones. Spots swam in front of my eyes.

Custos smiled like a child and clapped his hands, unaware of my distress. "Exactly. But this one does. The Vigil has hidden itself for centuries with good reason. Not only can they ferret out the truth no matter where it hides, they live for a very long time." Custos peered at me. "In forty years, he didn't appear to age at all. How old must he be?"

I fell against the table, but the impact might as well have existed only in the construct of Custos's mind. Nothing hurt, and after a brief jump the candles burned as steady as ever in disregard of my existence.

I would never possess the uncanny ability of the librarian, but my own memories served to confirm what he'd said: Bronwyn's long, long suffering; Toria Deel's artwork and how it took so many years for her, a woman who appeared no older than me, to learn; Pellin's strange movements about the city, always hooded on the streets. What had he said? The last time he'd been in Bunard for Bas-solas, the sun hadn't gone completely out. Oh, Aer, what a fool I'd been. Yes, forty years, but I'd assumed he'd been a young man.

Bile built at the back of my throat as more puzzle pieces slipped into place: Bolt's discomfort in Gael's presence, the hitch in my guard's speech whenever he spoke of the Vigil, his resolute assertion I would leave her.

I spun and swung with everything I had, catching a glimpse of my guard's surprise before he fell back. My knuckles screamed in agony, and blood flowed from a cut on Bolt's lip.

"*Kreppa*!" I screamed.

Bolt rolled with the impact and came to a standing position a few feet away. I ignored my sword and advanced on him, my arms swinging, but I couldn't move them fast enough to express my rage. "Liar! Deceiver!" I yelled. My fists found nothing but air as Bolt backed away, slipping each blow. "When were you going to tell me?"

"When Pellin deemed you ready to shoulder the burden," he said as if I weren't raging.

I couldn't think. Tears flowed down my face as I continued to swing for my guard. "Why didn't you tell me? You were supposed to be my friend!"

A blow just hard enough to make me dizzy found my chin, and I dropped to one knee.

"I was never intended to be your friend, Willet," Bolt said above me. "I was supposed to keep you alive. That was all."

I buried my head in my hands. "Go away."

"Friendship came later," Bolt said.

"Go away."

He didn't move. "And despite everything I could do to keep from it."

I tried to keep my mind from one last horrible realization and failed. I would try anyway, though I knew it would fail. There was a chance the Vigil might be wrong in this also, but the small flame of hope in my chest guttered and died. Others would have tried before me. "Oh, Aer," I cried. "The heretics say there's no hell, but it's been right here all along."

I stood like a derelict, staggering on legs far too weak to sustain my one last hope.

"Where's Volsk?"

Chapter 51

I shambled back to the meeting room, but the Vigil had left. Bolt walked beside me, but I was as alone as I would have been if no one else had ever been there and all my memories of love and companionship were nothing more than desperate dreams born of unbreakable solitude. An acolyte in white, a boy of perhaps twelve or thirteen, came down the hall toward me, carrying water and candles.

Putting my hand on his arm, I pulled him to a stop. "I'm looking for my . . ." I stopped, searching for the right word. "Friends," I said, but the word twisted in my mouth. "Where are they?"

He blinked at me. "Your friends?"

I clenched my fists at the delay. "They're probably the only people in this building who aren't part of the Merum order," I said slowly. "Do you know where they are?"

Comprehension dawned in his eyes. "I'm taking these to one of them, good sir."

We stood regarding each other for a moment, with me waiting for him to proceed and him waiting for my permission. "If you'll get moving, I can just follow you."

His head bobbed, ruffling the fringe of hair they'd left on his head when they cut it with a bowl. Then he started off again, looking back over his shoulder as if unsure of whether he was permitted to walk in front of me.

"I can't lead if I don't know where we're going, lad," I said. "Make haste."

A pair of turns later, we came to a well-lit corridor with polished wainscoting on the walls and a series of arched doors extending away from us. "They're all here," the boy said, his head bobbing again.

I nodded. Housing the few people of the Vigil would have been simplicity itself. Centuries ago, the Merum had been the church's only order. With their numbers cut by two-thirds after the Transformation and subsequent Order Wars, space was hardly an issue.

The boy knocked at the first door. A moment later, it opened just wide enough to reveal Allta, his sword bared. Only after he and Bolt exchanged one of those irritating knowing glances and nods did he step back so that we could enter.

I didn't bother. I could see Pellin standing by a small altar, the implements of haeling gathered around him. How long had it taken him to accumulate the wrinkles around his eyes, the furrows across his brow? He was old but not doddering.

I pulled Custos's memories into view in my mind. Was there any perceptible difference between the two? The newer memory of Pellin revealed a man who appeared slightly older than the one previous, but I'd seen men appear to age just as much from a couple of nights of bad sleep.

He raised his head as if sensing my scrutiny, but I turned away to speak to the page. "Boy, I don't care how you do it, but I want a priest and a scribe as fast as you can get them here. If they need a reason, tell them someone gifted is dying."

The words hit the boy like physical blows. He set the water and candles on a small table by the entrance of Pellin's room and ran, his skinny legs flying beneath his robe. On both continents, the one guaranteed way to create haste in the church was to invoke the rite of passing.

I went to the next door and knocked, but not before noting that Pellin had left his communion and followed me with his guard just behind him. I gritted my teeth, angry that my request would end up being more public than I wanted. I owed the Vigil retribution on several counts, and I wasn't normally a man to leave his debts unpaid.

But none of that really mattered. Caught in their trap, I would have chewed off my own leg and thanked Aer for the ability to do it, if I could just get free.

Bronwyn's guard answered the door, her shriveled, age-worn face visible just past him. I cursed myself for not understanding the implications of what I'd seen while delving her earlier. No one could amass that many memories in a normal lifetime.

I moved to the next door and pounded so that anyone inside would think the cathedral had been attacked. A second later the door flew open, and Toria Deel's guard, Elory, stood before me, crouched in a fighting stance with both his sword and long dagger drawn. Behind him stood Volsk and Toria Deel, he with his sword drawn, her holding a pair of daggers.

"A priest and a scribe are on the way," I said to Volsk. "You can have it." I cut my eyes to Toria Deel. "And if anyone had bothered to show me the truth, you could have had it long ago. I have no wish to live for . . ." I faltered. "I have no wish to be part of the Vigil."

The air stirred behind me, displaced as the rest of the Vigil drew close, safeguarding me or hemming me in. I didn't know which.

Volsk's face twisted at my offer, his eyes holding too many different emotions for me to decipher any one. He shook his head. "You still don't understand." He turned away from me as if my offer didn't exist, moving to take Toria Deel in his embrace with his back to me.

Pellin moved around me to enter her quarters, her guard falling back to make way for the Eldest. Inside he turned to address those of us still outside, his face a mask of sorrow and resignation. "Come inside. The priest and scribe will be here soon, but we will have a moment together first."

The large room, richly appointed in Merum red, from the carpets to the tapestries, held several couches in a spacious sitting area in addition to a large burnished table that could seat at least a dozen. Pellin took a chair from the table and turned it so that it faced the couches where Toria Deel and Volsk had retreated, signaling us to join him with a wave. Allta remained by the door.

"The gift cannot be surrendered as others," Pellin said without preamble once I'd seated myself.

I flung my hand up in disgust. "I know that." I went on, my voice sharpening until it cut. "Otherwise the lot of you would simply have deceived me into surrendering it to Volsk at the outset." I shook my head. "It would have been easy. Simply tell me the gift would continue to drive me mad until I went insane, and I wouldn't have been able to get rid of it quickly enough."

"If you know this," Bronwyn said, "then why do you wish to attempt the rite of passage?"

"Because you've been wrong before," I said. "You're old." I looked at the three of them by turns. "For all I know, you're ancient, but you're not infallible," I rasped. "Or else you wouldn't have tried to poison me."

Bolt didn't say anything, and I couldn't feel the approval I'd expected.

Pellin nodded. If he took offense at my words or tone, it didn't show. He regarded me in silence before he dipped his head. "I am ancient, but perhaps not too old to accept correction and a lesson in humility. Very well, Willet, you may make the attempt with my blessing."

Volsk jerked upright, standing in denial. "No! It won't work." He turned to Toria Deel. "I would not tempt you with false hope for a fool's quest."

I shook my head. "You have no hope otherwise."

He turned to me. "You're wrong. You're brave, but reckless and foolhardy. You are gifted with domere but you've made powerful enemies. How many times in the past two weeks have you been close to death?" He shook his head.

"So you mean to wait until my past catches up to me?" I asked.

He sighed, shaking his head. "Do I have the means to prevent it? I'm surprised you've lived this long."

Any other time I would have laughed to hear my own thoughts spoken to me by another. Now they took on a whole different meeting. My training and experience as reeve kicked in, and I sifted through the last week, trying to see each confrontation again, searching for the reasons and motivations behind the actions of others.

"As am I," I answered. "I'm impressed with your faith. I thought Marquis Orlan to be the proudest man living before I killed him, but I think you surpass him. Of all the people in the six kingdoms, you believe that a single free gift will come to you." Now I did laugh. "Those are very slim odds, certainly slim enough to warrant attempting the rite of passage. You have nothing to lose. If it fails, you can always pray for my death at Laewan's hand come tomorrow."

Volsk stared at me blankly, but deep in his gaze I saw a flicker of fear. In the end he nodded. "Very well. Perhaps it will succeed. I pray it so."

I looked at Toria Deel, who sat by Volsk, her dark eyes luminous with hope despite their certitude. "Consider it my wedding gift to all of us," I said.

We waited until a knock at the door signaled the arrival of the priest and the scribe. Pellin stood and moved to the door without haste. I heard the murmur of voices and stood, accompanied by the rest of the Vigil. Pellin returned alone.

"There," he said. "I've sent them away so we don't have to worry about being interrupted."

I took a step toward the Eldest. Allta must have sensed my intention because, before I could take another, he stood between Pellin and me.

"Be at peace, Lord Dura," Pellin said. "You know a priest is not required. We would not have been able to maintain our secrecy for all these centuries if we were obligated to use any of the priests the church afforded us. Even with the confidentiality of the rite, some would have talked. And we shall have a priest at any rate." Allta stepped to one side and Pellin gestured with his hand to Bronwyn and Toria Deel. "I'm a priest, as are Bronwyn and Toria Deel. Which of us do you wish to officiate?"

I replayed the conversation with Ealdor. "Elwin wasn't really a Servant," I said. "He was Merum, wasn't he."

Pellin nodded. "As am I. I took my orders before I came into my gift." He smiled. "Bronwyn took her orders in the Absold, and Toria Deel received hers from the Vanguard."

I nodded. Nothing about their selection of orders came as a surprise. Given Bronwyn's past, I could see why forgiveness would be of such importance to her. And Toria Deel's boldness, even to the point of aggression, matched the zeal the Vanguard professed. I nodded to Pellin. "I'm acquainted with all of the orders, but I was only a week away from taking my vows in the Merum when Laidir issued the call to arms against Owmead."

Volsk shook his head. "Not just a rogue," he said, softly, "but a *threigean* as well."

I rounded on him, not caring if he could see he'd stung me. "Let me explain something to you, Peret Volsk, just in case you missed it. Collum is the northernmost kingdom on the continent. The growing season is short, and if, Aer forbid, we have a drought, we have to fight Owmead for our share of the most fertile valley we own. They outnumber us two to one. That means when the call to arms goes up, a man from every family must answer, sometimes more than one. No exceptions."

"I questioned the guards in Bunard about you," Volsk said. "You had a brother. You went to war while he stayed behind."

"You should have questioned them more closely," I said. "And you would have discovered that my brother died of a fever just after fighting started at the border." Even now the loss hurt as if I'd just returned from the field. "He contracted it a week before the call. This time I'll say it more slowly so that you have a better chance at understanding. No exceptions." I paused to bow to him. "I should commend you on your pretense. After the House of Passing, I thought I might have found a friend."

I turned to face Pellin. "I think you all deserve each other." I yanked off my gloves. "Let's get on with this."

I went to the table and lifted the chair, turning it so that it faced the rest of the room. Without speaking, I gestured for Volsk to have a seat. He walked to it like a man whose every muscle was clenched for battle, hands clenched, stride stiff, and mouth tight.

"Don't you need the Scriptures for this?" I asked.

Pellin smiled and his eyes crinkled. "I've read the liturgy every day since I was a boy, Lord Dura. I'm pretty sure I knew it by heart after the first two hundred years."

He held up his right hand in the sign of blessing and lapsed into a singsong, the words ancient but familiar to every soul on both continents. "The seven charisms of Aer are these: for the body, beauty and craft; for the soul, sum and parts; for the spirit, helps and devotion; for the safeguarding of the future, domere. The nine talents of man are these: language, logic, space, rhythm, motion, nature, self, others, and all. The four temperaments of creation are these: impulse, passion, observation, and thought. Within the charisms of Aer, the talents of man, and the temperaments imbued in creation are found understanding and wisdom. Know and learn."

I noted the difference from the version I'd memorized as a Merum acolyte and wondered just how old Pellin's version of the exordium was.

The Eldest looked at me. "Willet Dura, do you surrender your gift of your own free will to Peret Volsk, and offer him your blessing in its use to the glory of Aer?"

I nodded, desperate and impatient and scared to the point of numbness. "I do."

Pellin nodded. "Pronounce the blessing."

"Peret Volsk, I give you the gift of domere, to use to the glory of Aer, to witness and edify his people." My voice rose as I called upon the power every gifted person had possessed since the first. "The gift of Aer is bestowed upon you!" At this last I put my bare hand on Volsk's head.

I'd heard old men or women on the edge of death speak of surrendering their gift, how it tore away from their mind like a scab, giving pain and relief at the same time. I didn't feel either. Instead, I tunneled through Volsk's glare and into his mind, delving him.

Moving images of his life battered me as I fell into his present and past. I saw the six kingdoms that bordered the Darkwater and their chief cities as he followed the Vigil in his apprenticeship, witnessed the study that went with countless hours of sacrifice, but always there was the image of Toria Deel, either present in reality or present in his thoughts, her face luminous and as precious as air. I felt a need for her within Volsk so deep it went beyond love and firing devotion, so intense it surpassed mere faithfulness. Familiar. A dim part of me that I still knew as myself experienced all of this with Gael. Twinned with that desire was another—a promise of centuries together and a communion between two lovers such as had never been known before, a knowing so deep no poet, gifted or not, could ever hope to express it in words.

In that moment I felt a renewed kinship with him. He knew love as I knew it, deep and passionate and earnest. I stopped, halting the flow of memories as I beheld a construct he'd built in his mind. Though he'd never exercised the gift, some member of the Vigil must have taught him how to store his memories. Not all of them flowed past me in the tide that defined his life.

Nowhere in Volsk's mind did I see a memory of me, Willet Dura.

A bright sun shone through the windows of his construction, illuminating a study with open-air windows, an impossibility in the north. At the far wall, next to one of the windows, was a door. I moved to it, drawn by curiosity, ignoring the flow of memory and emotion that called to me, that told me I was Peret Volsk. Why were there no memories of the other me, of Willet Dura? The door retained its lever and I smiled. With a thought I reached out and turned the mechanism that opened the door.

And knew.

I opened my eyes and stepped back. "It failed," I said, working my mouth as if someone had filled it with ash during the delve.

"It always does," Pellin said, but by then he was already talking to my back. The door opened onto an empty hallway. Shaking my head and blinking, I turned to find them all staring at me, but my gaze landed on Volsk, then Toria Deel.

"I wish to heaven I could give you what you wanted, what I want for myself." I thought of every fight I'd won or endured to buy my future with Gael. In the last seven days I'd found the pit of hell and stepped right off its edge into the long, dark descent. Now I'd hit the bottom. And there was no way out.

I shook my head. Bereft of love or affection, only justice and duty remained. For a moment I considered holding my silence, but grace was for people with hope.

My arm felt as dead as my insides, but I raised it to point at Volsk. "I'm going to wager that none of you have delved him in the last week." His eyes widened in fear and recognition. Both emotions slid from me as if they were meant for someone else. I shrugged. "Or perhaps his particular brand of cunning is what you want in the Vigil."

I could have provided the details, but I'd already wasted more breath on them than they were worth. I shut the door behind me and hoped Bolt had the sense not to shadow me. Right then I would have killed him if I could.

Chapter 52

Somewhere in the labyrinth of the Merum cathedral I found a chapel. A wooden cabinet barely large enough for two people to stand in marked the confessional the brothers used for whatever sins they might conjure in their lives of relative solitude. It had only been a week or so since I'd last seen Ealdor, and there had been times in the last ten years I'd gone a month or more without visiting him, but this most recent gap seemed like an eternity.

I was alone.

I wandered up to the sacristy, vaguely aware of being hungry. Even here the ancient prosperity of the Merum church evidenced itself. The cabinets that no one except the brother who officiated the service would see were made of richly paneled wood. I didn't bother to admire the craftsmanship.

I found two sets of bread and wine. Choosing from the larger set, the one yet to be consecrated, I helped myself to a generous portion and retreated to the front pew. I took a bite and gave a small mirthless chuckle that echoed back to me as mocking whispers in the chapel. It was the best tasting communal bread I'd ever eaten. I washed it down and discovered the wine to be just as good.

"You know I never asked much from you," I said to the intersecting arcs that symbolized Iosa, suspended at the front of the chapel. "I always figured you wanted me to look after myself if I could while you took care of more important things."

The sigil didn't answer right away, so I sampled the Merum hospitality a bit more and waited. Maybe Aer was waiting for me. "I only wanted two things in my entire life," I went on.

Frustration and longing started to build in my chest, and I took another long pull from the wine to wash them away. If I let those twins loose I wouldn't ever be able to rein them in again. "When you or fortune took the priesthood from me, I thought I'd died. I couldn't understand why—when all I wanted to do was help people—you would allow circumstances to send me to war where I had to kill them instead."

Bitterness crept into my voice. "I know what everyone says about you—that you walked among us and know all the sorrow a man or woman can know—but I've read the liturgy. You never had to put your sword into another man, never had to listen to the squelching sound it made as you pulled it and his life free." I shook my head. "All because the weather didn't cooperate.

"You never warned me I had to sacrifice my humanity." I took a bite of bread. It didn't taste as good as I remembered. Neither did the wine. I peered at the sigil. It still showed no signs of answering. "After nine years of duty I found Gael and I started to believe you had something for me after all." I gave a sardonic chuckle that in the silence threatened to turn to rage or tears.

I sat contemplating the last thing I would have to do if I survived the next day, all the while hating the last vestige of humanity that would send me into battle once more.

Looking down a few moments or hours later, I was surprised to see my hand empty, the bread gone. When I lifted the bottle, a few drops splashed on my tongue. How had that happened? The door at the back opened, and Bolt stepped through without bothering to close it behind him. I stood on my feet, steady and surefooted as a goat, as hungry and thirsty as I'd been when I arrived. I left the empty bottle on the bench.

Bolt stood at my shoulder. "I searched most of the cathedral for you, Willet."

I nodded, then started toward the door. "I came for confessional." I paused to look at the symbol of Aer's love hanging at the front of the chapel once more before I left. "But there was no one here."

Mild curiosity nagged at me as I followed my guard, my friend, my traitor out of the chapel. "What hour is it?"

"Not the question I expected," Bolt said. He sighed, his lined faced as inscrutable as a carving. "One hour after midnight."

"Is that all? It feels later."

Bolt turned back toward the luxurious rooms the Merum had provided the Vigil and their guards, presumably to put me to bed. With each step his posture stiffened a bit more until frustration radiated from him. "Don't you want to know what happened with Volsk?"

I'd been perfectly serious that I didn't want to expend the energy it took to put my hand on his head—now I couldn't conjure enough motivation to shrug. "Not particularly." Against my own injunction I envisioned the scene after I left: Volsk being delved by Pellin, Bronwyn, and Toria Deel—his deliberate inaction during the attacks on me, and sometimes Bolt, laid before them, his motivation plain.

Then I imagined his plea to Toria Deel and her forgiveness and their subsequent embrace as she buried her head in his shoulder and forgave him. My face twisted. After all, it was all done for love. Volsk and Toria Deel had expected only Aer knew how many lifetimes of love and passion they would have together, knowing each other in a way most people could only dream about. By heaven's gate, I got nauseated just thinking about it.

"Your revelation tonight," Bolt said slowly, "may have handed Laewan the margin of victory he needed."

I stopped, grabbing a handful of Bolt's cloak to turn him to face me. "You're going to put this at my feet? That pile of dung in a tunic stood and did nothing while I . . ." I pointed my finger at Bolt's nose. "While *we* fought for our lives." I stopped as I realized I'd been tricked into expending energy on Volsk anyway. I let my hand drop away and continued on toward my quarters.

"Tomorrow we'll quarter the city. Aer willing, we'll find Laewan and kill him so that we can execute those who've been taken by the Darkwater." I made a motion with my hand as though I were tossing something away. "It's been what, three hours since I tried to give him my gift?" The word tasted like death on my tongue. "I'm sure she's completely forgiven him by now. And Pellin probably has as well.

After all," I chanted in a singsong, "he's the most talented apprentice they've seen in five hundred years." I let my voice drop back to its regular tone and cadence. "But if he comes near me, I'll kill him."

"You don't understand," Bolt said. "What he did went against everything the Vigil stands for. Their whole lives are a sacrifice, Willet. They live in seclusion because of the power they hold and provide justice and safety where others can't or won't."

"And they execute people who've been to the forest," I said.

Bolt nodded but didn't react to the scorn in my voice. "And every time they do, they carry the wounds in their soul and spirit. All so kings and nobles, merchants and peasants—and reeves—can sleep in safety."

I snorted. "Yes. I do feel so very safe."

Bolt shook his head in disgust. "They don't know what to do with him, Willet. The Vigil has had its share of eccentrics in its long history, the gift itself guarantees that, but it's never had a traitor. Pellin had him thrown in prison."

"I'm sure Toria Deel will find a way to have him released," I said.

He nodded. "You may not know Elanians very well," he said. "It was her idea, but after they took him away she looked as if her mind had been broken. I'll be surprised if she notices dawn tomorrow."

We turned the last corner and entered a room just before Pellin's. I entered into luxury that would rival a duke's, certainly more than I'd ever experienced as a reeve or the least of Laidir's lords. I unbuckled my sword, put my knives on the table, and fell onto one of the couches, eschewing the bed in the room beyond. Tomorrow we would hunt and be hunted. Somehow, I just couldn't conjure the energy to care.

Waking sometime later with the instinctual knowledge that dawn still lay in the future, I opened my eyes to the sound of Bolt running a stone along the edge of his sword—Robin's, actually. "Don't you ever sleep?"

He nodded as he peered at a nick in the blade before taking the stone to it in slow methodical strokes. "Whenever I want. I tend to sleep fast and hard, so I don't require as much. Contrary to recent circumstances, the life of a Vigil guard is mostly training and waiting. Laewan's corruption has put us all into uncharted country." He gave the sword one last swipe and wiped it clean with a cloth as he stood and sheathed it. "Pellin ordered us to meet for breakfast this morning before sunrise." He looked at me, his expression saying he half expected me to refuse.

"What's the point?" I asked. "We already know the plan."

Bolt nodded. "Whenever the entire Vigil is gathered, the Eldest commands us to eat together. It's something Cesla encouraged, and I think it started with Ian, who was Eldest before him. The members of the Vigil have few opportunities to just enjoy fellowship without being on their guard." He shook his head. "I can't remember anyone ever missing a meal."

I drifted over to the table to belt on my sword and stash my daggers into their usual hiding places. Breakfast with a bunch of people who had lived centuries longer than I had didn't sound like fellowship, especially when at least one of them despised the very sight of me, but try as I might, I couldn't just leave my responsibility and the city behind. Gael, Ealdor, Custos, and King Laidir would be in danger if I surrendered to despair. I wanted to tell my conscience to go away and let me grieve, but there was no time.

I followed Bolt into the hallway without shutting the door, and we made our way to the expansive rectory of the Merum cathedral. Priests, acolytes, and church guards filled some of the tables, talking quietly, but Bolt led us past them into a side room where members of the Vigil and their guards waited. But not Toria Deel.

As I entered, Pellin's head jerked up, away from his prayer, and I saw his mouth tighten even as he nodded recognition. "Fetch Toria Deel and her guard," he said to Allta. Sometime between last night and this morning his voice had lost its doubtful tenor. The Eldest of the Vigil no longer seemed inclined to second-guess himself.

I sat at the long trestle and ladled porridge into a bowl, doing my best to ignore Bolt, the Vigil, even the cathedral and its inhabitants. About halfway through the bowl, Toria Deel and her guard entered from the rectory. Custos's revelation had taken the shine from my eyes, but Toria Deel looked as if she'd been in a fistfight and lost. Smudges as dark as bruises lined her red-rimmed eyes, and her distress left her hair in disarray.

She sat at the table without acknowledging our presence, including me. Pellin's expression changed from soft to steel before he spoke. "Put a comb through your hair, Toria Deel, or I'll have it done for you."

"Thank you, Eldest, for acknowledging my loss," Toria Deel said, a hint of fire in her voice.

"Ah, child," Bronwyn said. "To be one of the Vigil is to know loss a thousand times over. Friends. Relatives. Husbands or wives we might have had. We watch them all wither and fade like wildflowers, ravaged and scorched by the passage of time."

I stabbed my spoon at the remnants of my porridge, hoping the clatter would keep me from hearing.

"For all of you, maybe," Toria Deel said into the hands folded in her lap. "But Peret and I had a chance at something more."

"And now it's gone," Pellin said, his voice devoid of feeling. Toria Deel jerked. "But our task remains. Will you let innocents die because you need to grieve, or will you fulfill your vows?"

She glared at Pellin with unalloyed hatred. I'd seen looks like that on the streets of Bunard. Someone usually died soon after. "Did I say I would not?" Toria Deel said.

Pellin turned his attention back to his porridge, dismissing Toria Deel and her loathing. "Then put a comb through your hair. If you're on the streets like that, you'll attract attention we don't want."

With jerks of her hands she brought forth a plain blue ribbon and pulled her hair back, tying it behind her. Moving with quick, birdlike motions, she met the gazes of everyone else present, daring them to say anything. But when she got to mine, too many emotions fought behind her glance for me to define any one of them. One moment she looked on the verge of apologizing, the next of railing at me. She looked away and busied herself with the simple meal in front of her.

A few minutes later, Pellin's spoon rattled against the bottom of his bowl, and he stood. "Come. We're supposed to meet Lord Dura's friends at full light. Aer willing, they have something to tell us."

Chapter 53

Rory stood at the east end of the yard close to the fortified gatehouse, flanked by three urchins. The dawn sun blazed over his shoulder, giving him the appearance of a stained-glass savior surrounded by undersized disciples. But the expression on their faces held neither hope nor condemnation, only the blank stare of fatigue.

We drew near, but before Pellin could ask a question Rory stepped forward, pointing to the first of the other three. "This is Lelwin." A girl of about thirteen stepped forward. If she'd been better fed, her face would have been heart-shaped. "She coordinated the watch over the upper merchants' section."

He shifted to indicate a boy a bit smaller than himself. He wore clothes that wouldn't have been out of place among any of a dozen types of apprentices, ill-fitting but decently made. "This is Mark."

"The Mark," the boy corrected.

Rory shook his head at him. "They probably won't understand or appreciate that. Just leave it at Mark." He turned back to us. "He had the lower merchants' quarter."

Rory pulled a breath and held it before introducing the last urchin, as if he expected a fight or an argument at the least. "This is Fess," he said pointing to a tall thin boy with blond hair. "He organized the watch here and by the tor."

Pellin's eyes narrowed. "He's wearing an acolyte's robe."

Fess stepped forward and bowed, wearing an insouciant grin. "That

I am, good sir, and I stand ready to run any errand you wish, especially to the market." He winked.

Rory closed his eyes and sighed. "And it begins."

Pellin's mouth compressed to a line. "He impersonates an acolyte so that he can trick the Merum brothers out of their coin?"

"Not just the Merum brothers," Fess said. "I wouldn't dream of discriminating, your honorship. I have a blue robe, a brown robe, and a white as well. Don't get to use that last one too often. The Vanguard are stingy with their errands, they are. You might want to talk to them about that."

Pellin looked on the verge of voicing the affront he wore on his face, but Bronwyn's laughter cut him off.

When Pellin turned to face her, her mirth only deepened. "Give over, Pellin," she said. "All four orders of the church have always spoken a good line about caring for the poor, even while they build grand edifices for themselves. Fess is just helping them keep their commitment."

The boy's eyes widened until they appeared almost comical. "Exactly what I've always maintained, my lady," he said with a bow.

"Humph," Pellin grunted. "And just how good for his soul is it to engage in theft from the church?"

Bronwyn shook her head. "Theft is theft, Pellin. Don't reserve your condemnation for specific cases." She looked back to Fess. "Still, according to the agreement, the church has to provide homes for each of the urchins who desire it. I think I know a place for this one. What's your full name?"

His grin returned, larger than ever. "Confession."

Rory spoke before Pellin could react. "That's really his name. I'm sure you can imagine a few reasons why."

Pellin's offense drained from his expression. "I think we'll just stay with Fess. Time presses on us. What did you and your compatriots see last night?"

Rory shook his head. "Nothing you wouldn't expect any other night in Bunard, mostly people conducting business they don't want seen in the daytime."

I must have muttered something under my breath, because Pellin and the rest of the Vigil turned to look at me for a moment before continuing.

"Laewan is much taller than an average man," Pellin said.

"You told me that, yah?" Rory said.

"Were there any men on the street last night fitting that description?" Bronwyn asked.

Rory sighed, turning to his companions. "Fess? Lelwin? Mark?" They all shook their heads.

We'd assumed Laewan would be out in the city the night before his attack, if he attacked on Bas-solas day, but did he have to be?

"He knows we're looking for him," Toria Deel said. Her voice sounded hollow, and the bags under her eyes came close to matching their dark color.

Pellin's gaze narrowed. "Go on."

Toria Deel didn't meet his gaze. "What about a stooped man with a cane?"

Pellin and Bronwyn nodded, but Rory just shook his head. "Do you not think we looked for that? We steal for a living."

I stepped away from the group, wandering as if my feet were in charge. Bolt gave me a quick look, but I waved him away. I needed to think. Pellin's desperate conversation and Toria Deel's grief kept me from focusing.

What did I know? Quite a few people from Bunard had somehow been deceived into going to the Darkwater. Bronwyn had said so, and I'd seen enough of her ability to believe her. Laewan had control of them. I'd seen as much myself after the attack on Braben's Inn. The one limitation was light. Those infected by the Darkwater couldn't abide it, which meant Bas-solas presented an opportunity to strike during the day.

While Laewan lived, he still had the gift of domere, held captive by the evil that had taken him from the Darkwater. The evil from the Darkwater wasn't just sentient, it had a purpose.

What?

Frustrated, I shook my head to clear the question away. I didn't need to know the purpose, only the most immediate threat to it from Laewan's point of view.

The Vigil. The entire Vigil was here in Bunard, ripe for the picking. "Brilliant," I muttered. "My impeccable logic has led me right back to what I already knew." How many ways were there for Laewan to win absolutely? I could only think of two. He could corrupt the entire Vigil or kill all of us at once. "We're all fools," I muttered. "We should get out of the city and not come back until after Bas-solas."

But I already knew the answer to that idea. Laewan held us captive by the very principles that threatened him. I'd run into that sort of man before. I turned back toward the cathedral, shaking my head. Built in a time when kingdoms and peoples expressed their religious differences with the point of a sword, it would be easily defended. A few dozen soldiers could hold it against hundreds.

I pulled early morning air into my lungs and tried to think. Bas-solas. Everything centered, I supposed, on the festival. Sometime during those two hours of darkness, Laewan's goal was to kill or capture the Vigil—while our goal centered on killing him. And despite the aid of the urchins, we didn't know where he was.

Stymied, I returned to the group, cudgeling my mind in time with my steps into some type of insight that would help us, but nothing came. The Vigil and the urchins all stood in silent regard of the morning while the sun inched higher into the sky.

"What are we waiting for?" I asked Bolt.

A clanking of iron signaled the opening of the broad gate leading to the Merum courtyard.

"Nothing any longer," Bolt said. Armed men and women streamed into the yard in colored rows, like blooms in a well-tended orchard, wearing surcoats of white, blue, brown, and red. Those wearing brown each bore a heavy leather satchel, but no weapons.

Pellin stepped to my shoulder. "I contacted the head of each order in Bunard and requested every man they could put under arms. The Vanguard has the most, naturally, but the Absold and the Merum are surprisingly well-equipped."

I nodded. "What about the Servants?"

"They do not fight under any circumstances," Pellin said. "However, every healer and aide is at our disposal."

I looked at all the rows of brown-clad men and women and my throat tightened. "Aer have mercy. I hope we don't need them."

Pellin nodded. "A worthy prayer."

I watched as he split the soldiers into four mixed groups, placing each group under the authority of a Vigil guard. Bolt took our group to the north end of the yard and set them in formation before addressing them in a voice like a trumpet blast.

"Your job is to do exactly what I tell you. Our expectation is that there will be an attack on the city during Bas-solas, but the attackers won't be from Owmead. They'll be your own people—friends, brothers and sisters, maybe even children. For the first time in hundreds of years, the church stands united against a threat—one church, despite the different colors you wear."

His voice dropped as he pointed at me. "Your first instruction is this—you will keep him alive at any cost. If I see any of you hesitating in fulfillment of that instruction, I'll kill you myself." His gaze swept across them. "Now, I want the best of each order in front of me before a minute has passed."

Each faction of the church grouped together, their differing colors making them appear as a larger-than-life formal garden, and a blend of muttered voices filled our area of the courtyard before three men and a woman separated themselves to come forward.

"Listen carefully," he said. "Along with me, you will each stay within three paces of Lord Dura at all times." He turned to the Servant, a slender man with the hands of a musician. "During Bas-solas, you and the rest of your order will be torchbearers." Bolt nodded at the satchel. "Do you have any solas powder in there?"

"No," the healer said. "Sprin powder works better at stopping bleeding."

"We don't want it for wounds," Bolt said. "We need it for light." He sighed. "Stupid, throwing a campaign together at the last minute." He pointed at the other three groups around the courtyard, each receiving their own set of instructions from a Vigil guard. "Send a runner from the Servants over to the others. Make sure every group has as much solas powder as they can get their hands on before dark fall. I don't care if you have to beggar every alchemist in the city."

Bolt turned to me, the lines in his forehead deepened by frustration. "There's any number of things we should see to, but—"

"There's no time," I finished for him.

"And that's the first sign that we've been outmaneuvered," he said.

An idea occurred to me. "What if we had run?" I asked.

He cocked his head at me, and I went on, giving voice to a notion as it formed in my mind. "You said we should have left the city. Where would we go?"

Bolt's shrug preceded his answer by a heartbeat. "To one of the outlying villages."

I nodded. "And if we left during the daylight, he couldn't have us followed, but Laewan had to consider that we might have run." I looked around at the array of soldiers in the yard. "It doesn't make sense. We've got twenty score soldiers here. If Bronwyn had tracked more than that coming back to the city from the Darkwater, she would have said something." I shook my head. "Somebody would have noticed."

Bolt called the signal, and we moved out of the courtyard and turned south toward the poor quarter. Lelwin appeared at my shoulder. She didn't exhibit any discomfort at being out of her normal setting or routine. Her brown hair was cut short, and along with her weight and height, she could have passed for a boy. I'd never met her before, but that wasn't unusual. The urchins were a large and fluid group.

"Rory told us things might get bad," she said. "But he didn't bother to explain exactly how."

Out of the corner of my eye I looked for the telltale signs of nervousness expressed or suppressed and didn't find either. The well-defined lines of her chin and jawline along with some seemingly accidental choices in clothing caught my attention.

I picked my way along my thoughts and words as if I were charting a maze. "We think a lot of people have been to the Darkwater Forest and come back. Do you know what that is?" At her solemn nod, I continued. "It's possible they'll attack the rest of the city at Bas-solas."

She absorbed that with the concentrated stoicism of a field commander. I noticed the backs of her hands were sculpted, well defined. "How old are you really, Lelwin?" Her head turned to me, and for an instant I glimpsed a hint of the story that landed her with the urchins.

"You have a good eye," she said. "I'm eighteen. I've been with the urchins since I was thirteen." She raised a brow at my implied question. "I'd rather take my chances begging or stealing than take up trade as a night woman." Her delicate, almost frail, shoulders lifted in a shrug. "During the winter, I hardly ever have to beg for a full day. A smudge here and there and a bit of artistry with the clothing to hide my age and I can make enough in a few hours to feed three or four of us."

I smiled. "Those are the types of skills that could take you far as a merchant."

She nodded at me, all seriousness. "That's why I begged Rory to let me volunteer. I've watched some of the women at market bargaining for the best price on their wares. Humph. Amateurs. If I can get with a family of merchants that will take me on as an apprentice, I could set up my own house in ten years."

"We think the brunt of the attack will come in the merchants' or nobles' sections," I said. "I don't think the poor quarter will be a target."

She nodded. "Then why are you searching there?"

I sighed. "Because we don't know. The man we're looking for has disappeared, and we can't find him. We're going to continue searching every quarter of the city right up until Bas-solas."

"What if you don't find him?"

I sighed. "We go back to the cathedral."

We passed over the bridge that led into the upper merchants' quarter. Scores of people were already stirring in the streets. The countryside for ten miles or more around must have converged on Bunard, and I quailed at the opportunity for slaughter it represented. The press of people would make it almost impossible to move quickly. A few of the street vendors paused to look at us as we passed, but few took more than a passing note. Bas-solas always presented something new.

"And then?" Lelwin asked.

"If I'm right, every man and woman infected by the Darkwater will be trying to kill me."

Her eyes widened as she waited for me to finish the line of my blackhearted joke, then realized I wasn't kidding. "Why didn't you run?"

"Because there are other people in danger too," I said.

We didn't talk anymore. When we got to the bridge leading to the poor quarter, I took off my gloves.

Chapter 54

Rain had yet to wash the burn marks of Myle's phos-fire from the stones on the bridge, and I was grateful for the reference. I stood on the spot to orient myself, then walked diagonally across to the last place I'd seen Laewan. I put my hands on the weathered stones of the railing and closed myself off from the sounds and smells of life around me.

Partial images and emotions came to me, but nothing more than the detritus of a thousand lives that crossed the bridge each day, and I struggled to sift through that morass to find the one remnant that belonged to Laewan. Bits of memory floated across my awareness, pieces of life and love, overflows of jealousy and despair, and nearly colorless scenes of people focused on simply prolonging their existence from one day to the next, all subtly different. How many shades were there to human existence?

A hint of something darker flowed past me, and I stopped, reversing to find it. *There.* Some memories, in accordance to the emotion, were darker, but only one flowing past had been shaded in black so deep it swallowed light. I sifted it, holding it within my mind to see its owner.

Laewan. The ghost of a memory, as much as the stone of the bridge could hold, conveyed nothing more than his presence and the towering rage that consumed him, me. My insides rebelled at the spite and malice that defined him. I thrust the memory away and let the stream of memories pass by me once more, searching while my heart struggled to find its rhythm once more. An idea blossomed as

I watched the flow. Perhaps there was a way to narrow the search for Laewan after all. If I was right I should see . . . There.

Another impression as black as the first flowed by me, this one more defined, more recent. I pulled it from the flow, checking to make sure it belonged to Laewan himself, and staggered again as his rage and hatred became my own. Hurriedly, I released it and dove back into the stream of memories and time until I came to the present moment.

Pulling my hands from the rail, I motioned to Bolt, and we stepped away from Lelwin and the rest of our escort. "There's no point to searching the poor quarter. He's not here."

He shook his head. "I don't know how the Vigil delves memories from stone," he said softly, "but it's always taken longer than this."

I nodded. "I didn't sift through all of them, just the ones from the attack to now."

"How does that help?"

Time pressed on and against me like a merciless guard prodding me with the tip of his halberd, but I recognized the importance of checking my assumption. We couldn't afford to be wrong. "That night on the bridge," I said. "Which way was he headed?"

Bolt pointed toward the crowded buildings and alleys of the poor quarter—then understanding lit his eyes. "There's only been one memory since then, yes?"

I nodded.

He turned and shouted orders to our contingent to reverse course back into the lower merchants' section of the city. "Can the Vigil do as much on the other bridges?"

My satisfaction evaporated. "I don't know. After that night, he covered a lot of ground in the city, maybe too much to track." I shook my head as doubt deepened within me. "And he knows what we're capable of."

Bolt nodded, his face grim. "A man can't fight what he can't find."

"That one is worth keeping." I sighed. "And I sincerely hope you have the opportunity to come up with more."

Some instinct for danger, like animals seeking shelter before a storm, might have impressed itself upon the people in the lower merchants' quarter. The crowds filling the street for the festival no longer smiled at us as we passed in our panoply of colors. Perhaps our faces were so grim they could feel the threat without understanding it. Even so the press of people made it difficult to move despite the escort of church soldiers.

A half mile from the next bridge we caught sight of a Vigil guard standing over a hunched figure, hands splayed across the stone of a large inn, their escort fanned out around them.

Toria Deel.

Why couldn't Pellin have assigned someone else to this section? Bolt ordered our escort to the other side of the street while we went to coordinate our efforts. We stopped three paces short and waited for her to finish the delve. Bunard was well over a thousand years old. When the founders of the church came north to spread the Word, they found wild tribes who worshipped tales and legends amid ruins that hinted at civilization ancient beyond reckoning. What memories might be hidden in the ancient rock of Laidir's tor? Curiosity battled with caution as I pondered what a man might learn.

"Lord Dura?" A voice made of formality and frost pulled me from my reverie, and I blinked to see Toria Deel facing me.

Grief and loss had been pushed aside for the sake of her duty, just as she promised, but even a fool could see the price she paid. Lines radiated from the squint of her eyes, as if she were engaged in a constant struggle to keep from crying, and now that she had finished delving the inn, her hands were clenched into fists, the knuckles stark and white beneath the skin.

"He's not in the poor quarter," I said, and then before she could respond, I explained.

"Very well," she said. "But why did you come to me?"

Her question carried the sharpened edge of an accusation, but I responded to the words instead of the tone. "This is the next section up. I thought to help you search. If we double up here and find nothing, we would have three people to search the next section."

She stared at me, her expression almost blank, before she nodded. "If we have time." She paused to look at the sun. "Which I doubt."

Toria Deel shook her head, and the hair she'd hastily tied earlier threatened to come loose. She ignored it, pointing. "Work the east side of the main street heading toward the next bridge. It's slow going. He could have taken any side street or alleyway. Unless you have any additional insight, we'll have to search them all."

Without saying anything more she turned from me and moved north to the next building.

With each fraction of the sun's climb I could feel panic building in my chest, the tightening sensation growing until it radiated out to my legs and arms. I turned right off the main street and breathed a sigh of relief at the sudden decrease in noise. I moved to a small cobbler's shop and put my hands on the wood frame.

Wispy tendrils of emotions and images floated past me, too insubstantial to make out, colorless, each shaded gray, many of them disappearing entirely as I watched. I lifted my hands from the shop with a sigh of disgust. Bolt stood at my shoulder, but instead of moving to the next building, I shifted to the end of the cobbler's shallow porch and sat.

Bolt sidled over, giving us space to talk, but didn't bother to join me on the stoop. "Only the greatest stroke of luck will allow us to find Laewan before Bas-solas," I said. I wasn't really talking to anyone, but I needed to hear my thoughts out loud before I could frame a response. "Wood is too temporary to hold memories well enough for us to track his passing." I shrugged. "Not for me anyway. Bronwyn might be able to do it."

I thought back. "Is his goal to kill all of us?" I asked Bolt.

He pursed his lips but nodded. "Pellin thinks so, and it makes sense. If all of the gifts go free, there will be no one to train anyone who receives one."

"Except the southerners," I said.

Bolt nodded. "But it might be years before they noticed the lack of communication, and decades more before they could find all the free gifts and re-form the north back into the Vigil."

"All right." I sighed. "I'm convinced. Laewan wants to capture or kill the lot of us."

"Else he wouldn't have tried to burn down Braben's," Bolt said.

I snapped my fingers. "There's the problem. If he wanted to kill us, why did he not do it then? He put a few arrows into the tavern, but if Bronwyn's correct and there are scores of people in Bunard infected by the Darkwater, he could have thrown bodies at us until we were overwhelmed. It would have been easier to do it then. Now we're on our guard."

I looked up for an answer, trying to ignore the sun's ascent. "Those two pieces of the puzzle don't fit together."

"Even the strongest warrior has a flaw," Bolt said.

If my mood had been less dark, I would have laughed. "Is that one new?"

His expression stilled for a moment as he thought. After a moment, he shrugged. "I'm not sure. After a while they all sort of run together in my mind."

"I pity the one who ever makes the mistake of delving you," I said. Over on the main street, the crowds continued to thicken as merchants hawked their wares and each parish church made its own preparations for the festival. What would it be like to have the person closest to you go mad?

"We can't just stay here," Bolt said after the silence between us had stretched to breaking.

I frowned. "Yes we can. This is as good a place as any"—I waved an arm toward the southeast—"and better than the poor quarter."

Bolt drew breath to reply, but I held up a hand. An idea flashed in my mind, a way to make the puzzle pieces fit. I held my breath as I searched for flaws, then stood when I couldn't find any.

"What?" Bolt said, searching my expression.

"He can't be everywhere at once," I said, my voice almost a whisper. "That's why he couldn't kill us at Braben's. His reach only extends so far, and it's less than the distance across the city." I growled my frustration. "He must have been close by, near enough to find and kill."

"But those infected by the Darkwater before now went insane wherever they were," Bolt said.

I nodded. "But only one by one, and that was before Laewan had been corrupted, before whatever evil lived in the Darkwater escaped the forest, yes?"

The question wasn't lightly asked, and I waited while Bolt thought it through.

I saw him nod once, slow and unsure, before doing so again. "Yes."

Never before could I remember the sun climbing so quickly into the sky. The smell of roasted meat drifted on smoky wisps from the market, and I swallowed. "It's almost noon." My elation faded as I searched for a way to exploit Laewan's weakness. "Curse it! We're right back where we started. In two hours the sun will go out and we'll be fighting people who can see in the dark."

Bolt watched me, his soldier's gaze narrowed until I finished. "Yes, but we'll know which way he's moving. As he calls the madness out, we'll see insanity wash over the crowd like a wave." His eyes widened toward the end, as if his words had the power to appall him.

I gaped. "And you think I take risks? We would have to remain on the streets during Bas-solas."

He tilted his head to one side. "He can afford to wait. We can't. The Vigil will never be more than seven. In a few months the tide from the Darkwater could wash us under."

I shook my head. "Pellin will never agree to leave us exposed that way. Laewan can lead us around by the nose or into a trap and we'd never catch up to him."

He nodded at me. "Because you're used to thinking that way."

The hope in his eyes refuted my doubts. "What way?"

"That you have to do everything yourself because you don't have allies."

"All right," I said. "I've got three people working with me who love and cherish me and can hardly wait to commit to an idea I can't prove. How does that help? In two hours the streets are going to be darker than the inside of a pitch barrel. We could send up a signal, but Laewan will see it as well. He might not be able to interpret it exactly, but he'll still be on his guard. If we frighten him, he'll rabbit and leave Bunard altogether."

"Follow me," Bolt said, and before I could say yay or nay he stepped from the porch into the cobbler's shop. Inside, he pressed a pair of silver pennies into the palm of a stooped man with a pronounced squint. "I need to borrow your shop for a few minutes, good father."

The cobbler brought the coins close to his face, peering at them, and then jerked in surprise. "Assuredly, good sir. What can I show you?"

Bolt favored him with a good-natured chuckle. "We don't need shoes, father, just a few moments of privacy. Would you be willing to step outside for a bit?"

The cobbler closed his gnarled fingers around the coins and bobbed his head. "My shop is yours, good master."

When the door closed, Bolt stood so that no one looking through the window would see his hands. Then he reached into his cloak and untied a padded leather purse from within, the thong holding it closed, thick, too tough for a thief to cut without him knowing.

He pulled it open, and his hand dipped inside to retrieve a clear yellow crystal as long as his palm but no thicker than his finger.

I stared. Yellow diamonds were rare, scarce enough that Bolt's possession would have supported a wealthy noble's household for a year or more. "It's beautiful, but unless you intend to bribe Laewan into surrendering, I don't see how that helps us."

"The original diamond was much larger than this," Bolt said. A knowing smile wreathed his face as shock spread across mine. "Centuries ago, the finest jewel-smith in the world cut it into seven identical stones."

"A scrying stone," I breathed. "I thought only the kings and queens had them."

Bolt smiled. "We're not without resources, but you are almost correct. Other than the kings and the heads of each order, only the Vigil has them."

I looked out the window to see the sun standing as high in the southern part of the sky as it would get. In moments it would begin its descent, and soon after it would darken as the moon passed in front, its light narrowing to a splinter before it went out altogether.

Chapter 55

"No." Pellin's voice, smaller as it emanated from the stone but no less emphatic, didn't bother to elaborate.

"But we—" I began.

"I forbid it," he ordered. I stared at the perfect shard of yellow diamond that vibrated softly in my hands as if I could somehow will Pellin to agreement.

"Use your own argument," Pellin continued. "The tenor of the threat from the Darkwater has changed. If the Vigil is lost here in the north, the seven kingdoms are lost as well. Would you wish that on them for the sake of a single city?"

I looked up from the stone to see Bolt gazing at me, his expression a strange mix of what might have been anger, exhilaration, and other elements that were impossible to divine. "No," I said, finally. "The Vigil has to survive."

The emanations from the crystal ceased as I wrapped the diamond and put it away, breaking contact. "But I can't desert my friends," I said, knowing Pellin could no longer hear me.

"That's the sort of thing that puts him in a bad mood," Bolt said.

Through the open door of the cobbler's shop, I could just make out the stooped form of its old proprietor as he plied his wares on the church soldiers that awaited us. The ridiculousness struck me and I almost laughed.

I turned to Bolt. "I know you can force my obedience if you wish.

There's no power that can keep you from simply putting the hilt of your dagger to my head and carting me back to the cathedral on the back of your horse. But if you don't let me try to save my friends, I'll never be a willing member of the Vigil."

He reached up to adjust his cloak, then settled his weapons as if I hadn't spoken. "Where do you wish to begin?"

I stared, my instinctual distrust warring with what sounded like acquiescence on his part. "Here, I think. Laewan's forces are somewhere in the merchants' section, and he'll try to storm the cathedral. We'll want to stay behind him."

"I think I told you once that Robin could smell danger at a distance and avoid it," Bolt said. When I nodded mutely, he went on. "I didn't tell you of the times he refused to run because innocents would have been left at risk." His expression grew tight. "I think he would have liked you."

"Thank you," I said, acknowledging the magnitude of the compliment.

Bolt's expression twisted. "Of course, he might have rapped you on the head for being such an idiot."

A notch of light disappeared from the sun as if some creature in the heavens had taken a bite of it, and the people around us yelled. Everywhere, farmers and merchants, parents and children, began their reenactment of the ancient ritual. Donning fake blood and wooden knives, the participants divided into camps pretending to be evil spirits bent on killing or people trying to defend themselves. Laughter mixed with the phony screams of the wounded, either spirit or human, as the farce proceeded only to start again after a priest from one of the four orders offered a prayer for light for our world and for *the* light of the world.

I stood on the bridge between the poor section and the lower merchants' quarter as the sun's light faded. It carried a gray cast now, and between the leaves of the trees, dots of light no longer appeared as circles but as crescents. Northwest and southeast of where I stood, the plays started again. In keeping with tradition, the evil spirits would get stronger as the light dimmed, overcoming the people they fought until evil controlled the city completely. The last human standing, a priest of the four orders, would beseech heaven to send the light of the world, and after a period of darkness and mourning, the sun's light would return.

I knew the play well. I'd been a willing participant since boyhood and had reveled in the celebration as a young man preparing to take my vows in the Merum church. I had loved the symbolism, despite the inaccuracies of the performance.

A soft moan, almost a prayer, bubbled up from my fear. Bas-solas would be real. Caught between memories of the past and the present, I reached for a book of liturgy I hadn't carried with me since I'd gone to war. My hand landed instead on the scrying stone.

"Lelwin," I called softly, though there was no reason. Nobody thought our presence strange in the midst of the orchestrated strangeness of the festival.

The girl stepped close, joining Bolt and me at the apex of the bridge, the best viewpoint we could arrange and still maintain mobility. "Yes, Lord Dura?"

I nodded to the blindfold worn by her and the rest of the urchins—thieves and beggars gathered to act as runners—and cursed myself. When had I gotten desperate enough to let children fight with me? "They'll be able to see their way when the light goes completely out?"

She nodded with a smile. "This is their craft, Lord Dura. At times over the years I've seen a thief spend the entire day in a blindfold so that he could find his way in light too dim for others."

I prayed Aer would see fit to bless our thieves as he'd done once before. "Are they armed? This won't be like creeping around some merchant's house while everyone sleeps."

Lelwin gave me a penetrating look that could never have come from a child, and I reminded myself that she was eighteen, not thirteen. "We all know how to throw a knife and run."

"Just don't forget that last part," I said as I closed my eyes and lost myself for a moment. But even behind shuttered lids I could tell the light continued to fade. When I opened them, Bunard lay shrouded in unnatural dusk. Torchlight glimmered in the distance, winking like dots of phos-flies.

"How good are *you* with a knife, Lelwin?" Bolt asked.

Her eyes, a deep brown that indicated southern ancestry, grew intent. "Almost gifted," she said. "Only Rory is better." She opened her threadbare cloak to show a brace of five daggers tucked around her belt that I hadn't noticed before. The workmanship of the blades made my fingers itch to hold them, but Lelwin closed her cloak and I put the thought from my mind.

Up above, darkness ate the sun until only a sliver remained. Then it winked out.

"Aer have mercy." It took me a moment to realize the prayer had come from my lips. I turned, standing at the highest point of the bridge, searching first the poor quarter, then the lower merchants' section by flickering torchlight for some sign, hoping I might be wrong.

The air chilled and gooseflesh rippled across my skin as a northerly breeze flowed across the bridge, colder than an exhalation from the tombs under Laidir's tor, but all I could hear were the stage screams of revelers playing out their parts.

Had I been wrong?

A moment passed, then another, and my shoulders relaxed a fraction as the sights and sounds of Bas-solas continued and the scrying stone remained silent in my grasp. Bolt, at my shoulder, took my questioning look with a shrug and a shake of his head. The air continued to cool while we stood, waiting for light and a sign.

Then I heard it—a single cry of a reveler in the lower merchants' quarter, its pitch changing in midscream from mock pain to surprise, scaling upward in volume to agony before it faded and stopped. Even as I brought the scrying stone to bear, a second scream followed the first.

"It's begun," I said.

Bolt spun to the force we'd gathered with us, arrayed like a field of poppies in their colors. "Advance toward the keep at a walk. Stay close to buildings that offer defensible positions." His voice dipped until it sounded like rocks cracking beneath a hammer. "From this point on, trust no one."

We split into two groups and flattened against the shops and homes bordering the street, snaking toward the sound of the scream. I pulled the scrying stone from its hiding place. At a look from Bolt, I answered before he could ask. "We're cut off. Pellin's orders don't matter anymore, and he'll need to know what we see."

But when I unwrapped the stone, I heard Pellin's voice calling me in strident tones, as if he'd called for me before. "Dura!"

"I'm here," I said. "It's begun, Eldest. I'm sorry, I can't desert my people. We'll try to sneak behind Laewan and catch him outside the cathedral."

"That's what I've been trying to tell you." Pellin's voice sounded as sharp as the edges of the diamond I held. "We're not in the cathedral. Laidir sent reinforcements."

"We have the people I tracked from the Darkwater vastly outnumbered." Bronwyn's voice, stern with age and sorrow, came from another facet of the stone. "Even if they are gifted, they pose no threat."

"We will cast our net," Pellin said. "If what Lord Dura says is true, and I think it is, Laewan will be centered in the madness."

Toria Deel's voice came from the stone in miniature, reduced to the size of the diamond shard I held. "I hear it, but it's well south of me."

"I hear nothing yet," Bronwyn said. "My section is still quiet."

"As is the nobles' section," Pellin added.

Screams erupted north of us, echoing from the extensive market in the lower merchants' section. I heard the thread of children crying in terror and fought to keep from running headlong toward it.

"It's moving toward me," Toria Deel said.

Bolt's voice cracked like the tail of a whip, and we were surrounded by a trio of sword-bearing church guards and a healer. Around them, the rest of the church guards proceeded with short bows in one hand and arrows held between the fingers of another.

The bow had never been my best weapon, but I was familiar with their training. Holding three arrows at once between the fingers of their draw hand, a skilled archer could keep seven arrows in flight at the same time. I'd seen contingents of trained bowmen shatter a charge of foot soldiers in a matter of moments. Even the gifted couldn't stand beneath the onslaught.

But we weren't fighting to stay free or to safeguard what little food our kingdom had grown during a drought, we were going to be killing our own. I wanted to throw up. Bolt must have noticed my pallor.

"They're not countrymen anymore, Willet. Not if they would willingly go to the Darkwater."

I shook my head. "Is it possible for a brother to renounce his kinship?"

Even before we came to the main portion of the market, scared revelers were streaming past us like animals before a firestorm, their mouths agape, stretched by shock and horror. A man came stumbling from around the bend, his hands pressed against wounds in his neck and chest. But he couldn't cover several others that soaked his clothes with vermillion. Three paces away he took a final stumbling step and dropped to the cobblestones.

"Don't stand there," I yelled at the healer. "Tend him."

"No!" Bolt snapped, turning to me. "You've been in war, Willet. We can't delay for the dying."

The man on the ground lay still, his breathing stopped though blood still filled the cracks between stones beneath him. For a moment I saw color that had nothing to do with heart sap on the ground. "Then let's move." My voice came out as a growl. I meant to make Laewan pay, and right then I wanted to kill him myself and take my time about it.

We turned a corner and came into horror. Screams of women and children threaded through the deeper cries of men, and blood—not the brief swipe of pig's blood for show, but growing swaths of death—steamed in the air everywhere. Steel flashed as men and women, their eyes wide and unseeing, attacked the crowd with the businesslike strokes of a butcher.

A child collapsed a few paces away, slain by one perhaps a year or two older who cleared the body with a jump like a grasshopper to land on a farmer trying to escape. The swipe of his knife almost took the farmer's head off.

Five merchants, eyes vaçant of thought, cut their way through the crowd, their movements too fast to follow in the torchlight. Wherever they passed, people collapsed, falling like grass after a stroke of the sharpest scythe. The crowd of revelers collapsed as farmers and city dwellers fled into the side streets, but the attackers didn't follow. And the slaughter moved north, toward the tor.

"Stop this," I yelled. I could feel the muscles in my neck cording, but I had no idea to whom I spoke.

He turned to me, his face wearing fierce sorrow I'd never seen before. "No. Use your eyes, Willet. They're not attacking us because their focus is on getting to the north part of the city. If we make them fight us, we can't win."

Bolt pitched his voice to the squad of church soldiers hugging the shadows on the sides of the street. "Follow, but don't engage unless you have to. Don't attract their notice."

My breakfast roiled in my stomach, and I bent double, retching my disgust and horror into the street.

"Use the stone," Bolt told me.

Grasping the shard of yellow diamond as if it had somehow betrayed me, I relayed our position to Pellin and the rest of the Vigil. Pellin's voice came back at me in a staccato burst of sound. "Who fights for them?"

I didn't understand the question. Like a fool, I shook my head at the stone. "What do you mean?"

"Merchants, farmers, urchins, night women," Pellin's voice came. "We need to know who we're fighting."

I studied the maelstrom of carnage that engulfed the lower merchants' section of the city, searching out the attackers. "They're all low merchants or workers," I said. "One or two out of the poor quarter. No farmers."

"Do you see Laewan?"

"No." I turned around, but in the dim light of the eclipse I couldn't see past ten paces. "Lelwin," I called. The urchin shouldered her way between two of the church soldiers guarding me. "Send one of the urchins south. I need to know if the madness has passed from any of those who've been doing the killing." I clutched her shoulder, willing her and the urchin she sent to obey me. "No risks. I just need to know what's happening."

She melted between the soldiers and approached a skinny boy who wore a dirty blindfold over one eye. At her command, he whirled, removing the cloth, and set off toward the south at a run.

Bolt pulled one of the Servants close, the man's torchlight bobbing with the motion, casting lurid shadows across our faces in the gloom. "Fire the buildings to the south."

"No!" I screamed.

"We have to keep them in front of us."

The Servant looked at us, waiting.

"I gave you an order," Bolt snapped.

"Stop!" I grabbed Bolt's tunic, pulling him close. "We'll lose the entire quarter, maybe the whole city."

"We're not trying to save the city."

I spun, searching for an alternative. "There." I pointed. The broad market street had been lined with carts, the transportation and shops of the farmers and merchants who'd brought their goods to Bunard. "Put them in the street and fire them. The light will keep them north of us. If you need to, you can block the side streets and alleys as well." I pulled a deep breath that held the taint of pitch smoke within it, as if I'd already lost my argument.

Bolt nodded. "Do it," he ordered, "but if the carts fail, put a torch to the buildings."

Lelwin's runner came sprinting out of the gloom to tell me what I'd already suspected. "The madness is fading south of us."

A small measure of relief blossomed in my chest. "The killing has stopped?"

She shook her head. "The townspeople are going after anyone with a dagger in their hand. All those who were under the madness are being slaughtered. The farmers and the people from the villages have fled."

I'd taken a step back toward the south when Bolt's hand stopped me from behind. "There's nothing you can do back there, Willet. One way or another, it's going to be the sword for anyone who's been to the Darkwater."

A voice, small and tinny, came to me, and I lifted the scrying stone up to eye level.

"They're here!" Toria Deel's voice screamed from the crystal. "People at the north end of the lower merchants' quarter are attacking everyone. They're crossing the bridge."

"They're coming for us," Pellin said. "I want everyone to meet at Criers' Square. Bronwyn, wait for Toria Deel to meet you in the upper merchants' quarter. When you get to the square, split your forces and fill the east and west lanes," Pellin ordered. "Lord Dura, follow and fill the south lane between the Vanguard and Absold cathedrals. Cut off their retreat."

We followed the tide of slaughter north toward Criers' Square, but the dim light kept me from gauging the numbers of the mad.

Chapter 56

Moments later a faint call brought me to the realization that I'd been hearing noise from the scrying stone for a few moments without realizing it. "What's happening?"

Toria Deel dropped some uncomplimentary observations on me. "If you can't remember how to use the stone, give it to Bolt," she said. "The road north through the upper merchants' quarter is clear, but Laewan has us flanked in the nobles' quarter, and we're losing people."

Bolt swore under his breath. "They're trying to take the Vigil in pieces. We have to hurry or we'll never get them bottled up in Criers' Square." He turned to one of the soldiers trailing us. "Burn whatever you have to short of setting the torch to the city, but I want as much light in the streets as you can create."

I looked up into a star-filled sky. No light showed from the sun, not even a silver outline around the moon that had covered it. Any other time, I would have watched in amazement.

"Run in formation!" Bolt's order cracked through the moans of the dying like a verdict of indifference, but I picked up my pace to stay in the protective cordon he'd placed around me. To my left, Lelwin and the half-blindfolded urchins ran with the light, springy steps of the young.

We passed through deserted streets littered with the dead and dying until we came within sight of the bridge that spanned the branch of the Rinwash separating the upper merchants' quarter from the nobles'. By flickers of distant torchlight I could see Toria Deel's retreat, her forces trying to maintain order. Blurs of motion and screams testified to the losses they were taking, and they were still two hundred paces from Criers' Square.

"Archers front," Bolt yelled beside me.

Two dozen men and women advanced with short bows held in one hand and arrows gripped in the other.

Bolt pointed forward. "Fan out and fire a full volley on the run."

A Merum soldier jerked as if he'd been slapped. "We might hit our own."

"If you don't fire," Bolt rasped, "they can't hold."

A swarm of arrows hissed through the air as each archer drew and released, their hands swift in the torchlight until each had put four shafts in the air. The arrows disappeared into the gloom, and I watched the seething mass. "Oh, Aer, please let this work."

The men and women attacking Toria Deel's soldiers paused, their movement slowing. Here and there bits of red, blue, and white showed among them.

A space a score of paces wide opened between the church soldiers and their attackers, allowing Deel's men and women to bring their own archers to bear. But they couldn't kill them. I saw men and women who otherwise appeared ordinary move as quickly as the gifted, dodging arrows that should have put them down.

I searched the darkness for a tall, gangly figure. Somewhere close, Laewan was orchestrating his attack.

Our losses twisted my guts. We were losing ten men to each of his, but there was no way he could win. We crossed the last bridge, stepping over our dying, some of them felled by bow fire. Even in the dim light I could see the mass of Laidir's soldiers, men from the garrison, filling the alleys that led from Criers' Square, pulling Laewan's forces into a killing field.

The last of Toria Deel's soldiers retreated into the east lane, clearing the square. I looked at the figures attacking them, some two hundred in all, their movements quick and jerky, as if they were trying to leave their shadows behind.

Brazen-throated yells went up from in front of us as we filled the southern lane. Bakers, tanners, smiths, and other men and women moved like phantoms from a nightmare, trying to dodge scores of black shafts that streaked toward them in the muted light of torches. One by one they went down until the archers ran out of arrows.

Bolt pointed forward. "Swords out and hold the line."

Looking at Laewan's army, an array of common men and women, some whom I knew, I wanted to puke. Some three score remained, clustered around a central figure as we moved forward to finish them.

Surrounded by thick cordons of Laidir's men and church soldiers, the Vigil guards stood sentry over their hooded charges, each flanked by an urchin with a blindfold over one eye.

I pushed my way through the Servants holding torches and then the Merum, Vanguard, and Absold soldiers with their swords pointed forward, ignoring Bolt's gritty remonstrations. "Let them go," I yelled to the tall figure in the cloak at the center of the mass.

The hooded figure turned away from his study of Pellin and the rest of the Vigil to face me but other than that gave no acknowledgment that I had spoken.

"It's over," I yelled. "You're going to die, but there's no reason to keep them entrapped." I pointed at the threescore commoners crouched and feral around Laewan, their eyes dark even when flickers of torchlight illuminated their faces like swipes of a dagger.

A deep tone sounded from the top of the keep, a single strike of a massive iron bell that fell on my ears and then resonated against my skin. A moment later it sounded again, and then a twin joined it with its identical lament.

Pellin's voice came through the fragment of yellow diamond I held, though he was close enough to me now to be heard without it. "Laidir is dead."

A shout from the far side of Criers' Square, a mix of grief and rage from the commander of the garrison, echoed against the buildings. A moment later Laidir's soldiers, all of them, departed at a run for the keep, sprinting away to safeguard the heir and Laidir's queen from whatever danger had felled the king.

I knew better. I squeezed my eyes shut and clamped my mouth over desperate curses that tried to tear a ragged hole through my throat. *Aer, why?*

"You were there," I said to Pellin through the scrying stone. "You could have protected him."

"Everyone was ordered from the royal couple's presence, even the personal guards," Pellin said. "There was nothing I could have done."

"Nothing?" My hands gripped that perfect fragment of yellow diamond as if it were Pellin's throat. "You wield more power than the head of any of the four orders. I watched you and yours order him about as if he were a servant." My voice rose until it raked across my throat. "Don't tell me there was nothing you could have done!"

Hands pulled me around, and Bolt's face filled my vision. "Grieve later," he said, his voice as hard as his countenance. "Your king is dead. If you want to do something about it, finish this."

"*Kreppa*!" I spat. "You've taken—" I looked over his shoulder toward the bridge that led to the ostentatious estates of the nobles within the city. Hints of motion in the darkness, like shadows moving in a darkened room, obscured the bridge as if mere suggestions. "The farmers."

Pulling a dagger from my belt, I spun and threw, the blade tumbling end over end in the dim light. Without transition, Laewan stood before me with his hand raised, holding the dagger as if I'd placed the pommel within his hand.

Casually, he reached up with the other hand to push back his hood. "Greetings, brothers and sisters. It has been a long time since our last communion." He turned a slow circle, pointing to each of the Vigil or the street they guarded. "The need for bloodshed has passed. I grant permission for you to throw a single torch into the darkness behind you." He held up a finger. "But a warning, more than a single torch and I will kill everyone who stands with you."

I already knew what we would see even before Bolt took the torch of the nearest Servant and threw it back toward the last bridge. The flame wheeled and spun in the darkness of the eclipse, the fire hissing through the air before it landed. Behind us, scores upon scores of farmers and villagers blocked our escape, far outnumbering the church soldiers remaining with us. Around the streets that defined Criers' Square I could see a thick ring of commoners clutching knives, hemming us in.

"The farmers and villagers didn't run from the slaughter," I said. "They shadowed us in the darkness."

Bolt nodded. Then he swung his sword toward me, the point trained against my chest just beneath my left shoulder. I'd be dead before I felt the thrust. "The gift has to go free," he said.

"Not just yet," Laewan said, but he turned, taking in the rest of the Vigil guards who all held swords against their hooded charges. "There is an alternative to death." He beckoned us forward. "Come, let us parley. Perhaps you will find a more attractive choice for yourselves than the infinite night."

I raised the scrying stone, holding it close. "Pellin?"

"Approach," the Eldest said through the stone. "Bolt, Elory, Balean, do not allow Laewan to touch any of us."

The farmers and villagers hemmed us in, forcing us to edge forward. I tried to ignore the way my heart threatened to escape from my chest. "How good are the four of you together?" I whispered to Bolt.

He shook his head. "Not good enough to win."

The cadence of his answer told me what I needed to know. Bolt would never allow Laewan to touch me. Five paces away, the point of his sword shifted, coming to rest against my throat. A trickle of blood worked its warm way down my neck.

He was gifted, able to position the point and edge of his sword within a hairsbreadth of where he wished. The only reason to mark me would be to prove to Laewan the earnestness of his intent, but Laewan had to know it already.

He turned a circle, as if taking our measure before dismissing us. Under my breath, I prayed to Aer that Laewan's gloating would be his undoing, but an instant later I saw him glance skyward. I followed his gaze. The barest hint of corona shone, a feeble wisp of light against the darkness. The eclipse still had half an hour to run.

"Time marches on," Laewan said, then smiled as if he'd assayed a jest. "Lady Bronwyn"—he held out his hand—"you are the mother of my heart if not of my body. Let me show you what we were intended to be."

She shook her head without bothering to lower her hood. Balean's sword point at her throat never wavered. Laewan turned to regard

Pellin, silent and unmoving. "Come, Eldest. From the moment my servants surrounded you, death or alliance were all that remained for the Vigil. And if you did not wish alliance, you would not have lived this long. The guards hold the swords, but you still hold their leash."

Pellin didn't answer.

"Look at you." Laewan laughed.

Skittering chills raced up and down my spine at the sound. Contempt and disdain had no part in it, nothing but the cleanest joy filled the air, accompanied by the funereal sound of the iron bells in the tor above us.

Laewan shook his head. "Even now, defeated and on the edge of death, you attempt to preserve the anonymity the Vigil has used to cloak itself for uncounted centuries." He paused. "Lower your hoods." He raised a finger and a thousand daggers trained themselves on us, the eyes of their bearers black and vacant.

As one, Pellin, Bronwyn, and Toria Deel reached up to unveil themselves. I gasped and started, the movement reminding me of Bolt's sword, a steel thorn in my skin. I couldn't see his face yet, but the hands that lowered Pellin's hood were clean—not one age spot marked them. The faces behind the hoods were unknown to me.

Criers' Square erupted.

The church soldiers wheeled outward to fight the horde surrounding us. Bolt's sword disappeared from my neck as he and the rest of the Vigil guards launched themselves at the ring of bodies surrounding Laewan. Lelwin and the rest of the urchins dropped to a crouch, hiding.

I drew my sword. My blade was the least in the square, but I pulled Lelwin's head close so she could hear me. "When I go down, hide beneath my body. Make sure you get plenty of blood on you."

But she pushed me away.

"Fools," Laewan screamed as the first Vigil impostor went down. "Do you think you've escaped me? I will show you the fullness of your diminishment." He cut through a trio of his own men, his blade disappearing into motion and then reappearing as if by magic.

Bolt and Elory closed to within two paces, then tensed, their bodies coiled in preparation. Behind us, the farmers and villagers cut through the cordon of church soldiers so quickly a ring of bodies hampered their advance. Even so, we only had a dozen heartbeats of life left.

An Absold soldier crumpled and fell back across my feet, his blood pumping out through the slash in his neck. I grabbed Lelwin's arm, tried to push her down toward the dying man, but she threw me off with a blow that sent me reeling.

Then she gathered her legs beneath her and leapt, disappearing up into the darkness.

Chapter 57

A knife blossomed in Laewan's neck. Quicker than sight could follow, his hand flew to the wound as his head jerked up, searching the darkness. Faster than thought, knife blades buried themselves in each eye, with more appearing in his neck, chest, back.

He fell where he stood, the clatter of his sword lost in the toll of the bells. Around us, the sound of knives hitting the cobblestones of Criers' Square mixed with the moans of the dying and the ragged breathing of the rest of us.

Sometime after the appearance of the last knife in Laewan's body, I became aware of a figure dropping out of the darkness to land by me, surefooted and light. Lelwin. Scores of blank-staring men and women stood around us, waking to a nightmare of carnage.

Bolt barked an order that cut through the tolling bells, and the surviving church soldiers fanned out to herd everyone toward the Merum cathedral.

Then he came toward Lelwin, moving for the first time like a man his age. "I'll need my gift back." He paused to look at me, and his eyes grew still in the torchlight. "At least for a while."

Lelwin stared at her raised hands, staring at them as she flexed the fingers. "Does your gift make you feel like this all the time?"

Bolt's mouth pulled to one side. "Age takes a bit of the shine off, but yes, mostly."

She stepped close and put her hand on his head. "I'll miss it." A moment later her shoulders dropped a fraction and she stepped back with a rueful smile. "I'd better retrieve the knives Pellin gave me. They have the finest balance I've ever seen. Rory and Fess and Mark might be tempted to add them to their own." She paused. "They are thieves, you know." The smile she attempted never quite made it to fruition.

Across the square, I saw Allta, Elory, and Balean standing close and holding hands with the urchins who'd accompanied them, their heads bowed. "I should have seen it," I said to Bolt. "Pellin would never put the entire Vigil at risk." *Only me.*

Bolt nodded. "I'm sure you want an explanation." He pointed at Laewan's body. "It's right there."

He led me to the tall, almost-gaunt figure lying on the ground, his form riddled with the myriad dagger wounds he'd taken in a fraction of a second. Without care or respect for the dead, Bolt knelt and began searching through Laewan's clothes, ripping the cloth when impatience led him. Then he reached inside the dead man's tunic and with a satisfied grunt pulled a shard of yellow diamond free from its hiding place.

"It was a trap all along," I muttered, then shook my head. "But they couldn't be certain I would insist on staying on the streets."

Bolt straightened, tucking the resonance stone away out of caution or habit, but his expression became almost sympathetic. "They were, Willet. They delved you."

I sighed. "And if the Vigil guards and I all perished, we could be replaced."

He nodded. "There were other reasons as well, but I will let Pellin explain them."

"Where are they?"

Bolt pointed west. "Downriver, where no one who might have been to the Darkwater could find them."

I looked up to see a hint of the sun's corona brighten on one side, a harbinger of the light to come. It would take years and years for Bunard to heal from this year's Bas-solas. Up on the heights, no longer Laidir's tor, the iron bells continued to toll their dirge for the dead king.

Bolt gripped my arm. "I was ordered to bring you to the Merum cathedral."

I almost laughed. "If I survived."

"Yes, if that."

Within the windowless room of the cathedral, the four of us who comprised the Vigil met, flanked by our guards, who once again owned the physical gift of beauty that made them the deadliest men in the world. Yet as I played the events of the previous hours over and again in my mind, their subterfuge frightened me. It meant they believed Laewan overmatched them.

"You could have told me," I said to Pellin.

His brows lifted. "Of our plan? No. We needed your reactions to be genuine. Laewan, though he was the youngest of us, had over a century with which to hone his insight. And he had delved you as well when you first came back from the Darkwater." He stopped, settling himself in his chair as if it didn't quite fit.

I wondered at Pellin's sudden discomfort. Guilt or fear? "There was another reason, wasn't there?" I asked. Pellin looked at me without answering, his former indecisiveness returning in that moment.

"We weren't sure of you," Bronwyn said. "Of those who have been to the Darkwater, you are unique. You might have been the weapon Laewan held in reserve, waiting for the moment when we took you into our trust so that he might destroy us."

"The viper to our chest," Tori Deel said.

I nodded, but just enough anger burned inside me at being used that I refused to let them off the hook. "I'm young, but I know doubt. This hasn't erased it for you. Doubt doesn't work that way."

The fact that no one bothered to answer me was all the confirmation I needed.

A moment later Pellin sighed. "We'll have to break the vaults of all those taken by the Darkwater."

Bronwyn's bleak nod lent her agreement. "It will take days, even if we manage to gather them all. How will we hide this, Eldest?"

"Time, of course," he said. "Though we may need centuries of it."

Urgency filled me, fighting against the bone-deep weariness that threatened to drop me where I sat to sleep on the stones of the floor. "How is it done?" I asked her.

Bronwyn looked to Pellin for approval before answering.

"He is truly one of the Vigil now," Pellin said, but the statement belied itself. He turned to me. "You'll have to leave Bunard and Collum eventually, you know. In a few years, people will notice you're not aging."

Bronwyn put a gloved hand on my arm. "You've seen a vault, yes?"

I nodded. "It looks like a sealed black scroll."

She nodded. "Just so. Destroy it. You can tear it or burn it."

"Is it not possible to read it?" I asked.

Pellin shook his head. "We've tried. The script is unknown."

I rose and made to leave.

"Where are you going?" Pellin asked.

I fought back a surge of grief that threatened to rob me of my voice. "I am the king's reeve. I will dispense justice for my king." I took a breath. "I'm going to kill a queen."

How many levels of grieving would there be? I climbed the steps of Laidir's tor, barely conscious of placing one foot in front of another. My king, a man I'd considered a father in place of my own, was dead despite my best effort to warn him.

My mind tried to refute the guilt my heart laid at my feet and failed. I should have done something to save him. The queen would be dead in moments. If I had forced my way back into her presence and broken her vault earlier, Laidir would still be alive, kept safe by the four guards who would never have been ordered from his side.

As bad as it hurt to dwell on the king's death and my part in it, I preferred it to the alternative dilemma that pounded at the doors of my mind like ocean waves intent on eating the shoreline. Gael.

I thrust the thought of her away as I ascended past the hall of legends to the highest level of the tor, where Laidir had held court and lived. *Had*. The iron bells continued to toll, and people scurried through the halls like ants whose nest had been brushed aside by a careless foot. Who had inherited Laidir's gift, the gift of kings? I threw such thoughts aside. Perhaps I alone among the people within the tor possessed clarity of purpose. Sevin stood guard outside the throne room, his face a mask of duty that hid his grief.

"Where is the king?" I said.

Sevin looked at me, blinking as if he had trouble recognizing me. "He lies in his quarters. The castellan has taken charge of the tor's staff."

"What of the queen?"

Sevin's face pinched into suspicion and doubt. Rumors would be flying through the keep faster than messenger birds. "She is with the king. Duke Orlan has called the court in session." He swallowed, then licked his lips. "There are whispers, Willet."

Not Lord Dura—Willet. I acknowledged his trust with a nod. "There are always whispers, Sevin. I'll take care of it," I said as I turned right, away from the court and toward the king's quarters.

"How?" he asked after me.

"I'm the king's reeve."

I passed the entrance to the king's library and for a moment felt a stab of loss. The king's living quarters lay just beyond, a series of high-vaulted rooms with windows overlooking the city or the gardens at the top of the tor. I'd been in them a couple of times over the past year, when the king desired more discretion than his audience chamber allowed.

Two of his personal guards stood at attention outside the wide double doors, as if Laidir still lived and breathed. I bit the inside of my cheek to keep from crumpling into sobs. I stepped inside to see Castellan Baelwer standing over the queen, who sat in a richly embroidered chair a few paces from the mammoth bed where Laidir's body lay. He turned to bar me from entering, but Laidir's guards made no move to support him.

"Why are you here, Lord Dura? The tor is the province of the castellan. Me," he said, but threads of hesitation betrayed his doubt, and behind the façade of his eyes I could see him pleading.

I nodded my agreement. "Though I am the least of his nobles, I swore fealty to him, and I am the king's reeve." I spoke to the nervousness and fear he wore like a second tunic. He'd never dealt with regicide before. "I am well acquainted with murder, Lord Baelwer, and my help is yours for the asking, else I wish to pay my respects to my king and queen and withdraw."

I wasn't sure how Pellin and the rest of the Vigil opened doors and demanded cooperation and obedience, and I didn't have time to find out. If they decided the queen was guilty—and plenty of people would wish for such a verdict—she'd be summarily executed. And Laidir's son was too young to ascend, whether he'd inherited the gift or not.

That thought drew me up short. If I killed the queen, the boy would be in jeopardy as well. I didn't need to refresh my knowledge of history to know the lad didn't have better than half odds of making it to the throne even if the gift of kings had come to him.

Baelwer looked at me, his fear threatening to burst loose from behind his eyes. "What can you do?" he asked.

"I can talk to the queen, alone," I said.

Baelwer couldn't help but know my reputation, and he spoke to it. "You can't just kill her if she's guilty."

I nodded. "I swear the queen will live. After I speak with her, I will submit my findings to you, Castellan Baelwer."

He straightened at the use of his title, accepting the subordinate role I took upon myself. "We will withdraw. How much time will you need?"

"No more than a few moments."

I waited until the heavy door closed before I took the glove from my hand and went to kneel before the queen, who sat in her chair, her gaze fixed upon the bed. "My condolences, Your Majesty," I said. "My heart grieves at the loss of the king. This has been an evil day, but I trust Aer will help Bunard and all of Collum heal."

She looked at me, her passive façade restored once more. "I hope so too, Lord Dura. Who could have done this?"

"Only someone harboring a kernel of evil in the heart," I said, my gaze direct.

She couldn't afford to show the intelligence that would allow her to perceive the accusation, but I saw her eyes widen a fraction in anger regardless. A wave of fatigue passed over me. Duty and love and grief combined into weariness beyond any I'd ever endured, and I wanted nothing more in that moment than to leave the fate of the queen and the kingdom to someone else, to save or condemn as they chose.

"There was blood on my knife," she whispered.

I started, shocked to see the queen's gaze upon me, her mask of distraction gone. "But I don't remember the attack, Lord Dura. I swear it."

She stared at me, weighing, and then licked her lips with a pale tongue before speaking again. "I'm no fool, Lord Dura, and I know you are one of the very few to realize it. My life is in your hands, and perhaps the life of the heir as well. What will convince you of my innocence?"

Nothing. I walked over to the bed where my king lay. There was less blood than I'd expected. Cailin had struck true, and Laidir probably never saw the stroke that stopped his heart. Someone had closed his eyes.

I felt no pull from the stare that witnessed the limitless reaches of eternity. But I knelt one last time to show him my obeisance and loyalty. "I am proud to be the least of your nobles, my liege," I whispered. I attempted the antidon I'd learned as a Merum acolyte, but it stuck in my throat and I abandoned the effort. "If Aer wills, I will see you again and tell you how much you meant to me, though I imagine you know it already."

I rose, pondering the mystery that had been my king, that he should be so adept with people and so completely misread the distant queen he'd tried to love. She still sat in her chair, pale with the expectation of justice in my presence, the one her subjects had called the king's assassin.

Had Laidir misread her? He had been king, with all the power and loneliness the position required. I took another step toward Cailin's wan form, brushing the dagger at my waist with my fingers. I wouldn't have to kill her. Her mind would break if I destroyed her vault, and she would be dead in all but name. The healers could come and give their medical opinion, but there would be no poison to find and no blame to fall at my feet, only rumors that my visit to Her Majesty had been an unfortunate coincidence.

"Will you kill me, my lord?" she whispered.

I brought my eyes into focus. "I warned him," I said, "that he might be in danger by your hand, told him that you had played a game with him for years, hiding who you truly were." I took a step closer, the fingers of my right hand brushing each other, feeling the warmth of skin to skin. "He didn't believe me."

She stared, offering no defense or explanation. Outside, full light shone upon the city as if it were just another spring day. "I could not bring myself to trust any man."

I knew that to be true. With a nod I lowered myself to kneel before her on one knee. "Then we will trust Aer, Your Majesty." I extended my hand as any devoted subject might.

At the last, I thought she would refuse. There was too much purpose and intensity in my simple gesture for a woman of her intellect not to suspect some motive or action. But Cailin had no alternatives. She took my hand as she held my gaze.

I fell through her eyes and into her memories, but I had no desire to sift through the horrors of her childhood or the ploys she'd used to survive her father's court. Despite my resolve, Cailin's past became my own, each cut to her soul and worse washing through me until Willet Dura was forgotten. Strong. A king's daughter must be as indomitable as iron, immune to hurt or damage of any kind.

Somewhere beneath the tide of memories my true self raged at Cailin's solitary abandonment. With no friend or companion within her father's court, no sympathetic ear, every wound had been hidden behind her abstraction, unseen and unhealed. In the midst of living her memories as she had, acting as magistrate and executioner, I grieved the child that she had been.

As Willet Dura of the Vigil, I had no right or desire to extend mercy to the killer of my king. I found the black scroll and tore it to pieces, smaller and smaller, slashing through the obsidian parchment with my mind until it turned to dust. Only then did I see the thousand strands of coal-black tying it to every other memory in Cailin's mind.

With a mental surge, I returned to myself. No wonder those who had a vault destroyed lost themselves—the scroll encompassed everything they were. I rose, turning to leave Cailin where she would remain until someone moved her. The castellan would be free to interpret the queen's condition however he wished.

"How will Aer rule, Lord Dura?"

I turned, gaping. She stood now, still pale, her hands clutched before her, the fingers in motion over each other, working to wring security or solace from them.

With a nod, I forced myself to speak. "Aer has ruled, my queen. You are innocent of the king's death." I put as much forbidding and threat into my gaze as I could dredge from my exhausted body. "But if you ever return to the Darkwater, Your Majesty, *I* will rule. In the meantime, I will tell the castellan the truth: You are not responsible."

The air in the king's chamber smelled of blood and death, but perhaps I imagined a hint of grace and redemption in it as well. And possibly hope for myself within the queen's survival. I would have to remain in Bunard long enough to deflect suspicion from the queen and direct the watch's search for a killer we would never find. I had time for now.

A lump I couldn't swallow formed in my throat. I would have to find a way to persuade Gael to marry Rupert.

I put my hand on the latch and opened the door.

ACKNOWLEDGMENTS

As always, there are many people to thank, friends and relatives who have given unstintingly of their time to help make this a better work. I want to thank my wife, Mary, and my son Daniel, who helped edit the galleys, searching for the minute errors that I could no longer see. I owe a debt of gratitude to my sister, Ramona Dabbs, who remains my biggest cheerleader even when I'm struggling to get the plot to come together. I also need to thank my critique partners Austin Deel and Tori Smith—you're both awesome. And lastly, courtesy demands I give my fellow teacher Jesse Tidyman a huge thanks for his time and input at the very beginning as I struggled to leave the world of The Staff and the Sword behind and forge a new and completely different one. Jesse, your input was invaluable and you are, quite possibly, the coolest English teacher in the world.

ABOUT THE AUTHOR

Patrick W. Carr was born on an Air Force base in West Germany at the height of Cold War tensions. He has been told this was not his fault. As an Air Force brat, he experienced a change in locale every three years until his father retired to Tennessee. Patrick saw more of the world on his own through a varied and somewhat eclectic education and work history. He graduated from Georgia Tech in 1984 and has worked as a draftsman at a nuclear plant, done design work for the Air Force, worked for a printing company, and consulted as an engineer. Patrick's day gig for the last eight years has been teaching high school math in Nashville, Tennessee. He currently makes his home in Nashville with his wonderfully patient wife, Mary, and four sons he thinks are amazing: Patrick, Connor, Daniel, and Ethan. Sometime in the future he would like to be a jazz pianist, and he wrestles with the complexity of improvisation on a daily basis.

More Fiction to Enjoy!

As a dynasty nears its end, an unlikely hero embarks upon a perilous quest to save his kingdom. Thrust into a world of dangerous political intrigue and church machinations, Errol Stone must leave behind his idle life, learn to fight, come to know his God—and discover his destiny.

THE STAFF AND THE SWORD: *A Cast of Stones, The Hero's Lot, A Draw of Kings* by Patrick W. Carr
patrickwcarr.com

Only two men were brave enough to tell the truth about what awaited the Hebrews in Canaan: Caleb and Joshua. This is their thrilling story, from the pits of slavery in Egypt, through the terrifying supernatural experience of the plagues, and finally, to the Hebrews' dramatic escape in the Exodus.

Shadow of the Mountain: Exodus by Cliff Graham
SHADOW OF THE MOUNTAIN #1
cliffgraham.com

This tale of power, truth, and the consequences of our choices will grip your imagination as Callie, a desperate woman trapped in a dangerous world, must find her way back to our realm with only a few cryptic words to guide her. Will she decipher the clues—or will she fall prey to the deception of the Arena?

Arena by Karen Hancock
kmhancock.com

BETHANYHOUSE

Stay up-to-date on your favorite books and authors with our free e-newsletters. Sign up today at bethanyhouse.com.

Find us on Facebook. facebook.com/bethanyhousepublishers

Free exclusive resources for your book group! bethanyhouse.com/anopenbook